"I REFUSE YOU AND YOUR SUIT!" TIFFANY CRIED DEFIANTLY.

"I do not love you and I do not want you. Find yourself another possession, Your Grace, for I am leaving and it appears you are short one betrothed. I will not whore for a title my father covets."

"Princess, you have not the sufficient experience . . . yet . . . to perform such a service. In time perhaps," Clinton said, his eyes glinting devilishly.

Spinning around, Tiffany slapped him soundly across his cheek.

Clinton merely stood, holding her eyes with his.

" 'Tis a shame we'll never disprove your words, for I have no intention of marrying you!" she cried.

In a voice that brooked no argument, Clinton quietly said, "But you will marry me. And you will be the one to decide to do so."

Other Books in
THE AVON ROMANCE Series

Defiant Angel

Stephanie Stevens

AVON BOOKS NEW YORK

For my nephew Mimmo, my dear, dear friend Eileen, my husband Ray, my children Mark and Ashlee who prayed every night for "mommy's book," and for the romantics of the world.

DEFIANT ANGEL is an original publication of Avon Books. This work has never before appeared in book form. This work is a novel. Any similarity to actual persons or events is purely coincidental.

AVON BOOKS
A division of
The Hearst Corporation
105 Madison Avenue
New York, New York 10016

Inside cover author photograph by Kiernan Photography
Published by arrangement with the author
Library of Congress Catalog Card Number: 90-93620
ISBN: 0-380-76449-0

First Avon Books Printing: June 1991

Printed in the U.S.A.

RA 10 9 8 7 6 5 4 3 2 1

Prologue

The pink dust of dawn stole across the sleepy meadows. High in the sky, the fading silhouette of a crescent moon disappeared as the shades of twilight gave way to morn. The sharp, blustery wind whipped through the boughs of stalwart oaks, their bare limbs beginning to show the promise of green buds.

Tiffany crawled from her warm bed to venture forth on this unusually cold March morning to view the new foal Moria had delivered the night before. She quickly donned her clothing and ran from her bedroom. She eyed the newly polished banister that ran the length of the broad, curving staircase. A twinkle gleamed in her brilliant sapphire eyes as she looked over the railing below, finding no one about. Raising her leg over the banister, she straddled it and slid backward down its length, pushing herself off as she reached the end. She turned and headed toward the double oaken front doors.

"And where ye be goin', child, not properly dressed and without a proper breakfast?"

Tiffany turned, her unbound raven tresses cascading about her face. She looked at the old woman, the only female she had known since her mother's death. "Oh, Clarissa, Moria delivered a foal! I must see it before I do anything."

Clarissa was unable to resist the pleading look reflected

in the eight-year-old's eyes, and with a shake of her head, she said, "Ye know how yer father is about ye bein' at the stables, lamb." She waddled over to her charge, pushing errant curls from Tiffany's face. "And look at yer hair; now, ye know yer father is finicky about it not bein' combed and bound, lamb."

"Oh, Clarissa, I'll let you fix it later—I promise. I'll only stay a moment, that's all, I swear." She raised her hand to emphasize her promise.

"Ye just stay out of yer father's way, ye hear me?"

"Oh yes, I will be as quiet as a mouse, I'll not be a nuisance. I'll be as Papa says, 'seen but not heard.' Thank you, Clarissa." She threw her arms about the nurse and hugged her. Then she pulled open the doors and began to leave but was stopped once again by Clarissa.

"And, lamb, ye stop shinnin' down the railing. We don't want another broken wrist."

Tiffany smiled at Clarissa, nodding her head. Closing the door behind her, she bounded down the stone steps two at a time. Lifting up her skirt to her knees, she ran down the crushed stone drive. The wind whipped her hair about and pinkened her cheeks with its bite. Reaching the stables, she paused at its threshold. She dropped her skirts, patted her hair in place, and took a deep, calming breath. She hoped her appearance would pass her father, the earl's, muster. He constantly made her aware of how badly she disappointed him by her dress. She calmly walked into the stable, trying to act demure and feminine when really she'd love nothing better than to burst in and run down its corridor. Suppressing this urge was pure torture for the exuberant eight-year-old.

As she approached the stall where Moria lay, she overheard her father. "Once again, it's bloodlines, I tell you. The dam was unproven. She had no lineage, and the result of it lies here—an unfit colt!"

Hearing him smack his gloves against his leg, she moved cautiously forward, knowing the tone of his voice, a tone he often used when she displeased him. And she displeased him often, for she heard that tone in his voice regularly. She was not proper—knew nothing about decorum or propriety, whatever that was. Tiffany moved quietly to the open door of the stall and was as yet unseen.

"I should never have listened to Percy Engstrom. What the hell does he know about breeding? He let that son of his marry some Irish lass! Hell, he's got the worst stable in all of England!" He threw his hands up in disgust.

Aeyhish El-Kadin, the master stable hand, stood at her father's side. He had been a slave whom her mother had saved from certain death and had felt he owed her mother his life, serving as horse trainer even after her death eight years before. Tiffany could not hear what Aeyhish said to her papa, for he spoke in soft tones as was his habit.

"Bah! No matter that she looked the part, the mare failed. The proof is lying there!" Her father waved his hand across the stall.

"They say from an acorn a mighty oak grows; perhaps he just needs time. There is no harm in giving him time, for his sire's blood is traced to Alexander the Great's stallion, Bucephalus."

"Are you daft? You heathens place everything in the hands of fate. His sire, Ghengis Khan, you say—now, there is a bloodline proven. The mare, nay, she was useless. Look at him." William Courtland pointed and he continued. "Too weak to even raise himself. No, I'll not waste another shilling on him."

For the first time since her arrival, Tiffany moved into the stall. There lying on the floor was Moria. Tiffany thought she was so still, as if sleeping. A few feet away lay a scrawny black colt. Tiffany smiled, never before having seen a newly born foal. In her eight-year-old eyes, the foal was beautiful, bearing a shiny coat as black as her own hair, long, gangly legs much like her own, even a proud, angular face. She fell in love with him on sight.

"Put him out of his misery and haul the dam's carcass

out of here as well. I want the kill clean. Use a pistol and do not slit its throat as is your heathen practice."

Upon hearing her father's words, Tiffany involuntarily cried out. "No, Papa, please don't kill him!" She ran to him, clutching his pant leg.

William Courtland glared down at his daughter and, as always, took in her appearance, noting her improper attire, her untidy hair, and her being where she should not be. He pushed her away from his leg. In a disapproving voice he asked, "And where are your manners, young lady? I've told you you're only to speak when addressed. And what are you doing out here? Have I not told you numerous times that the stables are not a proper place for a lady of your breeding?"

"I . . . I wanted to see Moria's new foal, Papa," she stammered, but looked him in the eye, raising her chin slightly.

"Well, see for yourself." He waved his hand toward the foal. "A perfect example of what I have been trying to drill into that head of yours. This is the result of a tainted bloodline. A freak of nature, worthless because he has no breeding!"

"But . . . but surely, Papa, he has some value."

"No, my dear child, he has none. He is tainted. His lack of breeding prevents him from rising, for he is too weak. There is none to feed him, and I'll not have him taint my blooded stock." He turned from her and began to give further instructions to Aeyhish.

Tiffany pulled at his hand, causing him to turn to her. "Did I not tell you to leave?" he ground out sternly.

"Papa, please, I will care for him. You need not spend another shilling on him." She saw him narrow his eyes, but ran on anyhow. "I promise I will practice my scales diligently, I'll even eat the meat at dinner, and I'll fold my napkin." Seeing a weakening in her father, she quickly added, "Why, I'll give up my bonbons for a whole month, just please don't kill him."

The earl considered her words and promises. He was about to reply when a servant informed him of the arrival of his solicitor. "Do what you will, daughter, but he'll die, mark my words, and if he does, I'll nonetheless hold you to your promises. His survival, it's meaningless; if he lives or dies matters not, for he cannot bring me the promised coin any longer." With that, the earl left, dismissing both the fate of the foal and his daughter.

Tiffany stood to the side as Aeyhish directed the stable hands to remove the dead mare. After they left, she struggled to lift a fresh bale of hay. Aeyhish helped her, bringing it to the stall, where she spread it abundantly on the floor.

Tiffany stood back, watching the foal, who still had not risen and lay, his chest heaving. She turned to Aeyhish, asking softly, "Do you think he'll live?"

Aeyhish smiled at her, thinking how she resembled her mother, a mother she never knew. He did not much like the earl, finding him to be a cold, hard man, as evidenced by his handling of Tiffany. Aeyhish had stayed at Courtland Manor because of Amelia's daughter, finding in the little girl a spirit and courage her mother had only partially possessed. "It is in the hands of a power greater than ours, child," he said softly. "But we could not do harm in helping, although the outcome we cannot control."

His words gave her a flicker of hope, which gleamed in her blue eyes. "I'll do whatever you say; why, I'll even appeal to your Allah."

He silently prayed Allah would intervene and save the colt, for he knew the price her promises to her father would cost her. She was full of life, full of spirit and courage. She would one day be a woman of strong passions, and he hoped she would find a man who could cherish and cultivate her essence, not stifle it as her father tried to do. He watched her kneel on the newly strewn straw and place the foal's head on her lap, stroking his muzzle. Silently he left.

''Why, you feel just like the soft velvet of my dinner dress.'' She tentatively raised her small hand and touched his forehead. She saw his small body shivering with the cold and laid her body on him to share her warmth. She whispered to him in her child's voice, ''You know you must get up. All horses are supposed to do so. Why, it will be impossible for us to ride like the wind with you lying this way.''

Throughout the day, she kept a watchful vigil over him, offering comfort and company to the abandoned foal. She never left his side; he was not alone.

By afternoon, when most had given up on the colt, Tiffany held on. She told him stories, made plans for him, gave him warmth. By early evening, all had given up, but only she continued to coax him to take nourishment into his weakened body; when he shivered, she shared her warmth, and when he would have let go, she gave him strength. And when he struggled to a sitting position, his flanks heaving with the exertion, she encouraged him and never lost hope, even when he lay back down.

As darkness began to fall, all that could be done, had been; his fate lay with God. Salty tears streamed down Tiffany's cheeks. The foal was still, as if dead. Cradling his head in her arms, she cried softly. ''Please don't leave me. You can't leave me alone.'' She sniffled and wiped her eyes with the back of her hand. ''I believe in you. I'll name you after the magical kingdom of Xanadu that I believe in and love. It is a place of kings. Don't leave me, stay, we will ride there, you and I. I love you,'' she sobbed.

Aeyhish stood quietly in the passageway, concealed by the lengthening shadows of dusk, tears filling his eyes as he watched the child willing her spirit into the dying colt.

The colt's breathing was shallow, his sides barely rising. He opened his large, liquid black eyes, and gazed up at Tiffany. A tremor shook his frail body, and with a surge of strength, he pushed into a sitting position, and with the spirit drawn from his mistress, he righted his wobbly front legs, bringing his hindquarters up. Standing shakily, he nuzzled Tiffany's face.

It was as if they shared a soul; both cast motherless and alone into an unkind world, which had no meaning or place for them until they found each other. It was destiny that a lonely girl and an orphan colt should find each other.

They grew together, complemented each other, shared common traits of spirit and determination. As youngsters, they were unruly, mischievous, needing a firm but gentle hand. As adolescents, they were high-strung, temperamental—seeking understanding and encouragement. Through their growth, there was an ever-present, unquenchable need for freedom. Xanadu's pursuit of it was purely instinctive, while Tiffany's quest was fired by self-preservation.

On a blustery March morning, as rider and mount moved rhythmically over the endless hills, their black manes flying out behind them, the wind roaring in their ears, and the blood coursing through their veins, they sought their elusive butterfly.

In a burst of spring, they raced across the lush new grass up to flower-laden fields to pursue it and found it in a flower chain necklace hung regally about the horse's neck.

They glimpsed their butterfly on a warm July day under a scorching summer sky and chased it into the cool woods, grasping it as they frolicked and splashed in the ice-cold waters of a brook.

It caught them as horse and rider moved from a canter to a flowing gallop, racing the autumn breeze and leaves. And over every hedge and wall they jumped, they chased it. They saw it hide as they watched the squirrels forage, the birds fly south, and the earth prepare to sleep.

Their endless pursuit of it took them across the crest of a hill, silhouetting them against an autumn night lit by a harvest moon. And when the earth was shrouded in a blanket of white, the snow-laden branches of a tree would beckon them to find it. And they found it while a rider sat catching snowflakes on her tongue and a horse with lowered head blew inquisitively at the snow-covered ground. They hadn't really needed to seek it, for it had always been with them—it was interred in their souls.

Chapter One

The black cloak of night which covered the sleepy land began to rise. The moon fading and the stars dimming, the black curtain lifted in the hour before dawn. Creatures of the forest began to stir in anticipation of a new day.

The thundering of hooves echoed in the stillness as a lone rider on a mount as black as the night, save for its hooves and blaze, raced over the newly fallen dew which covered the high meadow grass. This solitary figure leaned close to the neck of its mount as they plunged headlong into the wooded area, avoiding the low-hanging branches of trees.

The rider's thoughts were racing as fast as the magnificent beast. At a glance, the rider appeared to be a young lad of twelve or thirteen, dressed in breeches, with a cap atop his head. In actuality, it was a girl, Tiffany Elizabeth Courtland, a countess and last in line, directly descended from Robert Marlowe Courtland, seventeenth earl of Courtland Manor.

As the horse pushed toward its destination, Tiffany shot a glance up at the sky, noting that the inky blackness had turned a light purple. "Oh, it will be beautiful this morning," she said to no one. She squeezed her mare's side, increasing the wild pace, and thought it seemed like ages since she'd felt this free. She had been severely reprimanded and punished by her father, William Courtland, over an incident involving Miriam Wareingham. She shook her head lightly, recalling her father's anger, which had not yet diminished. It was not her fault that Miriam didn't hold her seat, and how was she to know that Miriam was on the other side of the hedge when she'd jumped Xanadu? Miriam was not really hurt, only her pride, for she was trying to show Alan how well her gelding responded to her. Well, she certainly did show him! Tiffany smiled wickedly, remembering the image of Miriam sitting, legs sprawled, in the midst of a large mud puddle. Tiffany's smile faded, recalling the fuss Lady Wareingham had made over the incident—advising her father that Tiffany was nothing but a wild hoyden who needed to be sent to a convent school, where her behavior would be molded into that of a demure, feminine young lady of her station. What ensued after Lady Wareingham left was nothing that had not happened a hundred times before in her fifteen years. She was punished and ordered to refrain from riding; Xanadu was off limits entirely, and her bonbons were taken away. Her father again reminded her of her position, her bloodlines, and how the family name would be dragged through the mud by the gossip mongers. As if it were her fault that they were making wagers at the local tavern as to how long it would be before she pulled another stunt.

The sky began to change its hue from the deep purple to the dark blues and grays that would soon lighten. She pushed Touche faster, wanting to reach her favorite place—the bluff, where she had, for almost seven years, religiously watched the day break. She knew her sentence had not been lifted, but could not take another day of imprisonment. The only thing missing was Xanadu; she would not place Nathan, their groom, in jeopardy, and so did not go to the stables. Instead she took Touche, who had been grazing in the paddock. Tiffany knew if she timed it right, she would be able to return undetected. Laughing aloud, she was smug in her belief that she could pull this escapade off cleanly. But then, with a frown, she wondered why she had to pull anything off. Alan had told her that she had to start acting like a lady—had to repress some of her rebelliousness and take on, at least for appearance's sake, some decorum. But why? Tiffany never understood *why* she had to be someone she wasn't. And as far as titles went, she never understood what some people saw in a title. As far as she was concerned, the titled persons who visited Courtland Manor were stuffy, old, pompous people, impressed more with who they thought they were than with what they actually were. "Bah, titles! Position means nothing to me!" she shouted to the birds that flew overhead, disturbed by the pounding hooves of the horse that raced through their wooded domain.

"I wonder what my great-grandmother, Katherine Courtland, would have said." Often she heard the lecture from her father about Katherine and her wild, outlandish behavior. How she kept the gossip mills churning! As Tiffany's father had pointed out, she had inherited not only her great-grandmother's sapphire eyes and natural ability to ride, but also that damn tainted Irish blood of hers. Tiffany loved those lectures, because she felt a closeness to Katherine. She did not like the fact that her great-grandfather, Robert Marlowe Courtland, had abducted Katherine and made her his mistress until she finally agreed to marry him. She would never have given in to any man's demand. No, she had found the man for her, and he was nothing like her great-grandfather. He was kind, understanding, and considerate of her—Alan Winston Thurston. Yes, someday she would marry Alan, and with her father's blessing, for Alan was a lord and would someday be an earl, so that would make her father happy—her husband would have a title. Actually, Tiffany could care less if he was nothing more than Alan. As a matter of fact, she would prefer it, for it would mean she would not have to live within the strict confines of the peerage.

The light shades of gray streaked across the horizon as Touche broke through the woods onto the headland of the bluff. Tiffany pulled her mount to a halt and sat astride, looking at the sky, waiting for the first pink streaks of dawn to appear. Touche pawed the ground, eager to stretch her legs, but Tiffany checked her and the mare stood. Tiffany's cheeks flushed with color as a fine sheen of perspiration glistened on her face. Leaning onto Touche's neck, she looked with anticipation at the horizon.

"I know it will be beautiful," she whispered to Touche. "I wish Alan had reconsidered, and ridden with me." Tiffany pondered Alan. He was her only friend and confidant. She was not friendly with the other titled girls, for they found her behavior to be shocking and thought of her as a misfit. Alan did not seem to be overly bothered by her riding astride, bareback and barefooted. Her breeches never seemed to disturb him either. But of late, he seemed to be busy elsewhere, escorting this young lady or that one to soirées. Of course, he was a man of twenty, and his interests were different now. "Just you wait, Alan, until I am old enough to make my first season, and then you'll escort *me* to all those silly balls. I will bedazzle you with my charm and wit, and you'll be so enamored with me, you'll ask for my hand. And I will wave my fan and contemplate your proposal, batting my eyelashes coyly, and then throw my arms around your neck and scream, *'Yes!'* She giggled at her words, but wondered briefly if she was pretty enough for Alan. She was not like Beth Applegate or Miriam Wareingham—small, curvy, and blond. She was too tall, too long-legged, and dark-haired. She shook her head. She did not fit the current mold of beauty. Well, maybe I'll look different when I'm older. She looked up and saw that the sky was changing. Brilliant yellows mingled with pink as the sun crept over the horizon. Tiffany's eyes, the windows of her soul, spoke as no words could. They sparkled and gleamed in happiness. All of what she was, who she was, what she felt, was revealed in her sapphire eyes. The golden rays of the sun stretched out toward her, bathing her face in their glow. She reached up, grabbing the brim of her wool cap, and pulled it off. Long, raven tresses cascaded down her back to her waist. She swung her head from side to side, her hair swinging like black silk, catching the sun's rays, which reflected the blue-black hue. Here is where she felt wanted, loved; here is where her spirit was free.

She flung her cap skyward, swung her leg over Touche's neck, and leaped to the ground. Then she spun a cartwheel, standing upright, arms outstretched, to embrace the morning. Laughing gaily, she joyously greeted the day.

Unobserved, at the edge of the woods before the clearing, stood a man whose own thoughts had been interrupted by the sound of pounding hooves. He glanced up to see a rider and mount gallop past him, heading to the headland. He watched the lad pull the mount to a halt, noting the antics of the horse and the subtle checking of the reins by the lad. He moved quietly through the woods and stopped, resting against a tree, and coolly gazed at the intruders. His gray eyes passed hurriedly over the figure clad in breeches, resting for a moment on the lad's bare feet.

When the sun kissed the twilight good day, the gray eyes moved to rest on the profile, which appeared very soft, very feminine, and an easy smile lifted the corners of his mouth as he realized that the lad was no lad, but a lady. He moved closer, quietly, so as not to disturb the solitary girl. He saw the flush in her cheeks and the fine sheen of perspiration that covered her lovely face. His eyes were drawn to the rapid rise and fall of her breast, and when she raised her arm, the cloth of her shirt stretched taut, revealing the young, round fullness of her breast and the pert peak of her nipple. His attention was reluctantly drawn by the tumbling of her glorious mass of raven tresses that fell to her waist, a waist, his experienced eye noted, he could span with his hands.

He grinned when she leaped to the ground and went head over heels and back upright again. His eyes traveled the length of her as she walked to the edge of the bluff, taking in her long, coltish legs, round, soft buttocks, and the carefree, almost provocative sway of her curvy hips. He smiled, watching the bewitching girl in her childlike embrace of dawn.

He thought her to be around fifteen or so, a bit thin, he smiled crookedly, but in time, she would fill out quite nicely. He noted a natural grace and sultriness to her walk. He eyed her rounded hips, nicely displayed in the breeches, imagining the young woman this girl would become in two years time. She had something else, something inborn, like a pervading spirit; passion, it seemed, ruled her, as if it was in her nature. Now it was young, innocent, virginal, in its essence, but in time, with the right tutelage and the right man, it would blossom and burst forth like a newly tapped well from which a man could drink forever.

He watched her and thought he could do so all day. He saw her curtsy to the sun as it came fully above the horizon and could not suppress a throaty chuckle from escaping his lips.

Tiffany spun around when she heard the laugh; the sparkle and gleam in her eyes fled, as fear of discovery took over. She saw a man unknown to her, leaning negligently against a tree. A myriad of expressions washed over her face, relief finally settling on her features when she realized she was not in danger of being discovered by her father. The rapid display of emotions did not go unnoticed by the intruder, nor did the return of the sparkle and gleam in the sapphire eyes that regarded him.

Tiffany placed her hands on her rounded hips, raised a delicately arched brow, and indignantly said, "Pray, sir, what do you find so amusing?"

A gleam of admiration flickered in the gray eyes as they moved casually over her. He missed nothing in his perusal, absorbing the wild disarray of tresses, which tumbled about a delicately carved oval face and raised brow above an almond-shaped, sapphire eye. He grinned broadly in admiration and let his gray gaze course from her cheekbones to her fine, straight nose, whose tip turned up to the small, slight tilt of her chin—a sign of pride. But it was her mouth that held his gaze. Her hidden passion and vulnerability were revealed in its fullness and softness. It was inviting, and he suppressed the urge to taste it. She promised to be exquisite.

"You," he replied to her question as he unfurled himself and stood at his full height.

As he slowly moved toward her, Tiffany's eyes widened, taking in his full measure. He was uncommonly tall, and she instinctively took a step back, feeling small and vulnerable.

He stopped, smiling at her reaction, causing Tiffany to stand her ground and tilt her head defiantly toward him. He moved with casual grace toward her, and she noticed the broadness of his shoulders and the rippling muscles of his arms. She fought the urge to retreat, in spite of the power and forcefulness he exuded.

"What governess have you escaped, child?" he slowly drawled as he stopped a hair's breadth from her.

Child! Tiffany bristled, and all caution fled, along with any thought of retreat. She tossed her head and replied indignantly, "I am not a child!" She brushed a strand of hair from her mouth with her hand. "And I assure you, sir, I have no need for a governess."

He deliberately let his eyes slowly roam over her form as if considering her claim. His mouth curved into a smile as he spoke. "That's debatable, little one."

Tiffany's eyes narrowed at the affront of this man. She took note that he was older, with dark, winged brows, arched above the most piercing, penetrating gray eyes she had ever seen. She shivered involuntarily, feeling as if they touched her soul. Composing herself, she sarcastically retorted, "No doubt someone of your advanced years would think so. Age, I'm told, distorts the body as well as the mind."

Amusement gleamed in the gray eyes. A grin flashed dazzlingly against his tanned skin in response to her words.

She realized that he was laughing at her and became more angry. "Obviously in your case, sir, your mind has been affected."

His response to her words was to throw his head back and laugh. She had a sharper wit than most of her age, and he appreciated a woman with wit.

Tiffany, too naive to appreciate the compliment, again felt that she was the brunt of his laughter. She responded in anger, which now flared in her stormy eyes.

Realizing she was angry at his laughter, the man with the gray eyes attempted to make amends, but Tiffany spoke first. "Stand aside, you . . . you . . . hyena, and let me pass!"

"Little one, a hyena, you say." He spread his arms and continued. "What you see here is a man, flesh and blood." He moved slightly to let her pass.

With all the dignity befitting a queen, she brushed past him, her head held high, raven tresses rippling as she strode barefoot to her mount. Before jumping onto Touche, she turned back to him and called out, "A man, aye, but sired by a hyena." She leaped up, kicking her mount into a gallop, hearing mocking laughter trailing behind her.

Chapter Two

"Jacob, kindly awaken Lady Tiffany. The hour grows late and she should break the fast soon."

"Yes, my lord," Jacob replied as he refilled the earl's cup with tea. "Will you require anything else, sir?"

The earl gazed up from his paper to regard his servant above the rim of his spectacles, shaking his head, dismissing the servant.

William Malcolm Courtland, nineteenth earl of Courtland Estates, sat enjoying his second cup of tea after having finished a substantial breakfast of eggs, cold pork pudding, and sweet muffins. He withdrew a pocket watch from his vest, snapping open the gold lid, noting the time, before returning it to his pocket. He continued to read the financial column, intermittently sipping his tea.

At fifty-five years of age, the earl still cut a fine figure of a man. His raven hair, although dusted with gray, was thick and plentiful. While he required spectacles for reading, his brown eyes were alert and ever shrewd. His broad shoulders, while not as firm as they had been, did not stoop with age. He took pride in his appearance and attributed his well-preserved looks to generations of careful breeding. His lineage was impeccable, tracing back to William the Conqueror. His face bespoke character and expounded aristrocratic beginnings, evidenced in its bone structure and aquiline nose.

William continued reading, but again withdrew his watch, noting ten minutes had passed. He wondered where his daughter was. He had risen early, as was his custom, believing one did not manage estates indolently lolling abed. He had instilled this in his daughter as well. He folded his paper neatly and looked across the table, seeing her place setting. He had expected to see her up and about. "Must be some female disorder this morning," he spoke aloud, and picked up his tea, sipping it.

His thoughts traveled to the work he had scheduled to complete. He had amassed a fortune in his lifetime and had increased the wealth of Courtland Estates when, on the untimely death of his older brother, Robert, he took over the title and handling of Courtland Manor. *Robert.* It was not often William allowed himself to think of the past—he found no percentage in it and felt it was a waste of a man's energy. However, today he allowed himself the luxury. Robert had had everything—looks, charm, and title. He had won and married Winifred Channing, a beautiful, gracious woman. William had always held a tender for her, even though she was four years his senior. He had loved his brother, admired him and envied him. He had been crushed by his death, and after the shock wore off, he'd damned him for being so imprudent as to accept the bet to ride the stallion that had trampled him to death. Robert had been tainted by their grandmother's Irish blood, just as his daughter, Tiffany, was. Her wildness was more pronounced than Robert's, for she flaunted all social conventions, while Robert had lived on the edge of them. Thoughts of his daughter caused him to withdraw his watch again. He frowned, wondering where the hell she was.

After leaving the breakfast room, Jacob ran to locate Godfrey, the butler. Wringing his hands nervously, he said, "His lordship has inquired of Lady Tiffany. Has she been seen?"

Godfrey shook his balding head. "I will inquire of Clarissa if she knows of her whereabouts."

A much-relieved Jacob returned to the kitchens.

Godfrey walked up the staircase, down the long hall, seeking Clarissa. He was the epitome of an English butler, liking things to run smoothly—with no snags. He somehow doubted today would run smoothly. "Madam!" he called to Clarissa, who paused, waiting for the butler to reach her. "His lordship requests the presence or knowledge of the whereabouts of Lady Tiffany."

"I know not where she be, Godfrey."

Godfrey pursed his thin lips. "She is your charge, is she not?"

Clarissa nodded her capped head. "That she is," she replied somewhat tartly.

"Then I suggest, madam, that you locate her posthaste, or else there will be hell to pay." He turned stiffly from Clarissa and walked away. Clarissa engaged the help of Jimmie, the cook's son, to run to the stables to inquire after Tiffany. He returned to inform Clarissa, who stood near Godfrey and Jacob, that Lady Tiffany was nowhere to be found.

Jimmie retreated, and the three servants stood regarding each other, digesting the information at hand. Godfrey cleared his throat and quite pompously stated, "Since his lordship specifically made his request to you, Jacob, then you will inform him that Lady Tiffany cannot be found."

"Damn that chit, I know where she is! Out riding like a banshee. And punished to boot. Well, I tell you!" He slammed his hand on the table, rattling the china. "This time she'll pay. I will take measures to ensure that she does, dearly!"

With that, he stormed out of the room, calling for Godfrey and Clarissa. After a brief conversation, he turned from them, charging into his study, slamming the door behind him. The household staff quickly spread the word throughout, and all held their breaths, knowing their mistress had certainly done it this time. The staff moved silently within, all walking on eggs, knowing the earl's tendency to misdirect his anger, and thanking God that they were not standing in Lady Tiffany's shoes.

Tiffany dismissed the incident on the bluff quickly from her mind when she saw how high the sun had risen on the horizon. "Oh my God!" she cried as she squeezed her knees against Touche's flanks, moving her into a wild gallop.

Maybe, just maybe, she hadn't yet been missed. But all hope fled when she pulled a lathered and winded Touche to a halt before Nathan, the stable hand. The look etched across his sun-wrinkled face was not hopeful. Her worst fears were reconfirmed when she watched Clarissa, walking as fast as her large bulk could carry her. The worry evident on her beloved nurse's face, and the nervous wringing of her gnarled hands, diminished any last remaining hope Tiffany held.

"Lamb, yer father wants you in his study immediately."

Tiffany ran up the stone U-shaped driveway, taking the steps two at a time. The door was opened by a dour-faced Godfrey. She entered the marble foyer, heading to the staircase, when she was stopped by Godfrey's words.

"Lady Tiffany, his lordship awaits you in the study. You are not to bother to change."

She stepped off the stair, nodding her head to Godfrey and making her way barefoot to the study door. She stood before the oak door, patted her disheveled hair, rubbed one dusty foot against the side of her leg, and then the other. Taking a deep breath, trying to still the rapid beat of her heart, she raised her hand and then paused, reluctant to knock, a sense of impending doom surrounding her. She felt that when she entered this room, somehow her fate would be sealed. A long moment passed . . . her hand knocked on the door, the sound echoing, reverberating throughout the house.

Once he'd vented his anger, the earl had turned his energies to a calculated plan of action. He had written three letters; one to Winifred De Namourie, the dowager duchess of Breatoney, another to the Madame Dechamp Academy, and the last, a notice of sale.

He leaned back in his chair and closed his eyes, rubbing them with his thumb and forefinger. He reflected on his plan, a plan that was meant once and for all to straighten out his willful daughter. He grimaced with the painful recall of Tiffany's outrageous behavior and antics he had endured since she was able to walk. The day she jumped from the apple tree onto Duke Alsbury, the fox she hid from the hunt, the day she put the pepper in the salt cellar, and on and on.

He opened his eyes, gazing out the study window, thinking of the scores of governesses who had departed Courtland Manor. Slamming his fist in renewed anger, he said aloud, "Damn. I should have sent her away. But no, I thought she'd fill the void Amelia's death left." He stood at the window, cursing himself for his foolishness, for all Tiffany had brought him was disappointment. She fell short of all his expectations. No matter how often he drilled her on the importance of propriety and comportment, or the responsibilities her title and position demanded, the more unruly and impetuous she became.

He saw her run up the drive. Shaking his head at her attire, he commented to himself, "About the only thing she has is her beauty. And no doubt if she could alter that, she would!" He turned away from the window, thinking her beauty would ensure a good titled husband, for no one who had ever seen her had not remarked on her beauty. "Yes," he said aloud, "her beauty is her salable commodity."

He called out in response to the knock on his door.

Tiffany pushed open the heavy door, standing at its threshold, watching her father. William's gaze traveled the length of her, coming to rest on her bare feet. He curtly waved his hand, motioning her to the leather wing-back chair in front of his desk. Tiffany closed the door and padded across the room, seating herself in the chair. Sitting primly, lost in the oversize chair, she consciously placed one bare foot over the other, tucking them under the chair. Tiffany saw her father's stern expression and read the disapproval in his eyes. She nearly jumped when his voice boomed out, "Well, what do you have to say for yourself this time?"

Tiffany squirmed uncomfortably in her seat and lowered her eyes demurely, unable to meet the unrelenting stare. A long moment of silence reigned, causing her to peak up from lowered lashes. She jumped, finding her father bending over the desk and inches away from her nose. He shouted, causing her to squeeze her eyes closed momentarily.

"Don't give me that sweet, innocent face. I am not a fool, girl, prey to your insincere acts of contrition." He straightened and slammed his fist on his desktop. "You deserve nothing more than to be beaten. It is my right and duty, you know. One I, unfortunately, never used and don't intend to start now."

Tiffany's eyes widened at his words. He had done many things to her, but never had he struck her. She watched him move behind the desk and lower himself into his chair. He smiled an awful smile and continued calmly, "No, I won't have your actions reduce me to such behavior." He leaned back in his chair, a smile of smug satisfaction on his face. "Oh no, my dear, don't look relieved yet, for compared to what I have planned for you, a beating will seem a deliverance."

She had never seen her father this angry before. He was not reacting as he normally did—she was not hearing the usual lectures of breeding, position, and duties. She was frightened.

William cleared his throat and began, "I admit, Tiffany, I had thought by your recent acts of compliance that you had mended your ways. Fool I was, but no longer, my dear. I have made plans for you. Plans that will turn you about, so to speak, break that spirit of yours, and allow your breeding to take over." He lifted three sealed letters in his hand, waving them in front of her. "Here, my dear, are letters to be posted today! One is to Madame Dechamp, who runs a school where the finer arts are taught and which you will attend. I am told that I shall be pleased with the results. They have handled many such as you. The second is to Dowager Breatoney, your Aunt Winifred, advising her that you will reside at her chateau while you attend the academy. Winifred is a titled personage of the realm and will see to your social obligations and education. You will be prepped, prepared, and presented to the crème de la crème of French society." He paused, as an almost evil smile crossed his face. "And this . . ." He waved the last letter in her face. "This is my coup de grace, as it were. A notice advising the sale of that beast that you are so fond of."

Tiffany's head snapped up, eyes widening in disbelief. The color drained from her face, leaving her ivory skin pale. She cried the first word since entering the study. "NO!"

A look of smug arrogance crossed the earl's face. With a triumphant look, he remarked dryly, "Oh yes, the beast goes." He sat down and began to give attention to the work he had scheduled to complete. He put his spectacles on to review a contract. He paused, looking over the rim of his spectacles, dismissing her with a wave of his hand.

Rising on shaky legs, Tiffany paused, wanting to speak, to plead, to beg, but was unable to push down the lump in her throat. She looked at her father, tears blurring her vision. She turned, walking toward the door, her heart breaking, her spirit battered. Before she put her hand on the doorknob, she summoned all of her courage and said, "Father, please don't sell—"

Without looking up from his work, he cut her off. "I said the beast goes."

Chapter Three

Sunlight filtered through the tall, leafy trees. The drone and buzzing of insects could barely be heard over the gurgling and bubbling of a brook that wound its way through the wood. The air was heavy with the humidity common to late summer, producing an unbearable atmosphere.

Tiffany sat on the grassy embankment of the rain-swollen bank of the winding brook, resting her head on top of her raised knees, arms wrapped about her legs. Her toes peeked out from beneath the sodden hem of her riding skirt. She had cast her stockings and boots aside under an old sycamore before wading into the cool waters of the brook. Touche grazed on the sweet clumps of grass, switching her tail and stomping her feet to ward off the bothersome insects.

Tiffany watched and pondered the fate of a leaf that clung bravely to the mossy side of a protruding stone resisting the churning waters. She likened the leaf's struggle to her own, fighting forces stronger than she, sighing in despair when the leaf lost its battle and was whisked away from the sanctuary it had clung to so dearly. She saw it surface, spin, and then swirl helter-skelter until the current caught it on a predestined course down the stream, out of sight. How like the leaf she was; wanting only to float free but instead being swept up and put on a course of another's choosing. Tears welled, threatening to spill as she contemplated her fate.

The insistent hammering in his head was aggravated by the pounding hooves of his mount as it cantered toward the brook. Baron Alan Thurston was suffering mightily from a night of extreme overindulgence of women and drink. He cursed himself silently for having agreed to meet Tiffany so early.

At twenty, he cut a handsome figure, being of common height for men of his day and possessing a pleasant face. He was dressed quite fashionably and befitting his class. A young man of his times, he was required to assume his father's title and the responsibilities that came with it. Thus, he was hell-bent on sowing his wild oats and enjoying all the pleasures his position afforded him: wine, women, and gambling. Considering himself a man of the world, he was a bit annoyed at Tiffany's summons, having no longer the time to devote to the girl.

The pounding in his head lessened as he breathed in the air and felt guilty over his thoughts. After all, there was a time when he truly enjoyed her company. He smiled recalling their first meeting. He had returned from a holiday from school and thought to ride. It was a brisk autumn morn and, to a fourteen-year-old, a perfect day to ride the courses. He had ridden to the meadow and saw a mounted young black stallion break through the woods. To his eye, it appeared as if the rider had lost control, for the stallion was tossing and turning its head, its eyes wild, and flecks of foam appeared at its mouth. He signaled his mount into a canter to try to reach her, but the stallion was galloping at breakneck speed. He watched, stunned, as the girl reigned her mount, clearing the first two jumps with a skill most boys his age did not possess. But it was the last jump, a three-foot-high stone wall, that caused his eyes to fill with fear, and justifiably so, as the stallion refused it, dumping the girl head over heels to the other side. He had nudged his horse faster to get to her side and was surprised when he saw her stand up, brush the seat of her britches, and glare at the stallion. She picked up a stick, remounted the horse, wheeling him back toward the wall. He recalled thinking she was foolish in attempting such a dangerous act. The stallion snorted and tossed its head trying to veer off course but was held in check. When it was two feet away from the wall, Alan noted the stallion's hesitation, and visions of a broken girl filled his mind. However, she anticipated the refusal and brought the stick down on the stallion's hindquarters when they were one stride from the wall, sailing perfectly over it.

From that day on, they became friends, riding over the meadows adjoining their properties. Whenever he was home from school, they'd meet at the bluff to explore the recesses of the glen and streams. She was a capital companion for a young boy; she didn't squirm when baiting her own line, could climb the stalwart oaks faster than a monkey, and was mischievous and full of pranks. But then his life had taken another course and he found stimulation on a different level, and no longer spent lazy afternoons in Tiffany's company but rather wild nights carousing with his friends.

The stumbling of his mount brought him back to the present. He shook his head, feeling decidedly better, and wondered where Edmund Rathsburn would venture to tonight. Possibly to London to one of the clubs to play a hand of cards or roll the dice.

Meanwhile, Tiffany, lost in self-pity, scolded herself, being ashamed of such feelings, knowing they were self-serving. She brushed the tears from her cheeks just as Alan came through the trees. Teary blue eyes lit up on seeing her love. She jumped up, watching him dismount and tether his gelding.

While strolling toward her, he spoke. "Well, sweetling, I hope this is good, for you have me up and about at this ungodly hour." He stopped, seeing the tears in her eyes, and caught her as she threw herself into his arms. Tiffany sobbed brokenheartedly, wetting the front of Alan's crisp white shirt.

"Whatever is the matter?" Alan pushed her from him, holding her at arm's length, so he might see her face.

"I . . . I'm . . . being sent *awayyyy,*" she stammered between tears, "to . . . to France!"

"That's wonderful, Tiffany; why, you'll love it, the court, balls, theater. Nothing to cry about."

She sniffled, wiping her nose against her sleeve. Alan frowned, withdrawing a handkerchief.

"Is that what this is all about?" he asked increduously, for it was every girl's dream to go abroad. She nodded her head, her tresses tumbling from their pins to her shoulders.

"My goodness, Tiffany, I thought something horrible had befallen you. France is the center of fashion, art, cuisine. Why, you'll love it!"

He pulled her into his arms, telling her all the wonderful things that would happen to her in France. Tiffany wept, not listening, just finding comfort in his arms.

Still leaning against him, loving the feel of him, she whispered, "But Father did it as a punishment, Alan."

Alan made a face, wondering how the earl could consider France a punishment. Patting her head absently, he said, "Well, take it from me, Tiffany, it will be a far cry from one. Why, France is quite enlightened, you know, not pompous and stuffy as England."

Tiffany leaned back to gaze up at him. She whispered brokenly, "And he sold Xanadu, Alan . . . he sold my horse." Fresh tears appeared in her eyes.

"Well now, sweetling, 'tis not as bad as it seems." He cupped her chin and continued, "After all, very soon you will be a young lady, a child no longer, and time to put aside such childish notions."

Tears dampened her thick, sooty lashes as she whispered, "I . . . I will always miss him. I . . . I don't think I can put him aside."

"But of course you can! Why, in two years time you'll be busy snagging all those French gallants, dazzling them with your beauty and wit, and not even have time to think of the beast."

She lifted her downcast eyes when he called her beautiful. Her cheeks streaked with the path of her tears, she asked, "Do you really think I'll be beautiful, Alan?"

He smiled softly. Looking down at her tear-streaked face, red nose, and disheveled hair, seeing the promise of future beauty, he said, "Why, of course, and when you return, you'll not even give me the time of day, I wager, for you'll have a line of suitors a mile long."

Startled blue eyes met warm brown eyes. Tiffany declared, "Oh, Alan, you will be above them all. I will always love you." She paused, searching for the words to express her feelings."Why, I will hold my heart only for you, for I love you above anything."

Her childlike sincerity tugged at his heart, and as he gazed at her face, he thought that one day she would be very lovely indeed. "Ah, sweetling, I, too, hold a special place in my heart for you." His words erased all the hurt and gave her something to hold on to, something to see her through her exile.

"Will . . . will you miss me? Will you wait for me?" she asked shyly.

He read the question in her eyes and gave her the answer she needed, although in his own mind, he knew that people's feelings for each other changed. But she would learn that as she grew up. Right now she needed something to hold on to, and so he gave her hope. "But of course, sweetling, but of course."

Tiffany slowly made her way to the window, resting her head against the frame, watching the first rays of sun kiss the earth good day. She thought this would be the last time for quite a while that she'd watch the sun rise over and touch the earth of Courtland Manor. Turning from the window, she made her way slowly to the table, where a small breakfast awaited. She sighed and poured a cup of hot chocolate, wondering if she would find her next bedroom as comfortable and inviting as this one. The back of her eyes burned with the start of unshed tears, and she shook her head trying to stop them.

Tiffany walked to the fireplace carrying the Dresden cup holding her hot chocolate. She had made all her farewells to the servants she had known for fourteen years, had patted the heads of all the mounts in the stable, and had looked at Xanadu's empty stall. The tears that burned her eyes now fell in droplets, clinging to her lashes. Xanadu. No matter what Alan said, she would never forget him and would always miss him. She placed her cup on the mantel and fingered the plate of chocolate bonbons. A soft, sad smile touched her lips as she recalled how she and Xanadu shared a passion for the confections. Her mind screamed for him, and no matter the changes or course of her life, there would always be a void that none save Xanadu could fill.

Tiffany's reverie was interrupted by Clarissa, who waddled in carrying her pale pink traveling dress. "Oh, lamb, yer up and 'bout; good. We best get ye ready. Yer father's already had breakfast, and checking his watch, he is."

A look at her charge told Clarissa everything, and she quickly deposited the dress on a nearby chair, calling, "Now, now, lamb, don't be working yerself up."

Tiffany rushed into the open arms, laying her head against Clarissa's ample bosom, taking comfort from the woman who had given her the closest thing she'd known to a mother's love. Tiffany's shoulders trembled, her voice muffled by the embrace. "Oh, I will miss you so much."

Clarissa patted Tiffany's head, and in a voice close to betraying her own sadness, said, "Ah, lamb, 'twill be all right, ye'll see. 'Tis time anyway for ye to be gone from this place. Time to grow up and become the lady ye are. Best you be gone from 'ere an' in France with the duchess.'' Tears sparkled in the maid's eyes. Speaking more abruptly than intended, for she was beginning to lose control, she added ''Now, lady, let's get ye dressed.''

Clarissa left sniffling, carrying the unfinished breakfast tray. Tiffany stood before her mirror checking her appearance and wondering if she would ever be fashionably beautiful. You silly goose, she thought, what matters is that Alan thinks I'm beautiful. She continued to gaze at her reflection, making attempts at appearing haughty, sophisticated, batting her eyelashes as she had seen women friends of her father's do. She struck a pose: her shoulders straight, her lips drawn in a fine line, a brow raised delicately over her eye, revealing a look of determination. Speaking to her reflection, she said, ''I am going to France, where I shall become a most beautiful, most sophisticated woman.'' Lifting her chin, she continued, ''And I shall return to England and to the man I love.'' She held the pose but for a moment, until the fourteen-year-old girl emerged giggling at her playacting. She heard the boom of her father's voice and ran for the door, opening it, raising her skirt above her knees, running to the end of the hallway, where she paused unseen. She patted her hair, dropped her skirts, and took a deep, calming breath, then turned, proceeding to descend the steps, seeing her father waiting at the bottom.

''Well, you're finally ready, girl, I haven't all day to dally,'' he announced, abruptly taking her hand as she stepped onto the marble floor. ''Now say your final goodbyes and let's be gone.'' He pointed to the line of servants who waited outside on the stone drive.

As the carriage pulled away, Tiffany pushed back the curtain from the back window, gazing at the line of servants who broke rank and were filing back into the manor. She watched for a long time until the figures became smaller and smaller. When she dropped the curtain, a lump formed in her throat and her whole world faded from sight.

The rap of the footman's stick against the carriage top brought Tiffany out of her reverie.

"It appears we are to arrive shortly, Tiffany." William turned, appraising her as he often did, looking for any sign of imperfection.

"Button up your pelisse, daughter."

She readily complied with his request, even though it was warm in the carriage.

"We will be met by the Devonshire family. Winifred made arrangements for you to travel with them." He cleared his throat. "It appears Charles and Carolyn Devonshire have been sent abroad on diplomatic services for the regent, and their daughter, Alysse, will be attending the same academy as yourself. They are close friends to Winifred, and you would do good to follow the example of their daughter." He peered sharply at her for any sign of disagreement. Tiffany realized suddenly her father was not accompanying her abroad, and in an effort to keep her emotions in hand, she bit her trembling lip to still it.

"It seems the girl is already betrothed to an earl," he said with a nod. "Yes, a fine example for you to follow."

Tiffany could not suppress her surprise. "Already betrothed? How old is she, Father?"

"Don't look so shocked, daughter. I have told you repeatedly it is a daughter's responsibility to marry to suit one's family. The girl is your age, and unlike you, has begun to fulfill her duty."

"But does she know him?"

"Matters not," he responded exasperatedly, "as it should not. One marries primarily for lineage and dowry. In your case, you possess both; however, you lack elsewhere, which I hope this stint in France will take care of."

Tiffany lowered her head at his comment but ventured

on, "Do you consider the Marquess Thurston to possess both?"

The earl furrowed his brow at her and replied, "Of course. A good match once the baron takes on a bit more responsibility and stops his—" The sudden halt of the carriage interrupted his words. "Damn, Mason drives like a demon from hell!"

George, the footman, opened the carriage door. The earl stepped out, giving instructions to the footman regarding the trunks, and then assisted Tiffany in her descent.

They were approached by a handsome young man in his early twenties who escorted an older woman on his right arm and a girl about Tiffany's age on his left.

"Sir," the young man addressed William. "I am Brian Devonshire." He extended his hand, which William accepted. "And may I present my mother, Countess Carolyn Devonshire."

Tiffany watched Lady Devonshire extend her gloved hand, thinking she looked like most mothers; she was pleasantly plump, with blond hair swept up in a matronly style, and she possessed warm brown eyes. "It is indeed a pleasure, Earl Courtland, to make your acquaintance. Winifred has spoken kindly of you in the past." She turned to face Tiffany, and smiled. "And who is this darling child?"

"Lady Tiffany Courtland, Countess," William answered, and nudged Tiffany with his elbow. "Mind your manners and curtsy, Tiffany."

A blush crept over Tiffany's features. She curtsied as requested.

Seeing the young girl's embarrassment, Brian quickly intervened. "And may I present my sister, Lady Alysse Devonshire."

Tiffany looked from under lowered lashes at Alysse as she curtsied in kind. She was a petite girl who stood four inches shorter than Tiffany. She possessed beautiful curly wheat-colored hair and large, round cornflower blue eyes. She exemplified everything Tiffany longed to be.

While William, Carolyn, and Brian engaged in light conversation, Tiffany watched the footman at the boarding dock unload the trunks onto the cutter *Raven.* She stood shifting from foot to foot watching the activity, thinking this was the ship that would take her from England. She gazed toward Alysse, surprised to find her regarding her. Alysse was also shifting from foot to foot!

"Alysse, please stop that! It is so nerve-racking," admonished Carolyn when Alysse inadvertently stepped on her mother's slippered foot.

"Yes, Mama." Alysse shifted her eyes to Tiffany. A look passed between them, and both covered their mouths to hide the smiles that crossed their faces.

"It appears the captain is awaiting our boarding," Brian commented. "I think, ladies, we should leave the earl and Lady Tiffany a moment to make their good-byes."

Alysse and Carolyn were escorted to the ship by Brian, who returned to wait a respectful distance from William and Tiffany, as he would never think of letting a young lady go unescorted around the docks.

Tiffany turned, looking up at her father, eyes glistening with tears. The earl, feeling uncomfortable and not able to abide an emotional scene, placed a perfunctory kiss on her forehead and hugged her stiffly.

"Remember who you are, your heritage, your position." His eyes became misty. "Now go! What I do today is far better for you than what I have done in the past." Shoving her gently away when she refused to let go, he headed toward the carriage and, without a backward glance, entered the coach, signaling the driver on.

Tiffany, through tear-welled eyes, watched the coach disappear among the hustle and bustle of the busy docks. She squeezed her eyes tightly closed, preventing the tears from falling. She felt, rather than saw, Brian standing near.

Brian took her hand, gently placing it in the crook of

his arm, and slowly leading her to the quay, said, ''The tide is high, lady, and the captain grows impatient. We must be on our way to another of life's adventures.''

Tiffany, biting her lower lip to stop it from quivering, inquired softly, ''Do you really think of life as an adventure?''

He paused before he responded. ''Well, why not? After all, life is what happens while we are making plans and dreaming dreams. And during the time we are not dreaming or planning, life sneaks in with an adventure or two on the road to our dreams.''

Walking up the gangplank and down the long companionway, Tiffany pondered his words, thinking, Why not? I have my dreams and plans. My trip, nay, adventure, to France won't alter them.

No longer as frightened at her future, she smiled.

The voyage across the channel took two days, during which Tiffany and Alysse became fast friends. They were as different as night and day, but as the adage goes, opposites attract, so they did. Alysse thought Tiffany to be everything she was not—bright, amusing, and beautiful, with her long, dark hair and sapphire eyes. She admired the spirit and courage her new friend possessed and was not taken back when Tiffany confessed how she came to board the ship bound for France.

''Heavens, Tiffany, you are so brave; why, I would still be in shock over it all. Of course,'' she stated sullenly, ''I've never had much spirit or courage, for that matter, to even consider such an escapade.''

A look of concern crossed Tiffany's face as she sat, legs crossed, on her berth, brushing her hair. ''Oh, Alysse, you have been the better for it; look where it got me. Exiled from my beloved Courtland, torn from my true love, Alan, and . . .'' She broke off, tears filling her eyes.

''Oh, Tiffany. Look what I've done making you remember sad things. Brian always says I don't think before I speak."

"It's all right, I have to get used to the fact that Xanadu is gone."

Alysse looked at Tiffany, wishing to kick herself for causing such unhappiness, although she could never imagine being so attached to a horse. God, she rode only because it was expected of her. Certainly not for any enjoyment. Pulling down the covers, she crawled between the cool sheets. "Will you get the light, Tiffany, when you're finished brushing her hair?"

Tiffany blew out the candle and slid into bed, feeling the lulling motion of the ship.

A long moment passed and was broken by Alysse. "Do you think men will find me pretty?"

Tiffany was shocked by the question, thinking Alysse to be what the time considered a fashionable beauty. "Oh, but of course! I bet your coming out will be such a success."

"I do hope so . . . for the sake of my betrothed, at least." Alysse sighed, turning in bed.

"Have you ever met him?"

"No, it was arranged at my birth. The Allistairs are longtime family friends, and my father had promised the Marquess Allistair his firstborn daughter. The marquess had lost all hope what with mother presenting father with three sons, but alas, I was born."

"Is he much older than you?" Tiffany asked, visions of a gnarled old man crossing her mind. She shivered involuntarily.

"He is twenty-six and holds the title. I overheard my older brother, Chad, say, 'He is quite sought after by the ladies.' " She sighed. "As soon as I am eighteen, the marriage will take place and the contract will be fulfilled."

Tiffany turned to her side, peering through the dark,

trying to see Alysse. "Does it disturb you that you had no choice in the matter? For it certainly would bother me."

"What can I do? It is how things are done."

Tiffany wondered about Alysse's calm acceptance of the situation. The rocking motion of the ship caused the girls to drift to the edges of sleep. But before falling off, Alysse softly asked, "Do you think we can have a few girlish adventures before I become a married woman?"

Tiffany smiled in the dark, saying, "Oh, most definitely!"

Tiffany could never recall feeling as anxious as she did this moment. The closer the carriage pushed onward to Paris, the more anxious she became. Her stomach knotted with each passing mile and she nearly jumped out of her skin when Carolyn leaned over to stop her hands from doing irreparable damage to the silk of her gown. "Now, Tiffany dear, don't fret so. Winnie and I go back eons. She's not an ogre, you know, dear."

Tiffany smiled tremulously and stilled her hands, folding them in her lap.

Brian spoke. "I believe we will be crossing the property line of Breatoney. Yes, indeed we have; see there." He pointed at the stone wall. "There lies the beginning of Breatoney."

Tiffany looked out in the direction of Brian's finger, seeing a high stone wall. Her stomach began to flutter anew.

"Oh, thank God, I shall be so grateful when this trip is over; what with all this bouncing around the countryside and jostling, my lumbago is flaring up," moaned Carolyn.

Three pairs of eyes regarded her, and somewhat piqued by their ill-concealed humor, Carolyn retorted, "Well, all this carousing is fine for you young people, but when you get to my age, it is not enjoyable." Waving a gloved hand at them, she continued, "Winnie has asked us to stay, and I thank goodness for it. Winnie will know exactly what to do to relieve my aching bones. Why, she knows exactly what to do and when. Never flustered, no, not Winnie. Why, did I ever tell you about . . ."

Resting his head against the squab, Brian rolled, his eyes heavenward. The girls had been treated to a number of Carolyn's long, confusing stories during the voyage, and prepared themselves for another. They happened to glance at Brian and, seeing his reaction, could not suppress a laugh escaping from their lips.

Carolyn was stopped midway into her story by their laughter. A confused expression crossed her face as she glanced between the girls and her second son, who sat beside her, a calm look etched across his face.

Brian responded with an arched brow and inquired, "Yes, madam, you were saying."

Tiffany was able to stifle her laughter, but Alysse giggled louder.

Still not understanding what Alysse found amusing, Carolyn quickly admonished her, saying, "Stop giggling for naught, Alysse; people will think you've gone daft."

Further comments were forestalled by the halting of the carriage. Tiffany's heart pounded harder and harder and her hands began to sweat when the carriage door was opened by a footman dressed in blue and white livery, the colors of Breatoney. Tiffany was assisted down by the footman. While she waited for the others to alight, she gazed up at the house that was to be her home. She took in the marble edifice three stories high. Terraced levels led to the front entry, which was covered by a large portico that served as a second-floor balcony, supported by large pillars, giving the relatively new building a Grecian flair.

An impeccably dressed butler answered their summons, taking their coats and hat. Tiffany stood in the foyer gazing up at its ceiling, which vaulted to a peak three stories up with windows, allowing the flow of light to burst onto the foyer. A balcony encircled the foyer, supported by carved columns. In the center of the foyer was a U-shaped staircase, which curved gracefully and met at the second-floor landing.

"Her Grace is awaiting you in the salon." The butler handed their coats to the waiting footman. "If you will kindly follow me." He proceeded up the staircase, leading them through an arched doorway to the gallery.

Tiffany stopped so suddenly when her eyes caught the extraordinary view of the formal gardens that she nearly stepped on Lady Devonshire's heel.

"Lady Devonshire and party have arrived, Your Grace." The butler stepped aside, allowing them to enter.

Winifred De Namourie, the dowager duchess of Breatoney, was sitting on a settee in front of a large group of windows. The sun streaming in behind her bounced off her graying auburn hair. Bright emerald eyes gleamed out, touching the assembled group before her. She rose gracefully, grasping Lady Devonshire's hands in her own. In perfect French she said, "Carolyn, you are looking as young as ever. It appears traveling agrees with you."

"Oh bosh, Winnie. You always say the nicest things, but I feel as old as Methuselah. Traveling is for the young, I keep telling Charles. I am practically worn out with all that bumping along, and do believe my lumbago is flairing up again."

Smiling gently, Winifred led her dear friend to a soft, comfortable chair. "I remembered your lumbago, Carolyn, and as we speak, water is being heated for a nice warm soak. But first, I thought you'd like a spot of tea."

Carolyn laughed. "Oh, Winnie, all these years in France and Italy, and still the proper Englishwoman. Perhaps a bit of sherry first." Carolyn settled herself comfortably.

Winnie turned to face the others, her green gaze resting on Alysse. "My child, you have grown. Do not worry. I won't bore you with the nonsense of how little you were the last time we met. You indeed are a lovely girl, Alysse."

Alysse curtsied and replied, "Thank you, Your Grace."

"Poo poo 'Your Grace,' Alysse; Aunt Winnie will do.

After all, Carolyn is the sister I never had.'' She directed Alysse to a chair near Carolyn.

''And you, you handsome devil, must be Brian. It is a pleasure to see you again.''

Brian, bowing over her hand and gently placing a kiss on it, replied, ''It has been over a year since my last tour of France.''

''Ah yes, a captain in the English military it is now. I had heard your regiment was instrumental in Napoleon's defeat.'' Winnie smiled.

''Along with a number of others, I must confess, Your Grace.''

Winnie smiled in response and turned to Tiffany.

Tiffany had been waiting, trying not to fidget or show her trembling hands. She discreetly wiped her sweating palms on her dress and licked her lips in a nervous reaction. When Winifred turned to her, she dropped into a curtsy.

Winifred reached out to cup Tiffany's chin gently with her hand. ''And you must be Tiffany.''

Tiffany swallowed, replying, ''Yes, Aunt, oh, umm, Your Grace.''

Winnie's smile broadened. Stepping closer to Tiffany, she enfolded her in an embrace and pulled away, holding her at arm's length. ''Now, none of that 'Your Grace' nonsense; Aunt Winnie will do nicely. I have waited a long time to be called that.''

Tiffany shyly smiled. ''Yes, Your . . . Aunt Winnie.''

Winnie brought her arms about Tiffany's shoulder, leading her to the chair next to her own. Tiffany sat primly while tea was served, hoping her manners were acceptable to her aunt. She listened with half an ear to the conversation, thankful she was not its topic.

The shadows thrown by the setting sun indicated the hour had grown late. Winifred stood, causing Brian to rise as well. ''How utterly thoughtless of me. I lost track of time and made my guests suffer through a long tea.'' She pulled the bell rope, summoning the butler, who returned posthaste.

''Oh, nonsense, Winnie; why, I'm quite comfortable now. Must be the sherry. Charles always did tell me I should stay away from strong libations. Makes me dizzy, a bit confused at times,'' remarked Carolyn as she sipped her second glass. ''It is quite medicinal, though. There was that time when Charles and I were in India . . .'' The timely appearance of the butler ceased any further discussion of the matter.

''Yes, Your Grace.''

''Jacques, kindly escort my guests to their rooms so they might refresh themselves before dinner.''

Brian assisted a tipsy Carolyn from her chair, leading her to the door. Alysse followed behind, as did Tiffany.

''Tiffany dear.''

Tiffany turned, ''Yes, Aunt Winifred?''

Winifred softly smiled before speaking. ''If you are not too tired, dear, I'd like to speak with you.''

Good heavens, what have I done? she thought, walking toward Winifred.

Winifred saw fear wash over Tiffany's face, and seeking to still her doubts, quickly added, ''I thought it would be nice for us to get to know one another.''

''Oh yes, I would love that, too.'' She smiled, her blue eyes reflecting relief.

Winifred was momentarily startled by Tiffany's smile; it was reminiscent of her dear late husband, Robert's. Having taught herself over the years not to betray her emotions openly, she quickly pushed the memory aside. They sat on the settee together. Winifred leaned back to regard her niece. ''So, dear, tell me a bit about yourself.''

Tiffany was in a quandary, for surely her father had written every horrible prank and episode she was guilty of. Winifred, aware of Tiffany's predicament, easily broke the silence. ''Of course, your father has written me, but men tend to have a different perspective on things. Don't you agree?''

A soft smile lifted the corners of Tiffany's mouth. ''Yes, I do think you are quite right about that, Aunt Winnie.'' Tiffany, feeling decidedly more comfortable, leaned back against the settee and unconsciously brought her legs up under her. When she realized what she was doing, she quickly rectified the situation, only to be stopped by her aunt's hand and accompanying words.

''Tiffany, if we are to be housemates, so to speak, I think it best we feel comfortable with each other. It makes living with one another far easier.''

Tiffany resettled herself, tucking her legs beneath her. Winifred smiled, cocking her head as Tiffany began to tell her about her love of horses, including Xanadu. Winifred listened with half an ear, for she had already learned a great deal about her niece prior to her arrival. And as Tiffany's sweet voice filled the air, Winifred watched this young child-woman, seeing the promise of exquisite beauty in her face, the passion and spirit so like Robert's that emanated from her. She was again drawn to her smile, the same full lips, the same shape but with a feminine flair. She thought it really incredible, but with that smile, Tiffany could almost have been Robert's daughter.

Thinking of Robert made Winifred's heart ache, for he was her first and true love. Memories, both bitter and sweet, flooded her mind. The only thing worse than his death was that she had had no children by him; children would not have lessened the pain his death had caused her, but they would have left her with a part of him.

Tiffany's peal of laughter brought Winifred to the present. A smile crept over her lips as she thought, Yes. While Tiffany is not our daughter, she shall be treated as if she were. She will have the happiness she's been denied by William.

She recalled the disparaging remarks William had written about Tiffany. Oh, yes, Winifred could see the impulsiveness and spirit, but would not break that spirit, nay, she would channel it, and Tiffany would be a success while continuing to be who she was.

Her thoughts were interrupted by Tiffany's question. "I'm sorry, dear, I must have been wool-gathering." Seeing the hurt expression cross her niece's face, Winifred smoothed over her remark. "When you smile, dear, you remind me of Robert."

"You really loved Uncle Robert, didn't you?" She rushed on as a fourteen-year-old usually does, not waiting for an answer but asking another question. "Was yours an arranged marriage like Alysse's, Aunt?"

"Robert's and my marriage was indeed a *mariage de convenance.*"

Seeing Tiffany's smile fade, Winifred added, "However, it turned into, as the French say an *affaire de coeur.*"

Tiffany clapped her hands in glee. "I knew it."

"Is there someone special for you, Tiffany?"

Tiffany rolled her eyes and leaned closer to her aunt. "Oh yes, Aunt, a very special man. Alan Thurston." She looked seriously at Winifred and spoke confidently. "He as much as said he'll ask for me when I return. But Father does not know anything about it."

"Would your father not approve?"

"Heavens no. Alan fits father's mold—lineage, wealth, and title. He will be a marquess someday. It is important I do well here, Aunt, for Alan's sake as well as Father's."

"No doubt more so for Alan's sake than your father's." Winnie smiled.

Tiffany agreed, "Most definitely."

"Is it the man you have a tender for, or his title, dear?"

Tiffany quickly responded. "Alan, of course. The title would only interest Father. I personally think titles are far overrated, begging your pardon, Aunt." Winnie smiled, waving her hand to indicate no offense taken. Tiffany rambled on, "And the dukes, why, they are the worst of the lot! Steeped in their misguided beliefs that they are above all.''

Winifred rose, taking Tiffany's hands in her own. ''Dear, we will make you a success. Never doubt that. Your Alan will not be disappointed.''

Tiffany rose, still holding her aunt's hand. ''Do you really think I will be a success?''

''Tiffany, there is no doubt about that, for no one ever disappoints me.''

France
1816–1818

Chapter Four

Paris, April 1816

"Oh, Aunt Winnie, she's splendid!" Tiffany exclaimed. She walked over to the black mare, stroking her soft velvet muzzle. Tiffany's eyes, filling with tears of joy, turned to her aunt. "Never have I been given such a birthday gift. I shall always treasure her."

A soft smile touching her lips as she watched her niece lovingly caress the mare, Winnie thought she could not have found a better gift. She had considered the customary pearl choker one usually presented a sixteen-year-old, but Winnie knew Tiffany's passion was not for jewelry. Winnie had been at a loss for a gift for Tiffany's coming out until she struck on the idea of a horse.

"I shall have Franz tack her so I might put her through her paces." Tiffany began to walk away and suddenly stopped, realizing how inconsiderate she was since in a few short hours she would be called upon to make her season's debut. A frown marred her otherwise perfect features as she bit her lip in worry. "How foolish I am, Aunt Winnie. What with all the things left to do for tonight, I'm sure tomorrow will be soon enough to try her."

"Now, now, Tiffany, by all means ride. All the preparations are in hand, and you will only fidget and get in André's way."

André was the temperamental chef who, since Tiffany's arrival, had to accommodate her repulsion to meat by offering a course of fish with each meal. Tiffany was the "proverbial thorn in his artistic side," and with tonight's preparation, he would not welcome her presence into his "domain."

Tiffany looked questioningly at her aunt. "Are you certain?"

A nod of the graying auburn head was signal enough for Tiffany to jump astride the mare and trot away.

Winifred watched her ride out of sight and smiled thinking how in the past year she'd seen a lovely butterfly emerge from its cocoon. Tonight, she thought, the butterfly would test her fragile wings for flight. Winnie sighed, her mind running over the past year. Ah, her little diamond, though rough, had lost her edges and was now smooth, polished, still sparkling with her special essence. The transformation from the child-woman to the young lady was absolutely startling. The long, coltish legs had matured to long, shapely legs, the straight, lanky body had developed into a tall, curvy, feminine form, and the raven tresses, in spite of the current mode, still fell in soft curls to her slim waist.

Winnie brushed a strand of hair from her face. Smiling crookedly, she recalled how the past year had not all been a bed of roses. The most difficult task was to channel Tiffany's spirit, not break it, and to give her confidence in herself and her femininity. Winifred had been able to succeed in both. Of course, like the fragile butterfly's wings, so, too, was Tiffany's confidence. But she grew more confident and socially graceful as she became a much-sought-after companion. Winnie turned, heading back into the house, thinking she had changed some of Tiffany's perspectives and attitudes save one that Tiffany tenaciously held to: her aversion to titled persons. She had learned to deal with them—for it was her lot in life to be among their ranks—yet it did not alter the fact she snubbed them and prejudged them and actually did to them what she accused them of doing to others!

Winnie stopped before turning the brass handle, speaking aloud, "Well, to be fair to her, I will say that episode with the duke of Tremyaine did not help." Entering the foyer, closing the door behind her, she smiled broadly thinking of the occasion. It was during the time when Winnie was trying to alter Tiffany's attitude toward the titled personage that the duke's riding invitation had come. Tiffany, armed with a new perspective on the ton, readily accepted, telling Winnie the duke was "a cute old man who reminded her of Nathan, the stable hand at Courtland." She innocently accepted his invitation, unaware that the "cute little old man" had an obsession for young women and had set his sights on her. Once they had ridden a distance, the duke had blatantly offered her the power of his title properties and name if she would consider a tête-à-tête. Tiffany had impulsively and foolishly reacted by swatting his aging mount with her crop, causing the horse to lurch forward, nearly sending the duke over its head. After that experience, there was no hope in altering her attitude.

Winnie's thoughts were interrupted by Marie's words. "Your Grace, André needs you immediately."

Winnie smiled, knowing how André must have the kitchens in a tizzy. She walked with purposeful strides across the foyer to the kitchens, thinking, After tonight, Tiffany will officially be launched into society, and knew for certain the sons of the powerful ton would be in pursuit of her niece. There was no denying her beauty; a man would have to be blind not to notice it, nor her sharp wit and charm. Marriage prospects! Ah yes, those surely will come. Of course, Tiffany had been steadfast in her devotion to her Baron Thurston; nothing, not even a year of maturing, had changed this. Winifred thought it odd that while Tiffany pined and dreamed of this man, not once in the time she'd been in France had she heard from him.

Winnie reached the kitchen door and heard the crash of pans and irate voices that followed. Well, she thought, I will not interfere where her heart is concerned, providing he loves her above all else.

"Shalimar. Isn't that lovely, Alysse?"

"Stop fidgeting, you goose; it's the third time I've tried to get this curl right," scolded Alysse.

"I think the name is beautiful, as lovely as she is, don't you agree?" Tiffany asked, turning to face Alysse.

"Damn! Look what you've done, Tiff." Alysse let out an exasperated sigh.

"Oh, poo, leave it as it is. My hair never does what it should. And anyway, this is all a waste." She opened her arms, indicating her appearance. "I'll never be a success—I'm too tall, my hair is too black, my eyes—" she peered into the mirror "—are not light blue as yours. It's hopeless. I wish it were tomorrow already."

"Tiffany, look at me." Tiffany, with a dejected look, turned to her dear friend.

"Tiffany, you look beautiful, and tonight is your coming out, and you shall be a success. All of Parisian society will be at your feet; you'll not sit out a dance, and your card will be filled before the first waltz."

"Do you really think I am beautiful? Only Alan has ever told me that." Tiffany wrung her hands. "I really do hate this! Presenting myself to the ton, whom I abhor and care not a whit what they think." She stood, anger covering her insecurity. "Why I even need their approval, I'll never know."

"Now, now, Tiffany, we've been through this before. A coming out is to formally introduce you to society. A society you, as well as your baron, I might add, are very much a part of."

Tiffany began to pace frantically back and forth. "Precisely my point, Alysse; I need no introduction to society to present myself. *Hah!* It's more like putting me on the block, like merchandise to be auctioned! I am going to marry Alan and need not be packaged and presented, for I am already spoken for.'' She stopped her pacing. ''Well, almost spoken for.''

Alysse watched Tiffany; she never understood Tiffany's lack of confidence. God, she had been the envy of the girls at the academy. So many would not befriend her, for they did not want to compete with her beauty. Alysse knew that even Brian had a tender for Tiffany, which he could not properly declare until she formally came out. She had even overheard Chad talking to one of his rakish friends, saying Tiffany was ''exquisite—a nice bit of baggage,'' whatever that meant.

Alysse walked into Tiffany's path, causing her to stop short. ''Now, listen to me, Tiff. All you say may well be true, however, even your baron would not accept you if you did not come out. It is what's done, and do it you shall, if not for yourself, at least for Aunt Winnie. She has a lot at stake here. You are under her roof, and she has graciously extended free rein to your whims and such. Now you must reciprocate and see this through.''

''I . . . I guess you're right, Alysse, but I don't ever want to be sold, *ever!*''

''Aunt Winnie would never do such a thing to you, and anyway, you're not some mare to be sold. You sometimes have the strangest notions.''

''No . . . no . . . you're right, Aunt Winnie would never sell me,'' Tiffany mumbled.

A soft knock on the door caused both girls to turn, seeing Winifred whisk regally into the room dressed in a dazzling emerald green gown gilded with golden threads.

Winifred stopped upon seeing the exquisite picture Tiffany presented. Who would have thought deep violet to be her color? Indeed it was, as would black be when she was old enough to wear it. The gown turned her eyes almost violet, and her dark hair gave a depth to the violet a lighter-haired girl would have lost. Tiny fresh violets were woven in her coiffure and entwined in the curls that brushed the nape of her graceful neck.

"Dear, you look gorgeous," Winifred exclaimed.

"I told her so." Alysse turned to Tiffany. "Did I not say just that?"

Tiffany smiled, confidence bursting from her.

Winnie pulled her eyes from Tiffany to address Alysse. "Dear, your mother has arrived and required your assistance. She's in the guest room." Alysse went to leave as Winnie called out, "Oh, Alysse, your fiancé is here in the library with Chad and Brian."

Alysse stopped brushing down her skirts, and touching her hair. "Do I . . . I look . . . ah . . . presentable?"

Tiffany nodded her head, saying, "Definitely so!"

Alysse ran from the room, closing the door behind her.

Tiffany went to her aunt's open arms and kissed her on each cheek. "You know, Aunt Winnie, Alysse adores Kent."

Winifred, smiling, remarked casually, "It is fortunate she does; few arranged marriages have anything more than dowry involved."

"You don't believe the Devonshires would have insisted if Alysse did not love Kent, do you?"

Winifred sat down at a nearby chair; Tiffany accompanied her, sitting on the floor, arranging her skirts neatly. "I doubt, my dear, they would have much choice in the matter. A betrothal is legal and binding, a contract which must be met and fulfilled."

Tiffany shook her head at the words, replying, "How awful for any woman to have to endure such a life."

"Oh, and what about the man, my dear? Does he not also lose?"

Tiffany snapped her head up vehemently. "Lose, hah! I see not how. He prospers with the money and property a woman brings and has the freedom to seek his pleasure where he may find it, while the woman must endure a loveless marriage and life at the beck and call of her husband."

"Well, Tiffany, what of the man and his loveless marriage? Does he not suffer as well?"

"Nay, he is compensated by the dowry, which is what in all likelihood drew him to her. She, on the other hand, must be content to be another possession of his."

Winnie thought it fortunate William never arranged a marriage for Tiffany, for her niece had strong opposition and no doubt would balk. She quickly dismissed these thoughts and spoke. "I brought something for you tonight, dear, something I'd like you to have and wear this evening."

"Oh, Aunt Winnie, you have given me enough," Tiffany said, laying her head in her aunt's lap.

"I insist, my dear." She raised Tiffany's head and extended her closed hand, opening it. Tiffany's eyes beheld the large diamond earbobs.

"Oh, no, Aunt, I couldn't." She looked up, wide eyes pleading. "They are your favorite. You always wear them; why, Uncle Robert—"

Winifred placed a finger on Tiffany's lips. "Yes, dear, but you are the daughter Robert and I always wanted. My daughter would have had these earrings; so shall you."

Gently placing the earbob in the hole in Tiffany's ear, Winifred said "You know, Tiffany, your uncle gave them to me at my first season. They belonged to Queen Elizabeth I. There was a matching diamond necklace." She brushed a tendril aside and began working the earbob on the shell-shaped ear. "The necklace is said to be exquisite teardrop diamonds, each stone linked by fine silver filigree. It's a birthday necklace—a stone to be added each year."

Tiffany listened, mesmerized by the tale. "Whatever happened to it?"

Winifred placed the stud securely behind the post. "A most noble family was given it for its loyalty to the crown.'' Winifred finished, and Tiffany rushed to her mirror to look at the sparkling earbobs. ''They make me look beautiful,'' she whispered.

''Yes, you are beautiful!'' Winnie whispered, tears misting her green eyes.

The following day proved, to even a disbelieving Tiffany, just how successful she was. More than a success, she was a smash! Flowers filled her bedroom, foyer, and even the kitchen. The servants were at a loss where to place the arriving bouquets. The tray that held invitations to balls, soirées, and theater overflowed. Poems written by smitten hopeful suitors arrived hourly. Young, determined men were turned from the oaken doors of Breatoney by Jacques, who rigidly informed them ''Mademoiselle has gone riding.''

The gossip tabloids were filled with nothing save the ''exquisite, elegant beauty, whose wit was sparkling and beauty dazzling.'' They likened Tiffany's taking of Paris to the ''storming of the Bastille.'' She was considered incomparable.

Tiffany looked out her bedroom window, seeing another group of gentlemen turned from the door, and watched the gardener, Louis, chase an overeager suitor from the rose trellises with a raised rake.

''Well, I've done it!'' She turned from the window, throwing herself down on her bed, lying on her stomach, cupping her chin in her hands. A determined look etched her fine features. ''Now all I have to do is get Alan to ask for me.'' She smiled; with her success, it should be a piece of cake. She rolled onto her back thinking Brian had been right—life is full of adventures, and her dreams and plans had not changed one bit.

Chapter Five

Paris, 1818

During an intermission at the opera, Tiffany tapped her fan impatiently against her side waiting for Paul Dupre to return with her champagne. She smiled perfunctorily at a group of suitors and turned her head from them so as not to encourage their attention. "*Merde,* where is Paul?" she said under her breath.

The success she'd yearned for for so long was now beginning to wear on her. She sighed, letting out a long breath. At first she loved it, reveled in it. It made her feel valuable, wanted. Now she could go to Alan as a success, and her lifelong dream of becoming his wife would indeed become a reality. While the success she found served her purpose, the rest that came along with it was boring and trite. She no longer had a private life outside the ten-foot walls of Breatoney. She laughed cynically when she read in the tabloids someone had seen her riding, not driven in a carriage. And suddenly what was taboo became acceptable to the fashionable ton. Hah! A bunch of hypocrites impressed with their own self-importance, she mused.

She made a very unbecoming face recalling that just today she read in the tabloid speculation was running rampant as to who the countess would marry. Why, those people had the unmitigated gall to even list possible prospects,

"Duke Clive Wetherstone, Earl Malcolm Teaksbury, Duke Wilheim Bruinston of Prussia." She snorted a very unladylike sound thinking she'd marry a stable hand before she'd ever consider one of them. Just thinking of marriage made her remember the incessant, unrelenting line of unwanted suitors that constantly trailed after her. No matter how often she told them she held her heart for another, the more ardent and insistent they became. She was ever thankful for the protective arm of the Devonshire men. At least having that threat kept most from trying to compromise her, and she was extremely cautious not to be found in compromising positions even though what the ton deemed compromising, she thought ridiculous. The last thing she wanted was to be forced into a marriage not of her own choosing.

If only she were back in England. She snapped her fan open impatiently, then checked herself. Soon enough; by June she'd return with Alysse for her friend's wedding, and she'd see Alan and Courtland Manor and the meadows, and, of course, the bluff and . . .

"Tiffany?" Turning at the sound of her name, she found Brian at her side. He was so handsome in his uniform, a lieutenant colonel now. She loved him like a brother, always feeling at ease in his presence, not like the way Chad made her feel. She couldn't put her finger on exactly how, but it was different.

"As always, mademoiselle, you look lovely," he said as she grasped his hands.

Tiffany laughed gaily at his comment. "As do you, Colonel, but then, I always did love a man in uniform."

Brian smiled warmly, thinking how he'd like nothing more than her comment to be true, for he had strong, genuine feelings for her. But being a military man, he was able to mask them, and Tiffany never suspected. He knew if she were aware of them, she would cease to see him. For the moment, he was content to stand by.

"You seemed a million miles away, Tiffany. Wool-gathering?"

"No, just reminiscing," she replied softly.

"Are you enjoying the opera tonight?"

"Decidedly so."

Brian looked casually about, noting the suitors who stood on the sidelines. "With whom are you here? Percy? Marcel? Which suitor tonight?"

"Aunt Winifred." She smiled mischievously. "I rejected their invitations and took up Aunt Winifred's instead."

Responding to his quizzical expression, she added, "The French tend to be so insistent, it's no wonder it took so long to defeat Napoleon. They wear on me so." Waving her fan, she continued, "Of late, I've been homesick thinking of the endless rough terrain of Courtland Manor and how one could ride forever. France is so manicured, so 'just so,' not that that it isn't beautiful, but I long for the endless meadows." She sighed, lowering her eyes.

He lifted her chin ever so slightly with the tip of his finger. "Does this mean France could never be your home?"

She shook her head, her raven tresses catching the candlelight. She smiled lightly and said, "I guess you can take the girl out of England but you can't take England out of the girl."

"Ah, but France has been good to you, Tiffany."

"True, but my heart is in England, as is Alan." A bright smile lit her features.

"Of course, Alan," Brian remarked dryly. "The paragon," he said under his breath.

A perplexed look on her face, Tiffany was about to ask "What?" when Paul appeared, carefully carrying two glasses of bubbly.

"Sorry about the delay, but there was a line . . . Oh, Brian! Back from your campaign?"

"Obviously, Paul." Brian turned to Tiffany, slightly

bowing. "By your leave, mademoiselle." He turned, walking stiffly away, quite angry over Paul's presence, for rumor had it Paul had wagered that the countess would be his wife.

"Brian, ole boy, over here," called out Chad, who waved.

Chad Devonshire was twenty-eight and the eldest son of the Devonshire family. He would inherit the title and properties on his father's death, although he had in the last eight years handled the estates since his father had been called to diplomatic service. While Chad was a rogue, leading a carefree life, he never allowed it to interfere with the running of his family's properties. Chad's reputation was notorious, women flocked to him easily, and he was known to be among the elite group of titled men the ton tolerated. This group of men did as they pleased, having the wealth and power to do so.

The look on Brian's face caused Chad to remark, "Damn, Brian, you've the look of a sailor returning after months at sea and denied liberty." Throwing his arm across his sibling's shoulder, he asked, "Hell, what's wrong with you?"

"Nothing getting good and roaring drunk wouldn't help."

Chad raised his brows knowingly. "A woman, no doubt, has wounded your male pride." Blue eyes twinkled as he continued, "Now, I know a surefire cure and the place to purchase it. Madame Bouvier's, where the brandy, while not the best, flows freely, and the women, ah, the women, most willingly. We'll play a hand or two of cards, drink ourselves silly, and then ride the night away between the soft thighs of a warm wench. What do you say?"

Brian turned back, seeing Tiffany surrounded by a line of suitors, then looked to Chad, who had not missed the direction of Brian's gaze. "Sure. Why not?"

Before Chad and Brian took their coats, they were approached by Marcel Rousseau. "Chad Devonshire." Marcel slapped him on the back. *"Mon ami.* How long has it been? A year? Two?"

"Marcel, you old dog! Why, it's been more than that."

"Where are you headed?" asked Marcel.

Chad winked and whispered, "To Madame Bouvier's."

"Mind if I join you?"

"By all means," Chad answered.

The three of them exited the theater and jumped into the Devonshires' carriage. The ride proceeded in silence save for the striking of flint as Chad lit a cigar, puffing on it, savoring the taste of the aged tobacco. Marcel broke the silence. "Did you hear the duke of Chablisienne has a magnificent horse racing next week? Now, there is a bet I will cover despite the Dupres' mount."

"Really? I had not realized he returned to France. I know he had traveled to England a while ago to manage the estates. I met his brother, Austin, who told me he went to Italy. Then I lost track of him." Chad pulled on his cigar and continued, "Of course, I have been between England and France and have missed him. I understood he has offered his home for the hunt we are hosting for Alysse and Kent's engagement weekend."

"Mon ami, he has set himself up here recently due to his new mistress. A lovely petite redhead. The duke has always had excellent taste in flesh, both horses and women." Chad nodded in agreement, remembering all the wild oats they had sown together.

"Ah, *mon ami,* by your smile I know you agree. You shared many a year together, no?"

"And wine and women, ole man."

"Yes, rumor had it that you two had some interesting encounters."

"No comment, Marcel. It'd be like kissing and telling."

The carriage pulled to a halt, and before the footman opened the doors, Chad asked, "When's the race to take place?"

"Why? Will you attend?"

"Most definitely, Marcel, most definitely."

The door opened, and the three men bounded out into the night and through the welcoming doors of Madam Bouvier's.

"Demoiselle! You cannot refuse me again! Can you not feel the spring in the air? What better way to celebrate than a ride?" Paul Dupre finished in a pleading voice.

"Monsieur, indeed the air is uncommonly warm for March, but spring! Surely you jest." Tiffany adjusted her hat, which was askew from the gusty winds.

Holding his hand over his heart, Paul feigned a hurt expression and whined, "You wound me, you break my heart, demoiselle, if you do not consider my request."

A coquettish smile lit her face. She tightened the reins, holding a fidgety Shalimar in place, and adjusted her riding skirt over the sidesaddle. As if contemplating his request, Tiffany placed a finger on her chin. After a moment she replied, "Very well, monsieur, I suppose it would be unkind of me to break your heart over such an innocent request." She looked up from lowered lashes, continuing, "I've no doubt you've claimed as much to others."

"Demoiselle, you pierce me. Have I not said my heart belongs to no other?" He shifted in his saddle when his mount sidestepped.

"Why, Monsieur Dupre, only last season you said as much to Marie LeFuer!" Tiffany awarded him with a knowing grin.

"Ah, but that was before I made your lovley acquaintance."

"Very well, monsieur, we have a date," Tiffany smiled impishly and continued, "Say, three weeks from today at Breatoney. There is an excellent course of jumps in the south acre."

Paul Dupre, as Brian had surmised, had set his sights on winning Tiffany's hand and had been so confident in his goal, he wagered at the club in favor of himself. Paul knew of the many offers refused by Tiffany and had devised a plan to ensure his end. It was quite simple; he knew her passion for riding. All he had to do was to get her alone and detain her for an improper amount of time; she would be compromised and forced to accept him! He simply needed to preoccupy her during their ride. He broke on just the thing and ventured, "Possibly, demoiselle, a small contest of equestrian skill?" He smiled devilishly. "Perhaps a wager to make it more interesting?"

Tiffany knew the Dupres' stables were renowned, boasting some of the best horseflesh in France. Paul was a superb rider, technically sound, and his execution precise. She smiled. But he lacked the natural skill and ability she possessed. She never considered he had any other motive to his proposed riding date. She knew she could beat him and agreed, saying, "But, of course, wagering makes it more exciting. Shall we agree then, three weeks from now?"

The broad smile that etched his face disappeared. "Ah, demoiselle, any day but then. I am scheduled to attend a race." He puffed his chest out proudly, saying, "Caesar, my stallion, is to finally have some competition. An English mount with a most unusual name." He paused trying to remember the name and began to pronounce it. "Excaliber, no, it is most unusual, something Arabic, yes, yes, Xanadu, that's it, Xanadu." He smiled proudly, having remembered the name, and went on, "Perhaps in two weeks we . . ."

Anything further Paul had to say fell on deaf ears, for once Tiffany heard the horse's name, she heard nothing further.

Xanadu here! she thought. After all these years wondering what had become of him, and he was here in France of all places. *Dieu!*

"Where is the race to be . . . Paul?" Tiffany asked, her voice trembling with excitement.

Her use of his given name did not go unnoticed by Paul, making him believe he had progressed. "Outside of Paris. At La Fountaine."

Batting her eyelashes, a plan forming in her mind, she said, "Oh, Paul, I have never seen a real horse race. Would you take me, please?"

He was almost swallowed up by her wide, pleading blue eyes. "Ah, Tiffany, if I only could take you." He gauged her reaction to his use of her given name and saw none. Spreading his hands in a gesture to emphasize his regret, he continued, "The affair is for men solely and certain women of questionable . . . shall we say, women not of your standing." The look of disappointment caused him to offer, "Tiffany, I would escort you anywhere else, *chérie.*"

Realizing her hastily formed plan had failed, she tried another. "Who owns this Xanadu, Paul?" she asked sweetly.

"Ah, our most fierce competitor, the duke of Chablisienne. It is said the old duke was as fastidious about his blooded stock as he was with his own lineage. He had quite a fetish for that sort of thing. I am sure you English know the types."

Oh, Tiffany knew the types, all right, and the duke of Chablisienne no doubt fit the mold to a tee—an ancient, lecherous, hawked-nose man, probably stooped over, clambering about with a walking stick, intimidating his lessers. No doubt the duke intended to run Xanadu to the ground if he was fastidious about bloodlines. After all, Xanadu had no papers and would be no use to the duke other than as a possession that could increase his wealth. No doubt once Xanadu could run no longer, the duke would rid himself of him and purchase another possession.

Suddenly she realized Paul was awaiting an answer to his question and quickly responded, "Oh yes, England is indeed plagued by such fools."

Paul raised a brow at her remark, thinking Tiffany was

not concerned with the importance of title. He found hope in her attitude, for his own title was not impressive. He had dismissed the conversation about horses and was about to press for a riding date when the sound of hooves drew his attention. Chad Devonshire drew his horse to a halt before Paul and Tiffany. He quickly glanced at Tiffany, assessing her state, noticing she appeared preoccupied, but intact. Then he quickly turned to Paul, leveling a steady gaze at him. A smile that did not touch his eyes accompanied his stare. In a tight voice he asked, "Is there a problem, Paul? You seem to have dropped a ways behind us all."

Paul shifted uneasily in his saddle. It was common knowledge the Devonshire men were Tiffany's appointed protectors. Paul might easily dismiss Brian or Dalton, the former seldom available, the latter too young and inexperienced. However, Chad was neither; and while he was rumored to be among that elite group of men known to do pretty much as they pleased, he was also known to take his responsibilities seriously. Paul swallowed with difficulty. Chad was the one to deliver any recompensation to an overeager suitor, and Chad was not to be dismissed.

"N-no," Paul stammered as he looked at Tiffany for confirmation. "Demoiselle and I were discussing a future riding date."

Tiffany was oblivious to the encounter between the two—too busy formulating a plan to see Xanadu—to hear the threat in Chad's words.

"Really? Well, Monsieur Dupre, I suggest you enjoy the present riding arrangement." Chad paused, withdrawing a cigar and rolling it between his fingers. He lifted his eyes, pinning Paul's with his own, and said, "For there's to be no different arrangement in the future."

Paul stiffly nodded his head and said to Tiffany, "By your leave, demoiselle," and rode off.

Tiffany was brought back to the present hearing heard her name. She gazed over to Chad, who sat appraising her while he leisurely smoked a cigar. He nodded his head, indicating she should precede him, saying, "After you, Countess. I'll bring up the rear, so to speak." She smiled as if it was expected and daintily nudged her mare into a trot, once again lost in her own thoughts.

Chad watched her. Raven tresses waved from behind, beckoning. Her sweet, rounded derriere rose up and then down to the bouncing gait. He smiled wolfishly at the direction his thoughts took. Hell, he'd like to bring up that rear, all right! He couldn't blame Dupre, even Brian or any of them, for she could tempt the devil himself. By God, he was not immune! She stirred more than brotherly affection in him, and he was cast in a role as her protector! He tossed his cigar down and spurred his mount to a gallop. He laughed in the wind as he thought of the irony of his role, "the fox guarding the henhouse." How cruel life could be.

Tiffany tucked an errant curl under her cap while gazing in the mirror. She went forward toward the mirror, feeling the tightness of Dalton's britches. Standing to relieve the discomfort, she pulled shirttails out from her pants so they hung covering her derriere, hoping it would hide the way the breeches fit her like a second skin. She shook her head, deciding to tie the tails at her waist instead. Flying over to the bed, she sat pulling on Dalton's high black riding boots. Standing and pacing, she decided to wear socks, for while Dalton's britches were tight, his boots were large and loose. Opening the drawers looking for her heavy woolen socks, she gave up the search when Alysse flew into the room.

"Tiffany, please, I beg you not to do this. Reconsider; there must be a better place and time to do this."

"There is no better time. Aunt Winnie is at the Rothchilds' for tea. Xanadu is at La Fountaine, which is only an hour away." She turned back to Alysse, having given up her search entirely, and pointed out to her quite emphatically, "And Xanadu may never be this close."

"But, Tiffany, you can't possibly go to the race. Why—" she wrung her hands "—think of your reputation if you're seen. It is not as if no one would recognize you!" Alysse followed Tiffany to the window. "You are, after all, still the rage, you know, and if you were ever seen at such an affair . . ."

Tiffany moved across the room, oblivious to Alysse's pleading.

"Are you listening, girl?" Alysse stepped in front of Tiffany, grasping her hands, getting her attention. "Only men and their paramours go to such things, not ladies."

A frown marred Tiffany's brow, which was quickly replaced by a smile. "Of course I won't be recognized, Alysse, for no one will see me. If they see anything at all, it will be a young lad." Waving her hand, she added, "Anyway, I intend to ride to the stables, not the track area."

Alysse screwed up her face at Tiffany's words, thinking Tiffany's disguise made her look nothing like a lad, quite the contrary. "And exactly what will you do there?"

"Why, see Xanadu, of course, what else?" Tiffany asked innocently.

Knowing Tiffany as well as she did, Alysse was not convinced. "Are you certain? That's all?"

Tiffany could not miss the suspicion in her voice. "Well, I can hardly ride him now, can I?" she asked in a sweet voice. The look on Alysse's face caused Tiffany to regret her deceit and she rushed on reassuringly. "Really, Alysse, you worry for naught. I certainly don't intend to *steal him!*" Tiffany turned, for she was certain Alysse would read the lie in her face when she said, "I just want to see him and give him these." She turned and extended her hand, which was filled with chocolate bonbons.

An incredulous look crossed Alysse's face and she shook her head, her curls bouncing prettily. "How foolish of *me!*

Of course, why not risk discovery, reputation, one's whole life, to deliver bonbons to a beast that no longer belongs to you?'' Alysse threw up her arms. ''How stupid of me not to have realized.''

''There is no way I can make you understand, Alysse. Suffice it to say, I intend to go, and go I shall.''

The firm and determined tone Tiffany used convinced Alysse nothing she said would deter Tiffany. Instead she asked simply, ''Please be back before Aunt Winnie returns with Mother. Promise me at least that.''

Tiffany smiled and dashed over to Alysse, placing a quick kiss on her cheek. She ran to the door, opening it, looking down the hallway in both directions, and before exiting, turned back, whispering, ''I promise.''

Shalimar sailed over the last hedgerow, clearing the obstacle. In the process Tiffany lost the second boot, having lost the first a mile back. She shook her capped head thinking she should have put socks on. She dismissed the boots with a final thought—she owed Dalton a new pair.

She arrived an hour earlier and had the foresight not to gallop in at the track but came around to the paddocks. She patted Shalimar and whispered softly, ''So far, so good, girl.'' Although impatient, she walked the mare the remaining distance to cool her. She heard the yelling and cheering of the crowd, thinking that a good sign; the races were still in progress and she would encounter none save the stable hands.

Dismounting, she tethered Shalimar to a nearby tree, patting the mare. She walked from the wooded area toward the open paddocks, stepping on a sharp stone. ''Ouch.'' She grabbed her bare foot and turned the sole to check the damage. Satisfied there was none, she proceeded, thinking civilized life had made her feet tender as a baby's skin. The sound of voices close by caused her to duck behind a nearby water barrel, where she crouched down and peered out.

"Easy there. Easy, boy . . . damn you! Son of Satan, yer are."

Tiffany could not yet see who the voices belonged to but heard another curse.

"Goddamnit, Jim, grab the bastard's bridle before he kills me."

"I've got it, Toby."

She saw the grooms struggling with Xanadu, who was rearing and then bucking to break from their hold.

As they moved closer to the paddock, Toby asked, "Do ye 'ave 'im, Jim?"

" 'At I do; now, open the gate before he breaks me arm like he done to the jockey." Toby opened the gate quickly, and Jim maliciously hit Xanadu on the rump, causing the stallion to leap forward. They quickly closed the gate and moved back as a bared-toothed Xanadu ran toward them threateningly. Jim picked up a stone, throwing it at Xanadu, and both grooms left the area.

Xanadu pranced down the length of fence parallel to Tiffany's hiding place, stopping, his nostrils flaring, picking up a familiar scent. His ear pricked forward and he cocked his head in question. He whinnied, and when he received no response, he began to gallop up and down the fence, changing his gaits, then stopping, snorting, and pawing the ground.

Tiffany smiled, knowing he was trying to coax her out of hiding. Tears streamed down her cheeks. She rose on shaky legs, trying to whistle, but her lips trembled so much, she was unable. She tried again and a shrill sound escaped her lips. Xanadu reared majestically, pawing the air in tribute to his mistress.

Clinton Barencourte had left his carriage to collect his winnings and thought to stop at the stables to see the horse that had won him a fortune. He had seen the difficulty the grooms had with the stallion and thought to help them when he was waylaid by a group of gentlemen. By the time he had finished trading pleasantries, the stallion was already in the paddock area. He was making his way back to the track but stopped, seeing the stallion prancing up and down the length of the fence. He entered the corridor of the stable, making his way to the end, where he stood admiring the showy performance of the horse. He turned his head at the sound of a whistle. A grin lifted the corners of his mouth as his eyes leisurely appraised the tall, curvy figure approaching the paddock. He leaned against the support beams, hidden by the shadows of the corridor, smiling wolfishly at Countess Courtland.

Tiffany nimbly climbed up to the top rung of the fence, balancing herself. She stretched her arms wide, inviting Xanadu into her embrace. Xanadu complied, trotting from the far corner, tail arched high, tossing his head, whinnying to her.

Tiffany whistled at a different pitch, and Xanadu changed from a trot to a smooth, flowing canter, coming to halt between her arms, nuzzling her with his nose, almost causing her to lose her balance and fall.

Tiffany wrapped her arms about his large neck, tears making wet paths down his velvet black coat. She had imagined in her dreams such a moment and thought reality had exceeded her dream. Xanadu whinnied against her, remaining perfectly still as they shared their private moment.

After this, they broke from each other. Still balancing on the rung, Tiffany reached inside her cap, withdrawing the wrapped bonbons, causing the cap to fall off, releasing her raven tresses, which fell down her back. She extended a bonbon-filled hand to Xanadu and popped the remaining one into her mouth.

Xanadu nudged her, causing her to sit on the rung. He nudged her again. "Oh, you big bully, stop that before you knock me off." She laughed, filling the air with its pleasant sound. Xanadu nudged her again and then bent his foreleg and lowered his head in invitation. Tiffany quickly looked around, and seeing no one, decided to oblige Xanadu. She leapt onto his back, barefooted and tackless.

Clinton had moved back when Tiffany had quickly scanned the area. He wondered what she was about. His answer came quickly enough when he saw her mount the stallion. He suppressed the urge to stop her in fear of the stallion hurting her but did not realize the stallion was acting like a lamb. He questioned her ability to ride such a spirited horse, then reasoned if trouble arose, he'd be out there in a flash. Anyway, he was extremely curious to see what Countess Courtland was up to, and was content to watch her as he had done for the last two years.

Tiffany thought she had died and gone to heaven. She luxuriated in the strength and warmth of the flanks her legs wrapped about. As Xanadu moved, she felt the familiar movement of his well-honed muscles. She squeezed her legs, pushing him into a high, prancing trot, and then shifted her weight to rein him in the direction she desired.

Tiffany was jubilant. He responded to her as if they had never been parted. She was dying to put him through their old routine and pushed him into a collected canter around the ring. She idly wondered if he remembered the flying change and patted him when he performed the feat.

She felt the restraint of his powerful muscles, knowing she had not even touched his full potential. As if reading her mind, Xanadu tossed his head impatiently.

"Why not!" she cried, throwing caution to the wind. Hell, she was restless, tired of fences herself! She squeezed her legs, signaling him. Xanadu reared. She gripped him tightly, and when his feet hit the ground, he shot off into a gallop. Tiffany grabbed his mane, shifting her weight forward, freeing the stallion's hindquarters for the power needed to clear the fence she expertly estimated to be four feet in height. Their faces were turned to the wind, their mingled manes flowing back, as Xanadu gathered his hindquarters beneath him and sailed majestically over the first fence of four he had to jump to reach freedom.

A wide grin spread across Clinton's face as he watched the countess and the stallion take the last paddock fence to freedom. He was impressed with her skill and knowledgeable use of her hands, legs, and weight. He strolled casually out into the bright sunshine watching them gallop through the field, jumping anything higher than the stallion's hooves.

Clinton spotted Shalimar tethered in the woods and walked over to the mare, noting the fine lines indicative of good breeding. "Well, the countess certainly knows good horseflesh," he said aloud while patting the mare's neck.

He heard the sound of hooves and stepped back in the shade to observe Tiffany riding. Clinton pulled a cheroot from his pocket, lit it, puffing leisurely on it. His gray eyes followed the mounted figure. His keen observation gave him deep insight to the much-sought-after beauty. Horse and rider moved as one in fluid motion. Tiffany's body flowed, surging upward-downward, meeting the driving movement of the stallion. Her rounded hips arched forward, rocking with the rhythm set by the stallion, while shapely thighs gripped the heaving flanks. Clinton blew a stream of smoke out, his eyes held fast to Tiffany, who entwined her fingers in the black mane and dropped her head, arching her back, causing her breasts to strain against the muslin cloth. Clinton's gray eyes zeroed in on her taut nipples. His gaze moved upward to her parted lips, which she moistened with the tip of her tongue. As she moved closer, he could see the fine sheen of perspiration and the abandoned look in her eyes.

He felt a tightening in his groin imagining her body beneath his as he rode. He could feel her body surge upward to meet his driving movement, her hips arching forward, accepting his thrusting rhythm. He felt his blood boil imagining the tightening of those magnificent legs about his flanks as he sheathed himself within her. He smiled wickedly, almost feeling her fingers entwined in his hair as he dove deep inside her, before he lowered his mouth to capture her cry.

Tiffany lay spent on Xanadu's neck, thinking she had never felt so wonderful. She straightened up, an ache in her back causing her to arch forward. Her legs had gone numb and she stretched them trying to bring the blood back. She raised her hands to lift the heavy mass of curls off her neck, allowing the breeze to cool it. The exertion of the ride had dampened her shirt, causing it to cling, revealing the soft swell of her breast and the dusty rose of a pert nipple.

Clinton smiled appreciatively at the striking figure posed so innocently seductive atop the horse. He moved out of the woods as they passed.

After corralling Xanadu, Tiffany leaned against the fence, arms crossed on the top railing, admiring Xanadu.

"Horse-stealing, Countess?"

Tiffany spun at the sound of the deep, rich baritone voice. As she came around, her wide eyes rested on a man unknown to her who stood a few feet away. A devilish grin slit his handsome visage as he casually smoked a cheroot. A million questions rushed through her mind: How does he know me? I don't know him; why did he speak in English and not French? How will I get by him when he is blocking my way?

Clinton didn't miss the fear and confusion that crossed her exquisite features. Sensing a chink in her armor, he pressed on, "Are you not fluent in English, Princess?"

Tiffany, taking hold of her predicament and his implication of her illiteracy, retorted in flawless French, "I am quite conversant in the English language, sir!" She tossed her head and responded haughtily. "And I am not in the habit of speaking to strange men. Now, kindly stand aside so I might pass." She moved forward, realizing too late he had no intention of standing aside. As a matter of fact, by the grin on his face, it appeared he found the situation quite amusing. Her blue eyes glared at his amused gray ones. Tiffany bristled at his impertinence and cried, "Sir!"

"The name, Princess, is Clinton Barencourte." He made a mocking bow and added, "At your service."

She tilted her head back, looking into a pair of the smokiest gray eyes ever, and replied coolly in French, "Fine, Mr. Barencourte, now that we know each other, kindly stand aside." She made to pass him but found he still blocked her path. Fear began to surface, causing her to take note of him for the first time. He was tall, taller than most men, possessing a wide breadth of shoulders and chest. He had strong, classic features bronzed by the sun. It was his piercing gray eyes that shook the foundations of her soul.

"Do I meet with your approval, Princess?" Clinton asked, aware of her scrutiny.

Clinton allowed his eyes to casually roam over her feminine form, missing no detail, resting where her damp shirt clung revealingly to the pert rise of her young, full breasts. A wolfish grin split his handsome visage as he remarked, "You certainly meet mine."

Tiffany could not believe his audacity nor miss the way his gray eyes seemed to strip each item of clothing from her. Wrapping her arms to block his view, she met his stare with angry eyes.

Clinton threw back his head, laughing over her reaction.

"Your eyes are as misguided as your thoughts, Mr. Barencourte!" she said, tossing her head angrily to show her displeasure.

"Really, Princess, and how's that?" He pulled leisurely on his cigar, his eyes never leaving her.

"Contrary to your belief, I have no intention of stealing

the horse . . . I . . . merely am interested in purchasing him and thought to try him out."

A confused expression crossed Clinton's features. "I wasn't aware he was for sale."

"Heavens! Why not? Some infirm, doddering duke owns him!"

"I am fully aware of who owns him, Princess; I didn't know the 'doddering, infirm duke' was interested in selling him." He blew a curl of smoke in the air.

"Well, he certainly can't race him much longer."

The breeze lifted a strand of hair across her face, causing Tiffany no alternative but to drop her arms and brush the bothersome lock away. Clinton smiled, his eyes burning with lust over the bounty revealed to him. He ventured, "Possibly the poor man may wish to keep him to ride."

"Be serious! I don't think the poor man is able to walk him without assistance." She shook her head confidently. "I believe he can be persuaded."

With his cigar clamped between his teeth, Clinton considered her words, a mischievous gleam lighting his eyes. "Ah, Princess, the duke is known for his possessiveness and will not relinquish the stallion easily." Clinton rolled his cigar between his thumb and forefinger, observing Tiffany, who unconsciously bit her lower lip in thought. She was delicious-looking and no doubt tasted as much. He wanted nothing more than to plunder her full mouth and caress those soft curves.

Tiffany tossed her head, hair flying about her shoulders down over her breast, shielding them from his view. "Well, Mr. Barencourte, we'll just have to see if His Grace and I can come to some sort of agreement. Now, stand aside so I might pass." When he didn't move, she cocked her head, her eyes narrowing in anger.

"Princess, I know the duke quite well. As a matter of fact, I handle quite a number of his business transactions."

At her doubtful look, he added, "You know, the 'poor old man' not being up to snuff and all."

Clinton flicked an ash from the cigar, adding, "I personally know he is not in need of funds."

"So I'm to deal with his lackey! Very well, Mr. Barencourte. If the duke needs no funds, then possibly he'd be interested in another mount?"

A wicked smile appeared, accompanied by the nodding of his head. "Ah, yes, Princess, the 'poor old man' could do with a tender mount." His eyes raked her form shamelessly as he added, "Perhaps a night riding between your thighs would be the price. Are you interested?"

Her blue eyes widened in fury, spitting sparks in his direction. Tiffany suppressed the urge to slap the smile off his face. "You bastard! . . . You . . . you and His Grace can go straight to hell!" She made to storm past him and gave a cry of alarm when his hand encircled her waist, pulling her up against his powerful form. So incensed was Tiffany, she attempted to rake his face with her bare hands, but Clinton deftly caught them, holding them between their bodies.

"You see, Princess, 'the poor old man' prefers to mount the mare, not the stallion."

Tiffany struggled in earnest, and his words further incensed her, so she squirmed and twisted to be free. "You bastard, let me go!"

Clinton laughed at her attempts, feeling her body brush against his, causing a tightening and hardening in his groin.

Tiffany felt his hardness, saw the glint of lust in his gray eyes, and used any means available to extricate herself from his iron-clad hold. Since she wasn't wearing boots, the kicks she directed at his shins failed to prove effective. Stomping on his feet did nothing to deter him, and she was awarded with a challenging grin. Tiffany saw red and nothing else, and used the only weapon she had left. Like a bolt of lightning she bent, closing her mouth over his offending hand, sinking her teeth into it, drawing the sweet taste of blood on her tongue.

"Damn." Clinton released her and Tiffany took advantage, running quickly to Shalimar, leaping on the mare's back.

Recovering rapidly, Clinton grabbed the bridle, placing himself in front of Shalimar.

"Stand aside, let me pass!" she screamed in fury.

A glimmer of amusement flickered in his eyes. Bringing his hand to his mouth, he smiled as he said, "You little hellcat, I'll put that mouth of yours to better use."

Tiffany narrowed her eyes and looked down into his. "Remove your hand. Remove yourself from my path! I swear, *I will* advance through you, or over you. Trust me, Mr. Barencourte, I care not which you choose."

Clinton quickly tried to pull her from the mount, but she pulled away, causing Shalimar to sidestep. "If you persist, you best bind me, for I shall claw your detestable flesh from your hide and you will find you have bargained for more than an injured hand."

"We shall see, Princess!" Clinton lunged for her. Tiffany jerked sharply on Shalimar's mouth, causing her to rear. Clinton jumped from the dangerous pawing hooves. Tiffany wheeled the mare around, kicking her into a lunging gallop.

Clinton laughed, watching Tiffany disappear from sight. Then he looked at the teeth marks on his hand, and smiled.

Chapter Six

Clinton walked to the fence of the paddock, leaned against it, and watched Xanadu canter around the paddock.

His thoughts were on the dark-haired beauty when Keegan, one of the grooms, appeared at the fence. The red-haired man clucked to the stallion and held out a bonbon-filled palm.

With a raised brow, Clinton remarked dryly, "Bonbons, Keegan?"

Merry blue eyes regarded Clinton. "Let me tell ya, guv'nor, you laugh, but it works, it does."

Watching Xanadu walk toward them, Clinton remarked, "Obviously."

"I tell ya when we was sent to 'et 'im, he was no easy beast."

Xanadu nibbled up the bonbons as Keegan bridled him and Petey attached the lead rope, leading the stallion away.

"The earl fellow who we got 'im from was no help either, and the dark heathen fellow, well, ya know how's they be." He looked at Clinton for confirmation. Clinton nodded, remaining silent as Keegan told of the difficulty. "I remembers seeing a young pretty girl 'bout fourteen hidden in the earl's stable. Crying her 'eart out, she was. Thought she'd be a beauty someday; had big blue eyes, she did." Keegan stopped as if recalling the scene and then continued, "Well, anyways, we was led to the beast, and the minute I'd seen 'im, I knows he's trouble. Snorting, ears flat, and a wicked gleam in 'ims eyes. Was mean and ornery, he was. Nearly bashed Petey's skull, he did. Anyways, we finally got 'im bridled and was leading 'im out."

Clinton offered him a cigar, which he took, lighting it up. "Thank ye, guv'nor."

"You were saying, Keegan," Clinton prompted.

"Right, I remembers saying to myself, 'Self, why's the earl fellow holding the pretty miss, making her watch us take the beasty?' But it was apparent she was upset 'bout the beast." He blew a curl of smoke out, watching it dissipate in the air. "The earl fellow—" he turned to look at Clinton "—now, 'ats a cold man, making such pain for his own flesh and blood." He shook his red head slowly. "Anyhows, the beast sees the miss and rears up an' breaks from me, galloping hell-bent toward the miss! The earl tries to pull her away, but the maid won't have it. I recalls thinking she's to be run down, and guv'nor—" Keegan placed a wrinkled hand over his heart "—my ole ticker almost 'ave out, it did. But damnation! The beast skids to a stop not more 'an two feet from her." Keegan held his hands apart indicating the distance, and said, "Damn if he nudges her all gentle like. The maid, tears falling on 'er cheeks, hugs the beast and 'ives 'im bonbons! The maid, she leads 'im to the carriage and turns ta me an' says all proper like, 'He's a wretch without his bonbons.' "

Clinton looked at Keegan, smiling, his white teeth flashing against his leather-brown skin. "So ye laugh, guv'nor, but I gives 'im his bonbons 'ikes the maid says."

Keegan pushed himself from the fence and made to leave, but turned back to Clinton. "Guv'nor!" When Clinton turned, Keegan added, "Ye know the colt he sired, Kubla Khan?" At Clinton's affirmative nod, he continued, "Well, he 'ikes 'em, too!" Keegan turned, sauntering away. Clinton shook his dark head, a broad smile on his face, thinking he suddenly had a craving for some rich, dark chocolate in the form of Tiffany Courtland. He stood pushing himself from the fence, thinking she would taste sweet indeed.

Tiffany bounded up the steps, down the hallway to her room. The door opened and Alysse appeared, relief etched on her face. "You're back! Thank God, Dalton hasn't arrived, but Aunt Winnie and Mother have." Tiffany rushed past her to the privacy chamber and Alysse followed, having seen the distress written across Tiffany's face.

"Did . . . did everything go well? You weren't discovered, were you?"

Tiffany ripped off her clothing in a manner indicating she was angry and lowered herself quickly in the tub.

"Tiffany, will you please answer me!" Alysse cried, fearing something bad had indeed occurred.

Sighing as the water lapped against her sore muscles, Tiffany replied, "Yes and no."

A confused look crossed Alysse's face, one often seen on Carolyn Devonshire. "And pray tell, what's that supposed to mean, Tiffany?"

"Just that I did get to see and ride Xanadu." She lifted a long limb, squeezing water from the sponge on it. Tiffany waited for Alysse's response, unsure if she'd tell her about the vile Mr. Barencourte.

As she expected, it came soon enough.

"*Ride him!* Heavens, you never said anything about riding him!" Alysse, pacing the floor, wringing her hands in worry, peered at Tiffany, who laid her head against the rim of the tub with her eyes closed.

Tiffany let the water soothe her unpleasant interlude with Mr. Barencourte, pushing him from her mind. "Oh, Alysse, it was wonderful. There he was prancing in the paddock." She opened one eye to gaze at Alysse. "He knew I was there; he had to cajole me out of hiding. And you know how impatient I am, but wait I did till the coast was clear.''

Good, thought Alysse, she had hidden herself, and with this knowledge, she began to breathe easier. She sat upon the stool near the tub, listening with half an ear as Tiffany rambled on and on about her ride. Alysse was thinking of her upcoming engagement party but was not lost enough in thought to prevent herself from jumping up when Tiffany got to the part about Mr. So-and-So. She cried, ''Tell me you didn't, Tiffany!''

Water sluicing down her body as she stepped from the tub and padded to her room, Tiffany spoke over her shoulder confidently. ''I most certainly did!''

Stepping behind her dressing screen and before bending down, she added, ''And glad of it, I am.''

Alysse rushed to the other side of the screen. ''But why?''

Tiffany's dark head popped up, and pulling the fine straps of her chemise over creamy shoulders with crisp movements, she retorted, ''He deserved it. He did.'' She disappeared from behind the screen again and reappeared, arranging the bodice of her dress. She stopped and, looking over the screen at Alysse, explained, ''He was most vile . . . decidedly awful.'' Then she bent out of sight, pulling on her stockings, fastening them with a lacy garter, all the time feeding her anger at his impertinence. She stood up and with a defiant snap of her head, said, ''Yes he most certainly deserved to be bitten!''

Alysse stood facing Tiffany, her mouth agape over Tiffany's verbal confession.

''Whoever deserves to be bitten, dear?'' asked Carolyn Devonshire as she waltzed through the open door, surprising the girls, who spun to face the unexpected visitor.

Carolyn came to stand before the girls, noting Alysse's open mouth.

Sternly admonishing, Carolyn said, ''Alysse, close your mouth. It is not at all becoming.'' She turned to Tiffany, who now stood beside Alysse, and asked, "Who deserved to be bitten, dear?"

Tiffany stammered, "Ah . . . ah, Jacques's son, Lady Devonshire."

The furrowing of Carolyn's brow indicated her confusion and prompted her to ask, "What about him?"

"Just that he deserved to be bitten; you know the saying 'let sleeping dogs lie.' "

"Dogs! Egads, I never could abide them." Carolyn shook her head, placing a finger against her lips in thought, and ventured on, "Which Charles was it who had an affliction for the creatures, the First or Second?" She paused, hoping the answer would come.

The girls breathed a sigh of relief at deterring Lady Devonshire.

"You know, Alysse, your father's sister Gertrude had a tenderness for the beasts. Why, I dreaded my visits there, those yapping dogs at my ankles. Why, did I ever tell you girls when Charles and I were guests . . ."

The timely interruption of Winifred prevented Carolyn from expounding further. "Ah, here you are, Carolyn. Girls, did you enjoy your afternoon?" Winifred looked to them for an answer.

"Yes, we did, Aunt Winnie. We played cards and read. A most sedate afternoon," Tiffany offered.

"Well, girls, dinner will be shortly, and André has promised us some delectable dessert this evening."

Winifred turned to Carolyn, "Jacques has prepared your room, Carolyn, since you and Alysse plan to stay the night."

The mention of Jacques caused Carolyn to pick up where she left off. As she and Winnie strolled from the room, the girls heard her ask, "And how is Jacques's son?"

"His leg is mending," Winifred replied. "How kind of you to inquire."

"Well, I certainly hope he has learned to let sleeping dogs lie."

Winifred shook her head wondering what dogs had to do with Jacques's son's broken leg, and asked, "Carolyn, have you been into the sherry?"

Tiffany bid adieu to Lady Devonshire and Alysse, watching their carriage disappear from view as it turned the bend, knowing she would not see Alysse until the engagement party.

She had an urge to walk the grounds of Breatoney, for the air was sweet and the breeze that lifted her hair held the promise of warm days to come. Paris in April is so lovely, she thought, her eyes scanning the landscape and gentle slopes where the brown covering was lightly dotted with green. She would surely miss Paris in April, and a soft tugging at her heart reminded her that next year she would not be here. She absently kicked a pebble with the toe of her satin slipper, watching it hit the wide trunk of an elm. Leaning against the tree, she thought how kind France had been to her. Her father and Alan were right, France had turned the wild hoyden into a sophisticated, elegant woman, if what the tabloids wrote were true! She felt no different really; she still loved to ride astride in breeches, racing the wind, still held the opinion the ton was a group of hypocritical fools, and wanted nothing more than to exist undisturbed in a married state with Alan. She rested her head against the tree, closing her eyes, imagining for the hundredth time her homecoming. England! Ah, that was where her soul lay, in the meadows of wildflowers, the wooded slopes and hamlets that dotted the countryside, the sound of the pounding surf breaking against the jagged rocks of the bluff. Yes, her soul ran free there. And her heart, left in England and with Alan.

A soft smile lifted the corners of her mouth as she envisioned a scene she often conjured up when she lay in bed before sleep overcame her. They would be on the bluff, the surf roaring in their ears. Alan with arms outstretched welcoming her. They would kiss and break and he would whisper, "I love you. Will you marry me?"

She opened her eyes, watching the puffy white clouds sweep across the blue sky. Raising her foot, bracing it against the tree, she wondered if Alan would still be waiting for her as he had promised so long ago at the brook. She shook the thought from her head, speaking out loud. "Of course, you silly goose, he as much said so."

The appearance of Marie calling out to her stopped her thoughts.

"Demoiselle, Monsieur Devereau is calling."

Pushing off the tree, Tiffany called out, "*Oui*, Marie, I am coming."

Smedly Doonesbury, a frail, bespectacled man, braced his hands against the sides of the lurching coach as it rumbled posthaste toward its destination. His briefcase slipped to the carriage floor, spilling its contents about. Smedly silently cursed his employers, his assignment, and the client. When the coach righted itself, he cautiously removed one hand at a time, gaining his balance and proceeded to pick up the scattered papers.

The firm Teaksbury and Jacoby had contacted his employer requesting an investigation. His superiors impressed upon him the need for secrecy. To make matters worse, his assignment had had to be completed in four days and given to their client, Mr. Barencourte.

Being fastidious, Smedly had compiled a thorough report on the subject he'd been assigned to investigate, but he had been unable to review the volumes of information pertaining to the client. What he learned was enough. Clinton Claremont Barencourte was a rogue, a rake, a member of an elite group of men who did pretty much what they wanted with no repercussions from the powerful ton. Mr. Barencourte was a successful, powerful, ruthless businessman whose ventures varied from shipping to owning the most powerful banks in England and the Continent.

Smedly gazed out the carriage window, noting it had turned down a tree lined drive whose branches met, forming a canopy over the drive. Yes, he thought, Mr. Barencourte, at thirty-two, was almost as powerful as the prince regent. His personal life was filled with speculation. Rumors of his *affaires de coeur* flourished. It was common knowledge he enjoyed the pleasure and company of beautiful women. His hunting grounds, it was rumored, were strewn with broken hearts.

Women flocked to him, eager to enter his bed, for he was rumored to be an excellent lover. He was considered an excellent catch and was much sought after despite his questionable reputation. Which is precisely why Smedly thought it odd Mr. Barencourte would bother with Lady Courtland. He pushed his spectacles back up, shaking his bald pate. The man could have any woman he desired.

As the carriage drew closer to its destination, Smedly pursed his lips wishing he had had the time to check further into Mr. Barencourte's mysterious ancestral beginnings. He had only gotten as far as the man being a formidable enemy, an expert in the use of firearms, and a skilled horseman. With an affirmative nod, he promised himself he would indeed find out exactly who this powerful man was.

The carriage drew up and was opened by a liveried footman who placed a stepstool in front of the door, assisting Smedly in his descent.

A stiff, aged butler admitted him, escorting him to the library, leaving him alone to view the room. Smedly's eyes fell to the paper-laden desk, giving evidence that the man ran his business from here. Shifting comfortably in the leather-back chair, he noted portraits of famous horses and priceless dueling pistols and rapiers decorating mahogany-paneled walls. He was disturbed from his observation by the opening of the door. He rose from his chair to look behind him. Striding purposefully across the room toward him, dressed casually in breeches and a cambric shirt, was Clinton Claremont Barencourte. Smedly rose to accept Clinton's extended hand, noting the young man's strong grip.

"Bring us brandy and two glasses," Clinton called to the waiting butler. His piercing gray eyes returned to Smedly. "Have a seat, Mr. Doonesbury." Smedly did as requested, pulling his briefcase onto his lap.

"You come highly recommended, Mr. Doonesbury. Let's hope you live up to your reputation."

Smedly, fumbling with the catch on the briefcase, briefly wondered if he detected a threat in those words. Finally opening the catch, he withdrew his report, turning it over to Clinton.

The butler returned and poured their libations. Smedly, for the first time, was able to take note of the man who sat casually on the edge of the desk, his leg swinging nonchalantly as he read the report. Smedly thought that mere words could never do justice to the man. He was uncommonly tall, at least six two. He was broad of shoulder, and the expanse of a hard, well-muscled chest strained against the fabric of his shirt.

Smedly took another sip of his brandy, hearing the flip of pages and a deep laugh from Clinton.

Mr. Barencourte was no indolent fop; his long legs were sheathed in bluff-colored breeches, advantageously displaying the broad sinews of his thighs, giving evidence to rigorous outside activity.

A roar of laughter startled Smedly, causing him to stare wide-eyed. Smedly took note of Clinton's face. Breeding was apparent in the classic features—high, sculptured cheekbones, chiseled, strong jaw, and a straight partrician nose. Piercing smoky gray eyes were offset by dark brows which Smedly imagined could arch in humor or draw together in anger. Hair the color of rich roasted coffee fell to his collar in deep, thick waves.

"Mr. Doonesbury." Clinton's voice broke the silence. "You have indeed met all my expectations."

The smile that broke the handsome face, Smedly noted, was devastating. White even teeth flashed against the tanned skin. Smedly had no doubt women fell to their knees for this man. For his whole being emitted an aura of aggressive virility, uncompromising authority, and commanding presence.

"Thank you, Mr. Barencourte."

Refilling their glasses, Clinton asked, "The time allotted to you was short. Is there anything else I should be aware of?"

Sipping his brandy and placing his glass carefully down, Smedly cleared his throat before beginning. "Well, sir, there is one matter not covered in the report which I learned of today."

"And what might that be?" Clinton finished his drink and lit a cigar.

"Well, the earl and Lord Thurston are preparing a betrothal contract between Alan Thurston and Lady Courtland. Lord Thurston is dying and has found himself the victim of creditors, due, shall we say, to his son's misspent youth."

"Gambling debts?" Clinton asked, puffing on his cigar.

"That as well as foreclosure on the properties. The dowry Lady Courtland brings will be enough to pay off the markers and reestablish the mortgage."

Clinton rose, walking to the window to stare out at the expanse of lawn, the cigar clamped firmly between his strong teeth. His voice broke the silence. "What is the extent of the debt?"

"One hundred thousand pounds, sir."

Smedly could not help but notice the staggering amount did not even cause Clinton to flinch, only proceed with another inquiry.

"How long is Lord Thurston expected to live?"

"Each day he lives is considered a gift; that is why the contract was drawn so quickly."

Clinton turned from the window. He held Smedly's gaze with his own and proceeded. "What I want you to do, Mr. Doonesbury, is to buy up every marker against Thurston, and I want it done yesterday."

Smedly rose, picking up his briefcase and nodding affirmatively.

As the carriage ambled posthaste down the drive carrying Smedly on another appointed task, Clinton sat deep in thought before the hearth, his long legs stretched before him, crossed at the ankles.

He had set the wheels in motion. His brother Brent should receive his missive by tonight and would arrive in France by the end of the week with the requested information. The letter to his solicitors requesting them to set up a meeting with Courtland and Lord Thurston was already posted, as was another letter to his French financier requesting the transfer of Le Petite to his mistress, and twenty thousand pounds to be deposited in her account.

When Clinton Claremont Barencourte set his mind on securing something, he was relentless, almost ruthless toward his end. He was not easily persuaded from not having it, nor did he waver from his pursuit of it. Right now his end was Lady Courtland, and have her he would. He lifted his drink thinking about lovely Monique. He would do right by her and give her the house and enough money to see her through. Even delectable Monique could not assuage the desire he felt for Tiffany Courtland. He had left Monique many a night with desire burning his loins after a robust romp with her that would have left most men exhausted.

No, he wanted Tiffany Courtland! He thought of the results of his forthcoming meeting with Courtland. The earl would have his daughter married; Thurston would be able to die in peace knowing his family estates were free of encumbrances, and in sound financial position even his wayward son could not undo; and Clinton, well—he smiled broadly—he would leave with the voided contract of marriage and the newly drawn one giving him the ultimate rights to Tiffany Courtland.

Leaning his head back, he closed his eyes, and let his mind wander back to when he had returned to France and had been playing cards at the club. Percy Winchester, who was at his table, had remarked to no one in particular, "Have you chaps heard of the Lady Courtland, newest item in the tabloids? Made her debut and is a smash."

Marcel Rousseau, a cohort, laid down his cards, winning the hand, and added, "My brother Pierre speaks of nothing but her." As he pulled in the pile of chips on the table, he continued, "He hasn't been the same; suddenly he wants nothing more than to settle down."

Percy smiled smugly. "Unusual, you know; you Frenchies prefer the petite blond types. Heard the lady is tall and dark-haired."

Rodrique Chevalier, dealing the cards, added, "Ah, but we French love women, we are the lovers of the world, no? While you English are more inclined to pale, insipid women of English stock."

"Hah! Heard your French charm has gotten you no further than we English," countered Percy, who turned to Clinton, asking, "Well, Clinton, ole man, what do you say to this?"

He remembered his response. "I think I'd have to see the lady first." Well, he had seen her at the opera with the Dowager Duchess De Namourie. When they had been introduced, she paid him scant attention, being surrounded by a pack of faithful admirers, but Clinton knew then, she was the spirited girl he had seen years ago in England on the bluff. Even back then he had seen the blossom of her passion and beauty. She had stirred his lust then. But he remembered thinking, that day, had she been older . . . He smiled wickedly. Well, she was older now, ripe for the plucking, and fair game!

Pouring brandy in his glass, he absently swirled the amber liquid, immersed in his thoughts. He had observed her from afar for the last two years. Always surrounded by suitors, always keeping them close with her beauty, charm, and wit, but at bay as well. His close observation of Tiffany gave him valuable insight. Her wit was alluring and sharper than that of most women, her charm was innocently refreshing, her beauty exquisite, elegant. Lifting the glass to his lips, he drank.

Tiffany Courtland was like night and day, a study in contrasts—she was bewitchingly innocent at one moment, then a passionate, exciting woman at the next. She could be cool and impertinent, then vulnerably defenseless. She was impetuous, yet restrained. She was titillating, tantalizing, temptation incarnate.

Their encounter at the races sealed her fate. Then he decided she was worth the pursuit; a pursuit on his terms, guided by his rules. Just thinking of the encounter stirred his lust. He felt the familiar tightening in his groin. Ah, she had even drawn first blood. He looked down at his hand, seeing the faint teeth marks that marred his flesh.

Clinton threw himself into a nearby chair, his leg dangling over its arm. Yes, it was time to fulfill his family obligations, to marry and beget an heir, and who better than Lady Courtland?

She would never bore him, either in or out of bed. She was filled with unleashed passion, and passion was a quality he welcomed in his women. Tiffany would be a challenging quarry even though the game was fixed. He grinned remembering her temper and thought how angry she'd be if the methods he used to stake his claim were ever discovered.

A fleeting feeling of guilt surfaced, but Clinton reasoned if she ever came to know how ruthless his pursuit of her had been, she'd not care. He was confident she would be passionately in love with him, exploring and enjoying the intimacies of their marriage.

He sat up and lifted Smedly's report, fanning the pages. There were a few items he had not been aware of till now—her lonely childhood spent with a cold, unyielding father, her infatuation for Alan Thurston, her passion for bonbons and horses, her abhorrence for meat, and a longstanding hatred of titled personages.

He read between the lines of the report. She was spontaneous and passionate, free in spirit. With him, free from all constraints, she would blossom, and he would reap a most bountiful harvest.

A knock on the salon door broke his reverie as he called out, "Enter." Bartholomew entered bearing a tray of invitations to various social functions. Every day Clinton scanned them, advising his secretary which ones to accept.

An envelope bearing the Devonshire seal caught his eye and he lifted it, opening it and withdrawing the note. A smile lifted his mouth as he quickly read it. Laying it down on top of the pile of unopened invitations, he steepled his fingers beneath his chin. In two months time, an engagement ball honoring Alysse Devonshire and Kent Allistair would be held.

The time and the place for the ball were perfect, for he would be back from his meeting in England by then. "And so the battle begins," he said, lifting his glass in a toast. "To the victor go the spoils." A broad smile broke across his handsome visage—the smile of sweet victory.

"Well, brother, here are the papers you requested. Our bank holds the mortgage and payoff, the liens total a small fortune." Brent Boyd Barencourte was the third son. Tall like his brother and possessing steel gray eyes, he carried the Barencourte devastating smile.

"Well done, Brent." Clinton looked up at his brother,

who took a seat in front of Clinton's desk. "Tell me, Brent, how long can we forestall foreclosure?"

"Hell, Clinton, we own the bank. I'd say we could forestall it for however long you wish."

A sound businessman, Clinton asked, "I am aware of that, Brent, but what do we lose in interest?"

"According to my calculation, nothing if our bank in Genoa transfers the funds to cover the interest period."

Clinton leaned back in his chair, mentally calculating the rate and principal. Satisfied with Brent's strategy, he replied, "All right, that's what we shall do." He wrote a quick note on a sheaf of paper, folding it and neatly placing it in the envelope. "Brent, did Teaksbury give you any documents?"

Brent withdrew a large legal envelope and handed it to Clinton across the desk. Clinton quickly scanned the document, nodding his approval.

"What is it, Clinton?"

Clinton, smiling at Brent, responded easily, "Insurance, dear brother, insurance."

"Well, you'll need it. It's not every day you break a legal betrothal contract . . . You know as well as I do, the first contract is ever binding."

"True, Brent—" he waved the legal document "—but this nulls the precedent."

Brent rose to leave. "Well, Clinton, my carriage awaits and duty calls."

Clinton rose, shaking his brother's hand. "Thanks, Brent, for responding quickly to my missive."

"Hell, Clinton, it's not every day one's older brother decides to pay off another man's debt and at the same time steal the man's betrothed."

Clinton playfully slapped Brent on the shoulder. "Will you be attending Kent's ball?"

Shaking his dark head, Brent replied, "No, someone has to mind the family businesses."

Both men regarded one another, and Clinton spoke first. "I know what I'm doing, Brent."

Brent paused before answering. "I have no doubt you do, brother."

"Then what concerns you?"

"The repercussions, Clinton. They'll come, mark my words. Maybe not today or even tomorrow, but come they will." Brent picked up the mortgage papers, packing them away, and looked up at Clinton. "When that day comes, you'll have a lot to answer for."

"And just maybe, Brent, when that day comes, the answer won't be important."

Chapter Seven

Thousands of stars twinkled like diamonds against the black velvet sky, illuminating the moonless May night. From the terrace, under the star-studded sky, Tiffany stood gazing into the night. She had slipped away unnoticed from her admirers, escaping to the far corners of the terrace. She sighed; she was beginning to hate all the homage her suitors paid her, thinking their words trite and insincere. Tiffany wanted nothing more than to be home at Courtland Manor with Alan.

The orchestra began to play again, and the faint sounds of gay laughter escaping from the ballroom drifted on the breeze. The warm night breeze caressed the trees, their limbs swaying softly in time with the music. Tiffany thought the night divine, a night made for lovers. Alysse could not have wished for a more perfect night. Why, the night was so romantic, so in tune with the couple it honored. She smiled recalling a flushed, elated Alysse in pure white silk which rustled softly as she took her place beside Kent on the empty dance floor and proceeded to waltz as if they were the only two people in the room.

As the strains of the waltz began, Tiffany, closing her eyes, began to sway to the music, dreaming for the hundredth time a vision so tender to her. The night in her vision was not unlike this night, and as the music played on, it tugged at the strings of her heart. Wrapping her arms about her, swaying to the tempo, she imagined being held in Alan's arms, waltzing under a canopy of stars. The vision took on clarity; the night would be warm, clear, not a cloud to disperse the joy she felt or the glow of Alan's unspoken love. She gave herself wholly to the vision, losing for a moment reality.

"Dancing or dreaming?" an amused voice inquired, shattering her fragile dream, bringing her back to reality.

Tiffany slowly turned around, peering in the dark, and only able to see the form of a man leaning against the terrace wall, his features hidden by the shadows. She answered icily, "In either case, sir, you are intruding!"

An amused chuckle from the shadows was her only answer. The man stepped out of the shadows.

"You!" she choked out, disbelief numbing her brain, and any appropriate retorts that came to mind quickly fled.

Standing arrogantly, not two feet away, was Clinton Barencourte. Clinton casually strolled to the terrace wall, leaning negligently against it, smiling. Mocking gray eyes held stormy blue ones as he spoke. "Ah, introductions don't seem necessary. I am honored you remembered me, Princess. I must have made a lasting impression. You certainly did."

"Your arrogance is beyond contempt!" Tiffany felt his gray eyes roaming leisurely over her form, appraising her from head to foot. She glared as his insolent manner, noting how he leaned casually, his arms crossed loosely over his chest. His gall appalled her. His arrogance was insufferable. She cried, "You scoundrel, you have the manners of an ass who knows no better than to gawk." Turning from him to make her way, she was stopped as Clinton reached out, grabbing her wrist, whirling her about, trapping her between his legs.

Pulling away from him only to be yanked back up between his legs, Tiffany struggled earnestly, growing more incensed by the moment.

"Why is it, Princess, whenever we meet, you wish to depart? I might begin to think you don't like me."

"I care not what you think, Mr. Barencourte. I must find Alysse. This is her engagement party, after all. Release me this instant!"

Instead, Clinton, in a deliberate display of his mastery over her, grabbed and held her other wrist, pulling her closer to his form.

Struggling ineffectually with him, Tiffany considered her options and how futile they were. Screaming would only serve to create a scene, which she certainly did not wish; kicking him was impossible, for he had her trapped between his legs.

Clinton held her securely by her wrist, watching her frantic struggles, idly wondering if her breasts would spill forth from her low bodice if she continued. The thought brought a wicked grin to his face, which Tiffany did not miss, and she ceased her feeble attempts.

Tiffany was frightened by his actions. Never had she dealt with a man so aggressive, so immune to her sharp tongue. She looked around for a champion, silently cursing herself for wandering so far from the ballroom.

Clinton watched the myriad of emotions cross her delicate features. He knew she was frightened, and was remorseful he caused such an emotion, but tonight the lines of battle must be drawn. He saw her questing looks and chose to replace her fear by raising her ire. "I would say, Princess, your attempts to escape the men trailing after you were successful." Sure enough, anger replaced her fear, and raising her chin defiantly and with an air of marked sarcasm, she replied cooly, "Not totally."

Clinton laughed, "Touché, Princess."

"Stop calling me that!"

"You don't like my pet name for you?"

Daggers of blue flames shot from her eyes. Struggling against his iron grip, she cried, "I am not a pet to be petted, mauled, or tethered. Now, let me go!" Clinton, holding her wrists capably with his hands, smiled, watching the volatile beauty.

Tiffany quickly bent her head to bite his hand, but Clinton was prepared and easily warded off the attack by standing and bringing her up against the hard length of him. "Oh no, my bloodthirsty wench, once bitten, twice a fool. I warned you I'd put your mouth to more pleasurable use."

Feeling his awesome strength and power, she gave over to scream, but Clinton's mouth captured hers, reducing the scream to a whimper. His body pinned her hands between them, freeing his own. His hand traveled to the nape of her neck, holding her head still as his mouth claimed hers in a bruising kiss. The force of his lips parted her own and his tongue plundered the soft recesses of her mouth.

Tiffany placed her hands up against his chest to push away, but his other hand moved against the small of her back, pressing her against him. Struggling impotently against him, she felt his kiss deepen, and with it, a warm sensation spread in her belly. She caught herself and renewed her struggle. His kiss became more punishing. The more she struggled, the more insistent and forceful his kiss became. She fought the assault of his kiss on her senses. She struggled for control and pushed herself off the pinnacle of sensation he had raised her to. She ceased to struggle, becoming like stone in his arms. Clinton knew he had touched her and knew the game she now played. Lifting his mouth from hers, he caught the dazed, confused look in her eyes. He smiled broadly.

"How dare you!" she hissed, slowly bringing herself under control.

"Quite easily, I'd say," he taunted. Tiffany did not mistake the silent chuckle that preceded his next words. "I warned you, Princess, I would put your mouth to more pleasurable pursuits."

Stepping back from him, having regained full control

of her faculties and feeling decidedly more confident, no longer held prisoner by him, she retorted coolly, "Pleasurable, hah, surely you jest. Perhaps a few more lessons in the art of kissing would do you good."

Turning on her heels with the intention of fleeing, she paused and foolishly, in an act of defiance, wiped her mouth with the back of her hand.

Like lightning she was jerked back into his arms, her breast crushed against his powerful chest, her body pressed intimately against his. Clinton encircled her slim waist, holding her tight against him. He cupped her chin, lifting her face, holding it so she could not turn her head. His steely gray eyes held hers in an unrelenting gaze. She had dropped the gauntlet, issued the challenge.

"A lesson, is it? Then let us begin and see how adept a student you are." The words were stated quite cordially, but she did not mistake the edge of steel behind them, nor the low, menacing way in which they were delivered.

"Lesson one, Princess." Clinton's mouth covered hers, possessing her with its searing insistence, forcing her lips to part under the pressure, and his tongue entered, ravishing its softness. Tiffany struggled against his assault, but he was so much stronger than she, and she was beginning to despair.

Clinton lifted his mouth and whispered hoarsely, "Now for lesson two." He lowered his mouth, capturing hers with a gentle kiss this time. His teeth tugged at her lower lip and he traced their pattern gently with his tongue. When she parted her lips to protest again, he captured them, moving his mouth softly, then deepening the kiss, caressing the sweet, warm recesses of her mouth. Tiffany's knees weakened and she whimpered as his tongue lightly stroked hers, gently coaxing it. She felt rising panic, feeling her body responding to his shattering kiss. Mustering every bit of her strength, she managed to pull her mouth away from his. But Clinton still had his arms around her. "You stir me, Princess, as no other," he said softly. Gripping her chin gently, lifting her head so he held her eyes with his, he said, "I've a mind to have you. Doubt not that I will." Her blue eyes widened as he continued, "I think it only fair to warn you, Princess, I am quite single-minded in my quest, relentless in my pursuit. I will give you no quarter until my goal is met. The rules are simply this—there are none. All's fair in love and war, and you, Princess, will decide which it is to be."

Realization of what his words implied filtered through her turbulent thoughts, as did his next words, said in a voice uncompromising, yet gentle.

"Heed my words well, Princess. Never mistake me for one of those mincing fops who have trouble finding their way out of their breeches. I am a man full grown and have no such trouble."

Despite herself, she shivered.

"Choose carefully the game, Princess. I am master of the game and play by my rules, with one end in mind—to win!"

Rubbing his thumb softly against her kiss-swollen lips, suppressing the urge to kiss them, he felt the light pressure of her teeth against his thumb. He smiled at her show of spirit, knowing he had chosen well. He held her gaze and she held his in a standoff.

Tears of fury burning her eyes, Tiffany suppressed the urge to bite down on the soft pad. Clinton felt the trembling of her lips against his thumb; not wishing to injure her pride further, he withdrew it.

The sound of approaching footsteps caused Tiffany to realize how precarious her situation was. Free from any restraint, she brushed past him only to be brought back up against him.

"Let me go! You've had your amusement for the evening." She pulled earnestly against his arms.

Unseen, Clinton moved her into the shadows and waited for the couple to pass. He enjoyed the feel of her pressed against him, not struggling. He was reluctant to loose her from his embrace and blessed whatever saint was watching over him when the couple paused to chat.

Tiffany groaned. There was nothing she could do but remain in his arms, hidden. The nearness of him, his scent, the rock-hard muscle of his chest, assaulted her senses.

Knowing he had the advantage, Clinton leaned, nibbling at her ear, sending delightful shivers down Tiffany's spine.

"You cad! How dare you?" she hissed, not daring to move, fearing she'd draw attention to their hiding place. Clinton pressed on, enjoying every moment, lightly caressing her spine, resting his hands just a few inches below her heaving breasts.

Tiffany endured his touch, and the minute the couple strolled away, she pulled away, crying, "You really are despicable, Mr. Barencourte! I loath you, nay, I hate you, you have no idea of the depths of my—"

"While we dance you can tell me all those endearing thoughts." A smile lifted the corners of his mouth, and before Tiffany knew it, he was leading her toward the French door.

"Dance with you? Have you gone mad?" she exclaimed increduously as he pulled her along. She dug her heels in, causing Clinton to turn to her. Blue flames blazing in her eyes, she retorted, "I most certainly will not now or ever *dance* with you!"

Blocking her escape, he stated matter-of-factly, "You misunderstand, Princess, I'm not asking you. I'm telling you I want to dance." Tiffany's mind screamed in rebellion at his arrogance.

"Of course, Princess, if you prefer, we can go back on the terrace and pick up where we left off?"

Tiffany narrowed her eyes at him, dangerous glints of anger shooting from them. Dance with him! Why, that conceited ass; of all the unmitigated gall. Never! She was about to protest but thought, what better way to be rid of him? He certainly would not be as bold and outrageous in a ballroom filled with guests. Besides, she mused, she would elude him once they walked in. He offered his arm, which she pointedly refused, instead charging ahead, entering the ballroom to flee. Clinton had anticipated her game, his arms shot out, capturing her wrists, spinning her around to face him.

A captivating smile lit his face just as he whisked her across the floor to the beginning strains of a waltz.

"Tsk, tsk, Princess, you have no honor?" he mocked.

"You're a fine one to talk of honor; why, I bet—" Clinton whirled her as the tempo increased, and Tiffany was unable to finish her sentence. The fast tempo of the waltz was not conducive to conversation, and as Clinton whirled her around and around, she truly began to enjoy the dance. Even as she thought how much she despised this arrogant man, she had to admit he danced divinely, as if he'd waltzed a thousand times, twirling and dipping her expertly.

As he led her through the intricate steps of the dance, Clinton observed her, appreciating the startling blue eyes which sparked with a life of their own, the faint pink flush staining her delicate cheeks, and the irresistible lure of her kiss-swollen lips. She was so young, he thought, he would have to be tolerant and patient with her.

Clinton whirled her around the floor and across the room in deliberate display. As the whirling couple passed, whispers, turned heads, and stares followed them. Tiffany couldn't help but laugh when he twirled her about, her gown flying out, her tresses flowing.

She didn't know where one waltz ended and another began, she was flying free! So free she failed to notice the pointed stares of the guests as Clinton whisked her about.

Vaguely she realized the set had ended and that she stood in the loose circle of Clinton's arms, in the center of the empty dance floor.

Shock slapped her square in the face seeing all heads turned in her direction. She glanced at Clinton, who smiled smugly at her. Her eyes widened, fury gleaming in their depths, as her thoughts rushed in. Why, he had publicly monopolized her! She made to pull away, but Clinton's words caused her to stop. "I wouldn't."

Slightly nodding his head in the direction of the guests, he continued, "For if you do, surely their tongues will wag."

She knew she was caught. Damn it! And he knew it, too. She glared at him.

"Smile, Princess." He shifted his eyes meaningfully, laughter gleaming in them. "They will wonder if something is amiss."

Tiffany quickly complied, affixing a weak smile to her lips. "You are contemptible, Mr. Barencourte," she whispered. Inclining her head coquettishly, she added, "You've knowingly placed me in quite an awkward position."

For the benefit of the curious stares, Clinton captured her hand, bringing it to his lips, placing a kiss upon it. Still holding it, he whispered, "Princess, I don't care what they think." Turning her palm up and before lightly tracing it with the tip of his tongue, he added, "Gossip has never interested me." He lowered his mouth to her palm.

Her smile belied the rage seething within her as his tongue swirled over her palm, sending unwanted shivers down her spine. She wanted nothing more than to wrench it away, but circumstances prevented such a display, for surely it would not go unnoticed. Clinton, having the advantage, took it, teasing her sensitive palm. Tiffany snatched her hand from him and dropped into a deep curtsy, as decorum dictated, and as she lowered her head, Clinton noticed the sneer on her face. He smiled mockingly.

Other than Clinton's obvious interest in Lady Tiffany, the guests watching saw nothing amiss in their actions; that is, other than Chad Devonshire. He leaned against a marble pillar, reading the truth of the matter. Barencourte was staking his claim, announcing to the male population his interest. His intent? Barencourte's reputation as a rake was explanation enough.

He watched Tiffany pause before stiffly accepting Clinton's proffered arm. Pushing himself off the pillar, Chad strolled toward the couple.

"Mr. Barencourte, I am sure you care not a whit for gossip because your reputation no doubt is as black as your heart. I, on the other hand . . ." Tiffany stopped when Chad Devonshire appeared.

Chad stood before her; she quickly dropped into a curtsy in greeting to his slight bow.

"Lady Tiffany, as always, you look lovely," Chad said politely.

Tiffany smiled weakly.

Chad turned to Clinton, extending his hand. "Clinton, glad to see you could make it. I heard you were abroad. I see you've made the acquaintance of Lady Courtland."

"Yes, we have met." Clinton turned, smiling at Tiffany, and then back to Chad. "Sorry I was late. I just returned from England this afternoon."

Chad raised an arched brow and asked, "Business?"

Before he could reply, Reginald Stanridge appeared.

"Devonshire, Barencourte." Reginald nodded stiffly in greeting. He turned to Tiffany, bowing. "I believe, Lady Courtland, you promised me the earlier set." He gazed at Clinton. "However, you were otherwise detained. I would seek recompensation with this set." Tiffany laid her hand on Reginald's arm, thankful for his rescue, and accompanied him to the floor. Chad did not miss the cold half smile that crossed Clinton's mouth or the piercing gaze leveled at Reginald's retreating figure.

Chad relieved a passing waiter of two glasses of champagne, handing one to Clinton. After taking a sip of the liquid, Chad asked, "Will I see you at the hunt this weekend?"

Never taking his gaze from Tiffany, who at the moment was surrounded by admirers, Clinton easily responded, "I won't be riding to the hounds. Some loose strings require tying up. I shall be late, but early for dinner."

"Loose ends, you say! As in flaming red hair and green eyes?"

Turning his head slightly to Chad, Clinton lifted a brow in inquiry.

Chad's mouth lifted in a smile. He paused, taking a sip of his drink, remarking, "I might be interested in offering her my protection for services of her body."

A knowing smirk crossed Clinton's face and he remarked, "We go back a long time, Chad; never have I known you to take another's leavings." Clinton lifted his glass, sipping his drink. When he finished, he added, "If memory serves me correctly, you were quite put out whenever we engaged a wench in a ménage à trois."

"Ah, true, my friend, but you also cared not for seconds."

Clinton returned his gaze to Tiffany, watching her banter with an ardent suitor, and countered easily, "But I am no longer in the market for used goods, and you are."

"So what I hear is true, Clinton! You've made a large cash settlement and given your mistress the title to the house." Chad rocked back on his heels, ready with his next question. "Have you found a replacement?"

A long moment passed before Clinton answered, and in that moment Chad watched Clinton's gaze follow Tiffany as she was whisked about the floor.

"You might say I have, Chad."

Clinton did not miss the sigh Chad emitted, and turned to him, saying, "Let's cut to the quick, Chad."

"You may not like what I have to say, Clinton."

A crooked smile appeared on Clinton's face. "That never stopped you before, my friend."

Nodding, Chad began. "We have been friends a long time. Shared many an adventure, many a woman, and drank ourselves silly." In a serious voice, Chad continued. "We have never judged or slandered one another." He paused, "Or crossed swords."

Clinton met his gaze, asking, "And you think now we will?"

Declining to answer, Chad explained further. "I find myself in an awkward position thrust between friendship and duty. For the last two years my duty has been to protect Lady Courtland's honor." He smiled roguishly. "A duty most difficult, for often I had to remind myself of my role and exercise extreme self-control." Clinton grinned, knowing his friend's equally strong appetites.

"Tonight, Clinton, I could not help but notice your attention to that ravishing creature who would tempt the devil himself. As a man, I'd say pursue her with all haste! But as her protector, I need to know your intentions are not to dally, for I rue the day we'd face one another across a dueling field over a piece of fluff."

Smiling, Clinton placed his arm across Chad's shoulders, and thinking of the betrothal contract in his breast pocket, confidently replied, "You have my word, as a friend, that day will never come."

Much relieved, Chad suggested, "If you're finished devouring her, we can leave and find something a little stronger and fortifying than this champagne."

They made their way, but Clinton paused, turning back before leaving the room. His gaze rested on Tiffany, who was amidst a group of gentlemen. She must have sensed his gaze, for she looked in his direction. Their eyes met across the expanse of the room; his the cool, predatory gaze of a hunter, hers reflecting the wariness of the hunted. Tiffany quickly looked away. Clinton smiled, knowing she understood the exchange, and left the room.

Chapter Eight

"Come, come, mademoiselle, time to get up!" Germane dashed efficiently about the room, opening the French doors, allowing the late morning sun to stream into the darkened chamber.

"Mademoiselle!! Up! Up! The carriages are loaded and awaiting you!"

Tiffany moaned, pulling the pillow over her head, blocking the sun.

"Go away, Germane." Her voice was muffled by the pillow.

Yanking the covers back, Germane scolded, "You have missed the hunt and you will miss the festivities if you don't get up."

Tiffany threw the pillow at Germane, who caught it undaunted, used to her mistress's mercurial moods.

Sitting up, drawing her knees to her chin, Tiffany cried, "I'm tired of hunts, balls, champagne, and waltzes!"

A barrage of servants entered carrying heated water for her bath while Germane laid a small breakfast on the terrace table.

With little energy, Tiffany rose, wrapping her robe around her lush form, and padded out to the terrace. She nibbled on a croissant and sipped her hot cocoa. Her appetite in the last few days had waned. She attributed this and her lack of energy to her coming monthly flux.

Tiffany padded back into her room, heading toward the bathing chamber. The smell of crushed violets, her favorite flower, wafted in the steamy air. She lowered herself into the warm, soothing water, laying her head against the rim of the tub, her raven tresses cascading down to the floor.

I should be happy, she mused. This is Alysse's weekend celebration and most likely the last event of her single life. I should be happy, for after this, I shall return to England, to Alan. Her monthly flux always made her moody, that was it. Well, that's part of it, she thought as she squeezed water from the sponge over a shapely raised leg. And the other part, well, she didn't want to think about it, but Mr. Barencourte's face kept surfacing. And why did Kent have to know the duke of Chablisienne? Why did that lecherous old man offer his estate? Why? Why? Why?

She threw the sponge forcefully in the water, causing droplets to splash on her.

"*Oooooh,*" she screeched. Barencourte, Chablisienne, a weekend surrounded by them. No doubt that ass Barencourte, the lackey he was, had dutifully informed the lecherous duke of her refusal of his despicable offer! How would she ever face him? Him! How in God's name would she face Barencourte after last night! What a pickle she was in. A lecherous old duke and a high-handed Barencourte!

Fortunately last night at the ball, any talk about her and Mr. Barencourte had been overshadowed with rumors that the duke of Chablisienne had pensioned off his mistress. Speculation ran rampant as to her replacement. The duke should present no problem tonight unless he was able to hobble down the steps. No, the problem would be Barencourte.

"Mademoiselle!" Germane's impatient voice exclaimed. Tiffany groaned but rose from her bath, restored, refreshed, and ready to do battle.

* * *

Tiffany impatiently slapped her gloves against her hand, tapping her foot nervously, wondering where the duke's ancient butler, Leavit, was off to. God, she thought, the poor man should retire.

While waiting, she took in her surroundings, noting the tasteful blend of architecture and furnishings. It was obvious what the duke lacked in moral fiber was made up for in his estate's decor. "Hummh," she snorted, noting the priceless vases and bric-a-brac. "All his possessions on display," she mumbled unkindly. She shook her head, thinking, what did she expect anyway?

The estate was indeed pretentious, gilded railings, priceless paintings, marble statues gracing the hallways, and rooms upon rooms. Goodness, it was staggering the number of rooms and servants. Her room was lovely; it faced a southeasterly direction, large and spacious. Rows of French windows let the afternoon light in. Soft lavender paper lined the walls, and much to her surprise, vases of fresh-cut violets filled her room.

Strolling across the foyer in search of the butler, she wondered what Aunt Winnie was doing. "Probably soaking in a hot tub," she said to herself. Aunt Winnie had seen her restlessness and suggested she ride Shalimar, who had been brought to the estate two days ago. Tiffany readily accepted Winnie's suggestion, knowing the others were still out hunting. Fortunately she had missed the hunt. Although she loved to ride, she abhorred hunting. She had never seen a kill but had heard her father and his friends discuss it. It sounded gruesome! She could not abide the slaughtering of animals for food. She certainly could not abide the running down of a fox for sport!

Turning around, not having found the butler, she decided, contrary to Leavit's admonition, she did not need an escort to the stables. With purposeful strides, she crossed the foyer and threw open the door, charging down the numerous steps onto the brick drive, making her way in the direction she thought the stables to be.

"Mademoiselle, mademoiselle!"

She turned, hearing the anguished voice of the butler. Leavit paused, stooped over, his hand clutching his chest.

"Leavit," she cried, running back to the man, thinking him sick. Reaching him, helping him stand, she asked, "Are you all right? My goodness, you should not be running about."

"Mademoiselle . . . please . . ." he gasped between breaths. "Please, I beg your indulgence, the groom was detained." Leavit, catching his breath, stood up. "He will be but a moment."

Smiling down at the old man, speaking softly, she said "Really, Leavit, I need no escort." She waved her hand in the direction of the stables. "See, I am almost there."

Shaking his head, he said, "No, no, His Grace was most explicit; 'an escort,' he said."

At the mention of His Grace, Tiffany stiffened and retorted unkindly, "*His* Grace no doubt has lapses of memory, a condition not uncommon in men of advanced years; however, I have no such affliction."

Turning abruptly from him, Tiffany made her way to the stables. Leavit looked increduously after her, shaking his head. Raising his hand to the sky as if asking for divine intervention, he commented, "No matter how long I live and service the wealthy, I'll never understand them." He made his way slowly back to the manor.

Tiffany leisurely wandered into the stables. The familiar smells of sweet hay, leather, and horseflesh filled her senses. The stables were excellently kept, indicating the duke spared no expense in maintaining them. Well, he wouldn't, she thought; it's another possession of his, another mark of his status.

She aimlessly walked, stopping to pat the heads of horses stabled within, wondering where Xanadu was kept. She began her search, lingering for a moment with a dappled gray mare who caught her eye. A whinnying drew her to a stall where a young stallion was housed. Her experienced eye placed him at three years. His face bespoke Arabian and thoroughbred bloodlines. He had a proud head, strong neck, and fine-muscled legs. Her contemplation of the stallion was interrupted by a voice.

" 'E's a fine beast. Fine an' fast, 'e is."

Tiffany looked up at a man with flaming red hair and merry blue eyes; for an instant she had a feeling of déjà vu.

"Oh, indeed he is, sir. I bet he is a joy to ride." She patted his soft muzzle. "What do you call him?"

"Oh, the duke's named 'im Kubla Khan, 'ady."

"A most noble name." Tiffany observed the stallion, thinking he was much like Xanadu, which prompted her to ask, "Sir, is the stallion Xanadu stabled here as well?"

"No, lady, the duke sold him."

"Oh. Do you . . ."

Her question was interrupted by the frantic appearance of the stable master, who hurried to her, crying, "Mademoiselle, here you are! I was told you had left, but when I did not see you, I became alarmed." He grabbed her arm, leading her outside. Confusion was written across her face at the actions of the man.

Claude, the stable master, relieved he had found Mademoiselle, called out, "I have found Mademoiselle; bring her mount, Franz, on the double!"

Claude made to leave her to see what the holdup was but stopped, turning to say, "Stay right here, mademoiselle. I will see what the delay is." Tiffany had never seen a household of such frantic servants, first Leavit, now Claude. She shook her head. The duke was no doubt an ogre to work for, expecting his every command to be carried out with precision that allowed no margin for error. He probably thrashed them with his walking stick for any infraction, no matter how small.

Shalimar was led out, tacked in a hunter's saddle and not the customary sidesaddle. A surprise look crossed her face, which did not go unnoticed by Claude. He was quick to explain. "My apologies, mademoiselle, but His Grace specifically instructed this saddle."

"No, the saddle is fine." Tiffany mounted Shalimar, and while she was adjusting her skirt, Claude informed her of an intricate course of jumps His Grace thought she'd love.

"This course is, how you English say? Jolly Good!"

She asked, "Really?"

"His Grace had it set in the western acreage . . . Your escort will show you the way."

"I don't require an escort." Tiffany looped the reins between her pinky and ring finger, slackening on her hold.

Claude, shaking his head quickly, insisted, "Mademoiselle, His Grace's orders are explicit. You are to have an escort."

Tiffany had had enough of *His Grace*'s orders. She smiled sweetly down at Claude. "My dear man—" her voice held a note of challenge "—prove I need an escort!" She nudged an eager Shalimar into a gallop, shouting over her shoulder, "By keeping up with me!"

Startled, but not befuddled, Claude took note of her easterly direction. Springing into action, he shouted for the grooms to saddle up and follow her. Claude stomped angrily up and down, threatening them with a long tour of stall mucking if she wasn't found.

A half hour later, Clinton strolled to the stables, having heard from a much-exhausted Leavit that Lady Tiffany had gone riding. Leavit had informed Clinton that his family had served the Chablisiennes for five generations, and most had been born and died in their service, a tradition that, until today, Leavit had hoped to carry on. Clinton recalled the astonished look Leavit gave him when he laughed heartily over Tiffany's referral to the duke's senility, and a proper Leavit had commented, "Mademoiselle has not the proper respect."

Turning the bend, Clinton saw a red-faced Claude stomping up and down in front of an exhausted group of men and horses. He caught sight of Keegan and walked over to him, asking, "What goes on?"

Merry blue eyes twinkling with amusement regarded Clinton. "Seems one of the guests 'as eluded 'im." Keegan pointed a gnarled finger in Claude's direction.

Smiling, Clinton ventured, "Let me guess. Lady Courtland?"

"Ya got it, guv'nor."

"Claude, saddle Mercury. I'll find her."

Relief washed over Claude's face and he quickly complied with Clinton's request, bringing out the chestnut stallion.

Clinton mounted, adjusting his stirrups. Claude paced back and forth, saying, "Mademoiselle went east, but the grooms could not find her."

Clinton spurred Mercury into a gallop heading west, hearing Claude shout, "No, she went east!"

Instinct told him he would find her at the course. Tiffany could not resist the temptation any more than she could resist her bonbons. No doubt "His Grace's" instruction caused her to bolt as she did, but "His Grace's" temptation would draw her back.

As the magnificent chestnut stallion galloped up the crest of a hill, the sun's rays reflected off its coat. Clinton headed the mount toward the grove of trees, pulling to a halt. Streams of breath escaped Mercury's flared nostrils. Smoky gray eyes scanned the field of courses, searching for his quarry. His eyes moved away from the courses to the nearby field, coming to rest on his Princess. Nothing could have prepared him for the scene his eyes beheld. He had expected to find her jumping her bloodied mare over the intricate course, at the very least putting her through a strenuous workout. No amount of research, no report, no matter how thorough, could have prepared him for what his eyes beheld. She was ever full of surprises. His gray eyes were touched by the gentle smile crossing his face as he beheld a most enchanting vision, one he would always cherish.

On a gentle knoll, which sloped toward the edge of a brook, under a majestic willow whose boughs entwined about, creating a bower, she sat, amidst a profusion of wild violets and daisies, weaving garlands of flowers. A band of daisies, interwoven with bluebells, circled her raven head, mingling within the soft curls, and where a froth of lace once lay, a necklace of violets adorned her throat and lay enticingly in the valley of her breasts. A soft breeze whispered through the high grass, molding her sheer blouse to the full, soft curve of her breast, and rustled long, curling strands of hair about. He watched her pluck a flower and press her nose against the full open blossom, inhaling the sweet fragrance. He was enthralled by the fairy-tale quality of the vision: she was all delicate, graceful, vulnerable, and so beautiful. He smiled watching her chase a butterfly, peer into the tinkling waters of the brook, and absently pluck the petals from a daisy as she sat in the meadow grass. He witnessed a different, unseen side of her: no longer the impertinent, furious kitten, but a sweet, gentle maid, innocent and vulnerable. She touched a tenderness, a protectiveness, he did not think he possessed. He dismounted, leading Mercury from the grove into the high meadow grass sprinkled with early wildflowers to meet his Princess.

Shalimar grazed peacefully while Tiffany finished the intricate pattern of the flower garland she wove. Lifting the garland, laying it about Shalimar's neck, Tiffany noticed it was similar to one she had made for Alan. Shalimar tossed her head, and Tiffany laughed at the mare's antics, exclaiming, "Why, you look like a queen decked out royally!"

Tiffany leaned back on her arms, lifting her face to the sun, looking upward at the blue sky and watching the white, billowy clouds move across it. Closing her eyes, she could hear the steady buzz of nectar-filled bees and imagined them flitting from blossom to blossom, collecting their ambrosia. Opening her eyes, she saw the lacy, dainty wings of the dayflies flitting about, rejoicing in their birth. The tinkling waters of the brook tripped and fell over moss-covered stones in its path; the croaking of a bullfrog calling its mate was music to her ears. All of it lent an air of tranquillity to her spirit, and her earlier trepidation fled on the wings of an elusive butterfly.

She plucked a flower, pressing it against her nose, inhaling the sweet fragrance. A daisy caught her eyes; she plucked it and twirled it between her fingers, watching the pollen-yellow center blend with the pinwheel petals. She regarded the flower and smiled remembering a childhood game, and began plucking its white petals, one by one, repeating out loud, "He loves me, he loves me not . . ."

So immersed was she in her play, in a world where she needed no barrier or wall to protect herself, she failed to hear or see his advance, and only when she discarded another petal and he said, "He loves you," did she look up.

He stood framed against the low sun, its rays streaming from behind him. The breeze softly rustled his hair and billowed his shirt open, exposing a well-muscled chest covered with a mat of dark hair. A stallion grazed behind him, its reins resting in his hand, a bouquet of violets in his other. She watched him bend down on one knee and extend the bouquet to her, a soft, disarming smile lighting his face, touching the depths of his gray eyes.

A long moment passed as if time were suspended. Suspicious blue eyes regarded smoky gray. Clinton, not wishing to spoil the moment, did not advance, nor did he retreat. Tiffany leaned back on her arms, ready to move dare he advance.

"Greeks bearing gifts, Mr. Barencourte?" Looking pointedly at the proffered bouquet, she said, "I think I shall beware."

Clinton sat down beside her, smiling as he laid the violets down between them. He realized the moment was shattered and his kitten was baring her claws. Stretching out on his side, he absently plucked a blade of grass, chewing on it. He noticed her bare toes peeking out from beneath her skirt when she drew her knees up, resting her chin on them.

Tiffany decided to take the bull by the horns. "Exactly what brings you here, Mr. Barencourte?"

Rewarding her with a dazzling smile, the blade of grass protruding from the side of his mouth, he explained, "It seems you left the stable without an escort, so I was summoned to the task."

Her laughter at his remark filled the air and was comfort to his ears.

"Hah! They were concerned for my safety and sent you to ensure it? Now, that I find quite amusing." She stood gracefully and brushed her riding skirt. Looking down at his reclining figure, shaking her head, her crown of flowers cocking slightly to the right, she raised a brow and remarked, "Sending the wolf to tend the sheep."

A wolfish grin was his reply. Tiffany glared at him, thinking he was the most infuriating man alive! In a huff she turned to leave, only to find that Shalimar, scenting the stallion, had moved a good distance away. Tiffany walked slowly, cooing softly to the flighty mare. As Tiffany advanced, Shalimar trotted farther away.

Clinton lay with his arms crossed behind his head, resting in the meadow, his eyes closed, a smile lifting the corners of his mouth as he listened to Tiffany's attempt to sweet-talk the skittish mare.

Unable to coax the mare, Tiffany cried in exasperation, *"Ooooh!"* Storming back, she glared at his prone form. How dare he lie there nonchalantly when he was the cause of her problem?

Feeling her gaze on him, Clinton opened one eye to find her standing above him, her fists resting on her rounded hips, and her bare foot tapping soundlessly against the ground. Such a lovely picture she presented. Her crown askew, the flower necklace rising and falling with her heaving breasts, and her locks falling beguilingly about her.

"Look what you've done, you cad!"

Innocently he asked, *"Moi?* Certainly, Princess, you know about the birds and the bees. It is not me, but the stallion." Smiling, he closed his eyes and added confidently, "She'll come around; they always do."

Seething with anger, Tiffany thought she'd love to wipe that grin off his face. She stood a moment longer; finally seeing the wisdom in his words, she tossed herself down in the high meadow grass, which she unmercifully began to pluck. Silence reined.

Clinton, lying prone with eyes closed, broke the silence. "Did you ride the course?"

Looking at the course, noting the manner in which it was designed, she answered him, "No, my mare took lame. I did not wish to inflict further injury to her leg."

Turning onto his side, he offered, "My mount is available for your use. Unless you find the course too difficult."

Tiffany rose to the bait. "Hah! Perhaps for His Grace! A child could figure out the best route for time and faults."

Clinton raised himself up. Standing above her, he offered his hand. "My mighty steed awaits your pleasure, milady."

Tiffany allowed him to help her up. They walked toward Mercury, who eyed Tiffany warily. While Clinton adjusted the stirrups, Tiffany proceeded to befriend the stallion, blowing softly on his muzzle.

"I'm afraid, Princess, the stirrups are too long and the saddle too big."

"Remove it; I can handle him without it." She returned her attention to Mercury, noting the fine lines indicative of good breeding. No match for Xanadu, she thought, but a worthy steed. Stroking the horse, she asked lightly, "A man at the stables said His Grace sold Xanadu." She turned her face to him. "I thought you said the duke was not in need of funds."

"He isn't." Pulling the saddle from Mercury's back, he turned to face her, noting the fleeting look of sadness pass over her. Softly he asked, "You remember the price, Princess, don't you?"

Sadness fled, an incredulous look crossing her face, a blush staining her cheeks. "A . . . a night . . ." She could not finish.

A wolfish grin split his face. "The price was upped and met. A lifetime, Princess, a lifetime." He cupped her foot, boosting her onto Mercury's back. His hand lingered and moved up her stockingless leg. She slapped his hand away, kicking Mercury toward the course.

Clinton watched her post up and down, zeroing in on her nicely rounded buttocks. He grinned, thinking she'd bear his weight quite well.

Coming down the broad, curving staircase, Winifred turned to Tiffany. A slow, beaming smile worked its way across her face as she thought Tiffany looked positively breathtaking. She asked, "Did you enjoy your ride this afternoon, dear?"

"Yes, Aunt Winnie, except for Shalimar's lameness." And a certain unwanted visitor, she thought. She had ridden Mercury over the course with hardly a flaw and was miffed that Mr. Barencourte had taken it flawlessly. Actually, the afternoon turned out quite pleasant. Mr. Barencourte had managed to act like a gentleman.

"Will Shalimar be sound?"

"Mr. Barencourte seems to think a day or two of rest and she'll be as good as new." Tiffany paused in her descent to look at the immense crystal chandelier, the likes of which she had never seen. The flickering lights of a thousand candles reflected a rainbow of colors off the tear-shaped crystal droplets.

Winnie stopped, seeing what had caught Tiffany's attention, and explained, "The duke of Chablisienne's home is a virtual museum of priceless treasures. Many presented for the family's loyalty and bravery."

At the mention of the duke, Tiffany bristled, doubting loyalty or bravery had anything to do with it. More than likely the whole family was self-indulgent, striving to possess anything, merely to possess it. She began again to descend the broad, curving staircase, touching the gilded railing. Sarcasm clearly etched in her question, she asked, "Has his royal personage made an appearance?"

Winnie cocked her head toward Tiffany, confusion clearly written on her face. As they stepped onto the marble floor of the foyer, Winnie answered, "Quite a while ago, dear."

Not looking at her aunt, she scanned the crowd, remarking dryly, "I can hardly wait to meet His Eminence."

Winifred drew her brows together, perplexed as she began to reply, "But my dear, you al—" Carolyn's sudden flustered appearance interrupted Winifred.

"Oh, here you are, Tiffany. Thank goodness. Please see to Alysse. Why, she's all aflutter, says she knows none of Kent's friends." Carolyn fanned herself furiously.

Tiffany left to find Alysse, and Carolyn turned to Winifred. "Oh, Winnie, were we as nervous? How will she ever make it to the wedding? . . . Oh my, what—"

"Now, now, Carolyn, all will be right, you'll see."

Tiffany found a very nervous Alysse wringing her hands; her flushed face had a fearful look on it. Spying Tiffany, Alysse let out a sigh of relief. "Oh, Tiffany, whatever am I to do? All of these sophisticated people are friends of Kent." Tiffany scanned the crowd, noting she was unfamiliar with many of the guests as well.

"I must appear the country mouse to them."

"Nonsense, Alysse, you look spectacular."

"Do you think so, Tiffany?" Alysse smiled at Tiffany's

nod, feeling decidedly better. "Oh, Tiffany, here comes Kent. Do I look all right?"

Tiffany winked at her and turned just as Kent approached them with two other gentlemen.

Kent bowed to them. "Alysse, my sweet, may I present to you and Tiffany, Nigel Hardwich and Charles Wainright."

Tiffany and Alysse lowered themselves in a deep curtsy.

"Tiffany, these fine gentlemen are your dinner partners, fresh from English shores." Tiffany smiled and extended her hand to each one.

"Alysse, my sweet, our host, the duke of Chablisienne, is in the upper salon, and I would honor him with your introduction." Kent turned to Tiffany. "Lady Courtland, I leave you in most capable hands." Kent bowed and, taking Alysse's hand, strolled away with her.

Tiffany breathed a sigh of relief. Thank God she wasn't called upon to pay tribute to the old man. With any luck, the pompous relic would remain closeted and not formally appear before his subjects!

"Lady Courtland." She smiled at the gentlemen, laying her hands upon their arms, walking into the dining room.

Seated between Nigel and Charles made dinner a delightful affair. The two very sophisticated gentlemen amused her with tales of adventure. As a result, dinner turned out to be quite enjoyable. That is, except for the presence of Mr. Barencourte, who sat across from her. He was flanked by two very sophisticated, very beautiful women, who, by their actions, appeared to be very familiar with, and comfortable in, his company.

Often she felt his gaze on her, and when she glanced up, she'd find him regarding her intently, a mocking smile etching his handsome face. She chose to ignore him but found it difficult, knowing he was observing her. During a brief respite between courses, Tiffany nonchalantly glanced down the length of the table, seeing if perhaps the duke had made a surprise appearance. Scan as she did, none of the guests remotely resembled her image of an old, gnarled, stooped man, wielding a walking stick.

When she glanced up, she found Clinton regarding her, a question poised in his smoky gray eyes. She quickly turned away and flirted shamelessly with her dinner partners.

"You say you'll be gracing England with your beauty soon."

She smiled at Charles, a blush staining her cheeks. "Yes, in less than two weeks I am scheduled to return."

"Well, we English have again defeated the French. England's gain, France's loss," remarked Nigel. Tiffany laughed, gaily bantering with them during the long dinner.

Clinton sat back observing Tiffany. Tonight she looked ravishing in the deep rose gown whose low-cut bodice afforded him a generous view of her young, ripe breasts. Midnight curls were loosely drawn up save for the errant wisps that framed her exquisite oval face. Her color rode high this eve, which he attributed to the heady wine she had consumed. Even his two friends, Nigel and Charles, were snared by her beauty, attracted to her rapier-sharp wit.

He smiled remembering the pleasant afternoon he spent with her. He knew he could spend the rest of his days in her company. She was emotion personified. Like the wind, she was spontaneous, ever-changing. She could be furious, with claws bared, when cornered, or cool, confident, when approaching a jump, proud and headstrong to a fault and vulnerable and defensive.

A tightening in his groin accompanied a train of more lustful thoughts. Chaneling all that passion and spirit to the bedroom was going to be challenging. By his hand he would show her the depths of her passion, teach her the roles of a lover, a mistress, a wife. The sound of Kent's voice broke through his thoughts.

Kent rose, a glass raised. "I'd like to propose a toast in

honor of our host, who has so graciously extended his home to us this evening.''

Tiffany absently raised her glass, her gaze moving from one guest to another in search of ''our host.'' Again she glanced up and down the length of the table, noting all glasses raised, except one.

He grinned and inclined his head in acknowledgment to her. Seeing confused eyes regarding him, amusement lit his eyes. The shock of discovery hit Tiffany full force just as Kent's voice called out, ''To His Grace the ninth duke of Chablisienne—Clinton Claremont Barencourte.''

England

1818-1819

Chapter Nine

England, June 1818

"William!"

Earl Courtland turned his head to Winifred, who sat to his right.

"Excuse me, Winnie, I have many matters on my mind." He lifted his teacup, indicating he required a second cup. Godfrey efficiently complied with the unspoken request. After sipping the brew, William replaced the cup on its saucer. Wiping the corners of his mouth, he said, "Now, what was it you said?"

"I said I think a respectable period of time has passed since Lord Thurston's death and we should pay our respects to his son."

"Yes, of course. You'll handle the arrangements?"

"I have already, William. We're to visit this afternoon."

"This afternoon!" William threw his napkin on the table. "Impossible, Winnie! I have a thousand things to do, contracts to review, correspondence . . ." William stood abruptly, pushing his chair out, looking at his sister-in-law. Seeing the determined expression on her face, he relented, "Very well, if you insist, you and Tiffany pay your respects." With that said, he stomped out of the room.

After Godfrey refilled Winifred's cup, he began to clear

away the earl's plates and carried them from the breakfast room. Winnie, holding her cup with both hands, sat contemplating William's recent behavior.

Something was amiss; her woman's intuition told her as much. She knew Lord Thurston had been a close friend of William's, and William was taking his death hard, but there was more. Ever since she and Tiffany had returned ten days ago, William's behavior was out of character, almost mysterious.

There was no doubt Tiffany's appearance had been a shock. Why, when she left, she was a young girl, and she had returned a young and very beautiful woman, possessing all the social graces of one of her class. William's mouth had been agape when Tiffany stepped out of the carriage, turned, and curtsied to him. He had been speechless. Winnie smiled, thinking William was seldom speechless. No, she shook her head in thought. She couldn't put her finger on it; there was an underlying current here, but for the life of her, she didn't know what it was.

"Good morning, Aunt." Winifred looked up, finding a bright-eyed Tiffany at her side. Tiffany leaned down, kissing Winifred's cheek, and then seated herself at a newly placed setting.

"Good morning, dear. Did you sleep well?" Winnie took in Tiffany's appearance. She was dressed in a white-and-pink-striped day gown. Her hair was drawn up from her face and plaited close to her head. Pink ribbon was intricately woven within the plait. Her cheeks had a faint blush to them and she looked fresh and lovely as morning dew.

Buttering a soft blueberry muffin, Tiffany looked up and replied, "Better than the previous nights. I imagine I have to get used to the bed. It's been years since I've slept on it."

Nibbling on the muffin, Tiffany reached for the teapot, filling her cup.

Grimacing at the taste of the brew, she gently laid her cup back on its saucer, reaching for the sugar, ladling two hefty spoons of sugar into it, mixing it with her spoon. Winifred watched Tiffany. She smiled to herself, wondering how her niece kept her trim figure with such a sweet tooth. Winifred began softly, "Tiffany, do you have any plans for this afternoon?"

Shaking her head while she delicately chewed a mouthful of muffin, Tiffany swallowed and replied, "No, Aunt Winnie, I thought only to ride later." Tiffany had ridden to the bluff every day since her return, hoping to meet Alan, but since his father's death, she had no chance to see him.

"Well, dear, I thought it appropriate if we pay our respects to Lord Thurston today. A proper amount of time has passed since the burial, and he should be receiving guests."

Tiffany nearly jumped for joy.

"Of course, Aunt Winnie. What time shall I be ready?"

"Teatime, dear." Winnie smiled seeing a bright smile light up Tiffany's face when she mentioned the Thurston name.

Tiffany was lost in thought. What shall I wear? My pink gown . . . No, the blue one shows off my eyes. Perhaps the lavender. Heavens no! Alan is in mourning. How about . . .

William sat behind his desk finishing the last of his correspondence. Withdrawing the betrothal contract from his desk, he scanned the form, thinking it odd the only dowry His Grace insisted upon was the bluff, a worthless stretch of property having no value to William's way of thinking, but he was not about to argue. For that matter, he did not protest over many of the strange "understandings" the duke insisted on. Hell, The duke of Wentworth was an extremely powerful man. William could not believe Tiffany had caught the eye of a duke. A duke whose blood ran bluer than most; a man who had been groomed to power and position at an early age.

A man who, at twenty-four, being the last surviving male heir to his French grandsire, Philip LaRougue, inherited the properties and title duke of Chablisienne. Five years later, his father, Bertram Barencourte, passed on, leaving the English title and property to his eldest issue, Clinton Barencourte. For the past three years Clinton Barencourte had held two of the highest titles, duke of Chablisienne and duke of Wentworth. A man that powerful and wealthy could be as eccentric as he wished, thought William. And he had indeed exerted his power and wealth in extracting the original contract from Winston Thurston by offering Winston free title to his properties, payment of all of Alan's markers, and a staggering sum of 150,000 pounds. Winston had seen the light and quickly shook hands on the deal, leaving William to negotiate with the duke for Tiffany.

For the most part, their negotiations had gone smoothly, with the understanding Tiffany was to retain her own dowry. William thought it foolish to allow any woman to be in control of money, but was silenced by the duke's piercing eyes. The bluff was part of the dowry Tiffany was to bring to the union, and finally, no word of the betrothal to Tiffany or anyone until the duke decided when it was to be announced. He was quite firm and unrelenting on these points. William readily accepted the terms of the betrothal, a betrothal that would forever tie the Courtland name to a powerful family.

William rose from his desk, walking to his safe, located behind the portrait of Amelia. Quickly turning the knob to the numbers of the combination, he opened the safe. Laying the contract within, he closed the door, replacing the portrait. He wandered to the window and happened to see Tiffany walking in the rose garden, picking roses, laying them in a basket she carried. He still could not get over the beauty that had blossomed over the last three years. It's no wonder she caught the eye of the duke, he thought. He turned from the window, sitting back down at his desk. He had observed her the last ten days since her return. The rebellious, unbiddable child he had sent to France had returned a beautiful young woman with perfect and acceptable social graces, in whose behavior he found no flaw. Evidently Winifred had tutored her in the proper conduct expected of her station. Withdrawing a contract he had yet to review, he pausing, thinking all was going quite well. Pushing his spectacles up, he began to read the contract, confident nothing would go amiss.

The coach swayed as they turned up the private drive to Thurston Manor. Tiffany's hand shook, her palms began to sweat, in anticipation of seeing Alan.

"Do I look all right, Aunt Winnie? You don't think the gown too . . . ah, bright?"

Winnie smiled, watching her niece, giving her a thorough appraisal, noting how flattering the buttercup yellow contrasted against her raven hair. Smiling at Tiffany, Winnie remarked, "I think when your Alan sees you, all his sorrow will fly."

The coach drew up in front of the manor. A footman opened the door, placing a stool for their descent. Tiffany gathered her skirts, stepping down after Winifred. Looking up at the manor she hoped would someday be her home, Tiffany took a deep breath and prepared to ascend the steps to the front door, hoping to find the love and warmth she remembered.

The door was thrown open, and at its threshold stood Earl Alan Thurston. Tiffany's breath was taken away at the sight of him; her heart fluttered at the pleasant image he presented. The sun reflected the sandy red highlights of his light brown hair. He was well groomed—his jacket and pants chocolate brown, offset by a yellow waistcoat.

Alan walked from the threshold; his handsome face smiled warmly at her as he stepped down to clasp her hands in his. The gold in his amber eyes flickered with admiration as he gazed at the exquisite beauty before him. For a fleeting moment he questioned the wisdom of the choice he had made.

"Tiffany," he said, and gently cupped her face with his hands, bringing his mouth down upon hers in a light kiss.

Tiffany always wondered what their first kiss would be like. On occasion she'd pressed her lips against her pillow, pretending it to be Alan. But this kiss, their first, while pleasant, was nowhere near the kiss in her dream. That kiss would be earth-shattering, not brotherly. She had never been kissed except by that fraud Barencourte, and, well, his kisses had been disturbing. She attributed Alan's lack of passion to the circumstances and Aunt Winnie's presence.

"It's good to see you again, Tiffany," Alan said, trying to force some formality into his words. "You have changed into a beautiful young woman."

Tiffany's heart sang as she heard the words she had dreamed. She smiled up at him innocently. "And you, Alan, ah . . . Earl Thurston, are still the man I dream . . . I remember." She gazed at the button of his waistcoat and, suddenly remembering her aunt, said, "Where are my manners!" Turning to Winifred, she began, "Aunt Winifred, may I present Earl Alan Thurston."

Alan turned to accept Winifred's hand, placing a kiss on it. "Now, where are my manners allowing two lovely ladies to stand in the hot sun? Please, after you." He extended his hand in a sweeping bow toward the door. Winifred and Tiffany walked through the portal, with Alan following.

Tea was served in the drawing room. Conversation was light after the necessary expressions of sympathy were made.

Winifred watched Tiffany watch Alan, who watched Tiffany. There was no doubt Alan Thurston was shocked by Tiffany's beauty and wit. On occasion Winifred detected a thread of disapproval in his comments to Tiffany's stories of her adventures in France. By the by, the earl seemed a fine fellow, perhaps a bit insipid, a bit too principled, but charming and quite pleasant-looking. Winifred was drawn from her thoughts by Tiffany's sweet laughter.

". . . The European women are so indolent, Alan. I must have appeared to be quite hasty. I fear their opinion of Englishwomen somewhat jaded."

"Now, now, Tiffany, because European women have not the same passion for riding does not make them lazy."

"I think, my lord, you tease me. You have often remarked how pleasurable it was to ride with one who enjoyed it as much as you." Tiffany smiled, challenging Alan to refute her remark. Alan chose not to and, smiling back, reached over, clasping her hand. Winifred thought, He is not teasing; he means exactly what he said and implies far more.

The time to depart drew near, and with saddened heart, Tiffany reluctantly rose. When they reached the carriage, she turned to bid farewell to Alan and could not keep herself from asking, "Perhaps we might ride together sometime?"

Alan, cupping her chin, smiled. "Yes, perhaps we shall."

Definitely not satisfied with his answer, Tiffany pressed, "Good, shall we make a date . . . say a week from today? You may pick me up in the morning."

Somewhat taken back by her aggressiveness, but knowing it would be impolite to refuse, he agreed. "Fine. I shall make it around ten in he morning." Alan, unable to help himself, leaned over gently and placed a kiss on her lips.

Before she stepped into the carriage, she turned, a dazzling smile lighting her face, and said, "Until then."

As the carriage ambled down the drive, Tiffany could hardly suppress the joy she felt. Her young heart was filled with hope as the promise of turning her dreams into reality drew closer.

Alan sat behind the desk his father once occupied. With quill in hand, hovering over the legal document, he paused in thought, remembering his father's words. "I tell you, son, if what I have done is not to your liking and you want the lady, she is still yours legally. The choice is yours. Her dowry will cover the debts, and the manor will produce enough monies to pay the mortgage and support you sufficiently. I am not long for this world. You are my only heir, and what I did was to see you safe, no more than that. But if you would choose to have done differently, then with my blessing, do so. The duke knows the choice be yours and awaits only to receive the paper. I ask only this. Think on it, and to your own self be true."

His hand holding the quill shook slightly and he laid it down on the desk, rereading the legally drawn document that, if he signed, would give him financial security during all of his life and that of his heirs. If he did not, it gave him nothing momentarily, only offered him the rights to a woman. He stood, moving to the hearth.

If only I had not been the fool trying to beat odds. If only what I know now, I knew when I foolishly placed the mortgage to Thurston Manor down to cover a bet I was so sure would come in! Damn! Damn all the ifs! He reasoned the predicament he found himself in was no other's fault but his own, and no matter how beautiful she was, or alluring, he owed it to his father, to his station in life, to his principles, to see the thing through.

Walking back to the desk, he thought, as he picked up the discarded quill, that he would ride with her one last time. Dipping the quill in the inkpot, he scrawled his name across the dotted line, ensuring his future and shattering another's dream.

Chapter Ten

"If you'll excuse me, Father," Tiffany asked, rising from her seat at the breakfast table.

William looked up at his daughter, a question written on his face. Tiffany explained easily. "Earl Thurston is coming. We are riding today, so I must go upstairs to change." She turned to leave the room, lost in thought over which riding habit to wear. Her blue or red? She failed to hear his first summons. The second one was loud enough to rattle the teacups, and his tone reminiscent of one used when she was a child.

"Tiffany!"

She turned to find her father standing, clutching his napkin in hand. His face red and in a clipped voice that forbade any argument, he said, "You will not!"

Angry at the tone used on her, as if she were a child, she retorted, "And why not? I have been closeted in this house for days. Surely you can't deny me a riding date?"

The only word William heard was "date." He meant to keep her safe for the duke and not jeopardize the contract in any way.

Whether she knew of the betrothal or not was of no consequence. He was going to see to it she behaved as a promised woman should. An engaged woman did not go galavanting across the countryside with another man. "You will do as I say, and when Earl Thurston arrives, you will inform him you are indisposed."

"I most certainly will not." She stood her ground. For three years she had been able to make her own choices, at least regarding riding dates, and she was not about to let her father tell her when, where, and with whom she could ride.

William strode angrily across the room, grabbing her arm sharply.

"Don't ever refute my orders. You will now go to your room, and Godfrey will inform the earl."

"The hell I will!" She yanked her arm from him, then stumbled backward with the force of the blow that struck her face. She brought her hand quickly to her injured cheek, tears spilling down the stinging redness.

William stood there appalled at both her disobedience and his action. As if to atone for his action, he blurted out at the top of his lungs, "I'll not have you jeopardize your betrothal to the duke of Wentworth to appease your desire to ride about the countryside with another man. Engaged persons do not conduct themselves in that manner, especially when they are betrothed to a duke."

The blow had stunned her, but his words numbed her so she did not feel him lift her abruptly and drag her to the door, handing her over to Clarissa with instructions to lock her in. All her mind cried out was, NO! Alan was her betrothed.

Tears running down her face, shock settling in, she allowed herself to be led to her room. She failed to see the redheaded man who stood at the front door.

Tiffany paced the length of her room for the umpteenth time, feeling the walls close in each minute she remained locked within their confines. She looked futilely at the oaken door, giving in to the impulse to run over again and trying the knob. She sank to the floor sobbing, tears of frustration coursing down her cheeks. With renewed spirit, she stood banging the door with her fists. Hands sore, she leaned against the door, an anguished sob escaping her lips as she slid to the floor and gave in to the deep, wrenching sorrow she felt. Cradling her head in her arms, she cried.

She picked herself up and walked slowly to the window, leaning her hot head against the cool pane. Lifting her eyes to the sky, she noted the heavy cloud layer moving in. A large raindrop splattered against the glass pane, trailing down.

Her tears spent, her rage under control, she mentally went over the scene with her father. Her cheek still smarted from the blow, but not half as much as the verbal blow he hit her with—betrothal! To a duke! The duke of Wentworth! God, the more she went over what she knew, the more she wished she hadn't. It was too astounding to believe. How could her father have done that? Who was this duke who had shown up and destroyed her life, and dreams? Damn his royal soul to hell!

Turning from the window, tears beginning anew, she wearily walked to the bed, flinging herself down onto its softness, burying her head in the pillows. She drifted off to a weary sleep, hoping she'd awake to find it was only a nightmare.

Waking to the rumble of thunder and the flash of lightning, Tiffany sat straight up. The room was lit in the unnatural light of the flash. Her head hurt, and she squeezed her eyes closed hoping to ward off the pain. Slowly she rose to light a candle. The cast of the light revealed the whiteness of a folded piece of paper near her door. She ran to the door, finding the handle unmovable, as she expected. Retrieving the note, she read it.

Dear Tiffany,

Sorry to hear you are indisposed. Hope you will be fit soon.

I intended to tell you this morning—I will be heading

this eve to London, where I am to leave on the *Falcon* for France to attend to some business matters which require my attention.

I shall be returning in two months, perhaps we can ride then.

Alan

Tiffany's heart plummeted. She lifted her tear-filled eyes to the darkening shadows of early evening. The rain fell, thunder boomed, and the lightning flashed. In that moment she saw her hopes and dreams crumble. She saw there was no one to help her. Alan had no idea what had transpired, and Aunt Winnie was visiting the Devonshires. Determined to change what the hands of fate somehow had altered, she sprang into action with conviction, but no real plan.

Opening the window, she climbed out onto the balcony and down the rose trellis. So singular was her purpose that she was unmindful of the rain, which had begun to fall harder. She did not care that the wind whipped sheets of rain against her or that when she jumped from the trellis, she fell to the wet ground. No! She was going to London to the docks to find Alan and leave with him.

She led Touche from the stable quietly so as not to awaken Nathan. She leaped on the mare's bare back and kicked her flanks, galloping from Courtland Manor and down the road to London.

Tiffany scraped back wet strands of hair which blocked her vision. Her fingers were numb and cold and her head hurt. The rain was relentless, drenching her clothes so they clung to her like a second skin, no longer offering her protection from the wind. She never remembered feeling so cold, and thought she would never feel warm again.

Squeezing the sides of Touche, pushing the mare into a canter, she withdrew into herself, escaping the effects of the elements. She would soon be wrapped in Alan's strong warm arms. She figured she had covered the distance to

London more than halfway in the last three hours. She had chosen the main road, although she was aware it was dangerous. Robberies and thievery were common, but the inclement weather, while a curse, proved to be a blessing, for any villain or robber would be sheltered by a warm fire this night.

Her head began to throb, and by sheer will she ignored it, concentrating on thoughts of joining Alan. He will protect me. He will give me refuge.

As she put miles between herself and Courtland Manor, she began to feel more secure knowing no one would miss her until Clarissa and Germane came to fetch her in the morning. Dear Clarissa, she thought, she'll be so upset. And Aunt Winnie. Oh, if Aunt Winnie hadn't decided to visit Carolyn, none of this would have happened.

Tears burned the backs of her eyes. Her father's actions were cruel blows to both body and spirit. She unconsciously touched her tender, swollen cheek where his hand had so cruelly struck her. She realized with anguish that she had always been only a piece of chattel, to be used or sold to gain position and wealth. Her tears fell, mingling with the rain. "Oh, God," she cried out into the night. All those years striving to please him, hoping to thus earn his love. How different the reasons, hers for his love and acceptance, his to be rid of her in a marriage that suited him. It was a bitter pill for her to swallow, but she knew now no matter who or what she was or did, nothing would change William Courtland. He had taken everything from her—her home, her horse, her love for him, and now any chance for happiness. She gulped hard; hot tears slipped down her windblown cheeks. She bitterly thought her father deserved what he had given her—nothing. She bit back the tears, for he deserved no more of her tears, and she turned her heart from him evermore.

Touche stumbled, nearly unseating Tiffany and bringing her from her thoughts. She saw the marker for London, pulling Touche to a halt. The wind picked up, blowing rain unmercifully against her soaked body. She looked at the sky and was unable to discern whether dawn was approaching or night still covered the land.

Nudging Touche forward into a gallop, she clung to the mare, ignoring the pounding in her head, and rode to meet her destiny.

"What is the meaning of this, Your Grace? Have you no common courtesy, barging into my home, demanding to see my daughter at this unholy hour?" Pulling his robe about his form, William continued, "I demand an explanation."

With long, purposeful strides, Clinton closed the distance between himself and William in seconds. "I demand to see Tiffany now, William."

William did not miss the narrowing of the gray eyes or the taut set of Clinton's jaw, nor his tone, which, though quiet, held an ominous quality to it.

"Are you mad, Your Grace? At this ungodly hour?"

A cold smile appeared on Clinton's face as he replied, "Mad? You have not yet seen how mad I can get. Now, you either summon her or I'll get her myself. Do I make myself clear?"

William sputtered in outrage but finally summoned Clarissa, asking her to bring Tiffany down.

While waiting for Clarissa, William ordered brandy. Godfrey poured, handing glasses to the men.

William, nervously sipping his, wondered if the duke had been informed of Tiffany's abortive attempts to meet the earl. Clinton downed the drink in one gulp, slamming the glass on a nearby table. He strode impatiently to the mantel, leaning his arm against it, gazing into the fire. The pervading silence was broken by a cry of dismay. Looking up, Clinton watched Clarissa enter the room, wringing her hands, instantly knowing something was amiss.

"My . . . my lamb, she's gone!" Tears brimmed in her eyes as she looked helplessly toward Clinton.

In turn, he leveled his gaze at William, who looked

astonished by the news. In a velvet tone, edged with sarcasm, he said, "Did I hear you say you thought my arrival late? Why, William, it appears I'm just in time."

Belying the rage and anger he felt, Clinton calmly withdrew and lit a cheroot. With the slim cigar clamped between his teeth, he inhaled deeply, slowly exhaling.

William felt Clinton's stare and met cold, steely eyes with a dangerous glimmer in their depth.

"Well, William, it appears you owe me an explanation . . . now."

William's explanation was quickly ignored when a lightly accented voice interjected, "Your Grace." Heads turned toward the petite maid Germane. "I found this in Mademoiselle's room." She handed the note to Clinton, who quickly scanned its brief message.

"Come along, Keegan, we've a long ride ahead."

Keegan shoved his hat on his head and walked behind Clinton toward the front door. Clinton opened the door but turned before leaving. His gray eyes narrowed and hardened when he spoke; his voice held a threat. "Be warned, William, there is still much you have to answer for." The slamming of the door ominously sounded like the last stone sealing a tomb.

Both men, unlike Tiffany, were appropriately dressed for the weather. Clinton figured they were about three-quarters of an hour behind her. Riding at breakneck speed and taking a shorter route should find them at the docks shortly.

Clinton rode ahead, for the road was not wide enough to accommodate two horses abreast. His gray eyes scanned the road for any potholes or rocks to avoid. With each closing mile, his concern for her grew. He pushed aside the fear and occupied his mind with the progress made up to date.

He had received the "insurance" duly signed and sealed from Earl Thurston, and once securing that, he had sent instruction to Brent to commence the transaction and notify the creditors.

His mother, Evette, should be boarding his brother Tristan's ship and starting the long journey from Genoa to England to help with the arrangements.

His brother Austin, who was also involved in the shipping business, would soon receive his missive with instructions to return to Chablisienne and pick up some priceless cargo to be brought to England. And last, word was out to all captains of ships sailing for America to locate Rory, the youngest Barencourte brother.

As they entered the outskirts of London, Clinton drew his horse to a halt. Turning to Keegan, he instructed, "Go to the town house, rouse Billy up to make ready the carriage." Looking up at the sky, noting the darkening clouds, he added, "Make sure he packs plenty of blankets and some brandy. When I find her, she will be wet and cold. Meet me at the pier near the shipyard with the carriage. I'm betting that's where the *Falcon* is berthed."

"Aye, think ye be right, guv'nor." Keegan paused, then continued, "Guv'nor, did ye think she found 'im?"

"Don't know the answer to that, my friend."

"What's ye to do iffen she's 'ith 'im?"

Without a pause, Clinton answered, "Take her. She belongs to me; she's mine!" He wheeled his mount around and lunged into a full gallop, the horse's hooves echoing as they hit the cobblestone street.

The incessant crash of waves against the dock resounded in Tiffany's already pounding head.

Mists of sea water and rain blew against her, the wind howled in her ears. She shivered with cold, her head throbbed painfully, and her cheeks burned.

"It must be close to dawn," she said aloud, her own voice hurting her head.

The dock area showed the beginnings of life despite the inclement weather. She passed the shipyard, seeing the skeleton of a ship resting on blocks. The sound of Touche's hooves clattering against the planks of the dock rang painfully in her head. She was grateful the rain had let up, for she was drenched. The wind, however, was fierce near the water and numbed her to the bone.

She pressed on, seeing two piers jut out into the harbor, where many ships were anchored. A sleek fourteen-gun frigate bobbed proudly, anchored in the waters. Gazing up at the mast, she felt an overwhelming sensation of vertigo. All around her were schooners, pinnaces, and brigs. "There must be hundreds of ships here, and the dock appears endless," she cried brokenly, feeling the awesome task at hand.

Her presence on the dock was causing quite a stir. Riffraff and tars common to the area watched as she rode by, noting her disheveled appearance. Had she not been so exhausted, the pain in her head all-consuming, she would have realized the potential danger she was in. A voice broke through the haze of pain.

" 'Ere, 'ady, where ye be goin'?"

Straining fever-bright eyes, she focused on the man to whom the voice belonged and asked, "Sir, the way to the *Falcon,* do you know?"

The wizened tar knew quality when he saw it, and this here lady was quality folk.

"The *Falcon,* she was docked over 'ere." He pointed a withered finger, which Tiffany followed.

She saw no ship at the dock. "Where?"

"In the 'arbor, 'ady, went out on the tide."

Tiffany looked out, a sob escaping her lips. She slipped from Touche's back and on shaky legs she walked to the pier, watching the sleek frigate majestically ride the white-capped waves, its sails unfurled, filled with the wind.

Stumbling down the pier, she tried to reach the end—to close the distance between herself and the *Falcon.* Tears streaming down her cheeks blinded her eyes as she watched the *Falcon,* its three tall masts rising skyward, disappear from the harbor.

She stared at it unseeing for a long moment, then her mind screamed, It's leaving! In its leaving it took her love, her dreams, her glowing youthful happiness. Crumbling to her knees, covering her face with trembling hands, she gave vent to the agony of her loss. With a rumble of thunder and a flash of lightning, the heavens opened, spilling its tears.

The wind whipped furiously around, the rain fell in a torrential downpour, streaks of lightning cracked against the sky. The rumble of thunder muffled the sounds of Clinton's boots on the planks of the pier.

He reached down, closing his hand over her shoulder, lifting her up, swinging her into the protective circle of his strong arms, pulling her against the warm corded muscles of his chest. He shielded her from the harsh elements, and Tiffany instinctively buried her face against his throat. The warmth of his arms and chest was comforting, and she briefly believed she was in Alan's arms and all that had passed was only a nightmare.

Tears streaming down her face, she lifted her head. When her eyes gazed upon his face, a shock coursed through her, her mind refusing to accept what her eyes beheld.

Clinton looked down into her fever-bright eyes with gentle understanding. He took her face, holding it gently.

Tiffany shook her head in confusion, causing the pain to nearly blind her. She cried out, "Why are you here?"

"I have come to claim what is mine, Princess."

Closing her eyes, opening them again, she looked at him and whispered, "No . . . I don't understand." Her head began to spin, her vision became blurry.

He spoke, his voice uncompromising, yet oddly gentle, and the last words to pierce her consciousness were "You are mine, Princess. I am the duke of Wentworth, your betrothed."

Chapter Eleven

When Tiffany first opened her eyes, her lids felt as if lead weights held them. Her eyes glanced about the room, seeing nothing familiar, yet surmising the room to belong to a man.

She became aware of the luxurious black velvet that draped the canopied bed and its matching bed curtains drawn and tied at the four bed posts, allowing the sun to stream across it. Her eyes rested on the black and gold marble fireplace at the foot of the bed, where a small fire glowed in its hearth. Over the mantel hung a priceless Italian painting.

The room was spacious and elegantly decorated in a combination of blues, black, and gold. A wall of French doors lined one side of the room, where a balcony ran the full length. Soft drapes of gold velvet which lined the French doors were drawn, allowing the sun to enter.

Chairs upholstered in striped patterns of gold and black were placed around the table, which held a brandy decanter, glasses, cigar box, and flint, confirming her initial impression that the room belonged to a man.

Tiffany started to sit up but stopped; her head began to spin, and every muscle seemed to protest against her intent. She slid slowly back into the downy softness of the bed. Raising a hand to still her spinning head, she accidentally brushed her cheek, causing her to grimace in pain.

My cheek, she thought through the haze of her befuddled mind. The pain momentarily cleared her head, and memories that rushed forward crowded her mind with images of Alan, her escape, her capture. She shook her head trying to sort the jumble of thoughts that pressed on, only serving to cause the dull ache to begin anew.

She glanced at her bedclothing and realized she was clad in a man's shirt; quite a large man, for the sleeves were rolled thrice to accommodate her wrist. Her eyes widened with realization, Clinton Barencourte; duke of Chablisienne, duke of Wentworth, her betrothed!

The pain in her head began to increase. She closed her eyes trying to block out the pain and reality, yielding to the void sleep offered.

Clinton rose from his desk, handing the sealed envelope to an awaiting Keegan. "Be sure you deliver this into the earl's hands only."

Keegan nodded at the instructions, stuffing the envelope into his jacket pocket. "Shall I return for ye, gov'nor?"

Clinton rose, walking to the table, lifting up his cup of strongly brewed tea, sipping it. "No, Keegan, I'll have Billy drive us back in two days. I need you to be at Wentworth. There is much to be done."

"Aye, guv'nor." Keegan doned his cap, walking out, closing the study door behind him.

Clinton stretched out on the leather coach, resting his head against his arm, rubbing his eyes with his thumb and forefinger, for he was tired and weary, not having slept in the last two nights. He had stayed with Tiffany until her fever broke early this morning and left, once assured she was no longer in danger, to write a note informing the earl of her safety. Now she was in the capable hands of Dolly, and he could seek his rest, knowing she was on the road to recovery.

As he closed his eyes before drifting off to a much-needed rest, his thoughts revolved around the woman who would soon become his wife.

* * *

The sound of a door opening disturbed Tiffany's troubled sleep. Her eyes fluttered opened to rest on a pleasingly plump older woman who regarded her with warm brown eyes. She tugged at her lacy cap as she came toward Tiffany, who could hear the swishing of her black skirts with each step.

Tiffany lay listlessly in bed watching the woman stoop to pick up clothing at the foot of the bed. After rising and tugging again on her lacy cap, the woman spoke. "Morn', yer ladyship. Feel'n better today?"

Tiffany remained silent. It mattered not to the woman, for she chattered on as she went about stoking the fire, opening the French doors to allow some fresh air to enter.

It was not until the woman, out of the corner of her eye, caught Tiffany struggling to sit up that she turned and scolded, "Now, now, yer ladyship, you don't want to be ge'in sick again! I tell ya, his lordship'l have ole Dolly's 'ide, he will, if I don't take good care of ye." Dolly tucked the covers around Tiffany, who did not utter a protest.

The fact of the matter was that she felt as weak as a kitten, both physically and mentally. Tiffany lay back against the pillows, watching Dolly go about her business, chatting all the while.

Dolly gazed upon her charge, thinking, His lordship's lady is pretty indeed, exceptin', of 'ourse, that bruise on 'er cheek. Dolly did not know the whole of it except that this woman was her charge and the duke's betrothed, and it was her duty to see her well. Dolly, a devoted employee of the duke's, intended to do just that! Now the ladyship was especially quiet, withdrawn, to Dolly's way of thinking, and not what she'd expect the fiancée of a much-sought-after bachelor to be like. Must be the fever 'at's done it, she thought.

Dolly broke the quietness. "I be think'n some of Mame's broth be doin' her ladyship some good. Mame makes the best broth, she does, says it's her secret ingredients 'at does it." Nodding her capped head, she pushed the window fully open. "Ah, just smell 'at fresh, sweet air; 'bout time the weather changed, 'tis." Turning about and walking across the room, intending to leave, Dolly paused, looking at Tiffany, "When I get back, I'll 'ave a warm bath drawn for ye. My mother always says a warm bath does one's spirit good." Receiving no response, Dolly left the room thinking it would take more than a warm soaking to lift the ladyship's spirit.

Her freshly washed hair hung over the rim of the tub; steam rose, carrying the fragrance of violets with it, filling the warm privacy chamber.

Tiffany lay submerged to her neck within the tub filled with bubbles. Her spirit battered, her body aching, and her heart broken, she withdrew deeper within herself to a place no one could touch. The bath soothed her body and enveloped her in a warm, safe cocoon that none could breach. Clearing her mind and thinking of naught save the physical sensations the bath offered, she closed her eyes, drifting off to a place where she felt nothing.

Dolly entered the chambers after an hour and helped Tiffany from the tub, drying her body with a warm, fluffy towel. Tiffany felt the ministrations of the maid and allowed herself to be turned and powdered and clothed in a fresh muslin shirt.

She was led to the fire, where she sat upon a stool, staring into the bright flames. Dolly droned on and on as she brushed the tangles from her hair. Tiffany drifted further and further into her shell. She was placidly led to bed, where Dolly tucked her in, pulling the covers about her. Tiffany gave in to the blessed escape sleep offered, where she could hide from the pain. She began to drift as if on clouds, feeling the pain separate itself from her. Lost to oblivion, she never heard the click of the door opening or the sound of footsteps across the carpet.

With eyes half-closed, she gazed up just before sleep

overtook her and saw him just as his finger touched her bruised cheek. She sighed. Her last thought as her eyes fluttered and closed, slipping into the healing potion of sleep, was that the look of concern on his face belied the anger she saw ablaze in his gray eyes.

Clinton gazed down at her sleeping form, thankful sleep offered her the escape and mending her spirit needed. He had become concerned when Dolly told him she had not uttered a word or protest since she had awakened.

His knuckle caressed her injured cheek, now a purplish color. Dark brows scowled. He could imagine, even sympathize with William, for he knew how her temper raged, but he held only disgust for any man who raised a hand against a woman. He could not prevent the curse that broke his lips at the thought of her being cruelly struck down. "William has a lot to answer for!"

He tenderly brushed away a curling tendril from her cheek, feeling its silky texture. He gently traced the delicately carved line of her jaw, marveling at the petal softness of her creamy skin. He watched the soft rise and fall of her breast against the muslin cloth of his shirt. How he envied that simple garment which enveloped her in a way he longed to do. He raised his eyes to her lips, parted in repose, and suppressed the urge, so strong, to cover them with his. He shook himself from where his mind led him. She was so small and vulnerable lying in his massive bed, and although the urge to sweep her into his arms and kiss her rode high, he did not, for he was not a man to prey on a woman wounded. Reluctantly he turned from the bed and walked over to the table, pouring a glass of brandy. Opening the French door, he walked into the night, sitting down in a wrought-iron chair on the balcony.

Night had fallen, with the promise of warmer nights to come filling the air. He withdrew and lit a cheroot, inhaling deeply. Letting out a stream of smoke, he resettled himself, stretching his long legs before him. Lifting his glass, he drank deeply of the brandy. His thoughts traveled. He wanted this woman even more now than he had in the beginning. He admitted that he was motivated by his lust. He would not deny he possessed a strong urge to bed her. God, she stirred his blood! Boiled it, to be exact. He could hardly wait to physically claim her, to satisfy his strong sexual need to have her.

He pulled on his cigar, blowing out a curl of smoke while vivid images of their coupling flashing in his mind. He knew as only an experienced man would know that she teemed with passion. He promised to stir and unsettle her until her desire for him overwhelmed her.

He stood leaning against the railing, smiling to himself, thinking, while all this is true, something else has happened. Feelings, alien to him, that he never felt before, nor possessed for any other woman, had begun. It happened at Chablisienne, in the meadow.

He lifted his glass, sipping his brandy, thinking of that afternoon. Yes, it was then when he saw a part of her, a side of her that touched his heart. That evening, at dinner, while he sat across from her watching her charm and flirt with his peers, he felt another alien feeling—jealousy!

He shook his head, and a smile crossed his face. A man of thirty-two who could turn the odds to his advantage, change the hands of fate, and make long shots pay off was passionately in love!

He laughed aloud thinking life had certainly been simpler when he wanted her. Instead, he found himself snared in her web, caught under her spell! And what had begun at Chablisienne, tonight he surrendered to.

He stood, tossing his cigar over the railing, watching its red tip disappear into the night, and shook his dark head, smiling. Only a fool would deny these feelings, but he was not a fool. He was in love with her and felt no less for it.

Inhaling the night air deeply, he began thinking her escape and unchaperoned presence with him would necessitate a speedy marriage. The time he wanted to court her properly, to win her heart and love, was no more. He had not wanted events to turn out as they had. He had hoped to win her, then offer for her and marry. Now he would have to marry first and then court and woo her to win her love.

While this did not meet with his plans, it did not prevent him from seeking this end, it merely changed his strategy. While he did not possess her heart, for she believed her girlish infatuation for Thurston was love, he blessfully had her body.

A grin split his face as he recalled her delectable body and sweet, tempting derriere. A blessing indeed! And while he was counting his blessings, he counted on his experience in knowing a passionate nature when he saw one. Tiffany possessed an earthy passion, much as he did, and he doubted not that once he released her libido, all reason would fly, and she would succumb to her natural urges.

Once she experienced the unbearable pleasure he could give her, she would become a slave to it. A very wicked smile crossed his visage as he lost himself to the carnal images his mind conjured.

Nodding his head in agreement with his thoughts, he began to carefully formulate his strategy. During their brief courtship, before they married, he would begin to tease, tantalizing her budding passion. He would create an ache within her and spark her tinder. After they married, he would fulfill the promise, release the ache, and light her a fire that would engulf her, a fire only he could ignite. And when her passion came full force, then he would have the key to her.

He wanted her body, her soul, and her love; not the girlish infatuation she felt for Thurston but the love that would blossom and open, enriching their life together as man and woman, a love that would take deep root and grow so they could feed from it in their golden years.

Aye he thought, I will love, cherish, and court her all the days of her life, and I will settle for no less than all of her, for I would give no less than all of me.

Chapter Twelve

Tiffany quickly entered the dark foyer, hoping to avoid Clinton, who was detained with his manservant by the carriage. She did not wish to endure his presence after the journey from London one moment longer. She paused a second, allowing her eyes to adjust to the dimness of the foyer light. She headed toward the stairs, intending to find refuge in her room. She needed to gather her wits about her and sort out her thoughts. She needed time to figure a way out of this mess.

She placed her foot on the staircase, but was stopped by her father's voice.

"Satisfied, daughter?"

At the sound of his sarcastic comment, Tiffany turned to face him as he stood near the study door. Looking at his chiseled cold features, she wondered how she could have ever yearned for this cold man's love.

"I asked you, *daughter,* are you quite satisfied?" Without waiting for a reply, William continued, his mouth set in a grim line; his brown eyes like hard pebbles scanned the doorway as if looking for something before resting on her. "You should be ashamed of yourself, daughter. You've ruined a very decent and profitable marriage offer." Moving slowly toward her, he taunted, "As well as dashing any hope of future ones!"

Tiffany stood ramrod-stiff, regarding her father's approaching figure, hearing the accusations as his voice stabbed the air. "You have once again dragged the Courtland name through the mud, sullying it with your shenanigans!"

His cold eyes pinned Tiffany; she was unable to move, unable to speak. "I have given you everything! All the creature comforts, a home, servants to answer your every whim, a *name* with the blood of generations of breeding, and a fortune making you an heiress in your own right. And what have you done? Brought disgrace to my doorstep. You have gone too far, *daughter!*" He screamed the last words at her.

Tiffany, rage welling inside, shouted at him, "How dare you!" Her blue eyes, dark and stormy with anger, stared at him. She stepped off the tread, walking to close the distance between them, her hands curled into tiny fists at her sides, and with scalding fury screamed, "Daughter, is it? Wouldn't chattel be more appropriate, *Father?*"

Standing a breath from him, she screamed with anger and hurt, "Chattel is what I am! To be either protected or cast aside, according to your whim." Shaking her head, her raven tresses flying about her shoulders, she continued relentlessly, "Nay, *Father,* I am many things to you: a stone about your neck, a troublesome bit of baggage, but never have I been a daughter to you!"

A hysterical laugh escaped her lips. "Given me everything; I guess you would think so. Why, you've given your name, your home, but never your love. We are father and daughter because of the blood which runs in our veins, for there is nothing more between us than that. I have been an outsider in your heart, an intrusion into your neatly arranged life." Tears of hurt, anger, welled and burned in her eyes when she spoke. "A real father does not take away all that is held dear as you've done. A father does not sell his daughter as you've done!" Tiffany screamed the last words at him.

William grabbed her arm, dragging her to the study,

shouting at her, "Enough, girl! I'll not have such distasteful scenes in the presence of the servants. Have you no decency?"

Inside the study, Tiffany struggled, freeing herself. Her blue eyes blazing with anger, she faced him and spat, "Decency! I am done with your sense of decency. Your decency has torn me from my home, my horse, and now from the man I love. Your sense of decency has caused me nothing but pain and anguish, and now you have arranged a marriage I want not and you had not even the decency to consult me." Sarcasm etched her trembling voice. "I am ever grateful, sir, I have not your sense of decency."

"You will cease *now!*" William said sharply. "Stop this foolish ranting." Pointing a finger at her, his eyes narrow and hard, he continued, "Your future is and always has been in my hands. Your duty is to marry to suit your family. And now that you have ruined it, I am stuck again with what to do with you."

"Do with me?" she cried increduously. "Whatever is left for you to do that you haven't already done? Nay! I'll not allow you to dictate to me any longer."

Standing tall, cold, and proud, she spoke. "I no longer wish to live on your bounty, under your roof or thumb. I shall seek another place to call home. I shall find a position where I can earn my keep." At William's questioning looks, she rushed on, "I am well educated and would seek a position as a governess."

"Such a noble cause, Princess."

Hearing the familiar mellow baritone voice and his pet name for her, Tiffany spun about, coming face-to-face with Clinton, who filled the study doorway. With an air of nonchalance, he pushed himself from the doorway, unfurling his tall form, and continued, "But one the lady of the household would no doubt refuse. You would be too tempting a morsel to her husband and might find your talents utilized toward the carnal instead of the cerebral."

Tiffany did not miss his gray eyes frankly admiring her form as they traveled slowly up and back down the length of her. The arrogant smile that crossed his face served to infuriate her. And as he slowly closed the distance between her and himself, he continued lazily, "I hardly think you'd find such a position. I do not believe you'd be considered the perfect role model, what with your riding and attire and all." He smiled at her, his eyes gleaming with amusement.

William was astonished that Clinton intended to uphold the contract and quickly asked, "Do I understand Your Grace intends to honor the contract?"

Clinton reluctantly lifted his eyes from Tiffany to William and responded without hesitation, "Nothing has changed except the banns must be read this Sunday." He returned his gaze to Tiffany, who was rooted to the spot upon hearing his words, staring with astonishment.

"Well, then, all is settled. I believe this calls for a drink. Godfrey! Godfrey! Damn that man, never about when I need him."

Godfrey, who had been eavesdropping, suddenly appeared with a tray of drinks. William's eyes narrowed knowingly, but he gestured for the butler to serve.

Tiffany, numb with shock, stood there with a bland expression, amazed and astounded, completely caught off guard. Wave after wave of shock slapped her until finally hitting her full force with the realization. Anger began to surface as she realized these two men had no regard for her own desire. The fact that they drank in celebration and intended to proceed as if nothing happened was her undoing.

Her face contorted with anger, she indignantly glared from one man to another and in a voice that showed her disbelief, cried, "Settled! Nothing is settled!"

Both men, who now stood in front of the desk, turned to her. William narrowed his eyes at her outburst while Clinton smiled in amusement.

"I have no intention of marrying him!" She looked at her father while pointing a slender finger at Clinton.

"The matter, daughter, is settled . . . You are betrothed to His Grace. There are no alternatives. You will marry and honor the contract His Grace most generously has offered to uphold in spite of your disgrace."

Tiffany's eyes widened in disbelief as her father continued. "His grace's offer is decent, to say the least, despite the scandal you've created."

A hysterical laugh escaped her lips before she replied, "Decent! You consider this rake, rogue, bounder, libertine—" she stumbled, not able to think of enough names to call him "—to be decent! Why, Father, his reputation speaks nothing of decency. Mothers hide their daughters from the likes of him. He has not a decent bone in his body."

"Enough, daughter," William growled, wanting nothing more than to shut her up before she pushed His Grace too far and out of the contract.

"It is hardly enough, Father, *I will not marry him,*" she screamed. "I'd sooner marry the devil." She walked toward William, pleading, "How can you do this to me? What have I ever done to deserve this?" She held out her arms in supplication.

"Are you mad, girl? Can you not see the benefits an alliance with a duke would offer? By God, girl, the man's a duke of two realms. He can provide for you, care for you as none other. Why, you would be a duchess!"

Angry with her father for not understanding her feelings, she responded recklessly, feeling she had nothing more to lose, "Nay, Father, if you force me to wed him, I would be a whore, not a duchess. For you would sell my body in exchange for a title you covet."

Aghast at what her words implied, William raised his hand to strike her, but Clinton, like lightning, grabbed William's wrist in an iron-clad grip. In a voice cold and threatening, Clinton warned, "Don't ever raise your hand against her. When you do, you raise it against me."

His eyes as dark as thunder clouds, William said tightly, "She goes too far."

"She goes as far as she wishes, as far as I allow. She'll have her say. She's entitled to that."

Tiffany did not view Clinton as her savior and turned her wrath toward him. "What manner of man are you who resorts to coerce my father to gain his end? I'll tell you! A man who preys on others' weaknesses. You are a coward for going behind my back, for you knew I'd not have you! You have lied to me. You have betrayed me, mocked me, deceived me!" Tears filled and threatened to spill from her eyes, but she rushed on, venting her fury. "I hate you, nay, I despise you! No woman would have you save for your titles, and I care not a whit for them! As a man, *Your Grace,*" she spat, "I find you lower than the dirt beneath my feet, and when in your presence, I have the urge to cleanse myself of the vermin which you are."

Clinton calmly stood while she spent her anger and merely responded, "As you say, Princess."

Disconcerted by his responses, she forged ahead, "I refuse you and your suit. I do not love you. I do not want you! I will not marry you. Find yourself another possession, Your Grace, for I am leaving, and it appears you are short one betrothed." Raising her chin, tossing her glorious raven tresses in what one would consider a defiant manner, she began to leave but stopped, facing Clinton. "I will not whore for what my father covets."

Taking a step, she was halted by his words. "Princess, you have not the sufficient experience . . . yet . . . to fill such a role. In time perhaps."

She spun around, her hand connecting soundly across his cheek. The slap resounded like the report of a pistol, breaking a stiff silence.

William gasped out loud and quickly lifted his glass, downing a good portion of his brandy.

Clinton merely stood, holding her eyes with his. Tiffany became increasingly uneasy under his scrutiny and blurted out, "'Tis a shame we'll never disprove your words, for I have no intention of marrying you!"

In a voice that booked no argument, Clinton quietly said, "But you will marry me. And you will be the one to decide to do so."

Seeing he had her attention, he continued relentlessly, "Princess, the facts speak for themselves. Even now the gossip mongers have spread the word of your four long nights unchaperoned in my company." Seeing realization take hold in her wide blue eyes, he smiled mockingly, adding, "As you say, reputation precedes me. And You, Princess, have been well compromised." Raising a finely arched brow, a smug smile lifting the corners of his mouth, he pressed, "Some say you are tarnished, spoiled, used goods, if you will."

Tiffany stood staring at him, disbelief etched across her face. Her thoughts were a jumble. He planned this, he knew what he was doing. All along he had turned the tables to his advantage. She was caught like a vixen in a trap he had set. She cried, "You planned this. You know in truth I was not compromised. It is all pretense. You never touched me!"

A devilish grin crossed his mouth, his gray eyes gleamed in victory. "Ah, but who's to say you were compromised in truth or pretense?"

She snapped. "You, of course!"

Smiling with satisfaction, he answered, "Now, why would I do that when circumstances speak for themselves and serve my purpose?"

It was all too much for her to absorb, to handle. Raising her hand with all the force of her body, her anger, her betrayal, she struck Clinton's other cheek. The sound reverberating in her ears, her rage boiling over, she raised her hand to strike again, but her wrist was caught in midair in a firm, strong hand which pulled her up hard against him. The amused look slowly left his eyes, which flashed a gentle yet firm warning. In an icy, yet authoritative voice, he spoke. "I have turned both cheeks to you for the wrongs you accuse me of, but I will not turn another. Never strike me unjustly, Princess. I will put up with a great deal from you, but I will not tolerate that."

Releasing her wrist but still holding her eyes, he saw the beginning of tears in her blue eyes. He spoke softly, gently, but his tone made it clear he would brook no arguments. "It has been a long day. You have many things to come to terms with, to sort out. Tomorrow, after a night's rest, I will come and we will talk again. I will answer all your questions after you are rested and refreshed." He lifted his hand, cupping her chin. "Now go to your room and rest. Despite your beliefs, you were quite ill, and I would not wish to see you relapse."

Holding back the tears that threatened to fall, she moved her chin from his hand and said in a defiant voice, "I go to my room, but not because you order me. You don't own me and never will! I go to my room not to come to terms with anything. There is nothing to come to terms with, for I am not going to marry you. What I am going to do is pack my bags to prepare to leave, for I will not stay here any longer." She turned and was about to open the door when his words stopped her.

"Splendid, by all means pack your belongings, your trunks, whatever. If your desire is not to remain here, then your wish is my command. My footmen will arrive on the morrow, along with my manservant, who will see to the safe delivery of your trunks to Wentworth Estates. And you, as you desire, shall depart from the walls of Courtland Manor and take up permanent residence in your new home, in your new position as my duchess."

Throwing her shoulders back and assuming all the regal dignity she could muster, she threw open the door and turned to him with cold triumph in her eyes and said, defiantly, her tone hinting a subtle challenge, "Only when hell freezes over, Your Grace."

The last words she heard before the slamming of the door were "So you say, Princess, but I know different."

Clinton turned to William when the earl's voice breached his thoughts.

"She's never been a biddable girl, and as I told you at our meeting in April, she can be quite unpleasant." William refilled his glass and continued, unaware of the dark scowl on Clinton's face. "It appears you manage her quite well, if I say so myself."

William looked up and was aghast at the cold look on Clinton's face. Looking over the rim of his glass, William felt chilled to the bone by the gray eyes, hard like glacial ice, that held him.

"Why the hell did you not keep your mouth shut, William? I told you in April of the conditions, which you agreed to."

Somewhat indignant over the tone Clinton used, William shot out of his seat. "I beg your pardon, Your Grace. I thought to keep her pure, unsullied for you. I did not feel it proper for the chit to be out with another when she was betrothed."

In a voice filled with icy sarcasm, Clinton said, "What you have accomplished, William, is to make my task more difficult. While I don't give a damn what she thinks of you, I take exception to being linked in her mind to the likes of you."

Slamming his fist down on the desk, causing the brandy to spill from the glass, he went on, "I told you before I wanted to handle the situation. Now I am forced to court her after the marriage rather than before."

"Your Grace, listen here, I will not tolerate you speaking to me in that tone of voice. What do you think I can do about this? It was you who created it, not I," William said defensively.

"What you can and will do, William, is leave as soon as possible. I want you—" Clinton pointed his finger an inch from William's nose "—gone from here till the social engagements commence."

"See here, Your Grace. You will not order me about as your lackey. I am a member—"

"I don't give a damn what you are a member of. Listen well, William." Clinton gave him a black look and said threateningly, "Don't push me. It would be very unwise on your part. I want you gone as soon as possible. You will not cross swords with the lady again. You will leave. She needs time to come to terms with this, time we no longer have. Your presence here is not conducive to my ends. As long as she has two enemies in sight, I cannot win the battle."

"Now . . . now, see here . . ." began William, only to be silenced by the tone of Clinton's voice.

His words came slowly, uncompromising, uncoiling like a whip. "If you can't accept my terms, I shall have her moved *immediately* to Wentworth. There I will no longer need to concern myself with your interference or her safety from your heavy hand!"

William's face was red with rage. Clinton was deadly still, save for the muscle that twitched in his jaw. The air was heavy with tension.

Sweeping into the study, Winifred exclaimed, "That will hardly be necessary, Your Grace." She fixed an admonitory look on William, asking dispassionately, "Will it, William?" Without awaiting his reply, she turned to Clinton, saying confidently, "Let me assure you, Your Grace, William will take a holiday. He is long overdue and was just saying the other day he might retire to his Cornwall estate to check with his steward."

Then, in her most awesome and grand manner, she stated, as she cast a long, hard look at William, "I can promise you, as a woman of honor, there will be no further incidents or episodes."

William stared openmouthed at Winifred. Clinton did not miss William's response and turned to Winifred, asking, "I trust you won't disappoint me, madam?"

"Disappoint you, Your Grace? Hardly, for no one would *dare* disappoint you."

Clinton bowed to Winifred, saying "By your leave, madam," and strode across the room to the door, where he paused, turning back toward William. "You're a fortunate man, William; the women who surround you make up for your shortcomings." Clinton stalked out of the room.

Silence reined again in the study and was broken by William's outburst of righteous indignation. "How dare he tell me what to do! Duke or not! The gall of that man knows no bounds. I'll call my solicitors on the morrow and null the betrothal immediately."

Winifred whisked across the room, closing the distance between herself and William. Standing regally in front of his desk, in a voice firm but reasonable, she said, "You will do nothing of the kind, William. What you are going to do is have your valet start packing now so come morning, you can depart."

"Winifred! Have you gone mad?" William stood abruptly.

"No, but by your recent behavior, it appears you have. Now, sit down!"

The command in her voice caused William to sink into his chair, where he began to protest anew. "Winifred! You exceed your bounds here!"

With an aura of majesty and aloofness, Winifred, looking down the tip of her nose at William, replied icily, "In exceeding bounds, *dear* brother-in-law, you take the cake! You have harassed and abused your daughter, placed her in a deplorable situation, to which she responded desperately. You not only lost your temper, you *struck* her and then locked her in her room like an animal! You have treated us all to an embarrassing display of the type of ill-mannered and ill-bred behavior not befitting one of *your* station. You acted little better than an obnoxious boor!" She paused, pleased at his reaction, and continued, sparing him no quarter, "What you shall do is exactly as His Grace has instructed. Do not fool yourself in thinking you will outwit or outflank him. He will know the minute your messenger leaves for the solicitor and he will come himself, William. He will take Tiffany and elope before your man is two miles from Courtland property. And that," she stated emphatically, "I will not see happen." Turning from William, looking out the study door and then back to William, she replied, "Tiffany will marry him, no matter how unwilling, but she will not be abducted as a result of your foolish pride. For if she is, never can she forgive His Grace for his action, and never will she find the happiness that can be hers. So you see, William, I will not allow you to ignore His Grace's instructions. I will represent the family and handle the Courtland end during your absence." She turned to dismiss him and headed to the open door, where she paused. Turning back, looking at William, she added with disgust, "I never knew your father. But I knew Robert well. I fear you have been deceived in believing you shared a common sire."

She whisked regally out of the room, leaving William alone.

Dull shafts of early morning light streamed, in bathing the room in soft gray hues. Tiffany slowly opened her eyes, watching the light catch the small dust particles floating in the air.

Her head ached, her eyes ached, and she felt melancholy. Looking about the room, she saw her clothes thrown in a heap on the carpet. Her shoes lay at the threshold of her bedroom door, where she had angrily thrown them yesterday. I should move them so Clarissa or Germane won't stumble over them, she thought, and reluctantly rose from bed to do so.

She heard a commotion outside and ran to the window overlooking the front drive. Seeing the footmen load trunks and baggage, she became fearful Clinton had taken her at her word and sent his manservant to fetch her. She sighed with relief seeing her father alight into the carriage, and watched it pull away, feeling nothing. Turning from the window, she sat down in front of her vanity, gazing at her reflection. Her reflection confirmed the restless, troubled sleep of the night past. Her eyes were red-rimmed from crying, and her lids puffy and sore when she touched them. Her hair was disheveled and terribly knotted. Dark circles outlined her eyes.

Closing her eyes, the scene in the study came back vividly to mind, reminding her of the seriousness of her situation. She tried to shut out the reality of it, replacing it with her dreams. She failed miserably. Opening her eyes and picking up her brush, she began to work the tangles from her hair, thinking about her predicament.

Brushing and thinking, she assembled the facts at hand. The brush moved smoothly through the untangled lock. Alan was gone and was not due back for two months. She stopped brushing and gazed at herself again. Eyes filled with tears. Shaking her head, she scolded herself mentally. There was no point in crying over his not being here to help her. She had to rely on her own wit until he returned. Suppressing the urge to cry, she began to systematically move the brush through the long, dark tresses. The facts are such. She began again stilling her trembling lips. Alan is gone. Her hand stopped when a snarl caught in her brush. The duke of Wentworth is the duke of Chablisienne, and they are one in the same man—Clinton Claremont Barencourte! She yanked the brush through the knot, wincing at the pain it caused. Her anger began to surface and she quickly pushed it down, remembering a quote at Madame's school, "He who angers you wins." The fact remained he was her betrothed. She snorted thinking of all the proposals she had turned down only to end up with a duke. A libertine and a bounder. Unbelievable! Her brush snagged again, and this time when she yanked, she came away with strands of hair. Tears came to her eyes from the pain of ripping her hair out over him. Remember the facts! her mind screamed. Okay, the facts. The banns were to be read on Sunday, which means the prenuptial agreement and contracts had been drawn and signed. But when? Where? How?

The first time she had the misfortune of meeting Clinton was at the races. Is it possible, she thought, he had arranged all of this after then? Her brush paused while she tried to remember their conversation. Then, he had known who she was, yet she did not recall ever meeting him. He was a duke, he decided he wanted her for a possession, and ruthlessly sought to secure his end by waving his title and position at her father.

Her father! She did not want to think about him and his treachery. She attacked her hair mercilessly and held back the tears that thinking of him brought.

Swallowing down the lump that formed in her throat, she gained control and began to assemble her facts. She was alone, and although Aunt Winnie had come to her last night to soothe her, there was no convincing Aunt Winnie to aid her in escaping. No, while Aunt Winnie was not the enemy, she was not an ally either and chose to remain neutral.

She had explained through her bouts of tears that she had not been actually compromised, but Aunt Winnie, while agreeing with her, did point out she had been technically compromised. Aunt Winnie told her it would be best to come to terms with all of this gracefully.

"Well," she announced out loud, "I might be outnumbered, but I am not outdone." Eventually Alan would return, and if only she could just hold out for two months until she had Alan to help her.

In the interim, she'd have to fend for herself in thwarting His Grace. A wicked smile crossed her face. "I'll show His Grace just what kind of duchess I'll make for his illustrious name. I'll show him just how stubborn and willful I can be. He'll see I'm no simpering miss at his beck and call."

She reminded herself for a brief moment that he was indeed a formidable opponent. Had he not drawn the battle lines at the ball? Well, two can play at his game, and maybe he did indeed win every game and challenge, and perhaps he was single-minded as well. So was she, and she was not going to marry him!

Her spirits lifted as she began to devise a plan born more of conviction than strategy. I will refuse to see him and let him know right off he cannot control me. That ought to set him back on his royal behind a bit, discovering his "duchess" was not an amiable, complacent girl. I will refuse to marry him. He has yet to see the real me, she thought, smiling at all the ways she could shock him and thereby cause him to break off the engagement.

Her spirits lifted as she continued to brush her tangle-free tresses, confident she would win. With each long stroke she dismissed Clinton from her mind, assured that her simple plan could not fail.

Chapter Thirteen

Tiffany jumped at the sound of the light tap on her door. Leaving the windows where she hid, she walked to the door and threw it open.

Winifred whisked into the room, closing the door softly behind her. Turning to Tiffany, she gently inquired, "Do you think it wise refusing to see him again?"

Ignoring the question, Tiffany asked instead, "Is he gone?" knowing full well he was, for she had watched him mount his stallion and ride off. She hoped somewhere between Courtland property and his lair, he would break his neck.

Winnie graciously sat on the edge of the bed, regarding her niece. "I think, my dear, you know the answer to that."

Tossing her head, Tiffany turned away to pace the length of her room, exclaiming, "Well, good riddance. Now I can go to the stable and ride!" Rushing over to where her boots lay, she pulled them on over her breeches, which she elected to wear as a sign of defiance and rebellion.

Winifred, knowing her niece well, saw the signs of her temper and restlessness. It had been four days since the episode in the study, and Tiffany had not ventured from her room. Winifred had to give her credit for her perseverance, for it was indeed a difficult task for Tiffany to remain inactive. Tiffany was used to exercise and unaccustomed to amusing herself with womanly arts. Winifred had wondered how long Tiffany would last before she started to champ at the bit.

She ventured, "I asked you, dear, how long do you intend to refuse seeing him?"

"However long it takes for His Grace to realize I have no intention of seeing him or marrying him."

Nodding her head, Winifred watched Tiffany dash about the room.

"I see, and do you intend to remain closeted each and every day?"

Tiffany spun to face her. "I think he has gotten the message. And so I think it safe to venture forth. God knows I could not stand another day of this forced captivity!"

A smile crossed Winnie's face. "Self-imposed would be a better choice, my dear." Brushing her hair and tying it back with a length of pink ribbon, Tiffany looked at her aunt through the mirror, choosing to ignore her remark, believing her captivity, forced or self-imposed, was a direct result of His Grace.

Silence reigned until Tiffany, for some strange reason unknown even to herself, asked, "Was he angry?"

A twinkle gleamed in the green eyes. "I think a man of His Grace's caliber rarely shows his anger, dear, nor does he let it blind him from his purpose. That is not to say if he is pushed too far, he would not use his anger as a tool to gain his end. A man as he should not be easily dismissed, nor taken lightly."

Catching her aunt's eyes reflected in the mirror, Tiffany sat thinking about her words. She worried at her lower lip and turned to steal a glance at her. For a brief moment she had doubts about her plan but quickly shook them off. "Well, he has no reason to be angry with me. I have been indisposed, and Godfrey has told him as much. Not that it is any business of his." Tossing her head haughtily, she was quite pleased with her reasoning.

Winifred nodded her head in mock agreement, saying, "Of course, yesterday what was it Godfrey told His Grace? Oh yes, you ate something tainted and were indisposed, and the day before you had overindulged from your solitary celebration of your upcoming marriage." Regarding her niece, who quickly turned away from the knowing green eyes, she continued, "And today, well, what was it today? I seem to have forgotten."

Refusing to be drawn, Tiffany abruptly rose. "If you'll excuse me, Aunt, I think I'd like to ride."

Heading toward the door, she was stopped by Winifred's question. "And what excuse will you give him this afternoon?" Standing, Winifred closed the gap between them, continuing, "Or had you forgotten you're leaving for a weekend celebration at Chad Devonshire's?"

A look of despair crossed Tiffany's face, for she had indeed blocked out anything to do with His Grace and his arrangements. "Oh, Aunt Winnie, what am I to do? I am in such a pickle." Placing her hands over her face in misery, she whispered. "Why? Oh, why me? Why couldn't he have found another to possess, another to purchase?"

Winifred reached for Tiffany's hands, gently removing them from her face. Seeing the tears well up in the blue eyes, she brought her arms about her niece's shoulders and walked with her to the settee by the hearth. Sitting, she brought Tiffany in the circle of her arms.

Laying her head against her aunt's shoulder, Tiffany cried softly. Winnie gently smoothed her hair with a loving hand while Tiffany wept silent tears. Speaking softly, Winifred began, "When you came to me, I thanked God for sending me the daughter I never had. I love you more than if you were mine. I remember thinking that day how lovely you were. Like an uncut diamond; I saw its many facets, which with a bit of polish, would emerge brilliantly." Softly stroking her hair from her cheek, Winifred looked down at Tiffany's tear-streaked face, her own eyes beginning to fill. She sighed, "Over the years my little diamond lost its rough edges and became a gem so exquisite, so rare, so very priceless, for it shines brilliantly and sparkles with life."

Winifred lightly kissed the top of the raven head that lay against her breast as her own tears softly fell. "You know, dear, the diamond is a most desirable gem. All covet it for its value. Most lock this treasure away. But there are a few who value it above all else, for its brilliance and sparkle, and want to wear it, not box it. Your duke, my dear, is one of those special few."

Gently pushing Tiffany away, Winifred rose softly, leaving the room.

The wind in her face, her raven tresses loose and flowing, the warm sun caressing her, Tiffany rode with an abandonment she hadn't felt in days. Touche sailed over the last hedgerow, landed, kicking up her hind legs as if feeling the restraint as well.

Rider and horse recklessly rode, unmindful of the low branches of the woods they now entered. Suddenly Tiffany pulled sharply on the reins, halting the spirited mare just feet from the bluff's edge.

Dismounting and dropping the reins, unmindful that Touche moved away to graze at the grass near the edge of the woods, Tiffany walked quickly to the edge.

What a sight her eyes beheld. It was breathtaking. She looked upon the wonder with the eyes of a woman but the memories of a girl.

The bluff formed a sort of plateau three hundred feet or so above sea level. Its brooding, gaunt cliffs seemed barbaric, savage, almost ferocious, rising high, abrupt and precipitous. It was beautiful to her; the varied scenery, the clear and lovely light, the splendor of the cliffs whose ferociousness was softened by the fragile growth of wildflowers that dared take root.

Moving a tad closer to the edge, she heard the sound of breakers roaring, smashing against the rock, and the cry of gulls, music to her ears. She watched the sea beat on as it had against the wild coast all through time. Mesmerized by the sight, the smell, the sound, she moved dangerously closer to the edge, yearning for the freedom it offered.

Suddenly a hand, like iron talons, grasped her waist, lifting her back against a hard body, turning her easily so she faced her assailant. "*You!*" she screamed, pushing against his chest, then bracing her hands against him, leaning away while he held her firmly.

Moving away from the edge, carrying her against him, he spoke sharply, "What the hell were you trying to do? Kill yourself?"

Her eyes narrowed, seething with anger. "You egotistical bastard! Do you honestly think you're worth killing myself over?" She began to kick her feet and pummel his shoulders as he carried her away. Ducking her flailing hands, he moved his, cupping her buttocks and leaning forward slightly, causing her to fall precariously backward so instinctively she was forced to steady herself by her legs about his waist, her arms about his neck to regain her balance. Clinton held her buttocks tightly, pressing their loins together. His hardness pressing against her softness caused a surge of warmth to uncurl in her belly. She felt acutely aware of his swollen, hard manhood pressing between her spread legs.

Regaining her senses, she demanded, "Put me down this instant!" unwrapping her legs from his waist.

Clinton did not miss the quiver that shook her body on contact with his nor the sweet blush that crept up her cheeks.

A mischievous smile lit his face. "As you wish." He slowly lowered her so each part of her delectable body slid intimately down his length. Her hands glided down, feeling every firm muscle of his chest, touching the dark hair that lay exposed from his half-opened shirt. His hands remained possessively cupped beneath her buttocks, pressing her against his arousal.

Stains of scarlet appeared brightly on Tiffany's cheeks. When her feet touched solid ground, she leaned against him to steady her legs, still shaking from the erotic sensation, and then quickly pushed away from him, hoping she did not betray how unsettling the experience was.

"What are you doing here? Your actions are as misguided as your sense of direction, Your Grace. You are trespassing! This happens to be Courtland lands!"

Clinton had missed nothing of her reaction and smiled confidently. He leaned back against a tree, withdrawing a cheroot, lighting it. "This bluff, Princess, is the dowry you bring me, and as you are mine, so is it."

"A bit presumptuous, Your Grace."

"Not at all, Princess, it is a certainty." He blew a curl of smoke out, watching her toss her head at his comment.

Balling her hands on her hips, she retorted, "Nothing is ever certain, Your Grace."

"Ah, Princess, I beg to disagree. I was certain I'd find you here. And here you are."

Tiffany paused before asking, "Oh, and how did you know where to look?"

She was awarded with a devastating smile, one that made her feel weak-kneed and caused shivers to course down her spine. Before she succumbed to its effect totally, she caught herself, averting her gaze from his visage.

"You wound me, Princess," he replied mockingly, holding his hand over his heart.

"I only wish it were fatally, my lord!" she snapped, glaring at him.

Knocking an ash from the head of his cigar, he smiled, loving every minute of their bantering. He regarded her. "You don't remember, do you?"

"If it involved you, I thankfully forgot."

Ignoring her comment, he explained. "You know, Princess, as your soon-to-be husband, I really should take offense, especially since I've carried that fond memory for four years.'' Noticing her quizzical expression, he continued, ''I recall a very young girl doing cartwheels on the bluff at dawn.'' Her wide-eyed look gave him cause to refresh her memory further. ''Of course, I forgive you for defaming my sire then, for how were you to know it would come to this?''

Her mouth dropped as the memory of that day flooded back. It was him! He was the root of it all. The term ''full circle'' took on meaning.

''I was quite enchanted by you, even stirred by your innocent allure.''

Tiffany was aghast at his admission that he had desired her as a girl. ''You are despicable, my lord!''

''I take exception, Princess. I may be accused of many a sin or crime, but a seducer of children I am not,'' he quickly stated, defending himself.

Looking heavenward, Tiffany spoke her thoughts aloud. ''But if only I were a man!''

''Or that!'' He smiled devilishly. ''A pederast I am not.''

Narrowed blue eyes regarded him. ''Do you mean to say, my lord, you arranged the betrothal then?''

Drawing on his cigar, blowing the smoke into the air, he shook his head. ''Nay, Princess, the bloom was too tender to be plucked.'' He paused. ''I was introduced to you in Paris at the opera just after your season.''

At her skeptical look, he added, ''You were surrounded by your faithful admirers and paid me no notice. I, however, recognized the bloom on the bluff.'' Blowing a stream of smoke out, he leisurely ran his eyes over her length, a wolfish smile etched on his face when he said, ''Only, now the bloom has blossomed into a ripe, succulent fruit, ready to be plucked. You certainly ripened beyond my expectations.''

Angry that he referred to her as a piece of ripened fruit, she turned her back, affording him a lovely view of her derriere, where his gray eyes rested with appreciation. She asked, "Was it arranged then?"

Lost in carnal thoughts involving her derriere, he had to ask, "Was what arranged?"

She spun around, catching his unguarded look of desire. "The betrothal, you dolt!"

"No. I kept tabs on you over the next couple years, but it was not until after the racetrack encounter that I decided you would be mine."

"You did, did you?" Rage at his high-handness flew like sparks as she marched toward him, hating his arrogant manner, his nonchalance as he leaned against the tree. "Well, let me tell you this; you have interfered with my life enough. No more, do you hear me? I don't want to marry you. Now or ever."

Pulling at his ear, his cigar clamped between his teeth, he regarded her. "Why do you insist on fighting the inevitability of this marriage? A marriage I assure you will take place." His words, though calmly said, were stated as if etched in stone.

"Because I don't love you. Nothing will ever change that!"

"Princess, let me assure you. I will do many things that will change the way you feel."

Slow boiling rage churned at his conceit. His words held innuendos that she'd rather not think about! He shook her foundations, and it was frightening to her. Frustrated, she blatantly replied, "You cannot change my feelings. I love another. Nothing you do or say will change it."

Tossing his cigar down, he explained matter-of-factly, "You will discover, Princess, there are few things that are not changeable. Your professed love of another is not one of them." He crossed his arms negligently against his chest, seeing her anger gleam in her eyes.

Seethingly she retorted, "As are my feelings for you!"

Shaking his head in disagreement, he smiled confidently. "Now, that is precisely one of the few things which is changeable. You will come to love me above all else, Princess.''

''It's a shame, Your Grace, that the few remaining years you have will be wasted on wishful thinking.'' She smiled unpleasantly at him.

A gleam of amusement lit his eyes. ''In my dotage, am I? I imagine someone your age would think so.'' He closed the distance between them, a devilish gleam appearing in his eyes.

Suppressing the urge to step back, not pleased with the look in his eyes, Tiffany stood her ground. ''Well, you are quite old.''

''Do you fear, Princess, I'll not be able to perform my husbandly duties and leave you wanting?'' He smiled at the blush that crept up on her face as he stood a breath away. ''My age will in no way hinder my performance. Actually, my experience will compensate for your lack thereof.''

Tiffany's face burned at what his words implied. Straightening her back, which caused her breasts to press against her muslin shirt, revealing to Clinton's eyes their rosy tips, she taunted, ''Experience or not, Your Grace—'' she raised a finely arched brow ''—an unwilling wife makes for a cold one.''

A leisurely smile broke over his face at her challenging words. Cocking his head slightly, an eyebrow raised inquiringly, he asked ''Is that a threat?''

Giving him a cool stare, belying the spark of fear she felt, she retorted, ''Nay. A promise.''

''We'll have to see about that, won't we?'' He pulled her up against him, cupping her buttocks, molding their lower bodies together. At the challenging glint that lit his eyes, Tiffany flung her head away from him, struggling. In a husky voice filled with promise, he stated, ''You will be anything but cold.'' His hands slowly caressed her firm, round cheeks, pressing them intimately against his arousal, moving down so his fingers touched between her legs.

Tiffany struggled, then stiffened, feeling his fingers touching her from behind. "Stop touching me!"

Ignoring her, he whispered, "You will learn the pleasure my touch can bring you. You will find your woman's pleasure by my hand." He bent his head, capturing her mouth with his. Moving his mouth over her, his tongue caressed her lips, coaxing them to part beneath his. Tiffany felt his lips, warm, dry, and insistent. When his tongue lightly traced her lips, she felt an uncoiling in her belly. His hands caressed her buttocks, pressing her closer to his desire. She struggled to get away, knowing she didn't really want him to be touching her like this. But when he moved her hips to rub against him, an ache began between her legs so sweet, she parted her lips, feeling his tongue enter her mouth.

Clinton deepened his kiss; his tongue darted into the soft recesses of her mouth and then out and in again, an imitation of the act he yearned for. Moving his hands up her back to clasp her head firmly, he deepened his kiss, touching her tongue, drawing into his mouth, sucking on it gently.

Tiffany was intoxicated by his heated passion, feeling the tension flow from her as fiery sensations coursed through her.

Clinton moved his hands, sliding them to her sides and up, catching the soft underside of her breast, caressing its fullness, then splaying his fingers, stroking the sensitive nipples to a taut peak. He heard her groan as he moved his mouth, trailing kisses down the soft column of her neck.

Tiffany arched her back. Her nipples ached from his relentless touch, a burning sensation began between her legs, and she groaned.

Her groan was nearly his undoing; he was aflame but held his passion in check. His tongue trailed down to the base of her throat, where a pulse beat rapidly; his hands glided into her shirt, separating the material so he touched the bare skin of her breasts. He unbuttoned her shirt, laying open her charms. And lowering, claimed the impudent tip with his mouth.

Tiffany gasped at his touch. Shivers of delight centered at her nipple, which he laved with his tongue and tugged at with his mouth. She moaned in delight when his other hand cupped her one breast while his mouth and tongue paid homage to the other. He was seducing her into insensibility, causing her to moan and arch to accommodate his onslaught.

Clinton smiled at her near surrender and continued to seduce her erotically, moving his hand down her exposed belly and over her britches, between her legs. He could feel the heat emanate from her center and moved his finger, stroking her woman's flesh through her britches.

The movement of his finger and the material of her britches caused molten waves of sensation to begin. A sweet ache began between her legs. Her nipple ached from his mouth, her center burned from his finger, and the promise of unbearable pleasure burst through her being.

Clinton lifted his mouth from her breast; his finger still moved, wringing a moan from her. There was no mistaking the fierce hunger reflected in his gray eyes. His hands slid sensually over her breasts, up the soft column of her throat, and buried themselves in the thickness of her hair, holding her head, capturing her passion-dazed eyes. She was still in the throes of passion, her lips parted, her breathing heavy, her face flushed. He knew he must stop before he could no longer control himself; as it was, he wanted nothing more than to finish what he had started. Giving in to the need to taste her lips again, he covered them, forcing them to open wider, capturing her tongue, drawing it into his mouth.

Tiffany matched his movement, mindless, lost in raw, hungry desire. When he lifted his mouth from hers, she could not stand and felt him support her, bringing them down to the ground. She clung to him as he lay her in his lap, feeling his hardness press against her buttocks. Stifling a disappointed cry, she curled against him. Her body ached and throbbed. Currents of desire ran through her body crying for fulfillment.

She felt the light, feathery kisses he rained on her and the soft, gentle caress of his hands, wanting them to be as ardent and persuasive as before.

Clinton soothingly began to bring her down from the pinnacle of desire, gently smoothing her tumbled tresses, lightly kissing her temples as she gained a measure of control. He noted her lips, still parted and swollen, drawing air in short breaths, her eyes half-closed and dazed, and her face flushed with waning passion. He held her against him, watching her nipples, still taut, begin to slacken, and slowly, with deft fingers, buttoned her shirt. He smiled in consummate pleasure at her reaction to his touch. He lightly traced her parted lips, suppressing the urge to begin again. He knew she rivaled him in passion, and that pleased him so. She belonged to him, and he ached for the day when he would mark her physically as his own. He was a step closer in the course he had charted to win her heart—he had awakened her passion and was sure none other had before. His physical possession would bind her to him, and she would seek him for it. His smile widened at the thought of telling her so, but he knew her pride would force her to deny it.

The strong, steady beat of Clinton's heart was the lifeline Tiffany clung to as the hot tide of passion ebbed and flowed. With the ebbing tide, panic hit her as fragmented thoughts began to replace the mindless sensations. The ache in her groin had subsided to a twinge, the fire on her lips cooled, her throbbing nipples no longer sent shooting currents to her belly. The hand whose touch she found scalding was now soothing and comforting.

Her mind screamed of her body's betrayal to her heart. She pressed her hands over her face, feeling wretched as the stab of guilt pierced her, causing the agony of defeat to come clearly to light. She tore away from the protective circle she had clung to with a choking cry, "I hate you!" She glared at Clinton with burning, reproachful eyes which filled with tears.

Clinton had expected her reaction and grabbed her shoulders, pulling her to face him. "You might hate me, but your body does not. You resist not me, but yourself." He gently brushed a tear that fell on her cheek.

Tiffany slapped his hand away, shoving hard against his chest. She stood on shaking limbs. "If I were but a man, I'd call you out!"

Clinton effortlessly stood, a trace of laughter edging his voice. "I told you, Princess, there are many sins you could accuse me of, but that is not one of them."

Tiffany was furious at his cavalier attitude and could not utter a word. She could not believe he was so unaffected by what was so devastating to her. How could he make light of what had happened?

Clinton noticed how high the sun had risen, guessing the hour to be noon. "Come, Princess, it grows late and we have a party to attend." Seeing her readiness to reply, he cut her short, gently placing his hand to her back. "It is time to go. We must depart soon." Stopping because Tiffany did, he looked into her eyes, seeing her anger, and replied lightly, "You'll have the entire carriage ride as well as a whole lifetime to upbraid me, Princess."

She snarled at him as he moved her toward their mounts; the import of his words "a whole lifetime" caused her to slap Touche into a gallop, leaving him in her wake. She heard his mocking laughter behind her.

Chapter Fourteen

The elegant black coach edged in fine gold bore the duke of Wentworth coat of arms: two lions rampart on a field of *noir* with the mark of cadency, the File sign of the firstborn son. It moved at a steady pace, led by four magnificent matched blooded bays. Following in its stead was another coach bearing Tiffany's trunks as well as Germane and Clinton's manservant, Mortimer.

The Wentworth coach was well sprung and extremely comfortable, with its plush interior. Tiffany sat across from Clinton, leaning her head against the plush squab, pretending to be absorbed in the passing scenery. Actually, she was absorbed, but in her thoughts. She marveled at how only a few short hours ago she was at Courtland Manor having no intention of departing anywhere, and here she was now, trunks packed, loaded, and bound for Chad Devonshire's country home in Essex for a prenuptial celebration given by Clinton's notorious friends.

She could not believe the audacity, no, the high-handness of him! No sooner had she arrived at Courtland, jumping off Touche, than she saw the Wentworth coach in the drive being loaded with her trunks. She had stormed into the foyer to be met by Germane, who informed her her bath was waiting and her gown laid out. She was confused and speechless, but when Clinton strolled calmly in and Godfrey had informed him his bath was ready, well, that just undid her and she flounced up the steps to her room. She had hoped Aunt Winnie would be about, but to her dismay, found he had packed her off to Wentworth!

Musing, she lifted the glass of champagne, barely touching her lips to the rim, and sipped the effervescent liquid. She watched the sun, which had begun its westerly descent, cast the landscape in a reddish glow. She easily finished the champagne, it being her favorite libation. The sound of her name drew her head from the window to Clinton.

"Tiffany." Clinton called her name a second time. Having been preoccupied in her thoughts, she had not heard him call her the first time. She looked at his outstretched hand and briefly wondered what he wanted. She then noticed the bottle of champagne in his other. She handed him her glass, her fingers brushing his warm, tanned hand. The mere touch sent a warming shiver through her, and she blushed unwillingly as thoughts of the scene on the bluff flooded her mind. Whenever they touched, a light brush of his shoulder or his hand lightly riding her back, no matter how innocent, she felt a fluttering in her stomach.

Retrieving the glass from his hand, she quickly sipped the liquid, hoping to numb the sensations that had begun anew. She lowered her lashes, afraid her eyes would reveal how unsettling she found his touch, and chanced to observe him from beneath them.

He sat there casually attired, yet impeccably dressed in a gray jacket. The rich outline of his broad shoulders strained against the fabric. A crisp mat of black hair curled against the open neck of his shirt. His hair, the deep, rich color of coffee, was combed back in defiance to the current mode, yet errant soft waves fell at his temples, giving him a rakish air. He wore it longer than the style, so it fell neatly to his nape. His lips were firm and sensual, and she shivered remembering the feel of them against her skin. His mouth was full and curled as if always on the edge of laughter and of breaking into that devastating smile he possessed which made her feel like warmed honey. She sipped her champagne and continued her secret appraisal of him. His eyes were heavy-lidded, seductive, yet compelling. The corners were slanted as if touched with humor. He was devilishly handsome, there was no denying that! She had no doubt many heads turned when he entered a room. She was sure, even in a crowd, those compelling eyes, firm features, and the confident set of his shoulders caused him to stand out. His height alone would draw anyone's attention.

Clinton watched her regard him and did not miss the blush that stained her cheeks when his fingers touched hers. He was pleased she took the time to leisurely appraise him, for it meant what he suspected—she was not all that indifferent to him. He leaned over for the third time to refill her glass and smiled as he emptied the last of the bottle into it.

As she raised her glass to her lips, feeling a bit lightheaded, her eye caught the sparkle on her left ring finger. She lowered her gaze to the large oval sapphire encircled by twelve perfect sparkling diamonds—her engagement ring. She had received it today, just before they embarked. A Wentworth family heirloom, Clinton had informed her, which passed from generation to generation to the future duchess, only to be relinquished to the next heir's duchess. Sipping her bubbly, she gazed upon it admiringly. It was exquisite and no doubt priceless, but from the moment he placed it upon her finger, she felt marked as a possession.

The pop from a newly opened bottle caused her to start. Clinton raised a brow in question, looking at her empty glass. He complied by refilling her glass, which she extended to him, and asked, "Are you nervous about meeting my friends?"

She sipped her wine, relishing the calming and numbing effect it had on her. "Should I be nervous, or afraid?"

He smiled hearing the slight slurring in her words. He

saw the flush in her cheeks, caused by the effects of the champagne, and leaned over, topping off her glass. "You should feel neither, Princess."

"Then wherein lies your concern, Your Grace?" She flashed him a bright smile. He returned her smile with his own quite charming one, one he used quite successfully when seducing a nervous woman, one that disarmed Tiffany.

"Princess, 'Your Grace' sounds so formal. Why not try 'Clinton'?"

Tiffany, who was feeling quite giddy and disarmed by "that" smile, complied. "Clinton, wherein lies your concern over my meeting your friends?"

He loved the sound of his name as it tripped over her lips. Smiling, he said, "Merely that you would not know many since they do not frequent the events you are accustomed to."

Her blue eyes sparkled as her sharp wit cut through the champagne-induced euphoria. "Ah yes, how silly of me to forget the roaming rogues. Their amusements tend to run toward debauchery, seducing innocents, and frequenting brothels and other dens of iniquity!" She extended her glass, which he promptly filled. "Amusements you are so famous for." She smiled brightly at him, sipping her champagne, enjoying every minute of her play.

His gray eyes sparkled with the love of combat and he replied matter-of-factly, "Jealous, and not yet a wife, Princess?" He sipped his wine and added, "You will soon come to appreciate the wealth of my experience." Tiffany did not miss the promise etched in his voice nor the leisurely, appreciative way his eyes roamed over her form. But she was feeling too good to allow his words or eyes to spoil her fun.

Clinton knew the inordinate amount of wine accounted for her flirting, that her defenses were lowered. He felt his desire grow as he took note of her. She was absolutely alluring in the teal gown which, while not daring, was cut low enough to provide him with a spectacular view of the soft swell of her breasts. He pushed down the urge to lift an errant curl that lay lovingly against her ivory breast. His attention was diverted to her mouth. So full, soft; lips parted and moist with wine. He knew she'd taste good, too good to stop tasting her. Her cheeks were flushed like the flush of sunset on the snow. Her eyes were bright sapphire, sensuous and glazed from the wine. He felt his manhood stir. God, she boiled his blood.

As she raised her hand to brush a curl from her cheek, Clinton's eyes wandered to the Wentworth ring, and he thought how the sapphire brought out the color of her eyes. He remarked, "I believe the sapphire complements you, Princess."

"It is lovely, isn't it?" she mummured, holding out an unsteady hand to regard the ring. Noticing a slight blurring of her vision, she rapidly closed and opened her eyes, clearing them. Looking up at him, smiling impishly, she teasingly replied, "It's a shame, diamonds have never been my favorite, you know. Just another bit of your wealth I can't appreciate."

Clinton raised a brow in inquiry, "Really, Princess?"

A slow, steady smile drew on his lips as he leaned forward and brushed back a wisp of hair caressing her shell-shaped ear, exposing the diamond earbobs she always wore. When he touched her, she shivered in delight as if electricity flowed through her. She closed her eyes, reveling in the sensation of his finger as it outlined her ear, moving to caress her neck.

He felt her response. Leaning closer so his mouth was inches from her ear, he softly asked in a low voice, purposefully seductive, "Does my touch bother you so?"

She felt a shiver ripple through her when his breath, soft and warm, fanned her cheek. She felt drugged by his clean, manly scent. Heady sensations tripped over her as his fingers trailed softly down the column of her neck to rest inches above the swell of her breasts.

He whispered again and leaned closer, his breath hot against her. "Does my touch distress you?" He leaned forward, nibbling at her ear, tracing its shape with the tip of his tongue. Her calm shattered, she leaned her head against his as his tongue entered her ear gently. Goose bumps coursed down her spine. His lips moved to sear a path from her shoulder to her neck, where he stopped to kiss the pulsing hollow at its base.

Tiffany sighed, yielding her throat. His hands slid sensually to her breasts, massaging their fullness. His finger found her nipple and caressed it to a proud and taut peak. A current of desire rushed through her. She moaned in delight when his other hand touched her breast.

The tormenting sweetness of her moan caused him to slide his hand to her back, his deft fingers quickly unfastening her gown, slipping it off her shoulders. His hands slid inside her bodice, freeing her breasts. He felt her tremble when his hand touched her bare flesh. He caught an impudent tip, which he rolled between his fingers, rolling it until she cried out.

He heard her gasp when his mouth covered a taut, dusty peak, then felt her nails dig into his shoulders when she arched, giving him her full bounty. His manhood was hard, throbbing against his pants as his passion grew stronger with each whimper and groan. He lifted her head and traced her parted lips with his tongue, seeing her dazed eyes and flushed face.

Tiffany was lost in a malestrom of sensation. "Oh . . . oh . . ." she moaned as his tongue teased her parted lips. She didn't want to yield to the passion he aroused, but she felt so light headed and dizzy with confusing sensations all she could think to do was to wrap her hands in the hair at the nape of his neck.

His parted lips closed over hers, drawing her tongue into his mouth. She timidly parried with his tongue, bringing a groan of satisfaction from Clinton, who deepened the kiss and brought her up against his chest, feeling the twin buds of desire quiver against him. With her surrender, he gathered her in his arms, bringing them to the carpeted floor of the carriage.

Rising above her, leaning on his forearms, he gazed down at the bounty she offered him. Her breasts, full, pink, with their peaks hard and tight in desire, rose up in offering. He lowered his mouth, paying homage to one, then the other.

Tiffany arched her back, offering the fullness of her breast to his mouth. An uncoiling began in the pit of her stomach, a wetness between her thighs as his tongue stroked her nipples. With each stoke a current shot from her nipple to the aching place between her legs and she moaned, "Please . . . oh."

Each moan undid Clinton. His breathing was harsh and rapid. Fire burned within him and he whispered hoarsely, "I want you, Princess."

She whimpered at his words, feeling his raw, potent sexuality against her thigh. His hands charted a course over her breasts to her belly. She groaned. He nearly undid his breeches save for the sound of a bell which pealed, bringing him out of his own flame. He lifted himself up to his forearms.

Tiffany moaned in distress when she felt him rise. Looking up at him with passion-dazed eyes, she ran her hands up his exposed chest, running her nails through the crisp mat of black hair.

Hearing her moan, he gazed down at her. The need for fulfillment, for release, filled her eyes. She arched upward, wrapping her arms about his neck, bringing her bared breast against his naked chest. He cupped the fullness of her breasts and was awarded with a delightful moan. He lifted them and lowered his hair-roughened chest, pressing her down beneath him. As he rubbed his chest against her taut nipples, she cried out in longing for more, of what she did not know. Clinton knew, feeling her quiver beneath him and writhing against his manhood, which was close to bursting.

He nudged her legs apart with his own. When she felt his knee against her hot, throbbing womanhood, she felt sensation after sensation rivet through her. She whimpered. He looked at her and saw the exquisite torture, feeling his own need rising. As he slid his deft fingers along the tender skin of her inner thigh, Tiffany writhed mindlessly. Clinton's finger sought and found the eagerness of her desire. Finding her wet and moist drove him to exert controls he never knew he had. Her sweet essence was swelled and slick with her own desire.

Tiffany felt a melting sensation, a sweetness that ached for fulfillment within her. The world seemed to spin on its axis and the sounds of bells rang in her ears. Never had she felt so assaulted by her senses. She writhed under the onslaught of his fingers and cried out in passion; his tongue entered and withdrew from her mouth in mock imitation of an act Clinton craved, but had not the time to complete, hearing again the peal of the bells.

Tiffany arched against his fingers, bringing them closer to the source of her need. When he lifted his mouth from her's, she whimpered against his throat, "Please."

"Let me have you, Tiffany." His voice was a husky, promising whisper, his finger loving her. The web of sensation he wove, his hands, body, his voice, a deep, seductive whisper, urged her on, then held her back. "Easy, Tiffany, savor it, love. Let it build, then ebb to build higher—till you think you might die from the wanting." Groaning, she yielded.

He whispered in a deep, sensual voice against her ear, speaking freely of what he would do. "I would taste you, Princess. Moving my mouth and tongue where my hand now plays, and drink my fill of your sweetness. Can you imagine how good you would taste?" She whimpered softly at the image conjured by her mind. Clinton's own control was near breaking when he heard the peal, knowing the time was shortening.

"I want to be drawn deep inside you and look upon your face as I fill you." He felt her body tense, ready to convulse in climax. He pressed her closer, stroking her bud, now hard and taut, his voice a husky, commanding whisper. "Now, Princess, now." Shudders of pleasure washed over Tiffany, suspending her in a moment of infinity where the tolling of bells played madly. She opened her mouth to cry out. Clinton covered it, capturing her cry of release.

He lifted his mouth from Tiffany's, removed his hand, pressing her against him. He heard the peal of the bell and smiled in recognition to the final warning.

Tiffany, drifting in an endless moment, whimpered at the loss of Clinton's touch. She faintly heard the ringing of a bell. Clinton gathered her in, bringing them to the seat of the carriage.

Still dazed, Tiffany stared at him in confusion, watching him deftly fasten her gown. He said softly, "It appears we have arrived, and in a moment the door will open." He thought, God, she is beautiful. Soft with waning passion, lips red and kiss-swollen, the sunlight touching her tousled ebony tresses, which fell over her beguiling ivory shoulder like a mantle. Her eyes, vague, glazed, smoky blue.

He cupped her chin, reluctant to break the spell between them. "Come, Princess, let me help you; we have arrived." The halting of the carriage bore the truth of his words. A bell tolled loudly.

"Is that a bell ringing?" she asked softly, her voice confused.

"It's the fifth peal, to be precise."

Confusion quickly changed to a startled expression when the carriage door was yanked open by a footman in red and gold livery.

Clinton alighted first and turned to assist her in descent. Her feet touched the crushed stone of the drive. When she looked up, she found the tall, handsome form of Chad Devonshire, a knowing smile etching his face as he stood before her. His scrutiny of Tiffany's ruffled appearance, her tousled hair, kiss-swollen lips, and flushed cheeks, lent support to his beliefs, but it was her blush, as becoming as it was, that clinched it. He regarded Clinton, who smiled in return. Clinton was impeccably dressed, not a hair out of place, only an unusual look in his eye, one Chad had never seen.

Tiffany self-consciously smoothed her gown when Chad turned his gaze to Clinton. Just as Chad turned back to her, the shattering of glass provided a momentary reprieve as all three heads turned toward the sound. The broken remnants of an empty champagne bottle lay on the drive while another rolled and teetered precariously at the edge of the open carriage door and soon fell, joining the other. Tiffany closed her eyes as scarlet rose up her face to the roots of her hair.

A wicked smile etched across his face, Chad regarded them both. Clinton appeared not the least bothered by Chad's scrutiny, and Tiffany wished to thrash him over his nonchalance.

"Lady Courtland." Chad bowed. Tiffany sank into a deep curtsy, rising on shaky legs. "May I offer you welcome to Haverstone."

"It is lovely, Lord Devonshire," she replied perfunctorily.

His eyebrow raised inquiringly, one corner of his mouth pulled into a slight smile, Chad asked, "I trust the journey was pleasant?"

A touch of color rose to her cheeks at his simple question. She couldn't speak, taking a deep breath while a nervous smile appeared at her mouth. Clinton intervened, replying, "Short, but sweet." A satisfying grin lit his features. Tiffany's face brightened at his answer. She was saved from further embarrassment by the appearance of a servant inquiring about the trunks.

Chad turned to Tiffany. "Lest I be accused of being lax in my hospitality, I am sure you wish to rest after the exhausting journey and refresh yourself for the evening's festivities."

As she nodded her head in assent, Chad continued, "Let us go in and I will have one of the servants escort you to your rooms, where tea will be served." With all the dignity she could muster, Tiffany allowed Clinton to take her arm, escorting her into the country home, where a servant led her up the stairway. Both men's eyes were drawn to the provocatively innocent sway of her hips as she disappeared.

They headed to the study. Chad walked over to the table holding a decanter and poured out two glasses of French brandy. After handing one to Clinton, who stood with his arm leaning against the mantel, Chad crossed to the fireplace and sat in a butter-soft leather chair, stretching his legs before him.

Reaching, he withdrew a slim cigar from the box near him and offered one to Clinton, who accepted. After lighting the cigar and blowing a stream of smoke out, Chad said, "Well, aren't you going to thank me?" Clinton regarded his friend from under lowered lashes. He pulled on his cigar, which dangled from his fingers, the smoke curling upward.

"Thank you for the party, Chad," he replied dryly.

"That's not what I mean, Clinton." Chad sipped his brandy, looking over the glass.

"Then perhaps you can enlighten me."

"Ah, and here I thought you had accomplished far more in the coach then you had. She certainly looked disheveled enough."

Clinton walked over to the table, refilling his glass. He smiled down at Chad. "And how much do you think I accomplished in the carriage, my friend?"

"Obviously not enough to thank me for protecting your future wife's virtue before she became your fiancée. Surprises me, though you've always been quite expedient and efficient."

Placing the stopper back on the decanter, Clinton replied, "This one I intend to savor, my friend. If thanks are in order, I'll thank you after the wedding night."

Chad laughed. "Well, anyhow, it appears you won, my friend. The lady was dazed and disheveled, and you not in the least. I'm curious, Clinton, how it is you manage so much in so little time. Is the secret to right yourself at the second peal?"

"Just practice and good timing, Chad, 'tis all."

The men relaxed, talking over business and future investments. Chad changed the topic when he mentioned the evening at hand.

"I say, Clinton, George Stanton has arrived with Monique in tow."

Puffing on his cigar, thinking about this bit of information, he replied confidently, "Monique was always a resourceful woman; she presents no problem to me. We parted quite amicably."

"Barbara Markham is here as well. Managed to coerce Walter Thorton to escort her, don't you know." Chad knocked the ash from his cigar. "Heard she's quite miffed you didn't offer for her. You know she's been waiting for the day you stopped sowing your oats."

Clinton smiled at this tidbit of news, fully aware Barbara Markham had set her sights on him long ago. "Well, Brent is arriving; perhaps Barbara can amuse herself with another Barencourte."

Laughing, Chad said, "Surely you jest! Brent can't abide the woman at all. Says she gives new meaning to 'clinging vine.' "

"Did Brent say when he would arrive?"

"Actually, his brief note said something to the effect, someone had to watch the store, but wager on Clinton five hundred pounds and he'd be late."

"Good ole Brent. Always plays the winner, calculates

the odds, and if nothing else, makes sure his bet is placed at all cost,'' Clinton remarked, feeling a twinge of guilt that Brent was handling not only his own load of work but Clinton's as well.

''Brent is quite good at wagering, don't you know. Why, he bet on you and tripled his money while he's busy doubling yours.'' Chad crossed his stretched legs at the ankle. ''To be honest, I haven't seen much of him in London and know he is busy with the banking. Do hope he does show; the boy needs some relaxation, wouldn't you agree?''

Clinton nodded his head, took a seat, and stretched himself out. ''Definitely, Chad. A bit of wine, women, and song would do him good.''

''By the by, how's it going with the reluctant bride-to-be?''

Clinton, smiled, answering, ''Still reluctant.'' Lifting his glass to his lips, draining it, he added, turning to Chad, a smug smile affixed to his face, ''But coming along.''

Chad laughed, Clinton joined him, their laughter filling the study.

Chapter Fifteen

Germane dressed Tiffany's hair in a soft, loose coiffure; raven tresses cascaded down her back, wisps of hair framed her flushed face.

The soft knock on the door brought Tiffany from her thoughts. Germane walked toward her carrying a tray bearing a bottle of champagne, a single glass, and a bunch of violets.

"Ah, mademoiselle, champagne from His Grace. How romantic, no?" Without awaiting a reply, Germane poured a glass, handing it to her mistress. The bubbles tickled her nose as she brought the glass to her lips, sipping the delightful wine, savoring its flavor.

A becoming blush stained her face, for the drink was reminiscent of the carriage ride. She could not prevent the rush of memories that flooded her mind nor the earth-shattering sensations she experienced. She felt the fluttering of butterflies in the pit of her belly and a warmth spread in her groin. Shaking her head, she tried to clear it of the images that rushed forward. He had touched her where none before had, creating an ache she had begged him to release. She had longed for it, even encouraged him. She sipped her wine pensively as images of her writhing body came to mind, of her naked breasts pressed against his hair-roughened chest. Just the thought made her nipples rise. Germane refilled her glass and began to put the final touches to her coiffure.

How could she have been so wanton, so abandoned, with a man she despised? A tingling, almost a shiver, ran through her, causing Germane to ask, "Does Mademoiselle want a shawl?" Tiffany shook her head, and Germane continued her ministrations. It must have been the champagne! It certainly wasn't anything else! She'd have to be careful with him and watch what she drank!

"Voilà," Germane exclaimed, stepping back to regard her work. "Mademoiselle ees beautiful, no?" When she received no response, Germane said, "See for yourself!" Tiffany stood before the full-length mirror. She did not recognize herself. The woman who gazed back was seductive and passionate-looking. The sapphire blue of the gown enhanced the seductive quality of her eyes, and the raven tresses flowed about her beguiling shoulders, adding the perfect foil. Her lips were full, sensual, and inviting.

Turning to view herself, she caught the glimmer of the silver threads that shot through the blue silk and glistened in the candlelight. The gown was elegantly fashioned; its neckline daringly displayed the full satin radiance of her breast. Smoothing down the gown with her hand, she saw that the silver threads captured the sparkle of the twelve diamonds that encircled the large sapphire. Turning sideways from beneath her skirt, a neatly turned ankle could be seen above an exquisite silver satin slipper. Tiffany was as sparkling as champagne and as seductive as its effect.

Germane announced the arrival of the footman. Tiffany turned, placing her hand on his arm, leaving the room.

As the curtain of night fell, candles of a hundred chandeliers were lit, casting the rooms in a soft amber light. Champagne flowed freely and a sumptuous buffet was laid in place for a formal dinner. Merriment was heard from all the rooms, where separate activities took place.

Gambling was available for both men and women, the

more serious high-stake games left for later. Certain game rooms were off limits to her by Clinton's decree, and when she attempted to gain entry, the posted servants politely turned her away. Of course, her curiosity was sparked at what went on behind the closed door, and she promised herself she'd find out exactly what types of games were being played. Save for this exception, she was enjoying herself immensely, having gambled shockingly, rolling dice, winning five pounds from Percy. After learning the game piquet, she had managed to beat Clinton royally. She was quite lucky at roulette, winning a tidy sum at the table.

Tiffany had to admit she was indeed nervous over meeting this elite group of people who amused themselves with entertainment not socially accepted. Most were older, extremely sophisticated, and outrageous. Titles were aplenty here, from lords to dukes. Enough blue blood flowed here to make the ton green with envy. But there was no doubt the men were rakes, bounders, and rogues, not the models of propriety or decorum.

When she was introduced to a few, she recognized their titled names from rumors spread about their escapades or some unfortunate innocent who had been taken in by them. There was no doubt they all had one thing in common: their reputations. She had no doubt if Clinton had not been by her side staking his claim, she would have been considered fair game. As it was, she received some outrageous innuendos while dancing with a few, and though she prided herself on her wit and sharp tongue, she was definitely out of their league and welcomed Clinton's presence this evening.

The women were older and more experienced than herself. Most were widows, who had married older men and, after their husbands' deaths, felt they were young enough to still enjoy life, but not in the way the ton dictated. Others she found out were titled women who were married but enjoyed the current fashionable marriages where one did not attend social functions with one's husband, choosing one's own way. Another group was free from the restrictions of a loveless marriage after having performed their duty by supplying an heir. Probably the most shocking was Priscilla Mawbry, whose husband was killed in a duel by one of the roaming rogues, and who now had become his mistress!

Tiffany was by no means judgmental, only shocked. She nearly laughed aloud recalling how she intended to force Clinton to cry off the engagement by her shocking behavior! Why, she'd have to ride naked through town to beat these people, and somehow she doubted that would do the trick either. She felt her spirit plummet at the thought.

The sound of a throaty laugh brought her from her thoughts and she turned. Clinton stood leaning close to a petite, curvaceous redhead, who had just exited from one of the off-limit games. She wore an elegant ruby red gown which displayed her hourglass figure perfectly. She watched the woman touch Clinton, noting the ease with which she did it. Clinton's husky laugh broke the air and the redhead casually drew his arm to her. Tiffany could not help but notice the ease he had with women and the comfort that existed between himself and the opposite sex.

"I tell you, some people, no matter who they lie with, have no class." Tiffany turned to Barbara Markham, a striking petite blonde dressed in a gorgeous creation of amber silk and satin.

Tiffany, after being introduced to Lady Markham, found her to be the epitome of everything she despised in the title personage. Barbara was condescending, snobbish, and catty. Tiffany absently wondered how she fit into this elite group.

Tiffany was about to discreetly depart when an announcement was made for the women to adjourn to the salon. Tiffany had no choice but to accompany Lady Markham so as not to appear churlish.

As they walked, Lady Markham kept up the conversation with Tiffany.

"I tell you, Diana, Chad should have prevented that riffraff from being here."

"Oh, now, don't you get into a tizzy about it, Babs," Diana said, shifting her eyes toward Tiffany in warning to Barbara.

Barbara smiled evilly and continued once they were seated, "Oh, I am sorry, Lady Courtland, I didn't mean to upset you."

At Tiffany's perplexed look, Barbara sought to enlighten her. "Surely, dear, you know who I refer to, Clinton's mistress." She pointed her finger at the redhead who now entered the salon, the one who moments ago had been laughing with Clinton. Gauging Tiffany's response, Barbara smiled and continued, "Well, it seems Monique bet Clive at strip poker, you know that American game. Well, she has the nerve to boast about it!"

Turning to Diana, she added, "Why anyone would want to remove their clothes one piece at a time instead of wagering money, I'll never know."

Tiffany was shocked into silence. Her mind registered two facts: one, Clinton's mistress, and two, the game that was off limits to her! Taking one's clothes off, indeed!

The footmen appeared with trays of champagne, then departed, closing the double doors of the salon behind them. Tiffany was still trying to digest the information when she was interrupted again by Barbara's voice.

"Why in heaven's name they put us through this, I'll never know." As she fanned herself furiously, Barbara's brown eyes narrowed and gleamed wickedly. "Vicky, dear, did you arrive by carriage with any of the contenders?"

"Babs, you know perfectly well I arrived with Diana."

"Oh, yes, how remiss of me. Of course, Lady Courtland, you traveled with His Grace." Tiffany smiled weakly, a sense of anxiety turning her stomach in knots.

Unable to bear the smirk affixed to Barbara's face, Tiffany asked, "Why are we closeted in here?"

Raising winged brows, Barbara mockingly asked, "Really, His Grace has put you at quite a disadvantage, what with his mistress and now this." Shaking her head, she awarded Tiffany with a look filled with pity.

"Oh, really Babs, you make too much of it. I'm sure Lady Courtland isn't interested in men and their wagers. Especially this one. It's as old as time itself," Victoria quickly said, hoping to prevent Barbara from telling it all. Victoria was well aware of Clinton's power and preferred to remain on the good side of it.

Tiffany could not help herself; something inside her head said, Let it be, while another side, her curiosity, needed to know. "Please, I would know what this is all about."

Barbara tore her eyes away from Monique, who sat across the room watching the four women, and proceeded to explain, "Did you not hear the tolling of bells when you arrived?" At Tiffany's nod, she continued. "You are not that young not to know what a man may try in a carriage ride." At Tiffany's blush, Barbara smiled and rushed on. "It seems the roaming rogues were all quite efficient in the art of seduction in a carriage and devised a game they could wager on to see who was the master of the craft. The crux of the issue was how to determine if the man amused himself during the ride. Surely no proper woman would confirm her ravishment. So it was decided a five-bell warning would be given alerting the man his destination drew near. So when the carriage drew up and the occupants alighted, they would be judged by the degree of the woman's dishevelment and the lack of the man's." Fanning herself, she watched Tiffany's face, inordinately pleased by her reaction.

"So you see, Lady Courtland, at this moment the men are being advised as to the winner, and the wagers are being paid off." Barbara turned, catching Monique's eyes. A moment of silence passed before Barbara turned back to Tiffany. "Now, why they bother, God only knows! Clinton has always won, and by the look on your face, dear, it appears he has again."

The doors of the salon were thrown open and the roar of men's voices cheering and yelling could be heard, as they exited the study. Clinton stood amongst his peers, being slapped on the back while money exchanged hands. It was obvious to all he had won again.

The women began to rise to join the men, and Tiffany quickly stood, wanting nothing more than to escape, and headed through the ballroom, out the French doors leading to the terraced gardens.

Monique, who had watched Clinton's fiancée since her arrival, waited discreetly until Barbara was abreast of her. "Spreading your poison, Barbara?"

Looking down her nose at Monique, Barbara haughtily replied, "Not that it's any concern of yours, I was just enlightening the future duchess on some of His Grace's habits." A sneer crossed her face when she asked, "How does it feel to have been one of his 'has-beens,' Monique?"

A smile lifting the corners of her mouth, Monique replied, "Better than never having been, Barbara." She began to walk away and stopped to turn her head once again at Barbara. "And now you never will be."

Brent saw Lady Markham through the salon windows he passed, and decided he would turn around and enter through the gardens to avoid a confrontation with the clinging vine. When he turned and headed back, he stopped, seeing the exquisite creature sitting next to her in a confection of blue silk. Who is she? He had never seen her before and wondered what the elegant raven-tressed lady was doing here. When she lifted her hand, he noticed the ring and knew instantly her identity. He smiled devilishly. No wonder Clinton had moved heaven and earth to secure her; spent a fortune to obtain the rights to her.

Brent had no doubt he'd have done the same. Whistling, he headed to the gardens.

Tiffany, once she gained the cover of night, entered the first level of the garden, giving in to the boiling rage. Her steps quickened and her anger singed the corners of her control. How dare he! How dare he seduce me, and so thoroughly, for a wager! I hate him! Loathe him! So absorbed in her anger was she, she failed to hear her name called. She snapped her head up and peered in the darkness where the sound originated from. Climbing the steps, heading toward her, was none other than her betrothed. Hah! She couldn't miss him. Dressed impeccably in black, appropriately so, the blackguard! She saw the devastating smile cross his face, and the bright, even teeth as he approached.

Brent crossed the distance between them, his arms open in greeting at the figure rushing forward. "Tiffany?" he asked, seeing the silver threads of the blue silk. What he didn't see, though, was her hand raised, and only felt the sharp crack against his cheek when they came face-to-face. "Bet you didn't wager on that!" she cried as she flew down the steps to the second level.

Brent raised his hand to his face, a perplexed look crossing it. What in the hell was that for? She's right, he thought, he had wagered on a friendlier introduction, not on being slapped. He stood unable to move, unable to decide what to do.

Go after her? Find Clinton? What? Hell, he didn't know.

Clinton had seen Tiffany disappear from the salon. He searched the upper ballroom, dining room, and lower ballroom. He was waylaid by Chad and Charles in the library. When he finally left them, he decided Tiffany must have gone to the gardens for some air, for it was a devilishly warm evening for June. He walked through the ballroom and out onto the terrace, where he found a much-befuddled Brent.

Tiffany had flown down to the third level, negotiating

the dark stone steps surprisingly fast. Her anger had reached a pinnacle where it was consuming her. Her mind kept thinking of all the terrible names she could call him, and when she ran out of them, she thought of all the terrible things she'd love to see happen to him. So enmeshed in thought was she, she ran headlong into a form ascending the steps, causing her to tumble forward. Strong arms pulled her up against a rock-hard chest. His movements were swift, saving her from falling, and a protective arm pressed her closer as she regained her balance. "What's this? Manna from heaven." A velvet-edged, strong voice broke the quiet night.

Tiffany looked up at a ruggedly handsome face of varying planes. For an instant it looked vaguely familiar. Gray eyes like summer lightning, sharp and assessing, regarded her. He held her away so his eyes could freely roam over her form, then lifted his eyes to sweep her face.

Tiffany detected a gleam of laughter in those gray assessing orbs and knew it to be true when his face split into a wolfish grin. His voice lifted with a trace of amusement. "You're a fine piece of fluff. Perhaps you're the prize for the latecomer? Or perhaps I won the wager . . ."

The word "wager" did it. Her eyes narrowed, fury clearly in them. "Move aside, I'm done with you!" She struggled against his iron-clad hold.

He laughed at her futile attempts, saying, "Why, sweetheart, I've only just begun," and pulled her to him. Tiffany pushed her hands between them, pummeling his chest. Her attack caused him to laugh, his laugh causing her to kick. He was undaunted by her kick and grabbed her wrists, replying, "You're a lively vixen. I lay odds you'd be the first woman to exhaust me before the night's through."

"You're as bad as he," she spat. "Ooooh, if I were but a man, what I'd do!" At her words, his laughter ceased, and in the velvet-toned voice, edged with steel, he stated,

"Tell me, my beauty, who has angered you, and I will kill him."

"And commit fratricide?" A voice broke the night.

Still holding her wrists, he made the mistake of looking up, giving Tiffany the opportunity she needed. Just as Clinton's warning came, Tiffany sunk her teeth into the flesh of his hand.

"She bites, Austin."

Laughing and still holding her wrists, in spite of his injury, Austin called out, "A bit late, brother. The deed's done."

Clinton appeared out of the dark, coming to stand at Tiffany's side. Austin looked, noticing the Wentworth ring for the first time. A knowing smile broke his face. "So this is my future sister-in-law? I congratulate you, brother, on your exquisite taste."

"Thank you, Austin. I suggest you release her wrists. As you know firsthand, she has a tendency to bite."

"Best you bind them as well," called out Brent, who walked out from the shadows. "She has a solid right as well."

Tiffany felt her wrists released, but her mind could not register what her eyes beheld. She stood in the middle of three large, handsome men who all resembled one another, from the tops of their dark coffee heads to their gray eyes, which varied only in shade, to the devastating smile each presented her as she turned to regard them. Her hand itched to smack those smiles clear off each and every face!

"Beauty, spirit, and courage, an explosive combination, Clinton. Where did you find her?" Austin asked, amusement lighting his deep voice.

Clinton's voice broke into her anger. "Tiffany, as you no doubt guessed, these are my brothers." His hand rode her back as he turned to Brent. "Tiffany this is Brent Barencourte, third son." Brent bowed to her.

Tiffany thought, He is the one I slapped, thinking him Clinton. She realized he did indeed resemble Clinton, save his eyes were more blue-gray, not smoky. He appeared to be more reserved than the other two, not quite as dangerous, more charming. She felt remorseful she had struck him, for he appeared to be more the gentleman.

"And this is Austin, the second son." Now, this one, she thought, I'd never mistake for Clinton. He was brawny, broad, and solid. His arms were heavily muscled, his face ruggedly handsome. His eyes were a lighter shade of gray and reflected a dangerous glint. She imagined in the affairs of the heart, if he had a heart, he would be quite a dangerous adversary. For some unknown reason, she attributed a quick temper to him. She smiled at him, feeling no remorse for biting him!

"And this, gentlemen, is the future duchess of Wentworth, Tiffany Courtland," Clinton stated.

"Well, I can see why you've rushed the wedding date, brother. I certainly couldn't wait to claim her as my own," Austin replied, easily smiling down at Tiffany.

Tiffany seethed and stiffened her spine. It did not go unnoticed by Clinton. Brent saw the effect Austin's words had on her and shook his head, placing odds she wouldn't let his remark go unanswered.

Tiffany did not disappoint Brent and blurted out, "And you'd be unsuccessful as he, for there'll be no wedding. For in spite of my forced presence and your brother's forced company, I have absolutely no intention of marrying him, now or later." Crossing her arms over her breasts, blocking Austin's view, she tapped her foot impatiently.

"What say you of this, Clinton?" Austin asked, a smile lifting the corners of his mouth as he lifted his eyes to Tiffany's face.

Brent knew as well as Austin what Clinton's response would be and was not surprised when Clinton answered in a tone that brooked no argument, "She will."

Tiffany spun to face Clinton. "I will not!" she said, stamping her foot. "I will not say the vows!"

Austin pursed his lips, stifling the smile that threatened

to split his face. He thought her a ravishing creature, finding her fury seductive, her anger passionate, imagining it channeled in another direction.

Brent was taken by her spirit as well, thinking her to be quite alluring and vibrant.

Clinton smiled down at her. ''Ah, I see. Since you leave me no alternative, Princess, why wait! I'll have my manservant make ready the carriage.'' He grabbed her wrist, explaining, ''We leave for Scotland to a drafty castle I have in the Highlands.'' He paused, looking to Brent. ''We still own it, don't we, Brent?''

Brent nodded affirmatively, smiling at the wide-eyed Tiffany.

Looking at Tiffany, Clinton began to pull her along, explaining, ''There I *will* compromise you. No pretense this time, Princess. It's compromised in truth and nothing short of the truth.'' He paused, as if thinking, then asked Austin, ''I'll need a witness to confirm it's not pretense. Is your carriage available and have you the time?''

Before Austin could answer, Tiffany cried out, her eyes wide in disbelief and astonishment, ''You wouldn't!''

''I would.''

She looked at Austin; he tilted his head, pursed his lips, and responded to her unasked question, ''He would.''

She turned to appeal to Brent, gambling if any of these rogues had a shred of honor, he would. Had she wagered, she'd have lost.

His words confirmed it. ''The odds are not in your favor.''

In an effort to salvage some of her pride and knowing full well she could not go far, Clinton dropped her hand. She looked from one to another, and before she fled down the steps, she said, ''You mother never deceived you in believing you share a common sire. She only neglected to tell you he resides in hell.'' She flew down the steps into the night.

''Ouch, that hurt,'' joked Austin.

"Must be your cloven hooves pressing against your new boots," teased Brent.

"No, I think my spaded tail is pinching the family jewels." Austin smiled, turning to Clinton. "Oh, well, I guess the family skeleton's out of the royal closet. The Barencourtes are the spawns of the devil." Austin roared with laughter, shaking his head, "You'll have the devil's own time taming her, brother. Which brings me to another devil. Your lady's stallion has been delivered to Wentworth into the capable doting hands of Keegan."

Lighting a cheroot, pausing as he blew a curl of smoke out, Clinton asked, "I trust you had no problem with him?"

"Depends on what you call a problem, Clinton. I found him to be quite spirited, much as your lady here, but easily appeased with bonbons. Had him eating out of my hand. Mayhaps you should try them with Tiffany."

Clinton smiled, refusing to be drawn. Austin continued, "It's a good thing you didn't send Tristan to do the job. He has no love for the beasts anyway, and this one is not exactly endearing."

"Is mother at Wentworth?" Clinton asked.

"Aye. She arrived today from Genoa on Tristan's ship. Tristan was a bit put out having to relocate the harem girl the dey bestowed on him to another ship."

Brent spoke up, adding, "Mother is in a flutter. She sent word she needed certain services and could I lend her my secretary, Loomis, to help with the invitations. Incidentally, Winifred is there, and last I heard, she and Mother already had handled the wedding arrangements."

Looking at each brother, Clinton asked a question neither wished to answer. "And what of Rory?"

Austin volunteered, "None of our captains have seen hide nor hair of him, but word is being spread across the high seas."

"I think our little brother will receive word from our network, Clinton," Brent reassured.

Clinton nodded in affirmation, pulling on his cigar. "Tomorrow we will head to Wentworth. I want Tiffany to meet the family and staff before we set up permanent residence there." Letting out a thin stream of smoke, he warned, "Not one word about the stallion; he's her wedding present." He looked into the darkness below, then raised his eyes to his brothers. "I've taken enough of your time. Go inside and find yourself some libation and amusement, for I have a pretty angry lady wandering about the lower gardens whom I must find and make atonement to."

Both watched Clinton make his way down the garden steps. Austin threw his arm about Brent's shoulders. "I hear Lady Markham is here, old boy; got her sites set for you, now that Clinton's out of the picture."

Brent turned, awarding Austin with a look that could kill.

Austin laughed. "She might be worth a toss."

"Don't bet on it."

Tiffany stood near the rosebushes, their heady fragrance wafting in the night air. She was unsure what made her angrier, Clinton's deception, his high-handedness, or his brothers. *"Ooooh,"* she cried, thinking about that motley crew. One was worse than the other! How could a family be plagued with more than one rake? No wonder their mother chose to reside in Genoa. The poor woman probably received only pitiful looks from her peers. Well, they were the least of her problems, and she quickly dismissed them from her thoughts.

Her emotions were in a turmoil. She felt guilt over her body's response. She felt hate and loathing for Clinton and what he made her feel. Her face grew hot recalling her reaction to him in the carriage. She was not that foxed to have not known what he was trying to do, she was just unable to stop the delicious, unabandoned feeling he aroused. Tears began to well in her eyes as she acknowledged her lack of resistance, wondering how she could be so weak to succumb to a man's touch, any man's touch, while she loved another.

She broke a rose from its perch, twirling its stem, worrying at her lip. Renewed anger surfaced as she thought what a fool she was, and how he had played her for one. Breaking down her resistance—what resistance? Making her yield to unbearable pleasure, deceiving her with loving words. While all the time what was shattering to her was merely a wager to win for him!

She stamped her foot, then crushed the rose head in her hand, its petals falling like tears to the ground.

"Tell me, Princess, what has angered you, and I shall run it through with my sword." Clinton spoke in mock chivalry.

Spinning around, she cried, "You! 'Tis you!"

"Moi?" he asked innocently.

Tiffany dashed toward him, pummeling his chest, screaming, " 'Tis you, sir; run yourself through so I may gain some measure of satisfaction." He held her wrist in one hand, cupping her face with his other. He saw the tears in her knowing blue eyes. Pulling her up against him gently, he asked softly, "How have I angered you, Princess?"

"You deceived me, played me for a fool."

His questioning look caused her to run on, tears falling softly. "You are a master of deception, sir! You have repeatedly deceived me. At the track, at Chablisienne, and tonight." Her tears fell freely now and her voice broke. "I did not know you were the duke of Chablisienne, nor the duke of Wentworth. I do not want a marriage with either one, but no, you would bind me nevertheless, despite my wishes." She sobbed and choked out, "And you play me for a fool, my lord. You make me . . . forget myself and rav . . . ravish me on the floor of a carriage for a wager!" She pulled forcefully away from him, a blush touching her face. She was grateful for the cloak of darkness. ''You, sir, are a despicable cad!''

Clinton realized now where the true source of her anger lay—the stupid wager. He spoke softly, yet firmly. ''I think, Princess, you accuse me rightfully in deceiving you about my identity. But whether you knew who I was or not, you would not have changed your mind and welcomed my suit. I think, Tiffany, that nothing short of what I've done would have made you mine.''

She stiffened at his referral to her as his. ''I could not have put it better, my lord. You are right. However, it changes naught; the fact is, I don't want you for a husband.''

''You don't have a choice in the matter, Princess. It's been taken out of your hands. As for the carriage ride, innocent that you are, surely you felt the evidence of my desire as well. What happened between you and me is not something staged, something one can control. It's passion, love, pure, unadulterated passion.''

He moved closer, separating the distance between them in two strides. ''Passion not born of a wager, Princess. Hell, I don't need to prove I can win that bet; time speaks for itself.''

He could not miss the narrowing of her eyes or the scorn etched in her words. ''And so I have been informed of your expertise.''

Refusing to be drawn, he changed the course of the conversation. ''I won't apologize for making you forget yourself. I hope my touch makes you forget till you can't remember what it was you forgot.''

His arrogance, his confidence, was too much for her, and she retorted, ''You'll never have that power.''

Tiffany did not miss the challenging smile that lifted the corners of his mouth or gleamed in his eyes. ''One little finger, Princess, is all it takes,'' he said, raising his finger at her.

Again thankful for the night, her face burned with remembrance. "Your arrogance is beyond contempt, my lord. Your touch, I loathe. I cringe at the thought of your touch; even now my skin crawls. 'Tis all your touch does!"

Like a flash he grabbed her, pulling her against him, replying in an awful voice, "Once I told you I am master of the game, and play by my rules; tonight I shall demonstrate that mastery." He captured her mouth with a demanding kiss, parting her lips forcefully beneath his, plunging his tongue into her sweetness, drawing her tongue into his mouth. His hands moved freely over her breast, caressing her nipples to hard peaks, rolling them between his fingers as his mouth worked its magic upon hers.

Tiffany felt as if a bird of prey had swooped down and carried her along the currents of the wind as sharp sensations ran from her breasts to that secret place where the beginnings of an unbearable ache rose to burn. But she struggled to free herself from the pleasurable trap he was setting for her.

Managing to pull her mouth from his, Tiffany gasped, "Stop! You will never be my master!"

As if to disprove her words, he moved his hand up under her skirt, touching the soft inner flesh of her thigh. She moaned from the pleasure and the frustration he was causing her, but she refused to surrender to him. "Let me go!" she begged, tossing her head from side to side.

Clinton's finger hovered above the spot he knew would be moist and warm if he touched it. "No," he whispered, "not until you admit I have the power to give you what you desire." He looked in her eyes, seeing the answer he sought. He held the strings to her passion. He had a powerful tool by which he would win her heart. He heard her groan as his finger teased her and then withdrew. "I have the power to stoke that fire which is burning in the pit of your belly." He moved his hand softly up her thigh, hearing her whimper. "I have the power to quench and release you." He felt her lean against him, and held her steady. His hand moved over the ebony triangle of curls. "Aye, I have that power, the power to cause you to cry my name." He slowly withdrew his hand and gently pushed her from him, holding her steady. "But you loathe my touch."

Her senses reeling, Tiffany stumbled, but quickly her anger steadied her. "You're right. So remember never to touch me again!" She raised her hand to strike him. Clinton quickly caught her wrist in a steel-like vise. His lazy smile was replaced by fury. His gray eyes were icy, hard, and held her own.

Tiffany never saw such menacing fury so tightly leashed. The grip he had on her wrist never wavered.

"Never-misdirect-your-anger-at-me!" Pulling her hard against him, he continued, "For I am not the source, nor will I tolerate it."

His tone was uncompromising. "Do not condemn me for the wanting of you. Condemn yourself for denying your desire. Scream your childish rage, but direct it at yourself, not me! Deny your body's response to my touch, lie to yourself, fight your own will. Do whatever you deem necessary."

He pulled her closer, her breasts crushed against his chest. He said in a voice that brooked no argument, "Know this well; all your denying will not alter the fact you belong to me. You are mine. And above all else, I will have no less than all of you—body and soul and heart." He released her abruptly and with deceptive casualness turned, strolling away, leaving her with his promises.

Chapter Sixteen

England, August 1818

Tiffany gazed up into the sky. Stars, like pinholes in the black curtain of night, twinkled, filling the sky. It is a beautiful night, she thought, cloudless, warm, fragrant. A soft summer breeze carried the night fragrances. She looked down at the empty drive, where amber lights from the flickering lanterns paved its cobbled way for the carriages soon to line it. Liveried footmen, like sentinels, stood awaiting the moment of their appointed task. The whisper of the summer's breeze would soon carry stains of a waltz. She strolled slowly from her balcony into her room.

The manor was silent, save for the occasional sound of a footstep, rustle of a gown, or the soft closing of a door. All preparations, any last-minute detail, had been capably taken care of by Aunt Winnie.

She stole softly to the bouquet of violets Clinton had sent and lifted a delicate flower to inhale its light scent. She smiled thinking a bouquet had arrived every day since she returned to Wentworth. Her mind drifted over the last weeks. She had ridden every day with Clinton over the endless acreage of Wentworth Estates. They had picnicked on the edge of a lovely pond, watching the graceful swans glide across its surface. They had gone fishing in the salmon-stocked rivers. She smiled recalling his look of amazement when she baited her own hook and cast her own line. Her smile widened and a mischievous gleam lit her eyes as she remembered the day. While pursuing a frog, she fell headlong into the river, and when he grabbed her hand to pull her out, she yanked him in.

Placing the flower back in the vase, she realized the past weeks had flown by. Meeting his family at Wentworth, she had been shocked to discover there was another brother, Tristan, and still another she had yet to meet. Tristan had the same uncanny resemblance to his older brothers, possessing the Barencourte smile. His, however, was far more disarming. She liked him—he was carefree, having an adventurous love of life, sailing the high seas. He proved to be as roguish as the others, though his style was more distinct.

Clinton had escorted her to every soirée, ball, and evening given over the past month. Often they were alone, and many times accompanied by one or all of his brothers. Many an evening spent in the Barencourtes' company ended in a card game where she was paired off with either Brent or Tristan. Brent showed her how to calculate the odds, and Tristan showed her how to cheat. Many times it was not until dawn that the games broke up and she, heavy-eyed, was led to her room, sleeping away the day.

Every day something was planned, either a picnic, sailing, or just riding for hours. Each night they attended an affair or spent a quiet evening playing chess or cards. She realized there had been only two occasions when Clinton was called away on business, and to her dismay, she had felt disappointed, even though he had sent one of his brothers to replace him. There was no denying she began to enjoy his company more than she should have. She also realized that he kept her so occupied that all the plans, preparations, and details were made while she was busy. She never uttered a protest, because he kept her too amused to realize it was all happening.

Sighing, she realized nothing was in her control. Clinton had effectively made her ineffective. Nothing had worked out as she had hoped for. He had successfully diverted her attention. She bristled at his high-handedness. Somewhere in the back of her mind, deep in her heart, she hoped Alan or some miracle would intervene, putting a stop to it all. Closing her eyes, she thought, Here I am on the eve of his victory night, the night when officially the world will know I belong to him. A soft knock interrupted her musing.

"Yes?" she murmured.

A maid entered, bobbed a curtsy. "My lady, His Grace has arrived and awaits you in the upper salon."

Tiffany touched the fragile petal of a violet, fingering its velvety texture. "Inform His Grace I will join him momentarily."

"Yes, my lady."

Before the maid left, Tiffany instructed, "Be sure French brandy is available for His Grace." Tiffany was momentarily surprised. She had instinctively seen to his comfort.

"Yes, my lady." The maid curtsied and left, closing the door softly.

Tiffany walked away from the French door into the glow of the candlelit room, pausing before a full-length mirror. She gazed at herself. Her midnight hair was brushed away from her face and ears. Masses of spiral curls, lightly sprinkled with silver dust, cascaded down the bare plane of her back. Turning, she peered over a bare, beguiling shoulder, viewing the waterfall of silver-highlighted curls. She lightly tossed her head, the effect eye-catching—the black tresses glittered as if stardusted. Her eyes glided down the graceful curve of her back; a warm blush touched her cheeks as she saw the expanse of creamy skin exposed by the backless design of the gown. She wondered how she could have allowed the modiste to cut it so. At the time, her thinking was to upset Clinton with the gown, to show him she was not conventional, not the material for a duchess, but the vixen her father accused her of being. Now she had reservations about wearing it. She feared not arousing his anger, but his libido.

Turning, she studied her mirrored image. She wore an elegant French-fashioned gown of pure black silk whose narrow skirt flared out slightly at the hem instead of falling straight to the ankle like the English design. Its cut was exquisite, leaving her back, shoulders, and arms bare. The décolletage was cut daringly, barely concealing the soft beguiling swell of her breasts. Save for the fine silk straps resting off her shoulders, nothing more held up the gown. When she moved, the black silk came alive with the light reflected off the fine silver threads woven through the silk, causing the gown to shimmer.

Studying her face closely, with her hair drawn away, she caught the twinkle of the brilliant diamond teardrops that adorned her small, shell-shaped ears. Long, sooty lashes framed her dazzling sapphire eyes, providing the perfect foil to Tiffany's otherwise dark, sultry beauty.

She felt sinful—wickedly so! Like an evening star, glittering, twinkling, shimmering, against the black curtain of night, she made her way to the door.

Clinton stood at the fireplace, his arm leaning against its mantel, a glass in his hand. A pleased smile lit his face as he lifted the French brandy to his lips. He was inordinately pleased knowing Tiffany knew his preference for the amber liquor and had it delivered to him. Yes, he was certainly making progress! Sipping the brandy and laying the glass atop the mantel, he began to think of the progress he had made.

Over the past weeks he detected a softening, a lowering of her defenses toward him. Although she'd never admit it, she was beginning to enjoy his company. He had forced her to be in his company. His intent? He smiled, smugly. Other than the obvious, that he enjoyed being with her, he did indeed have an ulterior motive. To keep her occupied, so occupied she'd not have the time to interfere with the arrangements.

He had been successful in that quarter, for the weeks flew by without a protest from her, and this evening had arrived. Of course, it was not due to her change of heart, he was not foolish enough to believe that. She had yet to acknowledge the losing battle against the powerful tug of attraction she felt toward him. But he had seen the progress he was making. Often he'd find her regarding him from under lowered lashes, quickly looking away when discovered.

He had also made progress with her desire. A wolfish smile split his face. She didn't pull away from him as quickly, nor stiffen when they accidentally touched a shoulder or brushed a thigh. No, now when he wrapped her in his arms, she responded. She'd deny it, for it was still too soon; Tiffany equated any admission of desire with surrender. Knowing she was prideful, he took care not to injure her pride unnecessarily.

Leaning his back against the mantel, he crossed his arms loosely over his chest. He knew it was not love that caused her response, but passion. The passion he had awakened by his touch. The spark of passion he saw in dazed blue eyes. For now he was content, knowing the spark would flame once he had total possession of her body. And after he released her passion, he would have her love. Right now he was one step closer to his quest—her body would soon be his totally.

The past month had afforded him an almost uninterrupted view of the woman who would soon be his wife. A broad smile crossed his face. She had lived up to his expectations and then some. He had seen all the facets to her he had yet been able to explore fully. She was impetuously reckless, absolutely spontaneous, abandoned, and bewitching. He loved her laughter, her mercurial moods, volatile nature, and vulnerability. She made him whole. She aroused feelings of lust, love, protectiveness, jealousy. God, he could go on and on. He desired her company and was most reluctant to leave her, and only the assurance that soon, very soon, she would be his gave him the willpower. Tonight was evidence their days and nights apart were coming to a close.

Tonight would be hers to rein and lord over all those country bumpkins who had hurt her, laughed at her, made her lonely. Tonight she would shine like a star. He would give her tonight.

The soft closing of the door brought him from his reverie. He looked up; his breath caught in his throat as he watched Tiffany float toward him. She was bewitching—a sultry temptress, an alluring vision of shimmering darkness.

Tiffany stopped a breath away. Clinton's bright, unwavering gaze drank in her beauty. The black silk shimmered with a life of its own, molding to her lush form. Briefly he wondered what held the gown up.

"Princess, you take my breath away."

His voice, his words, deep, sensual, sent a ripple through her. Tiffany took in his handsome visage, the elegant cut of his clothes giving him an aura of understated elegance. His rich black evening coat fit his broad, muscular shoulders to perfection. The black silk waistcoat shot with silver threads tapered to his lean, masculine waist. Long, muscular legs were sheathed in tight pantaloons. His stark white cravat contrasted sharply against his tanned, masculine face. His gray eyes were smoky, seductive, as he looked at her from under heavy lids. Her knees weakened, her heart fluttered, as she beheld his devastating image.

She could hardly lift her voice above a whisper. "You are quite handsome yourself, Your Grace."

Pleased she was as taken with him as he was with her, his voice as soft as a caress, he said, "It's Clinton, Princess; say my name."

"Clinton," she breathed.

Reluctantly he turned from her to the stone mantel, retrieving a long velvet box. Facing her, he opened the box, lifting a sparkling diamond necklace off the satin bed. "I fear my gift too humble for your beauty."

A soft gasp escaped her lips. Tiffany beheld eighteen perfectly cut teardrop diamonds connected by an almost transparent chain of silver filigree. The sparkling stones glittered and winked at her, catching the light of the candles. "It's beautiful," she whispered.

"May I put it on?" Clinton moved behind her, noting for the first time the backless design of the gown. Again, briefly he wondered what held it up. Tiffany faced the mirror that hung above the mantel, watching him.

He lifted the heavy mass of curls at her nape. At his warm touch, shivers ran down her spine. She closed her eyes when his firm, warm lips brushed her nape. His soft kiss caused tingles to run up and down her arms. He fastened the necklace about her neck and drew back.

Tiffany fingered the diamonds at her breast. They lay beneath her collarbone, resting against the beguiling swell of her breasts. The stones glittered and sparkled as if alive.

She caught his eyes in the mirror. He moved up behind her, his hand resting on her shoulder, his fingers splayed down. She swallowed convulsively. He spoke in a silken voice. "Your beauty gives them life." He lifted a stone. "Before they were only stones; now they radiate with your beauty."

Caught in a spell, she allowed herself to be turned in the circle of his arms. She looked into his smoky gray eyes as he spoke. "It was given to my family by Queen Elizabeth I for our loyalty. It was her birthday necklace, eighteen perfectly cut diamonds, a new one to be added each year." His finger touched her earbob. "These are part of the complete set."

All her senses blossomed under his gaze. She was unable to unlock her gaze from his smoldering one. With a flutter of lashes, she received the gentle kiss she knew would come, feeling his lips move softly against hers. When his mouth left hers, she slowly opened her eyes.

"Come, Princess, sit while I pour us some champagne." His hand rode her back, causing her to shiver. A moment passed. Clinton popped the cork of a bottle of champagne, filling two glasses, handing one to Tiffany. They drank in companionable silence, and after he refilled their glasses, he spoke.

"I have been thinking, Tiffany . . ."

"A commendable pastime, my lord. I hope it was not an exercise in futility for you." Tiffany smiled over the rim of her glass.

Clinton smiled at her comment. Pouring more wine into their glasses, he continued, "That I should reconsider your position this evening." Laying his glass down and sitting back in the chair, he watched her. "Tonight was to be my victory celebration. You know, to the victor go the spoils."

Tiffany awarded him with a glare for reminding her of her predicament. "The war is not over, my lord."

"True, Princess, there is still another battle left. However, I have reconsidered your position and decided you are not to be cast in the role of the spoils, but rather the victor! I am aware of what you have suffered in the hands and minds of the vast group of acquaintances who will attend this eve. I will not add to the sins committed against you. Therefore, I concede this night to you. Tonight you are the victor and I the conquered."

Over the rim of her glass of wine, amazement was clearly etched on her face. Tiffany could not believe what she heard. Her the victor, he the conquered! "I don't know what to say . . . Clin . . . Clinton."

Her mind was in a whirl! What caused this sudden change of heart? Why tonight? What had she done to make him cry off? Who cares, she thought, the deed's done. Her heart leaped in elation and yet a sadness crept through. "You . . . you've taken me by surprise."

Clinton poured more of the effervescent wine in her

glass, asking, "Well, Princess, is my surrender accepted?"

"With honor for a most courageous knight." A smile lit her face, reaching from her eyes. She wanted to tell him nice things; if she had not loved another, she could have loved him. A twinge of remorse filled her for this powerful, yet unyielding, man who had tolerated her childish tantrums, cries of hatred, and indifference with humor, and patience. She wanted him to embrace her, kiss her one last time. But she said none of these things, instead replied softly, "I am truly grateful for your change of heart, for putting my feelings above yours, for I know it cost you dearly. I wish there was some way I could repay your sacrifice."

A slow, roguish grin split his face. "Well, now that you mention it. There is something you could do for my wounded pride."

A warning bell went off in her head. She quickly pushed it from her. She had nothing to fear. He had said he conceded. It was only fair and she readily asked, "What might that be?"

"A promise of sorts." A slow, appreciative smile worked its way across his face. His eyes rested on the creation of black silk, and he wondered how that damn gown was held up before he continued. "You are familiar with the old adage 'One hand washes the other'?"

An impish grin lit her eyes. "Or one good turn deserves another?"

"Precisely," he agreed. "I ask only this. You promise me the first and last dance."

Thinking the request harmless enough, she quickly agreed, "I would be honored."

The sounds of carriages lining the drive, the opening and closing of their doors, and the murmur of voices broke the night.

She drained her glass, and Clinton leaned over to refill it. He watched her. She was a natural temptress. Provocative sensuality emanated from her. His mind drifted to another night, soon to come, when her silken body would writhe beneath his in sweet, tormenting ecstasy. To break the course his thoughts traveled, he asked, "The necklace is enhanced by your beauty, Princess."

She fingered the diamonds lightly. "I have never indeed been given such a priceless, beautiful gift." She gazed up at him, a hint of regret in her eyes. "I shall be sorry to part with it."

His brows drew together in a mild frown. "Part with it? It is yours, Princess. My gift to you."

"Oh, it would not be proper . . . as much as I love it. By rights it belongs to your future wife, the duchess."

"By all that's holy, Tiffany, what are you talking about? You are my future wife, my duchess."

A feeling of impending doom shook her. She stood. "But no more."

At his confused expression, she rushed on. "By your own words, that has changed. You conceded the night, the betrothal is no more."

Clinton stood facing her, shaking his head. "I conceded the night, Princess, nothing more."

Tiffany broke into his words. "No, you said you yielded your victory to me."

"Aye. The night, Princess, only this night," he stated emphatically.

A look of stunned disbelief etched her face. "No! All you asked was for the first and last dance, that's all, nothing more!"

Clinton grasped her by the shoulders. "Tiffany, do you honestly believe I would give you up? You are mine. I do not give up what is mine." He drove his point home. "The first and last dance will forever be mine so there is never a doubt with whom you arrived or any question with whom you will leave—the first and last dance is for me."

"You deceived me. You are a villian, my lord," she snapped. "You conceded the night to me!"

"Tonight is yours, Princess, to shine, to conquer the small minds of this broad group of acquaintances, nothing more."

The butler knocked, and Clinton called to him to enter. "Your Grace, Lady Courtland, the guests have arrived." Clinton nodded in acknowledgment and the butler departed.

"Shall we, Princess?" he asked, offering her his arm.

Tiffany paused before accepting his proffered arm, thinking how utterly foolish she had been to believe him. Tonight was hers; well, she thought, it shall be a night he'll never forget. She intended to thoroughly enjoy herself at his expense.

A challenging gleam sparkled in her sapphire eyes, which she raised to him. Tilting her head, accepting his arm, she replied, "By all means, let the night begin."

While they walked to the door, Tiffany said, " 'Tis a shame you forfeited your night, my lord."

Clinton stopped, causing Tiffany to look up at him. His gray eyes gleamed and his voice held promise when he spoke. "Do not distress yourself. I forfeit this night for another soon to come to enjoy my spoils."

Two liveried footmen pushed open the double oak doors wide. Clinton and Tiffany entered the ballroom, standing beneath the amber glow of a six-tier chandelier. Hundreds of hand-dipped tapers burned brightly in golden sconces decorating the silk-hung walls.

The braided footman announced, "The duke of Wentworth, The duke of Chablisienne, Clinton Claremont Barencourte, and Lady Tiffany Elizabeth Courtland."

A collective hush fell over the room when the guests viewed the handsome couple. Sounds of appreciation filled the air when Clinton bowed to his lady, presenting her to them. The musicians picked up their cue and the sound of a hundred violins filled the air as the strained first notes of a waltz began.

Enthusiastic applause was heard as Clinton, taking the

lead, took Tiffany into his arms, whisking her across the floor. *Ooohs* and *aahs* were heard from the room when the black silk came alive as the silver threads caught the candle glow and her silver-dusted curls glittered with the swaying movement of the waltz. The diamonds shone brilliantly, and the candlelight cast a peachy hue to her skin. Admiring whispers and approving nods were exchanged among the guests.

Clinton waltzed her over and across the ballroom in grand sweeping, graceful circles, showing her off to the crowd. His eyes glided over her flushed face and wandered to the black silk gown the color which heightened the translucence of her bare neck and shoulders. "Princess, whatever holds that gown up?"

Tiffany, as always when she danced with him, was lost, for he danced divinely. Her eyes glittered more brilliantly than any sapphire. Tilting her head back as he swept her into another circle, she smiled impishly and replied breathlessly, "That is something, my lord, you'll never know."

Clinton chuckled, a pleasant rumbling sound, causing shivers of anticipation to course down her spine. "I wouldn't bet on it."

The final strains of the waltz found the couple surrounded by guests who applauded and whispered their congratulations. Tiffany, flushed and breathless, found her hand seized by Austin, and again she was brought to the floor to be swept into another waltz.

Clinton stood to the sidelines surrounded by acquaintances and friends engaging in small talk. His possessive, appreciative gaze never wavering from the dazzling figure in black silk.

"You know, if he wasn't my brother, I'd fight him for you," Austin teased in a tone filled with unmistakable promise.

"You are as incorrigible as he!" She awarded him with

a dazzling smile. "Is this some condition which runs in your family lineage?"

"Most assuredly, sweetheart, from the eldest to the youngest. The strain improves each generation." The Barencourte smile lit his face, making her feel like warmed honey.

"Rakes! All of you!" she bantered good-naturedly.

"We prefer 'connoisseurs' of women, sweetheart."

"You're impossible," she laughed. As he whirled her toward the terrace doors, his eye wandered to her gown. "Trust me, sweetheart, if you weren't Clinton's, I'd show you how impossible I can be." His eyes lingered at the bodice of her gown, making Tiffany grateful the music had ended.

Leading her back to Clinton, Austin paused, turning her to him. "Tell me, Tiffany, however does your gown remain up?"

Raising a fine brow and smiling at his inquiring look, she teased, "Wouldn't you just love to know." Before he could reply, another pressed her and she was again led to the floor.

Champagne flowed freely, as did wine. An elaborate, sumptuous buffet of English and French cuisine graced the table. An enormous dessert table, laden with every conceivable delectable confection, lay alongside the buffet. Musicians from two orchestras played endlessly, and the boisterous voices and smiling faces of the guests attested to the evening's success.

If the evening was a success, Tiffany was the star. She had conquered, as Clinton had predicted, the small minds of this broad group of acquaintances. The very people who had sneered and poked fun at the antics of a young girl. The very people who shunned her, isolated her, separated her, making her lonely and alone to face the world. These very people now whisked her from partner to partner across the dance floor, mesmerized by the spirit they once turned their snooty noses up at.

Girlhood acquaintances stood jealously on the sidelines marveling at the girl who left England in disgrace and returned betrothed to a much-sought-after duke. Any one of them would have given her right arm and leg to have made such an alliance with the handsome, dashing duke of Wentworth.

Hours later, Tiffany had managed to consume more champagne than she ever remembered. She had danced more dances than her feet could stand and had flirted outrageously with all. She smiled and laughed endlessly with the guests. She had observed Clinton watching her from the sidelines. He showed no signs that her outrageous behavior was upsetting him. On the contrary, he smiled a smile that warmed her to the core. Stopping a passing servant, she procured another glass of champagne and lifted the glass to her lips. Over the rim she caught Clinton's gaze. His gray eyes closed the distance separating them. He raised a winged brow at her inquiringly. Feeling the effects of the inordinate amount of champagne she'd consumed, she defiantly raised her glass to him in mock tribute and downed its contents.

He offered her a sudden arresting smile that sent her pulse racing. A slight frown appeared on her face, because she didn't understand his reaction or hers. Brent's appearance caused her to leave her ponderings.

"Come, little one. Dance with me and I shall protect you from the masses that pursue."

Laughing at his chivalry, she said, "Really? And who will protect me from you?"

He awarded her with an amused smile. "Over yonder, little one, stands the man who would protect you from me." Looking over Brent's shoulder, she caught sight of smoky grays smiling at her.

Meeting Brent's smile and the hand that he offered, she moved with him across the dance floor.

Coquettishly she asked, "Do I really need protection

from you, Brent? Of all the brothers, you seem most the gentleman."

"Had you not been claimed by blood, little one, I assure you, protection you would need. As to being a gentleman, never let appearances deceive you. Though my methods be different, the result would be the same."

The music ended and Tristan appeared by their side to claim the next set. As he swung around the floor, his gaze kept drifting to the bodice of her gown. Tiffany became uneasy and retorted, "Are you quite satisfied, Tristan?" Tristan awarded her with an exceptionally disarming smile, causing her to loose her anger. "You are a rake, Tristan."

"I prefer 'master of seduction', love." He whisked her about, taking care to pass Clinton and flash him a mischievous grin. "You know, love, had not older brother claimed you, I would have abducted you and sailed away on the *Wanderlust.*"

"Sounds like honor among thieves to me, Tristan."

"I guess you could say that, love." The music ended and Tristan detained Tiffany a moment. "Love, I would know the name of the modiste who fashioned your gown."

A puzzled look crossed her face. "Whatever for?"

Clinton's voice intruded. "To know how the gown remains up and win the wager." He smiled and turned to Tristan. "Is that not so, brother?"

"Well, to be honest, yes. Perhaps, Clinton, you know?" A twinkle lit Tristan's hazel eyes.

Clinton's eyes drifted to Tiffany's gown, then rose to hold hers with a compelling look as he said, "Let's say I have a theory, Tristan." Tiffany was caught in the spell his gray eyes wove and the promise in his reply, "Which I plan to put to the test this eve." Turning back to Tristan, he said, "Consider your wager as good as won." Tristan gave his leave.

Clinton took Tiffany's arm, asking softly, "Have you eaten anything, Princess?" as he led her to the long dessert table. He chose an orange section glazed in deep chocolate and brought it up to her mouth. Tiffany looked at his fingers that temptingly held the fare. She raised her eyes to find him watching her. His eyes, compelling, magnetic, caused her to feel a shiver of pleasure. With her eyes locked to his, she opened her mouth, closing it over the sweet, succulent orange.

Clinton watched her nibble on the orange, her mouth moist with the sweet juice that threatened to trickle from the corners. Gently he caught the liquid with his finger, bringing it to his mouth, licking the sticky sweetness from it. Tiffany was mesmerized by him and innocently glided the tip of her tongue over her bottom lip. A vaguely sensual light seemed to pass between them. The smoldering flame she saw in his eyes made her aware of the delicious tingling sensation spreading through her. Clinton was the first to break the eye contact when hearing his name, and once again he handed Tiffany over to another, who whirled her about the floor as he watched her from the sidelines.

Winifred stood near Evette, watching Clinton. She smiled thinking there was no denying the possessive gaze, the gleam of desire, the sparkle of love emanating from the gray eyes that never wavered from the exquisite black silk figure. Walking to him, she asked, softly, "She is lovely, isn't she?"

Without averting his gaze, he responded easily, "Decidedly so, madam." There was no mistaking the pride in those few words, and Winifred smiled. They silently watched Tiffany float over the dance floor, her laughter music in the room.

"You love her, don't you?"

"Above all else," he replied softly.

Winifred smiled softly, knowing in spite of all Tiffany's objections to this marriage, it was indeed the best thing for her, for she would be married to a man whose life would be *her,* his every breath *hers,* a man who wanted *her* above all other things.

"You will take care with her."

Clinton turned to regard Winifred. Smiling, he asked softly, "Have you any doubt?"

She answered with a smile, then left him to his stargazing.

The beginnings of the strains of a last waltz found Tiffany floating dreamily into Clinton's arms, dancing the last dance with him. She felt an unexplainable joy surge through her veins and she yielded to the temptation to truly enjoy the feel of his arms around her as he masterfully waltzed them across the floor.

Tiffany felt as if she were on clouds, her head light and her body tingling with his touch. Clinton gazed down into her star-dazed eyes thinking she looked provocatively lush and soft. He smiled softly thinking how malleable she was—thanks to the champagne! He waltzed them out onto the terrace under the starlit sky; Tiffany leaned her head back, her long, graceful neck arched, the swell of her breasts pressed close to his chest, as she looked at the star-spattered sky.

"Oh, it is so beautiful, Clinton!" she breathed, and he whirled her in a circle. "I wish the night would never end." She giggled at the sound of her slurred words.

Looking up at him, an impish gleam lighting her eyes, she asked, "Would you grant me any wish, Clinton?"

"If it is in my power. Save one, of course," he added in a husky voice.

A twinkle of starlight caught her eyes as she glanced at him, her vision blurry. "I wish I could ride to the bluff to watch the sun rise."

"So you shall, Princess," he whispered.

The final notes of the waltz put the night to an end. The guests departed, appetites and curiosity satisfied. The manor was again silent, the cobbled drive no longer lined with carriages, its lights extinguished, the footmen abed, and the soft summer breeze a whisper only carrying the night's fragrances.

Clinton looked down at Tiffany's face as he guided the stallion over the uneven terrain in the darkness. God, he thought she looked lovelier than ever.

Tiffany leaned her head against his strong shoulder, feeling the crisp mat of hair exposed by his open shirt against the soft skin of her back. She snuggled against it, feeling its hard muscle flex as he maneuvered the horse. Clinton tightened his arm about her waist, drawing her closer to him as the stallion negotiated the downward slope. A shiver of delight coursed through her. She was aware of his long, muscular legs when he clasped her waist, drawing her closer between them. She felt his legs tighten about the horse's flanks, urging the mount into a gallop, blowing her gown up, exposing her long, shapely legs. She laughed aloud as they galloped wildly through the night.

Resting his chin atop her head, Clinton inhaled the sweet fragrance of violets and smiled when she laughed in child-like abandonment. The pressure of her derriere against his loins and the inordinate amount of leg exposed ignited his desire, which coursed through his veins like a wildfire. He wondered at his madness in having her ride with him, knowing she'd entice his already suppressed desire.

Tiffany turned her face up to him, and he smiled down at the delicate features, seeing in them her childlike innocence and womanlike sensuality. He felt a sweet aching in the region of his heart and a tormenting tightening in his groin.

The stallion broke through the woods into the clearing. He brought the horse to a halt, dismounting, and turned, lifting her off. When her slippered feet touched the ground, she swayed forward. Clinton caught her about the waist, steadying her. Giggling, she brought her hand to her mouth and then clutched at his shoulders to regain her balance. She turned to walk toward the bluff and stumbled. She reached down, removing her slipper, tossing it aside; the other quickly followed.

She felt the cool night air tinged with the salty tang of the sea against her face. She began to turn in circles, gazing up at the stars. "Oh, Clinton, how beautiful it is." An overwhelming sense of vertigo came over her. She stopped. Clinton moved toward her. The roar of that pounding surf against the coast below drew her to the headland, causing Clinton to call out, "Take a care, Tiffany." The cool air cleared her mind from the effects of the champagne. Elation was overcome by a sense of melancholy.

Speaking above the roar of the surf, she said, "You need not fear, I have come here all my life and know the way of the bluff." Memories assailed her mind and senses and she said aloud, "I would sneak here, like a thief in the night, away from the manor and ride Xanadu to our magical kingdom to watch the dawning. Each breaking morn, I envisioned, was like the very first morn of time. I would hear the cry of the gulls in praise to the new day and I would stand on this spot waiting for the first gray lights to streak the horizon. I felt I was on the edge of the world, embraced by the heavens." She turned, facing him. The sound of the waves crashing against the coast roared in her ears. She said sadly, "This place offered me refuge, gave me hope."

She paused and then softly said, "It gave me everything and asked nothing in return." She look up at him, tears burning the back of her eyes. "But now I see it was foolishness on my part. All my dreams and hopes dashed like the waves against the rocks."

Clinton stood silent; the image of a lonely, spirited girl riding her mighty stallion to her magical kingdom, weaving her dreams from the threads of her unanswered needs, tugged at his heart. He silently cursed those who tried to batter her spirit and pride. He admired her undying, unyielding spirit, refusing to be broken, keeping her whole, for him. He moved closer to her, separating the distance, wanting to embrace her in the protective circle of his arms and assure her all her dreams would come true, for he would spend the rest of his life in that quest.

She gazed up at Clinton, blinking back tears that threatened to spill. Her voice soft but quivering with unshed tears, she said, "Above all else, I dreamed of love. A love I yearn for, but now—" broken dreams, bittersweet memories, flooded her mind, and her tears fell "—will never have." Clinton touched her shoulder gently, drawing her face to his. She averted her eyes, not wanting him to see the tears.

He spoke softly as he lifted her chin with the tips of his fingers. "I love you, Tiffany." She shook her head, not wanting to hear his words. He was not to be daunted and again replied, "I love you, Tiffany, above all else." He drew her into the shelter of his arms.

Memories haunted her and she turned up a tear-streaked face to him. "You . . . don't understand . . . I love another. I always will."

"I am not above doing anything to insure your love. I am not above making up for the love you're denying you'll ever feel for me. This is not a fight I will lose."

Tiffany pulled from him, fresh tears falling. "You refuse to understand. I saw my future as something vivid, and now I view it as something dark and dull. Oh, sir, if winning is what you want, then you have won the prize! But it is nothing more than an empty shell." She wiped her tears with the back of her hand, and her voice broke with sorrow and anger. "My body may be yours to possess, to own, but my heart, my soul, they are mine to give. They can't be bought or possessed."

Clinton ran his fingers through his hair. Shaking his head, he stated, "I once told you very few things are not changeable. Your future life with me is not."

"The past is my future. When you kiss me, embrace me, make a woman of me, I will be yearning for another, seeing another in your stead!'' She turned from him only to be brought up hard against him. Gray eyes, hard and challenging, held hers before strong arms scooped her up, carrying her to the copse of trees.

''Will you now, Princess? Your body knows differently.''

Tiffany struggled impotently against his strength, and when he laid her down, she sought to escape but found him pressing her to the ground. Before his mouth captured hers, he said, ''Deny me.''

His lips moved urgently over hers, down her slender throat, kissing the soft base of her neck. His lips, firm and warm, slid to the soft, swelling flesh that rose temptingly above her gown while his hands traveled over her, feeling her quiver. ''Deny me,'' he challenged. With the skill born of practice, his fingers found and released the tiny buttons of the thin silk straps. Sliding the gown down to her hips, exposing the rich bounty of her breast and belly, his fingers and hands tantalized her.

Nothing mattered to Clinton save that she respond to his touch. His male pride demanded it, his passionate nature desired it. He was a man set afire to erase her image of another while in his arms, erase her vision of a dull, muted life.

Tiffany's mind screamed, *No, no,* but her flesh was weak as it always was with him, and she yielded to the sweet agony of his touch and, bringing her arms about his neck, pressed her taut young body against his.

''Can you keep the past alive?'' he whispered hoarsely as his mouth covered a tempting nipple. Tiffany groaned. Any vestige of control Clinton had was waning, and his tongue swirled over the throbbing crest while his hand cupped the satin softness of her breast. He raised his head and held her gaze as his fingers played, teasing her aching nipple.

Clinton felt the ache in his loins, the stirring of his blood, call to his male needs. Holding himself in check, he raised himself from her. He heard her cry of disappointment.

Ripping off his shirt in an almost angry motion, exposing a powerfully muscled chest, he lowered himself against her soft breasts, challenging, "Deny me." Bracing himself on his forearms, he moved his hair-roughened chest erotically back and forth against her taut nipples.

Tiffany moaned in sweet, aching passion, arching her back, bringing her closer to his chest. Setting her flesh aflame, he pulled back from her aching form.

"Look at me, Tiffany." he commanded huskily.

Raising heavy-lidded eyes, dazed with passion, she gazed into smoldering gray eyes burning with desire.

"Your future lies with me. I would give you a taste of your future." Still holding her eyes with his, he flitted his fingers across her ribs and belly, down to the dark triangle of curls.

Helpless under his expertise, Tiffany yielded to his touch, her belly quivering, her limbs having gone limp. She breathed heavily and gasped when his fingers played havoc with her senses. She moaned deep from her throat and gasped when he lowered his head and his tongue charted a course from her breast slowly down her belly. Curling her hands about his shoulders, trying to stop his descent, she tossed her head, whimpering, "No, no," and then cried aloud when his tongue delved into the ebony curls. She shuddered, tossing her head wildly, and protested weakly as his tongue sought and fondled the tender of tenderest spots of her womanhood. Not able to bear it if he stopped, she closed her hands over his shoulders, pressing him on, bringing him closer.

Clinton slid his arms beneath her buttocks, delving deeper into her feminine warmth, feeling her tense and arch against his mouth. He heard her soft, breathless cry, "Clinton," as he drank deeply of her flowing passion. Moving up over her, seeing her in the throes of passion, watching her pleasure wash over her face, he drew her shuddering form close within the circle of his arms.

The first streaks of gray appeared over the horizon as a new morn broke. Looking down into tear-filled eyes, he spoke, his deep voice simmering with barely checked passion. ''You cannot deny your body. And where your body takes you, soon your heart will follow. Either by your choice or mine, all of you will come to me, for I am your future.''

Chapter Seventeen

Tiffany leaned her head against the cool pane of glass, closing her eyes against the afternoon sun that reflected off it. Vivid images appeared beneath her closed lids of her writhing in the throes of passion. She opened her eyes hoping to erase the images, shutting them from her mind. Even though it had been two weeks since the episode on the bluff, she could not shake from her mind the feelings she had experienced. Just thinking of it brought a weakness to her knees, a tightening in the pit of her belly.

Turning from her window, Tiffany walked to her bed, flinging herself upon it. When she closed her eyes, the images reappeared, along with an ache between her thighs. Her hand moved down, traveling over the soft rise of her breast to a taut nipple which rose proudly under her touch. Her mind and hand moved in memory of the night past, charting the same path till her hand lay between her legs. She sat up quickly, aghast at herself, the weakness of her body and betrayal of her mind. Pounding her pillow in frustration, she cried out, ''What is he doing to me? Am I so wanton, the mere thought of him causes my body to respond? Oh! I may not be a whore, but surely I have the soul of one.'' Shame flared up to stain her cheeks.

Drawing her knees up, wrapping her arms about them, she thought of Alan. The thought cooled her body and senses. She wondered, Where are you, Alan? If ever I need you, it is now. Resting her chin upon her raised knees, she closed her eyes, trying to bring his image into play. Her mind began to reconstruct his visage, warm brown eyes, sandy hair streaked with gold, his mouth full, and his smile—ah—his devastating smile. *No,* her mind screamed, her eyes flying open. Alan's mouth was not full, and his smile, well, he had a sincere, soft smile, not that arrogant, mocking smile Clinton possessed! Resettling herself, she concentrated and brought up Alan's image; a soft smile crossed her face, which was quickly replaced by a grimace as brown eyes turned to smoky gray, sandy hair changed to coffee brown, and the warm smile altered to a devastating grin. Jumping off the bed, crying, "No! No! No!" she spun in circles trying to push his image from her. "He plagues me even when he's not about!" Shaking her head in frustration, she refused to concede to the power he had over her.

Since the episode on the bluff, Tiffany had not seen Clinton and was glad of it, for she felt she could never face him again after that encounter. She had refused the companionship of his brothers in his absence, fearing one glance at her face would tell all. "I hope he stays in London forever," she cried, running to the window, looking out, seeing the Wentworth coaches lining the drive, being loaded with her trunks. She turned away, refusing to believe tonight she would be permanently ensconced within the walls of Wentworth.

She sat on the edge of her bed hearing the noises that filled the house. The hustle and bustle of packing. Aunt Winnie, who had been up since the crack of dawn, could be heard giving orders to the servants. Tiffany could not believe in two days she'd be married. She shook her head in refusal, feeling despair, feeling a need to escape her fate. She needed to be away from here, away from anything remotely connected to Clinton. Jumping up, throwing off her wrapper, she donned a pair of breeches and a lawn shirt.

Running barefoot past the busy servants and Aunt Winnie, she flew down the steps without a word. She pulled open the front door, nearly knocking down Godfrey, and ran out of the house, ignoring her aunt's voice calling, "Tiffany, where are you going?"

Tiffany ran to the stables, startling Jimmie with her abrupt entrance and curtly informing him to bring her mount. Desperate to be gone, she mounted Touche bareback and kicked her into a wild gallop. She pushed Touche mercilessly as if the demons of hell were in pursuit, their jaws snapping at her heels.

She rode with no destination in mind other than to escape. The meadows and fields were filled with images of gray eyes, the breeze lifted with mocking laughter, his essence was all around her. Tears fell and she cried to the wind, "There is no place he has not touched, he has not been!" All memories of old were erased, replaced by clear, sharp images of him. She pushed Touche faster, running from his consuming presence, escaping from her fate, her future.

"I swear I'll never make another pledge to Clinton. Not when it involves Tiffany!" Tristan remarked angrily, shifting uneasily in his saddle.

Rory, the youngest Barencourte, smiled crookedly, observing his sibling's discomfort, and taunted lazily, "Prefer the rolling decks to hours in the saddle, Tristan?"

Rory had just returned to England, having gotten word of his brother's marriage. He lived a wild and adventurous life in America and was undaunted by the hours they had been in the saddle looking for the errant future sister-in-law.

Tristan glared at Rory as he pulled his horse abreast and retorted, "I prefer hours in a saddle more tender than this one I now ride. Perhaps when this deed is done, I shall find some accommodating wench and ride all night long."

Rory laughed and Tristan soon joined him in male conspiracy over the evening's possibilities. Pulling a cigar from his pocket, lighting it, Rory blew a curl of smoke out. The Barencourte stamp was clearly etched in the arrogant smile and silvery eyes. Rory was perhaps the wildest of the brothers, the most unconventional, having preferred to settle in America, where he led a notorious life of adventure. Like his brothers, he was broad of shoulder and of equal height, cutting a fine figure of a man. He was perhaps more lean and lithe, mostly due to his rigorous living. His features were ruggedly handsome and his hair bore streaks of gold in the coffee brown hue.

Pulling his foot from the stirrup, he drew his leg up across the saddle and rested his arms on it, casually scanning the landscape, smoking his cigar. He had his own thoughts regarding women. They were necessary, having their place, but at this stage in his life, they had only one function, which he used frequently—to ease his needs. Other than that, women were nothing but a troublesome bit of baggage.

"You know, Tristan, I don't envy Clinton having to marry and beget heirs and fulfill his responsibility." Pulling hard on his cigar, he continued, disgust edged in his impatient tone, "Why the hell is this simpering miss out gallivanting across the countryside instead of doing woman things!"

Tristan, who was listening with half an ear, intent on shifting and trying to find a comfortable spot in his saddle, stopped and raised a brow at Rory's words. "Trust me, Rory, Tiffany is anything but a simpering miss. She is not, as you say, 'gallivanting across the countryside' on a Sunday ride. She is attempting to escape in order to avoid the marriage."

Rory raised a questioning brow, giving Tristan a look of smug disbelief. Rory thought it impossible any woman would not want to marry a Barencourte, not when their wealth and good looks were widely known. "So you say, Tristan. I happen to think differently. No doubt we'll find her unseated and dallying about picking flowers."

Tristan shook his head, thinking, She's more likely to have been kidnapped by a marauding band of gypsies before we'd find her unseated. He deigned not to express his thoughts to Rory, figuring he was in for a surprise.

"What do you make of that over yonder?" Rory pointed to the crest of a hill on Wentworth land where a rider was seen galloping across, raven tresses flying out behind her.

Tristan looked. "It's her."

Her decision to escape was merely a conviction, for Tiffany had no plan. Catching a movement in the corner of her eye, she saw two riders a good distance from her. She was unable to discern their features, but it mattered not—these were no friends, only foes. One waved at her as if beckoning. She whirled her mount around and fled down the hill away from them. "I figured she'd do that. All I want is to soak in a hot tub and improve my riding skills on a different mount," Tristan complained. He had hoped she would come willingly. Why he thought she might, he had no idea.

Taking a last puff of his cigar and tossing it on the ground, Rory turned to Tristan. "You follow her and head her toward the wall. She'll not jump it. I'll come in from her left flank and we'll have her cornered."

With a sigh, Tristan replied, "If you say so," and nudged his mount after her, his muscles protesting loudly. He muttered under his breath, "Oh, she'll jump it, all right, and anything else in her path."

Rory kicked his horse into a gallop, disgusted by Tiffany's childish antics. He leaned low on his mount's neck, avoiding the low limbs of the trees, thinking when one caught his shoulder, I certainly do not need this.

Tiffany gazed over her shoulder, seeing the lone horseman approaching. Briefly she wondered where the other was but dismissed him from her mind, realizing she had to veer to the meadow in order to gain more distance from the one in pursuit.

Looking forward, she saw, about five hundred yards ahead, a five-foot stone wall which ran the length of the field in front of her. She had no other choice but to jump it or go through the woods. She dismissed the woods, for it would take up valuable time. Knowing her mount would have to be collected, she slowed down to a canter.

Rory smiled, thinking his strategy infallible. His smile widened as he noted she slowed her mount as it approached the wall. He dashed out from the woods, and from Tiffany's look of surprise, he thought the game up. Tiffany did not recognize the rider. Fear coursed through her, but she kept a cool head, keeping Touche collected and reined toward the wall. Leaning forward, she felt the surging power of the hindquarters gathering and sailed clearly over the wall, landing soundly and galloping away.

The smug look of satisfaction Rory wore quickly turned to surprise, then anger, as he watched her sail over a wall few riders would have ever attempted and executed as perfectly.

"Oh, we'll just corner her. She'll never jump the—" Tristan mimicked. Rory leveled an angry gaze at Tristan, who threw his head back, laughing heartily.

It was a matter of pride—injured pride—that caused Rory to spur his mount forward and over the wall after her. Catching sight of his quarry, he noted he had underestimated her ability and courage. The thrill of the chase began to surface in him as he shadowed her every move. A glint of admiration lit his silvery eyes, watching her expertly ride. He had come abreast of her, for his mount was fresh, not winded as hers. He came up to her right in an attempt to grab the bridle.

Tiffany was fearful, and survival caused her to act desperately. Instead of pulling up or to her left, she headed toward him as if to collide. Rory, fearful she would be injured, was forced to pull up and watched Tiffany gallop ahead. Rory pursued her using every safe means available to him, but her riding skills were superior and she kept a level head.

The chase may well have gone on testing the riders and their mounts save for Touche's untimely stumble. Rory took advantage; he leaned over and, with one strong arm, reached out, snaking Tiffany about the waist, tossing her facedown across his saddle. He continued at breakneck speed toward his destination.

After recovering the breath knocked from her, Tiffany took note and exception to the ignoble position she found herself in and began to struggle, flinging her arms, trying to unseat the rider. Rory used his weight to offset her attempts. He looked down at his captive, her britches molded tightly to her sweet, rounded derriere, which temptingly rose. He smiled appreciatively, commending Clinton on his good taste, if not sense, in choosing women. As her struggles increased and her derriere rose, he could not suppress the wicked grin or raised hand which smacked her bottom soundly. His smile widened at her screech of outrage. When he drew his horse to a halt, Tiffany, in her haste to be free, fell unceremoniously onto her derriere. Red was the color she saw. Pushing her locks from her face, she came quickly to her feet, arms outstretched, nails bared at the stranger who stood negligently against his mount, an arrogant smile etched across his face. Familiar silvery eyes regarded her, and strong hands grabbed at her wrists. His eyes slowly traveled from her disheveled raven tresses to the rapid rise and fall of her breast, resting on the soft swell exposed from her open shirt, down long, shapely breech-clad legs to her dusty bare feet and back up to hold the stormy blue eyes glaring daggers at him.

"Your skills as a rider are commendable. I only hope you prove a well-spirited and satisfying mount for my brother."

Like a red flash, Tiffany bent her head, biting his hand. If Rory was surprised she bit him, he was stunned when her palm cracked solidly against his cheek.

He moved like lightning, grabbing her wrist. "Why you little . . ."

"Rory!" A silken thread of warning etched the deep, mellow baritone voice that broke through the red haze surrounding Tiffany and Rory, dissipating it.

Clinton approached them. Seeing Rory release Tiffany, he smiled and replied confidently to Rory, "I think with a little instruction, Tiffany will prove to be a most satisfying mount." He looked down at her and added meaningfully, "However, I have no aversion to be ridden on occasion." Riding his hand on the small of her back, he turned her to face Rory. He felt the stiffening of her spine and the anger course through her. "Tiffany, I would have you make the formal acquaintance of the youngest Barencourte, Rory."

Rory smiled. He bowed mockingly. "My lady, the pleasure is all mine." He reached for her hand to place a kiss upon it, but Tiffany snatched it, spinning to face Clinton.

Hands on her hips, her breast rising and falling with each agitated breath she took, she spat, "I wish to be escorted home, immediately!"

"Ah, Princess, but you are home. A bit late and somewhat unorthodox, but nevertheless, home."

Tristan, who had seen the whole of it, sat astride his mount. He bellowed aloud, causing all to turn to him. "Welcome home, Clinton! We have delivered your maiden." Wishing to salt Rory's wounded pride, he added, "No easy task. Why, had not her mare stumbled, Rory would never have caught her." Turning to Tiffany, he tipped his head in tribute. "My hat to you, madam. Your riding is only outdone by an excellent right uppercut."

Rory seethed with anger over Tristan's taunting. Tiffany seethed with anger at her near escape. And Clinton, aware of the turmoil of emotions, diffused the explosive situation. Whispering to Tiffany, "There is a warm bath, love, awaiting you. Come," he directed her away, heading toward the house. Casually over his shoulder he called to his brothers, "Suggest you cancel any plans for this evening. Mother is expecting you to dine at eight."

Tristan watched them depart with one eye closed and the other one aimed on the provocative sway of Tiffany's hips. Turning to Rory, who also watched, he asked, smugly, "Well, tell me, little brother. What do you think of our little sister now? Let's see, what was it you said?" A finger was pressed against his lips in mock thought. Rory narrowed his eyes at Tristan and began walking alongside him. Tristan was relentless. "Oh, yes, I remember now, a simpering miss, unseated and dallying about picking flowers."

Rory, who was walking at a slow pace to accommodate Tristan's pained gait, smiled snidely. "I think, Tristan, you'll not be riding anything more strenuous than your hand this eve." With that, he picked up his pace, leaving a laughing Tristan in his wake.

Tiffany was silent as Clinton led her to the front of the manor. "Did you miss me, Princess? I do apologize for leaving you, but business called me away."

"Hardly." Tiffany replied coolly.

He smiled softly, knowing in his absence she had erected her wall against him. "You know, Princess, they say distance lends enchantment."

"Then perhaps your enchantment should be distanced."

Clinton was about to respond but noticed Tiffany had stopped at the golden doors before them.

Tiffany looked at the doors, which loomed large and threatening. Knowing when she crossed through their portals, her fate would be sealed, her future settled, she hesitated.

Clinton, as if reading her mind, said gently, reassuringly, "It will not be bad, Tiffany. It is inevitable." Lifting her chin with the tips of his fingers, he turned her face to him, seeing her fear, her insecurity, her vulnerability. He sought to assure her, to make her feel safe. "When you exit these doors, you will be the same—only a woman."

Wishing she could believe him, wanting to believe him with all her heart, but unable to overcome the nagging fear, she replied softly, "Nothing will ever be the same."

"Mademoiselle! It ees getting late, *non?* His Grace is most impatient." Reluctantly Tiffany rose from the sunken tub, which Germane had likened to a small pond, not wanting to leave its safe haven. She had stretched full length in the luxurious tub made of white and blue tile. She marveled at how the temperature was kept constant, preventing the water from cooling.

"Mademoiselle!" Germane dashed into the bathing chamber. "After this afternoon, I do not think you wish to push His Grace further with your tardiness." Tiffany meekly nodded, allowing her maid to dry and powder her. Tiffany followed Germane and sat at her dressing table, remembering her brief reprimand from Aunt Winnie, who likened her behavior to that of a child in swaddling.

Absently she gazed about her room thinking at least her lifelong prison was decorated much to her liking, reaching for a bonbon, which she quickly dropped when Germane scolded, "*Non,* mademoiselle! You will spoil your dinner!" Placidly Tiffany removed her hand from the plate, ignoring the rumbling of her stomach.

"Does Mademoiselle like thees?"

Tiffany looked. Held in Germane's capable hands was a sapphire blue gown whose skirt was edged in blue lace and satin ribbons, which were caught up with bunches of rosebuds.

Shaking her head, Tiffany replied softly, "No, I never cared for the gown. Choose another."

"But, mademoiselle! I kept only three gowns, and the other two are not appropriate."

"Did my trunks not arrive?" At Germane's affirmative nod, Tiffany asked, "Well, are my gowns unpacked?" Again Germane nodded. "Then choose another."

When her maid did not do her bidding, Tiffany asked sharply, "Well, Germane, if my gowns are unpacked, what is the problem?"

"They are in your other rooms."

A slight furrow appeared on Tiffany's brow. "What other rooms?"

"The rooms in the East Wing, mademoiselle!"

"Well, then, silly, go to those rooms and get my pink velvet-and-satin gown." Tiffany leaned down, smoothing a silk stocking. Looking up, she saw Germane standing before her, wringing her hands nervously.

"Heavens, Germane. What is it? You're so concerned over my tardiness and you stand there. Go fetch my gown."

"I . . . I cannot."

"Why ever not?" queried Tiffany, sitting straight up.

"Because . . . His . . . er, His Grace is changing and it would not be proper for me to go to his apartments. I would be most embarrassed."

The heavy, sooty lashes that shadowed her cheeks flew up. The shock of understanding hit Tiffany full force. Tiffany stood up, shrugging into her white robe. The meek, mild woman had transformed into a determined, angry one. Walking with purposeful strides to the door, opening it, she turned to Germane. Tossing her head in a defiant manner, she replied with conviction, "We will have this situation rectified immediately."

With purpose in mind and all the self-righteous indignation behind her conviction, Tiffany charged down the elaborately decorated hallways to the East Wing. Stopping a passing maid to inquire directions to Clinton's rooms,

Tiffany proceeded, unaware of the stunned expression on the maid's face.

Reaching the door, Tiffany raised her hand, knocking. For a brief moment a surge of excitement coursed through her. The door was promptly opened by Mortimer. The staid and proper valet quickly opened and closed his eyes in a flash seeing Tiffany dressed in a robe standing at the threshold. "My Lady!" he cried in a surprised voice.

Clinton, on hearing his normally proper valet cry out, walked in from the terrace. He smiled as his eyes beheld Tiffany, clothed only in a sheer silk wrapper which clung lovingly to her tall, lush form, outlining and leaving very little to the imagination of what charms lay beneath its silken shroud.

Tiffany had given no thought to her state of dress until now, seeing Clinton's gentle yet intent perusal. Pride prevented her from crossing her arms about her breasts, whose nipples, much to her embarrassment, rose tautly against the wrapper.

"Princess, I have lived day and night waiting for the moment you would enter my room. And now the moment is at hand and I am at a loss of what to do."

Taking in Tiffany's attire, Mortimer felt the heat rising from beneath his collar and creeping in blush over his face. He turned stiff-backed, walking into the bedroom, leaving them alone.

"Please, take a seat, Princess." He waved his hand toward a chair near the hearth.

"No, thank you. I have something I wish to discuss with you and should not take long for you to rectify."

He smiled appreciatively at her, his eyes resting on the taut dusty peaks.

"A glass of Madeira perhaps?" he asked absently, thinking how he'd like to roll his tongue over her taut nipples.

Narrow blue eyes regarded the misdirection of gray ones and Tiffany spun around to face the fireplace, affording

Clinton a spectacular view of her shapely derriere, which the silk material clung to and outlined magnificently.

The silence was unnerving and she turned to look over her shoulder, catching his unguarded look and the direction of it. She spun around and walked to the chair, where she sat feeling safe from his probing eyes.

"Do I have your attention?" Her eyes shot blue daggers at him.

A smile lifted the corner of his mouth. "All of it, Princess."

"Well, you see, I am in need of a particular gown for this eve, and when I requested my maid to get it, she informed me it was in my apartments." She raised her eyes to look at him and was not prepared for what she saw. He was partially dressed and wore a short robe of black and gold velvet, belted loosely at his waist, exposing his bare chest and the mat of crisp black hair that covered it. She quickly averted her eyes to her lap, squelching the tingling sensation beginning in her belly.

"You were saying, Tiffany." Clinton urged her on, looking at the long, shapely length of her leg which the parting of her robe exposed up to her thigh.

Shaking her head, she looked up at him, seeing his gaze directed on her exposed legs. Snatching her robe together, she continued, "As I was saying, I needed a gown and my maid informs me it is in my apartments. I foolishly inform her we are in *my apartments,*" saying those words with emphasis. "My maid then informs me, no, the apartments I now occupy are not mine. Mine are yours!" Rising softly, intending not to lose her anger, she smiled sweetly. "Of course, I know there has been some error and that you will rectify this most improper arrangement immediately." Taking a deep breath, she continued, "Of course, I knew once you were made aware of this, you'd have it corrected. After all, it is highly improper and unheard-of." She graciously accepted the glass of Madeira he had offered, in spite of her refusal. Tiffany sipped her wine, grateful for its calming effect.

"I would think, Tiffany, you've come to realize I do not adhere to what is proper. I tend to make my own rules to fit my own situation. Never the other way around. There is no mistake, we will share the same apartments. I will not abide the current mode of separate bedrooms. We soon will be man and wife. We will share a great deal together, both inside and outside *our* bedroom."

Tiffany gave him a glance of utter disbelief, responding, "This is preposterous. I demand my own rooms be separate from yours!" Placing her glass down, she walked up to him, ready to do territorial battle. "As a matter of fact, I insist upon it."

"Give me one good reason why I should consider your request," he asked, softly.

A becoming blush crept up her face as she timidly replied, "There . . . ah, will be times during the month when even you . . ." She stopped, unable to go on, too embarrassed for words. Turning her head away from his probing eyes, she continued softly, barely a whisper, "Even you don't expect to . . ."

Clinton smiled softly at her bent head, realizing her humiliation, and saved her from having to further state her case. A warm hand cupped her chin, turning her face up to his.

Looking gently with understanding into her eyes, noting the slight trembling of her mouth which she tried to still, he said softly, "How callous of me to forget how truly feminine you are Tiffany. How truly innocent." His fingers brushed the silky skin of her cheek. "I do not wish to offend your tender sensibilities, but there is much I've to teach you. Much you've yet to experience. Trust me, Princess, your monthly cycle does not offend me. It is but a minor obstacle, not insurmountable to our pleasure."

He grinned down at her, holding her wide blue eyes with his. "I can be quite inventive, you know."

Tiffany paled visibly. "You beast!"

"The beast shall have his fill, Princess, nothing short of it."

Images of a carnivorous beast devouring her flesh, consuming her, caused her to shudder. He walked to the bedroom door and stopped to ask, "Which gown is it you require?"

Tears threatened to spill in her defeat. She was unable to speak for fear her voice would crack and merely shook her head. Finally, looking up at him with imploring eyes, she whispered brokenly, "I only require a room with a door which I can open and close at will, nothing more."

"There is no door that will keep me from you, Tiffany. Don't you understand that yet?" he asked gently. "Now, which gown is it?"

Without answering, she turned from him, walking to the door. Before opening it, she replied, defiantly, "There is still *this* door." She yanked it open. "And when this one is gone, there remains one which will keep me from you. Which you have neither key or wherewithal to open." She crossed the threshold, and just before closing the door, she said, "The one to my heart!"

Chapter Eighteen

"And to the new duchess of Wentworth and Chablisienne—" lifting his glass in toast, Austin looked down at Tiffany "—you have stolen the day with your beauty." The crowd of guests cheered in tribute. Austin cleared his throat, shouting above the roar of cheers, "And to the duke, well, ole man, while the day is lost, the night surely belongs to you." The crowd burst out into laughter and cheers. Tiffany felt the warm flush of a blush creep hotly over her cheeks and lowered her head in embarrassment.

Toast after toast was pledged in honor of the couple as the elaborate dinner came to an end. Dancing began and late afternoon waned to early evening.

Winifred noted the lateness of the hour. Her green eyes scanned the crowd of over a thousand guests, coming to rest on the couple standing at the doors amidst an array of acquaintances. A smile crossed her mouth as she regarded the tall, handsome form of Clinton clad in an elegant white and silver jacket and pants; his waistcoat was solid black, providing the perfect foil to his otherwise white elegance. She watched him, noting that his eyes often drifted to Tiffany, and his arm possessively rode the small of her back, keeping her close. The green eyes sparkled, resting on Tiffany, outfitted in a long white satin bridal gown with an equally long matching train. The gown was lavishly trimmed with lace and pearlescent soutache braid. Her hair was pulled away from her exquisite face, drawing attention to the elegance of her features. White roses were tucked in the gather of curls caught up, exposing the graceful line of her neck. When Tiffany turned, the tender smile faded and a glimmer of sadness crossed the green eyes.

Winifred could not miss the forlorn look, almost lonely, etched on Tiffany's face. And for a brief moment Winifred had doubts. Oh, Robert, she thought, I hope I've done right by her.

Tiffany, feeling Clinton's hand on her shoulder, turned. Smiling gently down at her, he repeated, "Come along, Princess, Mother is ready to retire. We should bid her farewell." She placidly let him lead her. Tiffany moved in a daze, aware of all that happened, but numb. She had risen this morn to find three twittering maids fussing about her. She had endured their ministrations and Germane's as they clothed her in her bridal finery. And when Aunt Winnie had come to her, gently preparing her for the day and wedding night, she had apathetically listened with half an ear. The full extent of what had happened, and was yet to come, did not penetrate her numbness. Somehow she had managed to arrive at the church, say her vows, and become Clinton's bride without a bat of an eyelash, or an utter of protest. She had stood, a smile affixed on her face, nodding to congratulations offered, extending thanks to those who shared in the occasion.

When they approached Evette, Clinton bowed, placing a kiss on his mother's extended hand. Evette turned, grasped both of Tiffany's hands in hers. Tears shone brightly in Evette's gray eyes and edged her soft voice. "I have waited a long time for this day. I am so happy to welcome you to our family. Finally there is another woman to help balance our predominantly male members."

Tiffany smiled perfunctorily, replying, "Thank you, Your Grace."

Evette said reassuringly, "I believe when all is said and done, dear, you will find all the joy and happiness I have found at Wentworth." On a lighter note, Evette ventured, "I hope Clinton and you will visit me in Genoa, for the weather there is conducive to my health and I leave on the morrow."

Clinton had watched Tiffany all day and was well aware of her state of mind. He smiled at her and then at his mother, replying, "Madam, we will come to visit. You need not worry."

"Ah, well, now that you have settled down, I've no doubt. I would like it to be soon. I've had little chance to get to know my new daughter and would like that luxury before you present me with a score of grandsons!"

Clinton laughed and teasingly said, "Perhaps they will be granddaughters."

Evette smiled broadly. "Now, that would be nice! The first girl in ten generations of male Barencourtes. Lord only knows I tried. But, alas, it was not in the stars. Instead I produced five sons."

"Well, madam, I shall try to accommodate you."

Clinton leaned toward his mother, kissing her on each cheek, before she departed.

Clinton turned Tiffany in to the loose circle of his arms, whispering gently, "Princess, the hour grows late. It is best we bid our good-nights to the guests and leave them to their celebration."

He saw a flicker of fear cross the sapphire depths and suppressed the urge to pull her closer to reassure her.

After making the necessary good-nights and listening to the harmless jests from the men, Clinton led Tiffany to the broad, curving staircase. The events of the last hours began to slowly burn away at Tiffany's numbness. When Clinton stopped before the large double doors of their apartments and turned to her, he saw the fear of realization in her eyes. When he opened the door but did not enter, he saw a flicker of relief pass over her face. His eyes spoke of his desire and understanding as he studied her. His voice confirmed what his eyes told her. "I will give you some time, Princess, and then I will come to you."

Cupping her chin, he brought his mouth down upon hers in a gentle, yet promising kiss, before leaving her.

Tiffany stood alone in the dressing chamber, having dismissed Germane. She unconsciously brushed her hand along the fine black silk belted robe, the only night apparel found. Her hair was pinned up after her bath, and wisps of damp locks curled about the nape. She approached the bedroom door with trepidation and tentatively touched the brass handle, quickly withdrawing her hand as if it burned. Her thoughts spun as her hand trembled before her.

She knew, once she entered *that* room, the man who would come to her would physically bind her to him. In *that* room, beyond those doors, she was legally his to take as he chose. Her hand trembled as it moved back to the handle. She swallowed the fear that had lodged itself in her throat. Taking a deep breath to still her racing heart, she reasoned: her body might be his to take, but giving of herself—her heart, her soul—lay in her hands. She vowed no matter what he did to her body or how her body responded, he would not touch her core. No! That belonged to another!

A sense of strength flowed through her. Straightening her shoulders, she turned the handle.

Whatever she expected to find behind the door or feared to find did not prepare her for the breathtaking sight.

French doors were thrown open, allowing the soft, whispering breeze to flutter the long, gauzy curtains that graced two full walls. Nestled between the two walls was a black marble fireplace, where a small glowing fire smoldered. Thrown invitingly in front of the hearth lay a sable fur rug of a proportion she had never seen. Large pink-and-black-striped cushions formed a cozy semicircle on the rug before the fire. She hesitated, but the desire to feel the soft, plush rug beneath her feet overrode her reluctance—her toes curled against the fur.

Turning, her eyes fell upon a giant bed. Fear rose as she gazed at the black ebony bed set upon a dais which rested on a lavish Oriental rug of black and mauve. Her eyes drifted to the mauve silk bed curtains tied back at each post and came to rest on the six plump pillows arranged at the headboard. A rich ermine spread was drawn back, and white satin sheets gleamed in the candlelight.

She turned from the bed, thinking too soon she would join Clinton on it. A prickly sensation shivered down her spine as she moved out onto the terrace.

The brick terrace ran the full length of the corner apartment. It was laden in a profusion of blossoms, late in bloom, and was as vivid and exotic as the bedchamber. Leaning against the terrace wall, she gazed at the full moon which hung heavy in the night, casting its silvery glow, its beams stretching into the recesses of the chamber.

The late summer breeze caressed her, lifting a wet tendril of hair, and rustled the silk of her robe, molding it to the soft contours of her body. She shivered, but whether it was due to the breeze or fear, she did not know. A sense of sadness crept over her, bringing tears to her eyes. Tears born of defeat. She had been forced against her will. She had fought as best she could and failed. She turned, walking back into the room, the bed again catching her gaze. Aloud she vowed, "No matter how I've lost the battle, I'll not wave the white flag and wait placidly in bed like a mare led to a stallion!" Turning to stare at the fire, curling her toes against the fur, she heard the soft closing of the door. Turning slowly around, she saw him. Leaning against the jamb, his arms folded across his chest.

Clinton smiled softly at her image. His eyes fell to her

long, shapely legs revealed by the subtle parting of her robe. His blood flowed hotly, knowing soon he would feel her legs entwined and wrapped about him. Slowly, his eyes roamed seductively upward, stopping at her waist, a belt about it which defined its smallness and accentuated her rounded hips. A breeze molded the silk robe to her full, tilted breasts, outlining her nipples. Passion inched slowly, burning its way through his veins, as he knew his mouth and tongue would soon feast upon the bounty. His eyes continued their upward perusal, noting the translucence of her delicately carved face and graceful neck, heightened by the blackness of her robe. His eyes moved to the temptingly curved, parted lips to travel over her pale, yet proud face, stopping to search her eyes.

Tiffany was acutely conscious of Clinton. His stance emphasized the force of his thighs and the slimness of his hips. The rich outline of his shoulder strained against the fabric of his black robe, whose vee revealed a muscular chest, covered with a crisp mat of hair. A tingling, an uncoiling, began in the pit of her belly at his virile appeal. Tiffany swallowed, sensing the moment was close at hand. His compelling gray eyes, his firm features, the confident set of his shoulders, just the way he stood there, told her the time had come when he would mark her, possess her. She could not dispel the hungry desire reflected in his eyes but spoke out, "You'll not possess all of me, my lord."

Clinton pushed away from the door, walking toward her. "I will have no less." A flicker of apprehension coursed through her, hearing the promise in his words.

When he stopped, he stood so close, their hips touched, and his voice was like a caress. "This night is mine. It's only you and I, and tomorrow is a long time away."

She shivered at the underlying sensuality in his voice. She felt the heat from his loins, feeling as if she were afire as he moved closer, making her fully aware of his thigh. Lowering her eyes, unable to meet his, fearing he'd see her reaction, she looked at the mat of hair covering his chest. Her fingers itched to run through the dark pelt. She felt her knees weaken, knowing her fingers would touch firmly muscled, warm flesh.

Clinton lifted her chin so her eyes met his. Reaching up, touching her hair, he said softly, "A virgin comes to her husband with unbound hair." She shivered at his words, at his touch, as he plucked the pins from her hair.

Seeking to gain some fraction of control over him, wishing to dispel his effect and reaffirm her own conviction, she whispered, "You cannot possess what I have already given. You'll not possess all of me."

His fingers ceased their plucking, his eyes searched her face. She saw a flicker of surprise in them. His fingers began again and her locks cascaded down her back, like a silken mantle. She felt his fingers run through their texture, his eyes holding her captive as his warm, possessive hands slid across her scalp, the raven tresses wrapping about his fingers.

Gently forcing her head back, he held her eyes captive, drinking in her beauty. He leaned so his mouth was a breath from heres. His lips brushed gently across hers as he said, "No matter if the wedding sheets confirm or deny your honor." Pulling her up against his chest, crushing her breast against the mat of hair, he vowed, "When you lie with me, no other will come between us." His last words were smothered on her lips as if sealing his vow with a kiss as promising as it was rewarding.

He traced the soft fullness of her lips with his tongue, then wound a path of shivery kisses up the column of her throat to nibble at her ear. She shivered and tingled with his assault. His hands remained wound in her hair, holding her steady. When his tongue traced the pattern of an ear and delved into its crevice, she felt an uncoiling deep in her belly. She squeezed her eyes shut trying to block out the sensations, only serving to heighten them. She unwillingly moaned when he seared a path down her neck, placing tantalizing kisses at the base of her throat, where a pulse beat rapidly.

When he lifted his mouth, she opened her eyes, locking with his hooded in desire. She began to feel herself becoming lost in their promising depth and she tried to will her mind to resist. Clinton smiled softly, and as if knowing, he recaptured her lips with a demanding mastery, savoring the rich bounty.

Tiffany sucumbed to the forceful domination of his lips parting hers. Clinton felt her surrender and gently plunged his tongue, exploring the sweet recesses of her mouth. A betraying shudder urged him on, sucking the tip of her tongue into his mouth.

Her knees weakened. Her fingers clutched at his arms for support. She yielded, meeting his tongue timidly at first and then more boldly.

Clinton groaned in pleasure at her innocent boldness and released her hair, running his hands down her back, cupping her buttocks, bringing them against his rising manhood.

A cold wave of fear washed over her feeling his desire, so hard, so threatening. She pulled back, but his hands firmly held her pressed to his desire. ''No!'' She moaned. She braced her hands against his shoulders, pushing her upper body away and inadvertently pressing her lower body closer. Her action parted the vee of her robe, laying her breasts open to him. Clinton buried his face in the soft valley and leisurely circled a dusty nipple with the tip of his tongue. He closed his mouth over an aching peak. Tiffany whimpered, clutching desperately at his shoulders as a tingle shot from her breast to her belly. She arched her back and in an utterly wanton motion, dropped her head, groaning deeply.

Clinton's desire rose, burning brighter with each surrender. He swung her into the circle of his arms, carrying her and laying her on the bed.

Standing there at the side of the bed, he stared, meeting

her eyes, now dulled with desire, and held them imprisoned with his. He unbelted his robe and shrugged it off so it slipped to the floor.

Tiffany was half-dazed with passion, the betrayal of her body forgotten by the beginning of an ache between her thighs that consumed her. She couldn't move and lay there in the downy softness of the bed. She wanted to close her eyes but was unable to draw hers from the gray eyes burning with unleashed desire. She could only stare at his towering form, so powerfully built with its broad, muscled chest, flat, hard belly, and his manhood—full, potent, rising triumphantly from the mass of black hair at his groin.

Clinton gazed down at the magnificent woman who lay before him. As he watched her eyes take note of him, his manhood hardened, and his hand reached out, untying the belt of her robe, flicking back the silk material, revealing the beauty he would never tire of.

Tiffany felt a warm blush creep from her toes to the roots of her hair when he parted her robe. She looked up, away from his eyes, feeling their scorching path. Gazing up, she caught her reflection in the mirror above the bed. She stared, the feeling so erotic, watching them as if she were removed from her body, yet feeling every nerve end tingle.

Clinton let his hand travel to cup the fullness of her breast and slide his thumb over a nipple, working it to a hard, taut peak. Tiffany moaned as she watched his hand move deliciously over her breast, seeing her nipples, feeling them rise proudly. Her breath caught in her throat, she parted her lips, wetting them with her tongue, for they had gone dry with her ragged breathing. Seeking to regain herself so as to rebuild her wall, she closed her eyes against the reflection. She felt his hand slide over her ribs to her belly; she squeezed her eyes tighter, hoping to shut out the sensations.

He watched her close her eyes, knowing she sought to erect a new stone to her already crumbling fortress. His voice husky with desire, he commanded, "Open your eyes." She complied and he saw their heavy lids, the glazed, haunted look in their depths. Triumph gleamed within his own.

His hand moved down the soft inner skin of her thigh, caressing the long length, and traveled back up, stopping a fingertip from her womanhood. He drew a deep, silent breath. His desire burning, a need to be answered, he felt the sweet agony in not taking her yet, as much for her pleasure as his as he delayed their joining. He saw the slight arching of her hips, the subtle twist of her body, all signs of her rising passion, her need to have him touch her. He smiled in triumph, moving his hand, splaying his fingers in the curls of her mound, feeling the muscles in her belly strain. "Watch." His words were as potent as the caress of his fingers as they moved within the ebony curls, stopping a breath away from her essence.

"Please do not," she whimpered, her words a contradiction to her arching hips. She yielded to his command and lifted here eyes to the mirror above.

A single finger slid sensually down between her legs, finding and stroking that most sensitive of spots. She moaned aloud and lifted her hips against his finger. She tried to fight against herself but instead lost herself to him.

Clinton watched her face in its battle to withhold and saw her yield, felt the sweet moistness between her thighs as his finger brought her to the edge of unbearable pleasure.

His finger stopped. Tiffany felt the white-hot pleasure recede, the ache strong and pleasurably painful. She looked at him, not understanding anything but the need to fulfill that ache. She watched him take his finger and bring it to his mouth, tasting the moistness she felt between her legs. She whispered brokenly, "Please . . . I cannot bear it," surrendering another part of herself to him.

His eyes, burning with desire, captured hers; muttering thickly, he said, "You shall not bear it any longer." He spread her quivering limbs, placing himself between them, sliding his hands under her, lifting her hips to him and closing his mouth over her, stroking her sensitive bud.

Tiffany twisted mindlessly, her hands clutching the bed sheets, her hips arching against his mouth. Closer and closer she came to the bright tunneling light, and as she reached closer to the edge and was about to fall into the abyss, his mouth left her. A frustrated moan escaped her lips.

"Tell me, Tiffany, tell me you want my mouth," he commanded in a voice simmering with barely checked passion. She tossed her head back and forth on the pillow. Her body, as taut as a bowstring, arched to him, begging him for completion.

"Tell me," he ground out, his desire near bursting, his restraints slowly crumbling. "Tell me," he whispered, his breath a caress against her cheek.

Unable to bear her agony, her lips formed the word "Yes."

Satisfied with her admission, Clinton gave her what she yearned for, closing his mouth over her, bringing her over the edge in a shattering release that left her body weightless.

She was crying aloud in her release. Clinton moved over her, receiving her cry in his mouth. He felt her shudders subside as she began the descent from the peak. He gently kissed the tip of her nose, then her eyes, and finally he satisfyingly kissed her mouth. He whispered his love in her ear, moving his mouth down the slim column of her throat. He worshiped her body with his mouth, he reveled in the depth of her passion. He rekindled the fire in her taut body.

The pulsating feeling deep inside which had been quenched began anew. Her world existed only in the molten sensations, setting her body afire. She whimpered and moaned when her nipples ached against the warm pelt of hair on his chest, and rose as he erotically brushed against them. She shuddered and arched when his mouth covered a breast, holding his head, clutching her fingers in his hair. The traitorous flame of her desire rose higher, singeing the edges of her control.

Clinton moved his hand, mouth, tongue, over every inch of her—biting, nibbling, sucking, tasting the heady ambrosia she offered, leaving no course untouched.

He could barely control himself. Her wanton wild tossings, her moans, the feel of her wetness, pushed his body to the limits of control. His voice, barely recognizable, whispered raggedly, "Do you want me, Tiffany?"

She tossed her head, whispering, "N . . . no," as passion raged through her body, chipping down the remnants of her will.

"Will you take me, Tiffany?" he ground out, rubbing his swollen member against her bud. She whimpered. He smiled between clutched teeth, and commanded, "Give me your all. No less." His voice was thick, unsteady. Circling his hips provocatively, his member touching her wetness, he said, "Will you receive me?"

Half-mad with need, white-hot sensations rippling through her taut body, desperate for release, she cried out, "Yes," and her walls tumbled down.

His hands slid beneath her, lifting her hips to receive him. He inched himself into her wet sheath, feeling it open, and he withdrew and poised himself to bury himself deep within. He was near bursting and drew upon the last of his reserves of control before he drove into her.

Tiffany cried out when he entered her, tearing through the thin barrier. Her fingernails dug into his arms at his invasion.

Clinton breached her maidenhead and held himself, feeling the incredible sensation of her muscles contracting against his pulsating shaft. She tightened about him and opened to accommodate him. He held her, whispering softly, "Hush, Princess . . . easy, it shall pass." He stroked her streaming hair and lightly kissed her tear-streaked cheeks. "Hold me . . . the pain will fade."

"Clinton . . ." she whimpered into the hollow of his throat, clinging to his strong arms. She felt him within her—possessing her. He seemed so alien, so very hot, too thrusting, too deep, as if he touched her soul. Her tears welled in her eyes at his possession. She could no longer think when his palms moved over her breasts and his mouth covered hers. She heard him whisper little things and then felt her body quiver at his words. His body moved over her in fluid motion, moving deeper and deeper into her until he was fully seated and she fully possessed. She could not remember when the pain ended and the unbearable pleasure began, only that her body moved and arched to meet his thrust and receive him. A throbbing began anew in the center between her thighs and turned to a hungry need which screamed through every part of her body for fulfillment. Instinctively, to bring him closer to her needs, she arched her hips, bringing their loins together.

She heard his hoarse whisper, "All of you, Tiffany." He felt her undulations beneath him, almost undoing him. He pressed on, long, smooth strokes demanding she give to him and hold back nothing. He kept his raging desire to spill himself in tight check till she surrendered totally. Moving his hand between their bodies, caressing the taut bud of desire, he plunged deeper into her. "All, no less."

Tiffany wrapped her legs about his trusting hips, capitulating, giving over to him.

And when he felt her give over, he gave of himself, unselfishly, as if in atonement for her surrender. He felt her nails scratch his back in abandon and her body ripple in convulsion. She cried out in a tumultuous climax as he released all his passion he had so torturously contained, spilling himself, flooding her with his seed, crying out in ultimate triumph.

Chapter Nineteen

Clinton reclined against the propped-up pillows, a smile of contentment spread across his unshaven face. Smoke curled upward from a cheroot lying in the ashtray. He lifted the cup of tea Mortimer delivered earlier with a pot of hot chocolate, sipping the strong brew. He replaced the cup on its saucer.

Sun streamed into the room. A slight breeze ruffled the curtains of the open French doors. He inhaled the fresh morning air deeply, feeling invigorated. He normally rose before the break of dawn, but this morning he slept later than usual. The reason for his laziness was tucked snuggly against his side.

He looked down at her. Her head rested against his shoulder, her hand lay trustingly over his heart, and her leg, bent at the knee, entwined about his. His eyes moved to her face. A tender smile curved his mouth. She was so soft in her repose. Her lips, red and swollen from their night of passion, were slightly parted. Long, sooty lashes cast shadows on her creamy, flawless skin. Tiny curling tendrils escaped the heavy raven mass of hair streaming across the pillows. Absently he touched a lock, which curled possessively about his finger.

Images of the night past flooded his mind, causing a dull ache to begin in his groin. His eyes traveled to the soft, sweet swell of her breast, its dusky tip hidden beneath the satin sheet. He pictured it, hard with desire. His blood moved thickly in his veins at the image. His eyes followed the beguiling line of her waist over a rounded hip, slowly down long, curvaceous legs. Again his mind betrayed him and his manhood rose in tribute, picturing those legs wrapped tightly against his flanks.

He drew a deep, calming breath and lifted his cigar, puffing thoughtfully. He was glad he had kept his raging desires in check and had given her release. He was glad of his wisdom, for it prepared her to receive him, and contrary to her claim, she was untouched. He smiled broadly, knowing that her first experience in lovemaking would remain indelibly etched in her memory.

Although he had tapped and drunk from her well of passion, he found his thirst unquenchable. She had rivaled him in passion, giving him consummate pleasure.

She had surrendered each and every part of her body to him as he knocked down every obstacle in his path. He had forced her to admit to the passion he stirred and she possessed. He had forced her to watch her own passion and his possession of her and brought her to high ground, sharing a shattering release. Afterward, he wrapped her quivering form in his arms, feeling her tears fall silently on his chest.

He knew while she surrendered and contorted in the ecstasy he gave her, she also withdrew from him, denying her love.

The corners of his mouth lifted as he thought she had yet to experience all she could feel. There was much he had yet to teach her. In bed, wrapped about his body, Tiffany would learn and seek him for her desire, accept him as a lover. She had, as of yet, to accept him as a companion, for there had been little time for wooing and courtship. A broad smile etched his face; that, too, would pass.

Clamping the cigar between his teeth, he leaned back, smiling as he made his next battle plans.

* * *

The sweet aroma of chocolate teased her nostrils. A soft smile touched her lips in her sleep. She drifted up from the depths of sleep, thinking soon Germane's accented voice would break into her semisleep, urging her to be up for her bath. Snuggling deeper into the mattress, reveling in its warmth which enveloped her, she waited. She heard a dull constant pounding. A frown marred her brow, the pounding getting louder as her senses began to awaken. Slowly she opened her eyes, the sunlight causing her to squint. Adjusting to the light, her eyes opened and she saw her hand resting against flesh. Flesh that was warm and firm under her fingers. Her eyes widened with realization, and with a strangled cry, Tiffany was fully awake, grabbing the sheet and scrambling to the far corner of the bed. Sitting on her haunches with the sheet clutched in her hands, under her chin, she stared at an amused Clinton. Her eyes widened when she realized she had yanked the sheet from his body and now he sat proud, indifferent to his nakedness, casually smoking a cigar.

She blushed. Images of the night past flooded her mind. Images too powerful, too erotic, to deny.

"Well, good morning to you, too, Princess."

Averting her eyes from his smiling face and form, they fell to a stain as red as berries against the whiteness of the sheet, proof of his possession. Raising her eyes, she glared at him. His face split into a wide grin. Enraged beyond belief, Tiffany gasped, grabbing the nearest item, a pillow, and hurled it at him.

"Is it something I've done?" he asked with mock innocence, catching the pillow with ease.

Images of her unconditional surrender flashed before her. She shrieked, grabbed another pillow, and flung it with all her might at him.

Raising his arm, he easily deflected it, causing it to crash against a priceless vase, breaking it. "Or didn't do?" he inquired dryly. He looked at the picture she presented.

The sheet no longer covered her, forgotten in her display of anger. Her black silken mane streamed about her like a mantle over her shoulders, down to the beguiling ebony triangle of curls. Her breasts were covered by her hair, but dusky rose tips peeked out from beneath its raven shroud with each agitated breath she took. Blue eyes shot daggers of flames at him. He smiled, his manhood rising to the tempting image he held.

The arrogant smile on his face only incensed her more. Her hand frantically searched and found a heavy brass candlestick, which she threw at him. Clinton caught the heavy missile easily, dropping it to the floor. A gleam of triumph lit his eyes. "Must be something I didn't do."

"*Ohhhh,*" she screamed, and lunged for him, hands curled, nails bared, ready to scratch his eyes out. Clinton saw her coming and quickly grabbed her, but not before her nails scratched his cheek, barely missing his eye. Tossing her easily on her back into the softness of the bed, he pinned her hands above her head with one of his own. Touching his hand to his cheek, coming away with blood on his finger, he smiled down at her.

"I guess one bloodletting deserves another, Princess." He sucked the blood from his finger. His eyes hooded with desire.

Tiffany struggled beneath him, thrashing her legs, nearly unmanning him, until he covered her limbs with his own. She struggled anew until she felt his hardness press against her belly and realized her movements enticed him. She arched to buck him off, trying to get as far away as possible from the branding heat of his rising manhood. Instead she came closer. Her breasts heaved in her exertion, rubbing against his hair-roughened chest. Her nipples tingled and rose.

Clinton felt them pressing into his chest. Lifting his chest, he peered down, and a wolfish smile crossed his face. "Ah, a succulent ripe cherry for the tasting." He blew a warm stream of breath on the nipple and it hardened. Looking at her, a gleam of mischief crossed his eyes. "But is it sweet?" Not waiting for a reply, he lowered his head.

Tiffany struggled, attempting to move away from his lowering head, fully aware of his intent. She moaned when his mouth closed over a taut peak, feeling a bolt shoot from her nipple to her belly. Clinton grasped her hands with his, holding them above her head firmly as he payed homage to her other breast, biting, sucking its peak into a tight, aching crest. Tiffany clasped her hands with his own when she felt a sparkling tremor between her thighs.

Raising her head, he leaned close to nibble at her ear and whispered in a deep, sensual voice, "I've a need to taste more of you." His tongue moved teasingly down and traced around her hardened nipples. "This is but an appetizer to the great bounty you bring."

"No . . . no. I won't let you." She reared her head back, renewing her struggles. He brought her hands, pressing them down, at her shoulders, laying his palms against her own. Her fingers curled around his as he parted her thighs with his knees, raising himself between them.

Before lowering his head, he promised, "I think you will, Princess. You know you like it." His knee rubbed erotically against her, feeling the beginnings of her wetness. She felt herself grown warm and pulsating with the movement and moaned in submission when he bent his head, tracing his tongue over her breasts, down her belly. He looked up at her, watching her toss her head lightly back and forth. He hovered over her sweet essences. Tiffany felt his breath caress her intimate flesh as she knew soon his mouth would do. She moaned. Clinton wedged his chest between her raised thighs, still holding her hands.

"Watch me taste you."

"No . . . no. Please, you shame me," she whispered brokenly, but even as she spoke, her eyes lifted to the mirror above. Unwittingly she arched her hips in invitation.

"Nay, Princess, I but worship you." Tightening his fingers about hers, keeping his eyes upon her face, he lowered his mouth, closing over her. He tasted her with scorching need, his tongue stroking her sensitive bud till it was hard and hot. Tiffany groaned, dug her fingers into him, arching fiercely against his mouth. He delved deeper and deeper into her womanly flesh, and when he saw her toss wildly upon the bed, he released her hands. Sliding his hands beneath her buttocks, he lifted her against his mouth and questing tongue.

Tiffany watched their reflection, seeing herself move in undulating, writhing motion against his mouth. She felt herself grow warm and her moistness flow. Arching, her fingers dug into the bed, her hips moved wildly against his stroking tongue.

"Aaahh."

Clinton felt the tensing of her legs, and pressed relentlessly on until her body shuddered and she cried out. Rearing over her and lifting her hips, he entered her in one smooth stroke, seating himself fully within her. He nearly spilled himself, feeling her muscles contract in release against his manhood. Then moving in long, slow, savoring strokes, he brought her back onto the precipice, hearing her moan, feeling her hips meet his thrusts.

Closer and closer Tiffany came to satisfying the delicious tightening between her legs, as his hands on her hips guided their movements and rhythm.

When he felt her begin to contract against him, he demanded hoarsely, "Look at me." She closed her eyes—her last defense before surrender. When she didn't comply, he pulled from her, holding only the engorged tip of his member within. She writhed beneath him—her body screaming, demanding completion. Desire, like liquid lava, ran through her veins, centering where he now held himself. Her eyes opened. He dove into her when she surrendered, grinding himself against her. Tiffany screamed out as her body convulsed, then stiffened in climax. He watched her pleasure wash over her and he in turn surrendered to the woman he conquered, exploding into a shattering climax.

Tiffany stretched like a contented kitten. Opening her eyes, she slowly surveyed her surroundings; mauve bed curtains billowed with the soft breeze, sun rays filtered through the gauzy material, casting a pinkish tinge to the satin sheets. Looking up, she caught her reflection in the mirror above; long, raven tresses were in a tangled disarray which would take hours to brush, her face had a rosy glow, her lips swollen and red. Running her hand down the length of her body, she noted all her parts were still intact. Outwardly, she thought, her body showed no change from the night past. Regarding her image critically, she decided she looked no different, despite her passage into womanhood. She moved to sit up and felt a strange warm stickiness and pleasant ache between her thighs. Sitting, she drew her legs up, resting her chin atop and wrapping her arms about them.

She stared, her mind reflecting. She had lost yet another battle. Her body had surrendered completely to Clinton and, in that surrender, betrayed Alan. This caused her to wonder. Surely she felt nothing for Clinton, least of all love! Her heart belonged to another, but her body acted on its own volition!

"*Bonjour, madame,*" greeted Germane as she walked into the room. Raising her head, Tiffany watched Germane place the tray of hot chocolate down and accepted a cup of the sweet brew.

Tiffany sipped her hot chocolate uncomfortably, noting Germane scan the room, as if she expected to unfold some secret of the night past. Scarlet rose high on Tiffany's cheeks, and seeking to change the direction of her maid's thoughts, she asked, stupidly, "What have you been up to?"

"What else, madame! Arguing with that pompous Mortimer.'' Germane switched to French since her English was limited, and continued in flustered speech, ''He thinks he will attend you. I say *'Non!'* No one but me attends you, and it would be improper for him to consider! *Non!*''

Tiffany blew on the hot chocolate, smiling; she could picture her fiery maid all afluster while dour-faced Mortimer stood stiffly in outrage.

''It will be very difficult, madame, with one chamber, not separate. *Oui?*''

Sipping her hot drink, Tiffany nodded in agreement and asked, ''Where is Mortimer now?''

Curling her pouting lips, Germane spat, ''Discussing the situation with His Grace.'' Gathering her mistress's robe and holding it up, she inquired, ''Would Madame wish to bathe?''

Aware of the stickiness and soreness between her legs, Tiffany nodded, rising from the bed.

Germane's eyes fell to the bloodstained sheets and she muttered to herself, ''I will see to the chambers as well.''

''Correct me, Clinton. I was under the impression the husband wielded the sword, the wife the sheath?''

''Now, now, Brent, let us be fair.'' Austin grinned at Clinton. ''There's no doubt the sword was wielded and the thrust parried, but the question is, was the sword sheathed?''

Tristan walked up to Clinton, looking at the long scratch on his cheek. Laughter twinkled in his eyes and filled his voice. ''Ah, no doubt the sword was sheathed, but tell us, was the prize worth the price of your flesh?''

''And is the sheathing worth the price of your flesh, again?'' Rory added.

Clinton sat, elbow resting on the desk, two fingers against his temple, regarding the gathering of his brothers with an amused smile. Leaning comfortably back in his chair, arms clasped behind his head, refusing to be drawn and awaiting their silence as if tolerating a bunch of small children, he asked dryly, "Are you quite finished? If so, I'd appreciate it if you'd all depart so I might enjoy my honeymoon. *Alone.*" The four laughed in male camaraderie and rose to depart.

Clinton smiled and then bent his head, beginning to arrange the shuffle of papers that covered his desk into tidy piles.

Brent casually walked over. "I've left the mortgage papers and financial arrangements here." He pointed to a folder.

"After I see Mother off, I'm to meet with the solicitors and bankers in Genoa. As you instructed, the Genoa banks handled the transfer of funds to our London office. Let me know what you think of the contract after you've reviewed it."

"Good, Brent. I think I'll get to them after I return from Wales." Clinton began to resume his work.

"By the by, the Thurston account will be paid now that the marriage has been consummated."

He grinned at Clinton, who merely smiled and replied, "Good. Now, be sure I receive a copy of the draft for a hundred fifty thousand pounds and a copy of the paid mortgage. Be sure Thurston receives notification."

"That will take some time. You know how slow the Italians are, but I am sure Thurston need not worry since the creditors are all paid and the Bow Street Runners have been called off. As soon as delivery can be made, it shall be done."

Clinton nodded at Brent's words, picked up the folder marked "Thurston Properties" and placed a copy of Tiffany's betrothal contract within, then placed the file in the top drawer of his desk. Looking up, he found Brent staring down at him. "Was there anything else?"

Brent withdrew a cigar from the box. Lighting it, he replied, "You know, Clinton, should Tiffany ever find out the means used, I fear the consequences, as you should.

She'll not see any more than your deception, ruthlessness, and high-handedness in the matter."

Leaning back in his chair, looking at Brent, Clinton nodded in agreement. "No doubt she would perceive it as nothing more than that. For Tiffany is just beginning to learn and feel many things and has yet to know herself and come to terms with her feelings. Eventually she must face them, admit to them. I think once she is true to her own self and her feelings, she will admit my means justified the end."

Shaking his head, Brent inquired, "And what if she finds out before she has admitted her feelings? What then?" A confident smile lifted the corners of Clinton's mouth. "Perhaps, Brent, that will be the true test—the final truth she must admit to—that her heart belongs to me."

"And if that is not the case?"

"Ah, Brent, but it is. The lady's heart will be mine. She has yet to admit it, but she shall."

After Brent left and Clinton finished the work before him, he summoned Mortimer. A brief, but enlightening conversation ensued, after which an indignant Mortimer left.

Clinton headed to his apartments, meeting Germane within the bedchamber. He briefly advised her of her new duties and those of Mortimer's. After Germane left, Clinton went to the wardrobe, pulling out his robe and a large box tied with a lavender ribbon, which he tossed upon the bed. Removing his clothes, he donned his robe, heading to the bathing chamber.

Through the mist he saw Tiffany lying with her head back in the sunken marble tub. Her hair was loosely pinned up, errant wisps framing her flushed face. The sweet swell of her breast rose beguilingly in the violet-scented water, and dusky pink nipples lay barely beneath.

He quietly dropped his robe and descended into the tub.

Tiffany was delighted with the large oval tub and bathing chamber. The whole room was tiled, and in the ceiling was a large window, allowing the sun to burst over the tub, making her feel wanton, as if she bathed outside. The room was warm and misty. She had settled herself in the tub, wanting to soak, and scrubbed herself vigorously, wishing to wash away his scent, which clung to her. The water was as potent as a heady wine, and a lassitude stole over her. The soreness between her thighs slowly disappeared, the stickiness long since removed. Closing her eyes, she gave over to the soothing powers of the water.

The rippling motion of the water caused her to open her eyes. Sitting up and grabbing a sponge, which she held modestly, although ineffectively, over her breast, she cried, "You!"

"Who else did you expect?" A mischievous gleam lit his eyes and he smiled as he squeezed water from a sponge over his hair-covered chest.

Her eyes were drawn to where the water clung in droplets on the pelt. His very masculinity was like a potent drug. She watched his chest muscles ripple with his movements and thought his body fascinating, compared to her own.

"Welcome back, Tiffany. I was told you required assistance."

"Certainly not from you! You, who have defiled me! Hah!"

"Moi?" he asked in mock innocence.

"Yes, most assuredly you."

Moving to cross the distance that separated them, he declared, "Well, Princess, let me make atonement, immediately." Before she could utter a protest, she found him so close to her that the hand clutching the sponge to her breast touched the crisp mat of black hair on his chest. Gently he removed her hand, bringing it to his mouth, nibbling and sucking each finger.

Tiffany was mesmerized and watched his face, his eyes, his mouth. Unmistakable desire coursed through her at his sensual play. "I . . . I don't require your services," she stammered, feeling his tongue track light circular patterns on her palm.

"No?" he murmured as he dropped kisses on her wrist, resting where a pulse beat wildly. Lifting her hand and placing it against his chest, he took her other, paying similar homage. Her fingers against his chest curled in the pelt, feeling the pounding of his heart. She was reeling from his touch and stared wide-eyed at him, as he placed her other hand on his chest.

"Where have you been defiled? Here?" He ran a soapy hand up and down her arm torturously. "Or here?" His hand ran the length of the other arm. Tiffany remained still, belying the rapid beating of her heart. Her fingers clutched his chest hair, the pulse in her throat beat wildly. She felt him lave a soapy hand up her long, slender neck and back down, stopping at her collarbone. He leaned forward, placing a gentle kiss at the base of her throat. "Surely here," he whispered, moving his fingers down, cupping the weight of her breasts and massaging them in circular motions, barely touching her nipples, which rose erotically in anticipation. She closed her eyes as sensations rippled through her, leaving her breathless and weak.

She whimpered weakly when his hands slid down her belly, stopping to tease the quivering hollows of her hips and navel. Her arms slid up onto his shoulders. "Yes, Princess," he murmured, feeling her response. "Ah, definitely here." His hands played teasingly along her belly, down the soft inner skin of her thigh. She shivered in desire, her lips parting slightly in anticipation of where his fingers lingered near. He heard her small cry of disappointment when his hands moved up, not down, caressing her shoulders, pulling her gently against him. Tiffany shuddered, feeling her nipples rub against the coarse wet hair of his chest, and she pressed against him, her head dropping back. Her eyes were heavy-lidded and closed briefly when his hands moved sensually down her back to cup her buttocks. Clinton felt her shiver and press against him. He furthered his assault, kissing the sensitive area between her ear and shoulder, while his hands roamed intimately. He gently put her from him and she leaned back against the tub, her arms stretched, her fingers clutching the edge so her knuckles were white.

Soaping his hands, he watched her: her breathing ragged, her head dropped back, her nipples' taut peaks rising above the water.

Grasping both her ankles, gently bending her legs, he charted a course up their long length, soaping her inner thighs, retreating and rising again.

"Oh, definitely defiled here," he whispered with each movement. He leaned forward, touching her parted lips, then thrusting his tongue deeply into the moist recess, while his hand moved up into the ebony triangle of curls.

"Oooh," she moaned as his hands played beneath the water and his mouth dropped kisses along the length of her neck. When his finger entered her, moving in and out, she brought her arms about his neck, crushing her breast against him, arching her hips against his finger, bringing it deeper within her. Buoyant, due to the water, she moved in unison with his thrusting finger.

"Do you want me, Princess?" He rubbed erotically against her breast, his finger delving deeper and deeper.

"Do you want more of me?" he whispered against her sensitive ear. "Just tell me and it will be yours."

The burning ache in her belly uncoiled, spreading between her legs. She groaned. "Do you want to take me inside of you, feel me deep where you ache?" he whispered hoarsely, barely able to await her consent.

"I . . . I should not want you so," she whispered brokenly, laying her head against the hollow of his throat, "but . . . but I do."

Pulling her to him as he leaned against the tub, he slipped his hand between her thighs, feeling her essence wet and slick—from the soap and from her own passion.

Grasping her hips, he lifted, poised her above him, and slowly lowered her so she felt every inch of his long, hard length. He felt her body open slowly as she took his aroused member into her warm, tight sheath. He emitted a deep groan when her walls stretched to engulf him and he pulled her upright to straddle him and raised his knees, impaling her further. She gasped, accepting the full length of him.

He drew a long, steady breath, feeling himself fully seated in her tight, throbbing sheath. He saw her dazed eyes and heard the sharp intake of her breath. Concern etched his voice. "Do I hurt you, Princess?" Shuddering and squeezing her eyes tightly closed, Tiffany tried to still the unbelievable sensation of being impaled. She heard his voice distantly. Feeling the hard, hot length of him and trying to adjust, she shuddered again and shook her head.

Grasping her hips, he lifted her up and lowered her back down onto his member, teaching her the rhythm. Her breasts rubbed against him with each upward and downward stroke, causing her nipples to rise to hard pebbles, burning the length of his chest.

Tiffany moaned, splaying her hands against his belly, feeling herself widen to accommodate his member. She dropped her head back, allowing him to control her movements.

"Ride me, Princess."

She did as he commanded, feeling the bathwater rush in as he raised her, out when he lowered her onto him. She groaned at the sensation, like the ebb and flow of a tide within her. She tightened her legs about his flanks, feeling powerful as she sat in the saddle and gave over to a primitive ride as old as time, increasing the gait to reach fulfillment. All her senses were assaulted; the water lapped against her as she drew him deeper and deeper within; his voice urged her on, resounding in her ears and singing in her veins. She closed her eyes, and her hands moved from the hair at his groin, sensually leaving a trail of fire on his chest. She lifted her arms to her head, her fingers running through her tresses, and rode him with total abandonment, seeking to quench the fire that blazed between her thighs.

Clinton felt the fires in his own body leap at her abandonment, and his mouth closed over a dusky taut peak. Hearing her moan, he took more of her into his mouth. He watched her as his tongue circled the hard peak and his mouth sucked upon the satin moistness of her breast. When she opened her eyes, dark with passion, he knew her to be lost to her need.

"Savor it, love; let it build, love," he groaned out, slowing her motion. He heard her cry of protest and felt her arch as her passion consumed her and him.

"Please, Clinton . . . oh . . . pleeeease," she said breathlessly in frustration.

"Reach for it, Princess," he whispered hoarsely. His manhood throbbed, near release. He wanted her own release to bring him along, but he could no longer hold himself in check. Moving his hand between their bodies, he caressed her.

Tiffany whimpered, begging for release, and when his fingers stroked her, she arched, drawing him deeper. He groaned from deep in his throat, her movement undoing him, and no longer able to hold back, gasped, "Now, Tiffany, *now!*" Tiffany yielded to him and her pleasure, shuddering in climax, feeling his seed, hot and forceful, spew, filling her. She fell forward on his shoulder, her hair cascading over them, its ends floating in the water.

Still within her, savoring the impact of their shared climax, Clinton lifted her head gently off his shoulder and, before placing a gentle kiss on her mouth, whispered, "I love you."

Wrapped securely and snugly in a fluffy towel, Tiffany leaned her head against Clinton's shoulder, asking drowsily, "Where are you taking me?"

Smiling down at his treasured bundle, he replied easily, "To our room, of course."

A blush crept up her cheeks becomingly. "No, Germane is there!"

Clinton kicked open the door, saying, "Not to worry, Princess. She and Mortimer have temporarily been assigned to other duties till they can come to some compromise."

Placing her on her feet and unwrapping the towel, Clinton proceeded to dry her damp body. "Stop that! I am capable of doing it myself," she cried indignantly.

Continuing, in spite of her protest, Clinton easily stated, "I'm only making restitution for dismissing your maid. Now, turn around."

She complied with his request, allowing his ministration until she felt him deftly place the towel over her buttocks and between her legs. Whipping the towel from his hands, she screamed, "Give me that!"

Clinton laughed, standing back, watching her perform the task. He quickly dried himself and, walking to his wardrobe, pulled out his clothes.

Tiffany wrapped the towel around her, securing an end under her arm. "But I don't know where my clothes are . . ." Her voice broke off as she realized she was unable to draw her eyes from his half-clothed body.

Clinton was aware of Tiffany's perusal of him, as he was of her delectable towel-clad form. Rubbing his hand across his furred chest, he smiled, noting her eyes following his hand. "Princess, on the bed you'll find a box. I took the liberty of purchasing a few items for you."

Brought from the perusal of his chest by his voice, she bristled at his words, once again reminded how high-handed he could be. Turning from him to the bed, she reached and untied the ribbon, lifting the lid. Her eyes widened at the contents—four pairs of breeches in different colors, along with an assortment of muslin shirts. Lifting the fawn-colored breeches out, she turned to him, a question in her eyes.

"I know your preference for breeches, Princess." A leer crossed his face and he continued, "And I find I quite enjoy the way they mold that sweet derriere of yours."

She glared at him and then turned, a smile lifting the corners of her mouth. She frowned for only a moment thinking his motives were self-serving. Shrugging that thought off, she quickly dropped her towel, bending to don her breeches, unaware of the wicked gleam that crossed his eyes and the unmistakable invitation she offered.

Clinton was much taken with the view, imagining the feel of her buttocks against his groin as he rode from behind. Her question interrupted his carnal thought. "Do you think it proper I dress as such?"

Walking over to her, watching her shrug on her shirt, he turned her face to him and began to button her shirt, letting his hands brush against the soft skin. "Princess, you are a duchess, and a duchess can do anything she wants." His hand slipped inside her shirt to fondle the weight of one of her breasts.

Tiffany slapped at his hand, walking away to the dresser, retorting, "I suppose that also applies to a duke?"

Grinning wolfishly at her, he responded, "Have you any doubt?" After awarding him with a look of exasperation, she turned and attempted to brush through the tangled tresses.

She felt his hand take the brush and perform the service himself. She could not help her remark to him. "The mighty duke reduced to a maid." She looked at him through the mirror to gauge his reaction and was awarded with his mischievous smile, making her heart lurch.

"Since I am the one who caused its state, I am the one to rectify it. Besides, I need the practice since your maid will no longer perform her services." At her wide-eyed look, he explained, "It appears Mortimer and Germane can't seem to share common ground, civilly. I have relieved them of certain duties.'' Brushing her hair in long, smooth strokes, he continued, ''Until they come to terms with one another, they will attend us only insofar as caring for the chamber, our clothing, and serving our meals.'' Laying down the brush, he placed a kiss on her neck. She felt goose bumps on her spine and moved from him.

''That is unheard-of! Highly improper, as well.'' She turned, finding he had not moved and was but a breath away.

''Improper? Hardly, Princess. A husband and wife should care for one another, see to their mutual needs.'' He winked at her knowingly. She glared in return. ''As far as unheard-of, well, I do what's best for us. Not what is mode or fashionable. Now, come here and let me finish your hair.''

Turning obediently, she taunted him, ''And how will the mighty duke style my hair? An upsweep, a cignon . . .''

''Nay.'' Kissing the top of her head, inhaling the delicate fragrance of violets, he reached for a bright blue ribbon, tying it around her hair. Standing back to regard his work, he said, ''Just like this. Flowing free and wild, like you.'' He turned her to face him and drew her up against his body, bending his head, capturing her lips in a gentle yet promising kiss. Tiffany was shocked at her own eager response to the touch of his lips and leaned against him.

He pulled away, knowing if he continued, they'd be back to square one.

Tiffany was startled back into reality and flushed with humiliation and anger at herself, turning her back to him.

Laughing, he said, ''Did no one ever tell you, Princess, that losing is relative? What's important is conceding with grace.''

Spinning about, she retorted, ''Then I suggest you start conceding gracefully, my lord, for you'll not win.''

Shaking his head, a smile on his face, he crossed his arms loosely. ''Ah, had I the time, we would see again who concedes. Perhaps later, for now I have other plans for you.''

Miffed by his threat, bristling at his arrogance, she stood her ground. ''I will not go.''

A smile ruffled his mouth. ''You will.'' He grabbed her arm and pulled her along, playfully.

''Wait, Clinton. Stop! I have no shoes on, you fool!'' Tiffany tried to dig her heels to stop him, but he was not to be stopped. Just before he grabbed her by the waist to toss her over his shoulder, he asked, ''Since when did that matter?''

Tiffany pounded on his back with her hands and kicked her feet, screaming, ''Put me down this instant!''

Clinton laughed heartily as he kicked open the door, walking past a startled Germane and a mortified Mortimer in the hallway.

''You are a beast, sir.'' Clinton patted her upraised derriere and she cried out. Clinton laughed as he carried her as if she were a sack down the broad, curving staircase, past the astonished eyes of the servants.

''You cruel, mean beast. Put me down this instant!''

''I hear you, love. All of Wentworth hears you, Princess.''

Approaching the front door, which was whisked open by a dumbfounded Bartholomew, Clinton exited, only to stop when hearing his name called. Turning to look back into the foyer, he saw timid Alicia holding a basket, her eyes wide as saucers. ''Your . . . er . . . Grace, the basket.''

''Ah yes, sweet Alicia, bring it over.'' Alicia trod carefully, seeing her new mistress thrash about on His Grace's shoulder, screaming at him. Clinton took the basket and, whistling, walked down the steps, carrying his bundles.

Blood was pounding in Tiffany's ears and her face was quite red.

''Please, Clinton, put me down. I am getting quite dizzy.''

"As you wish, Princess." He let her slide ever so slowly down the full length of him until her bare feet touched the warm cobble-way of the drive.

He began to walk and she began to slow her pace, hoping to escape him. As usual, Clinton was always aware of her and stated quite casually, never missing a step, "I wouldn't try it, Tiffany."

She glared at him. She was angry, dizzy, and her stomach grumbled in protest, for she had not eaten.

"I'm hungry," she blurted out.

Slowing his steps so she walked beside him, he smiled down at her pouting face and teasingly replied, "If you're a good girl, I might feed you."

"You beast! Does your torture never cease? First you rape me, then bathe me, dress me, drag me, and now you would starve me."

He stopped and she collided with his back. He smiled wickedly at her. "Starve you? Why, Princess, I thought I appeased your appetite quite well. However, I obviously failed." He made to grab for her arm.

Realizing his intent and the meaning behind his words, she screamed, "No, you cad! No, I say! I am hungry for food, you fool!"

Feigning mock innocence, Clinton replied, "How stupid of me, and here I thought you hungered for me. Oh well, perhaps later I can appease that appetite. Come along, I know a nice place for our respite."

Her hunger overpowering her desire to escape him, she followed.

They came upon a group of large willows. Clinton stopped, sitting down on the soft grass that grew beneath the trees. Tiffany stood pondering if it was indeed wise to sit down in the secluded area. Clinton laid out a sumptuous lunch on a white linen cloth. "Are you going to sit, Princess, or eat standing?"

"Only if you promise not to touch me will I sit."

"I promise I wish only to satisfy your appetite." He

smiled devilishly at her. Tiffany glared at him, refusing to sit. "For food, of course, Princess. Later I shall appease your more carnal appetite," he added.

The food was so tempting and she was so hungry, she dropped to the soft cushion of grass, accepting a plate filled with her favorite foods.

The afternoon was sunny and warm. A soft breeze which held the hint of autumn ruffled through the hanging boughs of the willows. After accepting a second glass of wine, she became more relaxed and comfortable and gave over to the tranquility the afternoon afforded.

"It is very beautiful here." Her voice broke the long silence. "France was lovely, but England is beautiful. Wentworth is indeed much different from Chablisienne." Turning her head to him, she added, "I think I prefer Wentworth's rolling hills to Chablisienne's manicured landscape. Do you own all of this?" she asked, sweeping her arm.

"Um-hmm, and about twenty miles north. It takes two to three days to cover the boundaries of the estate."

Tiffany watched him peel the skin from an apple with a sharp fruit knife. She shivered remembering the skill of his deft fingers on her body. Clinton handed her a piece of the peeled fruit, along with a slice of rich Brie. He smiled, watching her nibble the fare. "Have you ever been to Wales, Tiffany?"

Shaking her head and chewing her food, she looked at him in question.

"I thought we'd travel to my estate there. I think you'll like Wales with its rough headlands and coast."

Swallowing her food, she asked with interest, "You have an estate there, as well?"

"Ah, Princess, you have married a wealthy man. I have estates all over England and the Continent."

"What is it you do, Clinton?"

He smiled at her interest. "The family has lucrative holdings and businesses. Our main interests are banking, but we engage in shipping and horse breeding and racing, to name a few." Withdrawing a cheroot, lighting it, he leaned back against the tree. "You are a very wealthy woman, Tiffany. There is nothing on this earth you cannot buy."

"Save my freedom."

"Ah, that is true, Princess." He smiled and continued, "Brent handles the banking concern here and in Italy as well as the managing of the properties. Austin runs the shipping and fleets, while Tristan sails the trade route with the infidels in the South and handles the payment of tribute. Now, Rory . . . well, Rory is opening the lines to the Americas and the islands, establishing a base of operations in the United States. Our family businesses and interests provide all of us with wealth and futures so we can leave a legacy to our heirs."

Smiling at him, she declared, "I always imagined bankers as squat, stuffy, balding men with wire spectacles hanging on the bridge of their nose." Laughter spilled from her. "Brent and you certainly do not fit the mold."

"Or bent-over relics wielding their walking sticks?" he asked, teasingly.

Blushing, she recalled her description of a duke, she smiled brightly, replying, "Only time will tell."

Throwing his head back, he roared with laughter. Tiffany could not help herself and joined in.

"Come, Princess—" he stood, extending a hand to her "—an old friend of yours awaits."

"Where are we going?" she asked for the third time as she walked hand in hand with him.

"Has no one taught you the virtue of patience?"

"Nah! You're a fine example of patience, my lord. I'm living proof of your lack of it."

"Ah, point well taken. Betrothed, wedded, and bedded in less than four months does indeed show a lack of patience on my part."

Tiffany bristled at the reminder, and she snatched her hand from him. Clinton smiled.

They had reached the stables. Keegan walked up, tipping his hat to her. Tiffany smiled and, while he and Clinton engaged in conversation, wandered over to the paddock. Leaning against the rungs of the fence, she looked out over the paddocks.

She squinted her eyes, avoiding the low-hanging sun, looking at the horses that grazed peacefully within the field. She noticed a stable hand come out from one of the barns leading a large horse, which he released in the far paddock. The horse kicked up his hindquarters and began to race around the ring, relishing his freedom. Squinting, she saw the horse stop and tilt its head, then paw the ground with his forefoot. The sun prevented her from making out the features clearly, but a nagging sensation told her it looked familiar. Shading her eyes with her hand, she peered at the horse. The horse turned from her and raced away, making tight circles within the ring. She heard him whinny and saw him charge toward the fence, jumping over it. She saw his face, then screamed and leaped over the fence, toward the stallion. ''Xanadu.'' He snorted and whinnied as he stood, pawing the ground and tossing his head impatiently.

Tiffany reached him, tears misting her eyes. She opened her arms wide, and Xanadu situated himself between them, his velvety muzzle nudging her.

Clinton watched enviously as she opened her arms wide to embrace the stallion, longing for the day she would open her arms in welcome to him. Walking, he stopped a distance from them, not wishing to interrupt their reunion.

''Ah, guv'nor, ya did a good turn puttin' the two halves of the coin together.''

Clinton smiled and nodded in agreement. He heard Tiffany crying and became concerned as her sobs shook her slender shoulders. When he touched her, she immediately turned in his arms, willingly wrapping her arms about his neck. Tiffany buried her face against the hollow of his throat. He felt her tears fall on his chest and whispered, "I thought to make you happy, Princess, not sad."

"I . . . I am," she sniffled, and began to cry again.

He kissed the top of her head, inhaling the delicate fragrance of violets, and held her against him, caressing her hair.

"You . . . you," she sniffled, "said you sold him to . . ." She could not finish and began to hiccup.

Looking down at her tearstained face, wiping away her tears with his thumb, he said, "Yes, but I said the new owner met the price." Looking down into teary raised eyes, he explained, "A lifetime. Remember?" She nodded, recalling the moment in the meadow at Chablisienne.

Xanadu whinnied, breaking the moment, causing Tiffany to turn and find Keegan smiling at her. She blushed becomingly, and softly said, "I remember you. You were the one who took him away at Courtland."

"Aye, milady, 'twas me. And I been givin' 'im his bonbons like you said."

Tiffany smiled at him, and her voice broke. "You . . . you've taken good care of him. Thank you." Tears filled her eyes and threatened to fall anew.

"Was nothin', milady. A fine 'orse the likes of 'im deserves no less."

"Would you like to ride him, Princess?"

Turning to Clinton, Tiffany awarded him with a beaming smile at his suggestion, crying, "Yes!"

Clinton opened the gate. She rushed in, then turned to ask, "Will you not join me and ride?"

Touched by her offer, he shook his head, "Not today, Princess. I am content to watch you."

Clinton leaned back against the fence thinking she was a magnificent sight to watch. She was both beautiful and bewitching to behold as she rode. Her raven tresses escaped their ribbon and flowed loosely to her hips, blending with the horse's coat. And as she had ridden him this morning, so she rode Xanadu; flowing in abandoned unison, her hips moving with the motion of the horse, meeting their thrust. Holding her head high, slightly back, she exposed the slim column of her neck. Her breasts pushed against the soft muslin shirt as they had pressed against his muscled chest. He unconsciously rubbed his hand across his chest in recall.

His loins tightened as her legs, long and shapely, wrapped tightly about the horse's flanks, preparing to take a jump. He could almost feel them gripping his sides as she accepted his full length within her body. He drew a deep breath, still watching as her fingers wrapped themselves in the horse's mane much as they had done with her own locks this morning, when passion engulfed her being.

When she landed safely from a jump, Clinton watched her sit back on her taut, yet soft, buttocks he knew bore his weight well.

His body burned, aching with the need of her yielding against him, bearing his weight, holding him tightly within her while he spilled himself, marking her. He took another calming breath, letting it out in a slow stream when she collapsed on the neck of her mount, spent from her exertion just as she had done a few short hours ago. Her muslin shirt was damp and clung to her, revealing her breasts, almost as if she were naked.

Tiffany dismounted, walking Xanadu to cool him. Xanadu nudged her, causing Tiffany to lurch forward. Righting herself, she turned and scolded him. Xanadu curled his lip at her retort. Standing her ground, shaking a finger at him, she scolded, "Where are your manners, you beast? I have no bonbons!"

Clinton smiled at their playful antics, a bit envious over the carefree manner Tiffany displayed, one he was yet to share with her. In time, he thought, grinding out his cigar. Yes, in time she would accept his companionship, his love, and give him hers, in turn.

Chapter Twenty

Tiffany could almost hear the haunting music of the harp and voices singing the song of fierce bards, crying out their will to live in freedom. The wind whipped fiercely, causing her to pull her cloak abut her as she stood on the stone steps of a cliff-hung staircase which wound up the seaward side of the castle's keep. The land bespoke the unconquerable spirit of a warrior past in the raw, brooding beauty of its terraine.

"Here Kind Edward I built his fortress—" Clinton pointed to the turret towers that pierced the gray, stormy sky "—to consolidate his conquest of Wales."

Tiffany pictured strong-featured handsome men, unique and different, fighting to maintain their spirit and culture. She reached, brushing a strand of hair away from her face, turning her head into the wind.

"During the War of Roses, desperate men offered desperate resistance. This was also one of the last strongholds the Royalists held before it fell to the Roundheads."

Tiffany looked up at the castle sitting formidable and impenetrable atop the cliffs. The pounding of the surf resounded with the war cries of the men fighting desperately, taking their last noble stand. Tiffany envisioned the site and sympathized with their losing battle and understood the indomitable spirit that pushed them to fight odds they could never beat.

Turning to Clinton, who stood three steps down from her, she declared, ''Your family, they stood beside their king, against the Welsh, and destroyed the culture?''

''Aye, my ancestors were rewarded by King Charles II for loyalty to him. The castle and its lands were titled to us and have remained in our family since.''

Again Tiffany regarded the brooding pile of Halthorne Castle where it sat commanding the rocky ramparts overlooking the rugged coast below, which belied the bloody history of the shore. Looking up at her, Clinton thought she resembled the tone and spirit of the land. A sharp gust molded her clothes against her, revealing the soft line of a body he had come to know intimately. Shaking himself from the directions of his thoughts, he continued on with the history of his family. ''Most of our lands came to us as spoils of war. We have maintained them by knowing the fickle face of our politics.''

''Your ancestors were truly ruthless men, having no conscience, only ambition. I doubt it was loyalty, but rather greed. Yes, greed and the quest to be all-powerful which drove them to unspeakable deeds,'' she shouted above the roar.

''Ah, ruthless, relentless, and ambitious men, true. Greed? Nay. Wealth, spoils, or tribute comes the way of the victor. My ancestors strove to improve their lot, provide for their own, and to protect what was theirs to hold. What they spilled their blood for, they coveted. War, Princess, has no conscience, only victims and victors.''

''Then I am a victim?'' she asked above the roar.

Clinton refused to be drawn, wondering at her strange mood and at its cause. Tiffany rushed on, ''Or perhaps I am the spoils? Which is it, Clinton, victim or spoils?''

He turned to face her, weary of this argument. ''Nay, you are my wife,'' he stated simply, running his hand through his hair. She cast her gaze, watching the surf-hemmed swells pound and gnaw endlessly at the ragged shore below. A feeling of hopelessness prevailed over her as she likened the proud, yet futile, struggle of the ragged cliffs against the furious ebb and flow of the tide to herself.

"Wife, spoils, or victim." She turned to find him watching her. "Wherein lies the difference? None, I say. If I am one of them, I am all of them."

Tears filled her eyes. "Am I not the spoil? Don't I belong by right to the victor? You. Am I not the victim? One subjected to deception, sacrificed under conditions I had no control over?" Tears fell freely and etched her voice. "If I am your wife, then I am also a victim, the spoils." Turning away, she brushed the tears that fell with the back of her hand. She felt him touch her shoulder and turn her to him so he held her.

Clinton saw the pain in her eyes, the tears. "Those are your words, not mine. If you so choose to believe you are a victim, the spoils then so shall you remain. But I think only of you as the woman I love; a woman I want to love, cherish, and protect above all else."

Pulling from him, fresh tears spilling, she cried, "And above all else, I wanted another to love, another to cherish, another to protect me. Not you!" Turning, fleeing from his grasp, she ran up the stone steps wet from the mist of the churning waters below.

Tiffany reached the top, stopping, tears falling freely, her breath coming in short gasps from having run up the fifty-odd steps. She entered the keep and ran up to her chamber, where she flung herself across the bed and gave vent to her tears. Sobbing loudly, she clutched the pillow to her breast. Her tears nearly spent, she lay there, staring up at the bed canopy, her mind filled with memories of the last month. She had fought and lost the battles—all of them—and now it would appear the war also. Her body betrayed her at every turn, at every touch of his hand. She surrendered nightly to him and yielded easily every morn to his lovemaking. It mattered not how she set her will against him, no matter how often she summoned up her resistance, she would yield to the unbearable pleasure she knew she found in his arms.

She turned to her side, biting her lower lip, which trembled. She knew no matter how often she yielded, he was still not content with her physical surrender. No! Now he knew he controlled her body and he demanded more. Now he was driven in ruthless pursuit to possess all of her. He had told her, nay warned her, he would take no less than all of her.

Fresh tears sprang to her eyes. She slammed her fist against the bed in frustration, for she no longer knew what she wanted. She believed she could lose herself in the physical pleasure he offered, yet remain detached from him in other ways. Slamming her fist again, she realized he caused her to doubt her own convictions. She damned him and herself for the emotional turmoil she felt, and cried out. She needed to escape his web, to be free of his hold before he devoured her, leaving nothing but a shiny, yet empty, trophy to be shelved. And again with no plan, only strong conviction, she vowed her heart, he'd never have; as exhaustion overcame her, she drifted off, summoning Alan's image. Whispering ''my love,'' she strained, trying to recall his features, but instead a face with smoky gray eyes lulled her to sleep.

Clinton stood by the windows, his foot resting on the rung of a nearby chair. He lifted his cigar to pull leisurely on it as he stared at the gray sky which promised rain. His thoughts traveled over the past weeks. It had been three weeks since their arrival at Halthorne Castle and four weeks since their wedding. The sound of a servant bringing him brandy caused Clinton to turn. He gazed at the Great Hall, scanning its contents—a large open hearth, where a fire now blazed, took up an entire wall; a large coat of arms hung above the hearth; an immense head table with lower ones filled the hall. He looked at the richly carved inlaid chairs, designated for the lord and lady, and idly wondered what means his great-great-grandfather had used to finally tame the fiery Irish princess he had married. Walking to the hearth, he drew a chair and sat, stretching his long legs before the fire.

His thoughts, as always, came to Tiffany. He wondered at her swift mood swing and its cause. He knew she was mercurial, but today she had caught him totally off guard. Since their arrival at Halthorne, they had settled into a mutual routine, starting each morning off with a most satisfying romp in bed and moving on to improve their riding skills on a different mount. Each morning's ride found them traveling the course of the property, exploring the endless caves and bluffs. In the afternoon they'd fish in the cold streams, catching their night's supper, or walking the endless length of the coast. The evenings were spent having intimate suppers, which ranged from elaborate fare to a simple trencher of cheese, fruit, and bread, shared in front of the hearth in their room. Often the evening was spent playing chess or cards, accompanied by conversation. And while the days they shared were filled with delightful adventures, the endless nights were spent exploring the depths of passion.

He knew her body craved his, her passion as full as his own, her releases as shattering as his. She had never resisted him, but herself, and no longer even that, yielding to him the minute he touched her. She had as of yet to become the aggressor, but in time this, too, would pass. He smiled thinking this, and sipped his brandy in a silent toast. She knew his love, for he declared it often enough. That she believed it, he doubted. She believed his passion and her own. Her love? He knew her last barrier—her love—she withheld, believing it belonged to another. Smiling almost wolfishly, he silently predicted, "Where her body goes, soon her heart would follow," and he had her body with her consent now. He was making good progress and, being a patient man, would wait for her declaration of love, knowing it would come once she admitted it to herself. Until she realized that she loved him and not another, there was nothing he could do. Well, he grinned, he was not totally ineffectual. A broad smile lifted the corners of his mouth. He would help his cause along at every turn, and he had no doubt that what he pursued, he would get.

The fire crackled and spit as a log caught and he shifted his gaze to the flames. He grew weary of her arguments whenever she felt threatened, and today she felt threatened. But by what? Shaking his head, he surmised a part of it was her own doubts, and a major part was him. He had to admit she was right accusing him of being driven, ruthless, high-handed, and lustful. Oh yes! He was all those things and more! If he weren't, he would not be the right man for her, and by God, he was the man for her.

He knew what he wanted and worked to get it. She, on the other hand, was sheltered, young, and dreamed of what she thought she wanted. He'd give her all her dreams, save one—her girlhood infatuation, a love that dwelled in the mind, not her heart.

She considered herself a possession of his, and she was. She belonged to him as much as he belonged to her. He wanted her by his side, not behind him or on a shelf. She had yet to equate the freedom she longed for with him. For he, above all and anyone else, respected and loved her. He admired her spirit, pride, and courage. He loved her for who she was and had no expectations she had to meet; he demanded nothing save her honesty with him and herself. One day, he thought, she will realize that above all else, she loves me, and all my deceptions and ruthlessness will mean naught.

A sense of discomfort brought Tiffany slowly awake. She felt clammy, chilled, and crampy in the region of her belly. She stirred, feeling a moistness between her legs. Sitting up, she tossed aside the quilt that someone had covered her with. Slowly she became aware of the source of her discomfort—her monthly flux.

She padded slowly to the privacy chamber, quickly cleansing herself, and donning her black velvet robe for warmth. Tying the belt about her small waist, she stood near the blazing fire, holding out her hands against its warmth, trying to stop the shudders that coursed through her. She felt a cramp grip at her belly and instinctively wrapped her arms about her waist, bending forward as the contraction took hold.

At that moment, Clinton walked into the room and, seeing her thus, moved quickly to her side, drawing her about. A look of fear crossed his face. "Are you not well, Tiffany?" He saw the paleness of her face and felt her cold hands.

When the cramp passed, she moved toward the warmth of his body, shivering as she stood within the circle of his arms.

Clinton held her against him, feeling her tremors. Concern was in his voice. "What plagues, you, Tiffany? Something you ate?"

"I . . . I am indisposed." She stammered with embarrassment, keeping her head lowered from his prying eyes.

"That is evident, Princess," he retorted, angry that something should cause her pain. Placing a warm hand against her brow, he stated, "You have no fever."

"Just let me be, Clinton," she snapped, and tried to pull from him.

"Let you be! What kind of man do you take me for?" he replied, a bit too harshly.

Wanting nothing more than to be left alone with her pain and discomfort, and certainly not wishing to discuss this most intimate of intimacies with him, she pulled away and snapped, "A ruthless one!" Tiffany turned to face the fire.

Clinton ran his hand through his hair, a disgruntled look

etched across his face. He said, "Not that again! Cease with this argument that wearies me and gets us nowhere."

"Go away," she moaned as another cramp seized her and she bent forward again.

"Oh, I shall go away and return with the doctor." He headed toward the door with long, purposeful strides, only to be stopped by her plea.

"No, I tell you 'tis not necessary."

Opening the door, he turned and stated, "And I tell you it is."

"Please," she implored. She looked at him, stains of scarlet appearing becomingly on her cheeks. Closing her eyes tightly against his questing look, she whispered, "Please."

He smiled as realization swept over him, just as her words pierced the silence. "Must you know every intimacy? Can you not let it suffice, I am not truly ill?"

Closing the door behind him and walking toward her, he grinned, relieved. "Forgive me, Princess; as your husband, I should have realized your womanly inconveniences. After all, we are so intimate." He reached for her, but she stepped away, glaring at him, but refusing to be drawn, having neither the will or means at the moment to refute him. Clinton added two more logs to the fire, creating a blaze that licked high against the back of the hearth and quickly filled the room with warmth. Clinton turned and scooped her up, causing her to squeal. Placing her in a chair near the blazing hearth, he grabbed a quilt, covering her and tucking her bare toes beneath it.

"I shall return in a moment. I'll have our supper brought up." He left, leaving her snug as a bug in the chamber which grew warm with the blazing fire.

Tiffany sniffed the liquid in the glass, wrinkling her nose.

"Drink it, Princess. It will warm you and sooth your cramps." Tiffany looked up at him, a question in her eyes.

" 'Tis only brandy, Princess. Trust me it will do the trick." Although it was stated quite cordially, she did not miss the note of command that etched his voice. Knowing he would persist if she protested, she complied, sipping the amber liquid. Clinton moved to change his clothes. As she finished the draft and laid her glass down, she stared into the flames. She felt the brandy course through her veins, warming her, and thought it was indeed quite effective since she felt a lessening in her belly.

Clinton watched her as he tied his robe and walked over to refill her glass and pour a draft for himself. He joined her at the fire, sitting in the chair across from her. A soft knock interrupted the companionable silence and Clinton called, "Enter."

A servant brought in their dinner, serving them from the covered dishes. "We will not require your services for the rest of the evening," Clinton informed the butler, who quietly left the couple alone.

Tiffany's appetite, which at the best of times was finicky, now was almost nonexistent. She merely tasted the poached salmon and pushed the broiled trout about her plate. Instead she choose to drink the heavy wine provided with dinner.

Clinton ate as usual, enjoying the cuisine, but noted Tiffany's untouched plate. "The meal does not please you?" he asked over the rim of his glass.

"Nay . . . uh . . . I have little appetite, my lord," she stammered.

With understanding, he replied, "I see." Refilling her wineglass, he continued nonchalantly, "Is that normal during this time of the month?"

A blush accompanied her nod. So great was her embarrassment, she was unable to speak and wished fervently he would change the subject. Lifting the goblet, she finished her wine. "Do you become weepy and teary as well?" he asked as he handed her a cup of tea, liberally laced with rum.

"I . . . I guess so," she almost shouted, and than ran on, "Why all these questions? Can you not leave something to me? Must you pry even about this!" She spoke the last with anger.

Clinton smiled, understanding her mercurial moods of today were partially due to her flux. "Princess, I only wish to understand."

"Understand what?" She sipped her tea, frowning at the unusual, but pleasant taste.

"Why, your behavior today. Certainly out of character with past weeks, 'tis all."

Feeling a bit fuzzy, she put her empty cup down, which Clinton immediately refilled. "Sir, it has nothing to do with this . . . I mean that," she spat, coloring brightly.

Clinton watched her drink the tea, seeing a pink tinge color her previously pale cheeks.

Tiffany was feeling the effects of the alcohol she had consumed and was warm all over. Her discomfort became a thing of the past and she became light-headed and relaxed. "I'll ask again, Princess." He waved his hand before her face.

Tiffany focused on him, confusion clearly etched on her face. "I'm sorry, what did you ask?"

Clinton smiled, thinking the brandy, wine, and rum were doing their job quite nicely. "I asked if your condition has nothing to do with your behavior. Pray tell, what brought it on?"

"Why, *you*, of course," she answered as if it were obvious.

"Moi?" he asked with mock innocence. The alcohol had loosened her tongue and Tiffany ran on, sipping her tea between outbursts.

"It's always you . . . wanting more than I would give . . . demanding it in your high-handed manner . . . making me do and feel things I don't wish . . . It's *you!*" Tiffany raised her cup, nearling spilling its contents, and downed the remaining portion, thrusting it toward Clinton. Smiling, she asked sweetly, "Would you mind?"

Returning her smile, he replied, "Don't you think you've had enough?"

Steadying her head and focusing her eyes upon him, she replied, "Of you, most certainly . . . of the tea, hardly."

Clinton rose out of his chair and lifted her, heading toward the bed, saying, "Of me, you'll never have enough . . . Of the tea, you've had your fill."

Tiffany wrapped her arms around his neck, balancing herself against the spinning room. She spoke out against his high-handedness. "And just what are you doing?"

"Putting us to bed."

Pushing against him, uselessly, she protested, "No! You cannot mean to lie with me."

"And where do you think I shall lie?"

"Anywhere but with me . . . It is not right. Not when . . ." She could not bring herself to finish and turned her face in to his shoulder. When he laid her down on the bed and saw her struggle to rise, he stated, "I intend to lie with you, my body wrapped about yours, warming you to your precious toes."

"Nay!" she protested. "I will not lie naked next to you."

Clinton walked to his dresser, pulling a shirt from the drawer. "You shall wear this tonight and every night of your condition, but, lady, know this—I intend to sleep with my body entwined about yours." Tiffany shook her head adamantly. "Whether you wear my shirt or not," he added with a note of finality.

"You beast!"

"I told you your womanly inconveniences would not interfere with our pleasures." He smiled at the wide blue eyes which reflected her disbelief. "Relax, Princess, not tonight . . . but perhaps another night."

"Never!"

He laughed and promised, "I am sure after a night or

two of abstinence, your body will crave my touch." He smiled knowingly and added, "I trust I shall survive the drought, but will you?"

Snatching the shirt from his hand, she jumped off the bed, weaving her way to the privacy chamber, hearing his laughter echo as she slammed the door.

Clinton woke slowly, his body responding to the feel of warm, silky skin pressed intimately against him. He instinctively reached out, pulling Tiffany closer with the intention of slowly arousing her. His hand moved slowly over her breast, feeling its weight. His thumb moved over the nipple, which rose proudly. Tiffany snuggled against the warmth, rubbing her derriere against the source of heat—Clinton's groin. She turned, still asleep, in his arms, so she faced him, her head resting in the crook of his shoulder. She sighed, nestling against him.

Clinton became aware of his surroundings as he awakened. He stilled his roving hand, remembering her condition. "You randy goat," he whispered to himself as he lay there, trying to push down his body's urge to toss her on her back and relieve the burning ache in his groin which now rose hard and proud. He smiled thinking in time her inconvenience would not be an obstacle to their pleasure, but for the moment—well, hell, he wouldn't think about it. Tiffany moved, her arm coming to rest intimately against his groin, her fingers inches from his rising manhood. He took a sharp breath. Her leg casually moved so it lay between his. Clinton suppressed the urge to run his hand along the smooth skin of her thigh, up over her rounded buttocks. He groaned, fighting the desires of his flesh by occupying his mind with computations of figures. Failing miserably and believing discretion being the better part of valor, he slowly unwrapped her clinging form, and rose.

He stood on the stone floor, welcoming the cooling effect it had on his body. The fire in the hearth had burned down to only embers, but he welcomed its lack of warmth, for his body was a raging inferno. Taking a deep breath, he saw his breath in the chilled air as he slowly exhaled. Finally, when he was in control, he donned his robe, walking to the table, where he poured a liberal draft of brandy.

He sat down in the chair before the hearth, laying his head back, closing his eyes, concentrating on the brandy coursing through his veins, soothing his taut body. He remained as such, a slight smile lifting the corners of his mouth, wondering if he would indeed survive the drought which could last from five to seven days.

Shaking his head, he thought he could never get enough of her. Since they'd been married, he had her every night, every morning, and still he craved her. He smiled broadly thinking he'd probably die wrapped about her body. Soon he'd have to show her how her condition would in no way prevent them from their pleasures.

Suddenly his thoughts turned to a more serious course. He began to note the date and quickly compute the days in his head. He groaned when the realization hit him—if he continued making love to her as he had, there was no doubt a child would quickly result. While he would love a child of their making, to see Tiffany swell with his heir, he selfishly wanted more time alone with her. Sipping his brandy, he reasoned honestly, while his motives were selfish and self-serving, she, more so than he, needed time; time to adjust and accustom herself to him, time to grow, time to learn and know herself and her feelings. Nodding his head in agreement with his thoughts, he would decide what was best for her in this instance, and when the time was right, he would give her a child, but now was not the time for her to conceive.

With this conviction made, he planned the best course to take. Sighing deeply, he knew what it would cost them. Seven to ten days of abstinence to avoid the inevitable. He groaned, but then smiled broadly, thinking the abstinence might well serve another purpose as well—if he was right, and he seldom was not—Tiffany, his proud and very passionate wife, would no doubt revel in her newfound fortune. He smiled wickedly as his thoughts continued. But he had no doubt her passion, of which he had just scratched the surface, would feel the effects of the abstinence. He might just prolong it a day or two more till she had an itch only he could scratch. Yes, he leered, she would come to him in her need, and that is exactly what he wanted, for where her body led, her heart would follow.

He turned to the object of his thoughts, noting she shivered in her sleep and had wrapped her arms about, missing the warmth of his body. He stood, laying more logs on the fire, making sure they caught, and walked over to the bed, climbing in carefully, not to wake her. He drew the fur cover over them. Tiffany instinctively moved into his arms, and while he warmed her, she sighed.

A confident smile lit his face as he drifted off to sleep. His last conscious thought was of the night he would possess her, a night when her physical need would be as strong as his.

Chapter Twenty-One

Like crumbs falling from a moist whiteness, the snowflakes fell, shrouding the earth with a blanket. Snow-laden branches of the evergreens bowed under the weight of the flakes, their green needles poking out from beneath their snowy cover. Swirling winds drove the snow into smooth, curving drifts, rearranging the terrain. The gray sky peaked through the heavy curtain of flakes as the snow fell softly.

Tiffany peered out, watching the delicate pattern of a flake hit the frost-coated pane. Her eyes wandered over the snow-covered landscape and she marveled at the mercurial moods of nature, for just a few short weeks ago she had watched autumn leaves turn and fall to the brown earth. Standing like a sentinel at the bay window, behind the study desk, she glanced out at the glistening snow, thinking Wentworth appeared like a winter wonderland. She had come to know and love Wentworth Estates, with its ever-changing terrain and its never-ending boundaries. Its vastness overwhelmed her, for she never felt hemmed in, always able to ride for hours. She felt a sense of freedom she'd never experienced before, and a sense of wonder.

Its terrain, while seemingly endless, offered her every variety she craved: meadows, hills and dales, valley, and woods. She seldom thought of Courtland Manor and found she no longer pined for it.

Maybe later, if the snow stops, I'll go outside, she thought. She was restless, having been housebound since yesterday, when the snow began, and felt a need to stretch her legs. She could understand her restlessness, attributing it to her captivity; another feeling, frustration, baffled her. Pressing her nose against the cold pane, she continued to ponder the source of this unwelcome feeling. The more she thought, the more she disliked the conclusion, for she believed her frustration was born from the close quarters she kept with Clinton.

She groaned knowing that Clinton had kept her at a distance, not demanding his husbandly rights, and while she had initially been pleased, for it allowed her to gain some measure of control over her traitorous body, she now had to admit she found herself anticipating when the drought would end.

She sighed and shook her head. It was becoming harder to ignore her body's yearnings, for while Clinton did not seek his conjugal rights, he was always just a breath away.

Each night they bathed together, and now that her flux was over, she was forced to sleep naked, wrapped in his arms. Each night she wondered if the good-night kiss he gave her would progress to more, but to her chagrin, he'd drift over to sleep while she lay there feeling an uncoiling burning in her belly.

She blew against the pane, watching her breath cloud it. Since she was forced to endure his daily company, she found herself noticing small things about him: the way a small dimple creased his cheek when he smiled, or the errant lock of hair that fell on his forehead. And, God, how her knees weakened when her eyes followed the crisp mat of hair on his chest tapering to a thin line over his taut belly and disappearing at his waistband! She took a deep breath, yet felt her heart flutter, recalling the way his muscles rippled when he bent to stoke the fire. Even now she could smell his scent. A tingling began in the pit of her belly, and again she shook her head to push away her lustful thoughts. She failed in her quest and blushed over the shocking lengths her mind traveled. An ache began in her nether regions as vivid images of their last coupling came forth; his mouth covering a dusky nipple, his hands caressing and stroking her, his tongue . . .

"No!" she cried aloud, yet her body belied her words, for her nipples stood erect against the fabric of her gown, and the ache between her legs became unbearable.

"No what, Tiffany?"

She spun to see Clinton enter the room. He covered the distance to his desk, where he lifted the cover of his cigar box, withdrawing one, lighting it, while regarding her. She, in turn, watched him with a mixture of awe and longing. He was dressed casually in bluff breeches, which encased his long legs like a second skin. His shirt lay open at his throat, exposing black hair she knew covered his chest. Her fingers curled into her palms as she suppressed the urge to run them through the crisp mat. He looked incredibly handsome sitting on the edge of the desk, his leg swinging negligently as he regarded her with an arched brow poised in question.

Realizing he expected an answer to his question, she stammered, "Ah . . . nothing." Fidgeting with the folds of her dress, she dropped her gaze to the material her fingers had wrought damage to in their twisting.

Clinton watched her intently as he puffed leisurely on his cigar. Her hair was unbound as he preferred it, with a ribbon drawn around it in the same hue as her burgandy gown. Her tresses reached her waist, flowing freely. His eyes were drawn to a lock that nestled in the soft valley between her breasts. He noted her color rode high, almost as if she'd blushed, and wondered where her thoughts had been. He watched her, assessing her nervousness and unease, speculating on its cause. Perhaps, he thought, she craved him, for it had been a while since they had made love. He felt the familiar tightening in his groin, knowing today would see the end of their abstinence. He smiled at her.

Tiffany hated the silence and his knowing smile—as if he read her mind. Seeking to distract him, she said, "It's snowing."

Clinton's smile widened to a grin. Ah, he thought, she's got the same itch as I. His eyes moved slowly over her form, resting on the taut nipples rising against the material of her bodice. He saw her blush again as if her thoughts wandered to forbidden territory.

"Really?" he asked with poorly concealed amusement to her obvious observation. "Is that what has occupied your thoughts?"

"Of course!" she snapped, then wished she hadn't. She added lightly, "Whatever else would I be thinking?"

"Oh, how long it's been since you've felt me hard and throbbing deep inside you." Knocking an ash from his cigar, he watched the myriad of emotions cross her face and continued to verbalize her thoughts. "And how you'd love to feel my tongue travel over your breasts, down your belly, and stroke."

"Stop it!" she cried.

"Talking about it, Princess?"

"Yes, yes!"

"And start doing it?"

"Yes . . . no, damn you to hell, no!" she screamed, and headed toward the door but was stopped when he easily reached out, pulling her to him. Holding her between his legs, his arms about her waist, he pressed her against the evidence of his arousal.

"I think you lie, Princess." His eyes searched her face and she blushed furiously, pushing against his chest to be free. When her hands touched his chest, rivers of fire shot through her loins.

Clinton's eyes rested on her taut nipples. Raising them, he smiled crookedly and taunted, "Most definitely you lie. I think, Princess, your thoughts are filled with images of me doing all those delectable things which make you whimper and moan."

Shaking her head adamantly, she was unable to speak for fear her voice would betray her.

Clinton seductively rubbed his thumb across her full bottom lip, huskily whispering, "I bet, Princess, if I'd tip your skirts, I'd find you ready for the taking."

"You delude yourself," she managed to utter, as scarlet rose becomingly on her cheeks at the truth of his words.

"We shall see." He stood and tossed her over his shoulder, strolling confidently from the room as Tiffany pounded furiously on his back with balled fists.

Clinton kicked the bedroom door open, startling both Mortimer and Germane, who made a hasty retreat from the room.

"Put me down, you bastard, put me down!"

Clinton complied, slowly lowering her against his hard length, then holding her, pressed her against his swollen manhood. He released her and nonchalantly began to unbutton his shirt.

Tiffany watched him remove his shirt in a trancelike state, noting the play of his well-honed muscles. Shaking herself out of the trance, she stated, "It will be rape, you know."

Pulling his boot off casually, he stated, "I think not. It has never been."

Tiffany watched as his hand moved to his waistband. A pleasant ache at what was hidden and would soon be revealed throbbed between her legs. "You'll . . . not win . . . this time," she whispered.

Pausing, Clinton looked at her and smiled. "You always equate our lovemaking with winning or losing. Let me say neither of us lose. Both win." As he dropped his breeches, his manhood rose proudly, full and potent, from the nest of black hair at his groin.

Tiffany thought him to be a splendid specimen of manhood. She could not help but admire him, and a shiver of anticipation coursed through her. Closing her eyes, she felt his deft fingers unbutton her dress, which fell, pooling at her ankles. She felt, rather than saw him, kneel before her, and knew he had when his hands slowly unrolled her stockings and caressed her shapely calf.

"Admit it, Princess, you want me so badly, it hurts," he whispered. His tongue trailed a path from her ankle up her calf, placing nibbling kisses.

Tiffany was going mad with the wanting of him. His tongue trailed a fiery path up the soft skin of her thigh. She groaned, feeling herself becoming warm and open. She squeezed her eyes tightly, feeling his tongue inches from her desire. She felt his hands move up over her thighs and hover over her essence, and just when they would have touched her, they retreated and she moaned disappointedly.

Tiffany arched instinctively toward him as he knelt before her. His hands moved to grasp her buttocks and he whispered love words while his hands worked their magic, rubbing and kneading her buttocks, bringing her closer to his mouth. She felt him lift the edges of her chemise so her charms were exposed to him.

"Watch me, Princess; open your eyes, love." She felt him breathe, his breath inches from her desire, and knew what she sought would not be given unless she complied. She willingly opened her passion-dazed eyes.

"Can you imagine how good you will taste? Can you even now feel your own desire well up, longing to flow upon my tongue? Can you imagine the velvety feel of my tongue?" he whispered hoarsely. She groaned at his words and cried aloud when his tongue stroked her desire, sending electrical currents through her so strong, she thought her legs would crumble.

When he moved his tongue away, she dropped her head back, groaning in protest. Her legs weakened, threatening to buckle, but he held her still and lifted his mouth. She arched her hips to his mouth. "Please . . . don't stop . . . not yet." Her fingers gripped his hair, pulling him closer to her core of desire.

"Savor it, Tiffany. Let it build till it hurts." His tongue returned to stroke, to tease her, till the bittersweet pain became unbearable and she pulled his hair in need, yet he withheld from bringing her to release. "Not yet, love, not till you feel as if you'll die from the wanting." And then his mouth and tongue worked its magic, and when he felt her unfilled desire well and begin to flow, he brought her down to the rug, sliding her legs over his shoulders, and reared over her. His hands slid up her buttocks and lifted her closer to his mouth closing over her. Her legs stiffened as her body convulsed in a climax that sent her spinning slowly down into a pool of sensation as each shocking wave after another washed over her.

Keeping her legs over his shoulders, Clinton rose and entered her in a long, smooth stroke, feeling her muscles contract in climax. Tiffany cried out when he filled her. Clinton withdrew, concerned that in his need to possess her, he had hurt her. Feeling him withdraw, Tiffany whimpered in protest, again feeling the first of desire ignite.

"Please . . . don't go . . . oh, please."

Clinton groaned, a sound deep in his throat, and complied with her pleas. Grasping her hips firmly, he drove into her, watching her eyes darken with pleasure, feeling her body sheath him tightly. She moved, writhing beneath him, drawing him deeply into her warmth. Her eyes widened when she felt him plunge deeper and she contracted against his manhood, bringing them both to release.

Lying against her, he felt the rapid flutter of her heart. He shifted his weight onto his hands and gazed down into her glazed eyes. Still within her, he felt the final contractions of her muscles against his member, causing him to spill the last of his seed into her. Slowly withdrawing, he savored the sensation as much as when he entered her. He lowered her quivering limbs from his shoulders and withdrew from her completely. Tiffany moaned, feeling a sense of emptiness.

She felt his breath against her damp cheek as he whispered, "I love you," and then covered her mouth with his own in a gentle kiss. She tasted herself on his lips, a musky, bittersweet taste. She felt herself lifted in strong, warm arms and laid on the downy mattress, feeling it sag with his weight when he joined her. She curled against him, lying languid and content within the circle of his arms.

Clinton smiled down, softly stroking her tresses. The tension and frustration of weeks of abstinence behind them, they drifted off to a contented sleep.

Chapter Twenty-Two

Tiffany stood at the bay windows in the study watching two squirrels scamper up and down the trunk of a large sycamore. She suppressed a giggle watching them leap from branch to branch in pursuit.

The earth was covered in brown, still asleep, awaiting spring before its blanket would change to a mossy green. The trees were still bare of leaves, their limbs swaying in the March wind, showing signs of the promise of spring in the nubs dotting their branches.

Her cheeks burned from the cold winds and were apple red after having ridden an hour before. Today, unlike every other day, she had ridden along wildly over the endless meadows of Wentworth. Normally she rode with Clinton every morn after (as Clinton put it) their romp in bed, and then they'd breakfast in the conservatory, he leisurely reading his morning paper and she tending to the large assortment of plants and flowers that graced the room. She enjoyed the conservatory, for it overlooked the gardens, and often she imagined, come spring, the bay windows would be opened, letting in the fragrant breezes.

This morning she had cut her ride short and sought out the study—her favorite room of all. As to why Clinton's study was her favorite room, she could only speculate. It faced the eastern portion of the estate, and from where she stood, behind Clinton's desk, the bay windows offered an uninterrupted view of the rolling meadows that stretched to the paddocks.

There was something about the smell that permeated this room and which she found pleasing—leather, tobacco, and brandy. It was cozy to her, although its size belied the word. For some unexplained reason, she felt secure and comfortable and often sought it out.

The study incorporated a library within it whose walls were lined with rows upon rows of books. A spiral staircase wound its way to the second level, where a balcony ran. The remaining walls of the study were paneled in mahogany, which shone with its daily application of beeswax. Portraits of famous horses filled the spaces, along with dueling pistols and sabers. It was decidedly a masculine room, reflecting the master of the home. It was comfortable, lived-in, as evidenced by the well-worn leather chairs and couch arranged in a semicircle in front of the immense stone hearth, where a cheery fire always burned. Above the mantel of the hearth was a life-size portrait Clinton had commissioned of her; she stood at the bluff dressed in breeches and a lawn shirt, her hair loose, blowing in the wind, her hand at her head, holding back the strands. A plaque beneath the portrait read, ''Varium et mutabile semper femina,'' (a woman is ever a changeable and capricious thing).

Often when she sat curled up in the soft leather chair, a quilt tucked about her, reading a book, she'd glance up at the painting and wonder why Clinton had chosen that quotation. Once when she asked him, he smiled, saying, ''I thought you'd prefer it to the original quotation, 'Veni, vidi, vici' (I came, I saw, I conquered).'' With his reply, she had tossed her head and stormed away, while he laughed.

The antics of the squirrels caught her attention, breaking her thoughts until they disappeared from sight. She sighed, feeling a restlessness she had not felt since the very beginning of her marriage. Then she had used the freedom offered to its maximum, riding for hours upon hours, trying to escape Clinton's presence and her reality, seeking her elusive butterfly as she had done for most of her life. But of late, knowing she had the freedom, she no longer pursued it with a vengeance and instead found herself spending more and more time in his study.

She touched the leaded pane of glass and traced the initials T.B. She remembered the day she sat curled before the fire and Clinton had entered the study with a business acquaintance. She had risen to leave but was stopped by Clinton bidding her to remain, and when she sought to argue, he simply announced his business was hers as well. She had remained and henceforth used the room as if it were hers; never leaving when he worked alone or conducted meetings. Even now as she drifted back to the present, she heard the soft murmurs of conversation between Clinton and Mr. Boniface. Once she asked him what his associates thought of her presence, and he merely replied he cared not what they thought.

In this room she'd often sit going over the week's menus and invitations while Clinton worked diligently at his desk or conducted a business meeting. This room, save the bedroom, provided her with an insight to another side of her husband—the ruthless, ever shrewd businessman. She was amazed at the vastness of his empire, how diversified it was, and the staggering amounts of money made and spent in its running.

She could detect and recognize Clinton's position on a matter just by the tone of his voice. He could be coolly disapproving, or his tone could harden ruthlessly, and on occasion, a silken thread of warning would etch his voice. She shivered involuntarily as she thought of this other side of him. He was absolutely commanding, highly ambitious, extremely formidable. His decision-making process ran from quick to the point of astute consideration. He kept his own counsel, debating the pros and cons, and often, surprisingly, asked her opinion.

There was no doubt in her mind now, she never had a chance against him, for in business ventures, he was ruthless, driven to secure what he wanted. And after all, wasn't that what she was—a business venture? Bought and paid for. She frowned, not wishing to remind herself she was just another conquest, another addition to his worldly possessions.

Lifting her chin in a defiant manner, she remembered exactly the lengths this man had gone to to secure his prize, and again she congratulated herself over her decision never to yield her heart to him. God knows she had a difficult time in not yielding to him, for he was an opponent who gave no quarter. By God, she had already lost her body to him, unable to deny the unbearable pleasure he gave her. Her soul, alas, had yielded as well, for he nurtured and drew it from her. She sighed, remembering he had once promised her he would have nothing less than all of her—all that remained was her heart, but that she would hold from him, for it belonged to another—Alan.

Alan. I wonder where he is, she thought. She cocked her head, wondering, Does he ever think of me? When will he return? Does he know another claimed me? Her mind screamed out in defense, Of course not, you ninny! Else he would have returned, posthaste, to reclaim you. Biting her lower lip, which trembled, she allowed her mind to wander. Does he still love me? But of course he does; time and distance never changed my feelings. One does not just fall out of love. She chewed at her index finger, asking, Why has he not even sent a note or a letter? Probably, her mind rationalized, because Father would never forward them. Why else, you silly goose! Again she lifted her chin and refused to think any more about it.

She shifted from one foot to the other thinking of her mercurial mood swings of late, causing her to dwell on unhappy thoughts, attributing it to the coming of her monthly flux. Nodding her head in assent with her thoughts, she mused, I am acting like a ninny because my flux always puts a damper on my spirits, for it is a time when I am restricted.

And Tiffany hated being restricted. She balked at it, having lived most of her life under her father's forced restrictions. She had to admit even though Clinton was not her chosen husband and the marriage not her idea, the fact that she lived a pretty unrestricted life, within reason, was one positive side. She smiled, imagining her father's face if he ever knew of the activities she and Clinton had engaged in on some evenings. Why, Father would be aghast at the number of scandalous card games and games of chance she had learned. She smiled, remembering a game of piquet where she and Clinton wagered their clothing! Yes, she thought, the last few months have not been boring!

Yet the thought of her coming flux did dampen her spirits, for she would be unable to engage in their morning ride, nor—and she felt her cheeks burn with the thought—would she be able to satisfy the cravings of her body. God, how she hated to admit it, but she did crave Clinton and did miss their nightly coupling. She felt her face burn hotter as he had promised her monthly inconvenience would not hinder them from their pleasure, but he had as of yet to show her. She knew tenseness and frustration would come upon her, and she signed in resignation. What bothered her most was that even after her flux passed, Clinton would hold himself away for days till she thought she'd die from the cravings. She often thought about seducing him, but she couldn't bring herself to do it. A well-brought-up woman did not do such things! And if one did, one surely loved, and she did not love him. He simply did not hold her heart!

"Tiffany, love."

She turned at the sound of her name to face Clinton, whose hand was extended toward her. She smiled, gazing at his handsome visage, an unasked question on her face.

Clinton smiled softly in return, realizing she had been

off somewhere, and explained, "Mr. Boniface is leaving, love."

Placing her hand in Clinton's, allowed him to present her to their guest, Tiffany extended her other hand to Mr. Boniface, who placed a kiss upon it. "Your Grace, it's been a pleasure meeting you. I had heard rumors of your beauty, but mere words do you no justice."

"You are too kind, Mr. Boniface. I do hope you'll return to Wentworth; perhaps you'll be able to stay."

Mr. Boniface smiled and replied, "Hopefully, Your Grace, both you and Clinton will be able to attend a ball my wife and I are hosting when you arrive in London next month."

Clinton interjected, knowing Tiffany had not listened to their conversation. "We will let you know, Horace, once I have reviewed the itinerary with my wife. We are scheduled to go abroad to France, and perhaps we will be able to take you up on your invitation."

After the butler had shown Mr. Boniface out and they were alone, Clinton walked over to Tiffany, drawing her into the circle of his arms. He raised his hand and caressed her windburned cheek.

"You rode without me, Princess. Why?"

Tiffany shivered at his touch and felt a fluttering in her belly at his soft-spoken words. A delicious shiver went down her spine as she felt her body against his. "You had already ridden and were engaged with Mr. Boniface."

He smiled softly. "Aye, Princess, indeed I did ride a most tender mount this morning. A raven-maned, feisty mare with a soft saddle who I left quite exhausted and sprawled sleepily across my bed. So exhausted from her ride, I was unable to roust her up to put her in a different saddle."

Tiffany felt her cheeks pinken at his words. Refusing to be drawn, she asked, "You did not tell me we were going abroad. I felt quite foolish, you know, when Mr. Boniface asked.'' She broke from his embrace, turning her back to him, adding, ''Of course, what with your high-handedness, I should not be surprised. Just another flaw in your character.''

Clinton casually appraised her trim form, his eyes lingering in their travels on her rounded, enticing derriere, snugly encased by her breeches.

''A flaw, you say, Princess? Something like wrongingly accusing?''

Tiffany did not take the bait and remained silent with her back to him. Clinton continued, ''Princess, while you were wool-gathering at the window, all the arrangements were made in this very room.'' Still refusing to turn, Tiffany held her ground. Clinton moved to sit at the edge of his desk, where he withdrew a cheroot, tapping it against the desk.

''I thought, Princess, that is, in my high-handed manner, of course, that country life was dampening your spirits. Wanting nothing more but your happiness, I arranged a trip to France. On our way to France I thought a week in London, going to the opera, theater, and such, would be nice.'' He paused to light his cheroot; Tiffany began to turn toward him, her interest piqued. Clinton pulled leisurely on his cigar, blowing a curl of smoke. Smiling, he said, ''Then I thought we'd travel to Paris and attend a horse race.''

''A horse race! Really?'' Tiffany rushed over to Clinton and stood between his legs, her blue eyes as big as saucers. ''You're not teasing me, are you?''

Clinton smiled in response to her question and shook his head.

Tiffany squealed with delight, throwing her arms about his neck, placing a quick kiss on his lips. Clinton was pleased with her uninhibited response but would have liked to plunder her sweet mouth in a deep, passionate kiss. His hands encircled her waist, bringing her closer to him, as she rushed on, ''Really? You do mean it, don't you?''

Clinton nodded his head. "Have you a doubt?"

She laughed with joy; it was music to his ears. He vowed he'd take her anywhere, just to hear that sound.

Her laughter died with her words. "But Father always said a horse race was no place for a lady, that only ladybirds and paramours attended such." She frowned and rushed on, as if doubting her last statement. "Although the only race I attended, well, I really didn't attend it . . ." She stopped, realizing he of all people knew the race she referred to.

She shook her head, wishing to forget that incident, and asked, "Do we have a horse entered? Surely not Xanadu!"

Clinton smiled over her exuberance, and not wishing to put a damper on her excitement, made no mention of the encounter. He lifted her chin with his fingers and said, "Princess, you are a duchess, you can do as you please, no matter what your father's notions are. You are my wife, my lover, my paramour, if you will. And yes, we do have a horse entered, and no, of course not Xanadu."

"Which horse do we have entered if not Xanadu?"

Clinton loved the sound of the "we" she had used. He loved her abandoned joy and he loved her more than life itself. "You shall see, love, and there'll be no prying it from me."

Tiffany pouted at his words, but Clinton refused to be daunted, adding, "Our horse has better than fifty percent odds at winning but is virtually unknown. Rory and Brent will meet us there, for they are much interested in wagering some pounds."

Seeing the unasked question in her eyes and knowing her love of gambling, he answered her, "And, of course, Princess, you may wager all my worldly treasures, except, of course, yourself. That I would not allow." Tiffany stiffened in his arms, but Clinton held her tightly.

"You presume too much, my lord. You do not own me nor do you control me."

"Really, Princess? I beg to differ, for you own and control me as well." She pushed against him, wrenching free. Clinton smiled and she glared at him, knowing she was free because he allowed it.

"Princess, I control and own you body and soul, every morning, night, and often in between."

"Aye, but only then, my lord, never any other time." She stalked to the door, yanking it open, and before leaving, she turned and said, "Body and soul maybe, but never my heart."

As she walked out, she heard the underlying promise in the words that followed. "That, too, will pass."

Chapter Twenty-Three

Paris, Spring 1819

Tiffany stood on the bottom rung leaning against the fence; her sweet rounded derriere, clad in black breeches, rubbed against Clinton's groin as she turned to watch the horses approaching the finish line. The tail of her French braid caught Clinton's chin as she turned her head sharply. Her high black boots struck his shin when she jumped in excitement as Kubla Khan crossed the finish line first.

"Oh, did you see, Clinton!" Tiffany exclaimed. She turned in his arms to face him. He stood behind her, hands braced upon the fence.

Clinton gazed at her. She was refreshingly charming; her cheeks heightened with color, her eyes sparkled with excitement, and errant wisps of hair escaped her braid.

Impulsively Tiffany threw her arms around his neck, and he instinctively moved closer, pinning her between the fence and his long, hard form. "Wasn't he wonderful? I knew he would win. I told Brent he would, odds or not."

Clinton was inordinately pleased with her obvious happiness. "Yes, Princess, he is indeed wonderful, odds or not."

"Oh, Clinton, this is the very best birthday. How can I ever thank you?"

He grinned at her innocent question, thinking of a number of ways, none which were appropriate at the moment. "A kiss, Princess, would do it."

Without a pause, she leaned fully against Clinton's body, placing a sweet kiss on his lips.

"Ah, Princess, I know you can do much better."

As her fingers twirled in the hair at his nape, she considered his request. A teasing sparkle lit her eyes when she replied, "Clinton, 'tis not proper," and she gazed about, continuing, "What will all these people think?"

"I don't give a damn what they think. Now, give a proper tribute to your husband."

Still uncertain but more than willing to do his bidding, she leaned into him, parting her lips slightly and placing them upon his. When she would have lifted her mouth, she found his hand held her head. His tongue teasingly traced her lips, then plunged into her mouth, coaxing her tongue to play. Tiffany, stirred by him, kissed him back, her tongue boldly fencing with his.

Clinton felt the fire light in his loins, the blood rush to his manhood, which rose, pressing against Tiffany's belly. It had been almost ten days since he last lay with her, and three days remained in his self-enforced abstinence. With this in mind, he checked his desire and lifted his mouth reluctantly from hers. He saw the aroused passion in her dazed eyes and knew she felt the stirrings as strongly as he. Rubbing his thumb over her lip, he whispered, "Princess, if we continue, I shall embarrass myself. As it is, I pray you do not leave me at this moment, for my breeches are straining at the bit."

Feeling herself as if her knees would give out, Tiffany rested her head against his throat, willing her own desire to burn down.

"Merde!" Marcel Rousseau spat as he threw down his cigar, grinding it viciously with his foot.

Brent turned to him, a smile etched on his mouth.

Tauntingly he inquired, "Lose, did you now? Well, if it makes you feel better, I lost a tidy sum to my sister-in-law." Shaking his head, he muttered, "Should have never taught her about odds and all."

Marcel, his gaze resting on the figures embracing at the fence, replied, "*Mon Ami,* your brother has the devil's own luck when it comes to horses and women, *non?*"

Brent, looking in the same direction, nodded in agreement.

Tiffany, after having gained some measure of control, lifted her head and saw the many faces turned toward them. She whispered desperately to Clinton, "Everyone is looking."

Holding her close, he replied easily, "Let them. I told you, Princess, I care not what people think nor say." She smiled timidly at him, leaning against his tall frame, casually fingering the hair at his collar.

Seeing the horses lining up, Clinton asked her, "Which horse have you wagered on, Princess?"

Tiffany turned to lean against the fence, securing her feet in the rung. "I wagered with Rory over the gray," she replied, and turning to face him, added, "I did wager a large sum, though I think Rory goaded me into doing so. I fear he and I will always be at odds."

Smiling, Clinton remarked, "Don't worry, love, about the amount, nor Rory for that matter. He's always one to hold a grudge, you know."

"Well, had Touche not stumbled, I would have beat him, and well he knows it," she replied defensively.

"I guess you'll have to show him, won't you?" Clinton pulled a cheroot from his vest pocket and lit it.

"Would you really let me challenge him to a race?" she asked incredulously.

A curl of smoke drifted upward as Clinton puffed on the cigar. "Have you any doubt?" A smile lit her face at his words. The start of the race caused Tiffany to turn.

Once again her exuberance over the race caused her buttocks to brush against Clinton's groin. He groaned as she unconsciously rubbed against him. He thought, Only three more days, which at the moment seemed a lifetime.

"Pardon, Estell *ma petite,* I must collect my winnings," Rory said, looking appreciatively down at the redhead he had recently made his mistress.

"You will not be too long, *m'amour?"* she pouted prettily, batting her eyelashes at him.

Taking in her lush, curvy form, he remembered the delightful night past and replied easily, "No, *ma chérie,* just long enough to collect what's owed me."

While making his way to Tiffany and Clinton, he was stopped by a group of acquaintances.

"Say, Rory, ole chap," called Clive Thornton, "you could make me a very wealthy man today if you'd solve this puzzle for us." Clive swept his hand over the four men standing nearby.

"Alan here insists the lovely bit of fluff with your brother is his new duchess." Holding his head arrogantly, Clive snorted and continued, "I told Alan the nice piece of fluff is his new lovebird."

Now, while Tiffany, to Rory's way of thinking, was a troublesome bit of baggage, she was nevertheless family, a Barencourte, and *no one* gossiped about a Barencourte. In a voice edged in steel he replied, "That bit of fluff you refer to, Clive, is Clinton's bride." Leveling his gaze, holding Clive's, he added, "My family has an aversion to gossip . . . a deadly one." Rory turned, leaving the group.

"Tiffany, pay special attention to the horses parading by." Tiffany watched mounts passing, noting a solid black filly, fine-boned with four gleaming white hooves and a blaze. She watched the filly prance before her and sidestep daintily.

"Which would you choose? Which one would you bet on?"

Without pause, Tiffany pointed a slender finger at the filly, "That filly over there, Clinton, the feisty one."

He smiled and pulled on his cigar.

"I'll wager two hundred pounds on her, Clinton."

"Not until I've collected, little sister," interjected a just-arrived Rory. Tiffany pulled a face at him and withdrew one hundred pounds. Clinton stilled her hand. Both looked to Clinton, who explained.

"Perhaps, Rory, you'd wish to wager double or nothing on this race?" Clinton smiled down at Tiffany.

"Two hundred pounds?" Rory asked. Clinton nodded. Rory looked to Tiffany, who smiled and agreed.

Rory raised an inquiring brow and taunted, "But can you afford it?" He smiled at her, letting his gaze travel over the breech-clad figure, and taunted further, "I wouldn't want to deplete your allowance and deprive you of the means to purchase a proper wardrobe."

Tiffany glared at him, her temper, beginning to flare, reflected in her narrowed eyes. Clinton interjected, "Not to worry, brother, I'll cover her."

Rory had witnessed the public display between Clinton and Tiffany. He had noticed how Clinton had remained very close to her, even now as she was pressed against the fence by his body. He replied, sarcastically, "Cover her, yes, you've done that quite nicely today."

Not willing to be drawn, Clinton smiled easily, asking, "Which mount do you chose, brother?"

"Let the lady make her choice first; it's the least I can do before I take her money."

The lively twinkle in Rory's eyes incensed her. She permitted herself a withering stare before she turned abruptly, causing her head to bump Clinton's chin, and pointed. "The black filly with the white blaze and hooves."

"I prefer the strawberry roan myself."

Clinton grinned at Rory. "Yes, it appears you are partial to redheads today." His eyes pointedly came to rest on Estell standing a discreet distance away.

"It would appear so," Rory agreed, following Clinton's gaze.

The report of the gun signaled the race had begun. Tiffany rose to stand on the rung; her body rested against the fence, and her derriere rode high, brushing against Clinton's groin, which burned with the contact. Clinton, not the least bit interested in the race at hand, leered wickedly down at Tiffany's raised bottom, taking in its soft, rounded shape, while illicit thoughts and images ran rampant through his mind.

Tiffany turned quickly about, crying, "She won, Clinton! She beat them all!"

Clinton quickly masked his face against his carnal thoughts and led Tiffany over to the filly. Tiffany stood admiring the horse and rubbed the soft black muzzle.

"Do you like her, Princess?"

"Oh, she is splendid, Clinton. What is her name?"

"Duchess." Clinton paused to relight his cigar. With cigar clamped between his teeth, he added, "And she is yours."

Intense astonishment touched Tiffany's face. She breathed one word, "Mine."

He pushed a stray tendril of hair from her face. "Happy birthday, love."

Impulsively she threw her arms around his neck. Standing on her toes, she drew his face to hers and pressed her open lips against his mouth. She moved closer, molding her body against his, pressing her breasts to his chest, her hips to his, and slowly curled her fingers in his hair.

The kiss she had begun deepened, loosening the restraints of her passion, bound by their abstinence. Her tongue stroked his mouth thoroughly, as the flames of desire began to lick at her.

Clinton could no longer suppress his desire and kissed her, his tongue boldly meeting hers, stroking her mouth.

His hands moved over her back, caressing, kneading her, pressing her closer to his rising desire.

A discreet cough brought Clinton to his senses and reluctantly he lifted his mouth from a weak-kneed Tiffany, who leaned heavily against him, her face turned against his throat feeling his rapid pulse pound.

"Sorry to interrupt, brother," replied Brent, who looked anything but sorry, "but my intentions, while untimely, are honorable. I've come to pay Tiffany her winnings."

"As have I," added an even less remorseful Rory.

Tiffany at the moment could have cared less; she was still reeling from the effects of the kiss and merely smiled weakly at the intruders. While she had unwrapped her arms from Clinton's neck, she remained leaning against him until she was sure her trembling legs would hold her upright.

Clinton, for a brief moment, entertained the thought of fratricide and its consequences. His face reflected his thoughts as he stared at his brothers.

The moment was interrupted by Keegan, who strolled up to the group, a length of rope coiled in hand. " 'Ow'd you like 'er, my lady? Told the guv'nor she's a credit to her sire and you'd love 'er."

Thankful for Keegan's timely intervention and sure her legs would hold her, Tiffany moved closer to the horse. "Xanadu's the sire. I should have recognized the markings."

Keegan led the horse away as a group of men, who had remained on the sidelines, unwilling to interrupt, now joined them. Tiffany stood quietly at Clinton's side as the men conversed. Not paying much attention to the conversation or exchange of markers and pounds, Tiffany stood, scanning the crowd. Her eyes drifted over a group of well-dressed men who stood laughing and chortling. Her eyes stopped and moved back over the group, coming to rest on the slender figure of a man whose back was to her.

A nagging sense of familiarity oozed through her as she took in the light sandy hair, the lean, athletic physique.

As if feeling her eyes upon him, the man turned. His amber eyes arched slowly back and forth in the crowd, stopping to hold sapphire eyes. He turned fully to face her, and across the distance that separated them, Tiffany saw the face that haunted her dreams, and held her heart.

Chapter Twenty-Four

Tiffany felt as if she were in a dream. Her legs, though moving, seemed to drift, never closing the distance that separated her from him. She drifted over to him as he broke from the crowd, moving toward her. Like in a dream, the rest of the world ceased to exist, as if they were the only people who inhabited it. When they did meet, only a breath away, they feared to touch and awaken, they feared to speak and shatter the moment.

For Tiffany, the world came to a halt. Nothing existed save him! Nothing mattered but this moment! Yet in that moment two thoughts intruded: I remember him taller, and, Why doesn't he kiss me?

Thoughts also raced through Alan's mind: God, she is exquisite! What the hell is she doing here dressed like that!

Blue eyes misted with tears of love; a love of yesterday, of years gone by. Her heart sang, for nothing could diminish this moment.

Alan, on the other hand, asked sharply, "What the hell are you doing here, Tiffany? Why in God's name are you dressed like this?" He grabbed her arm with the intention of removing her from the track.

Clinton, acutely conscious of Tiffany at all times, noted her absence immediately. Looking up from the group of men, he scanned the crowd. His hand, which idly rubbed his chest, stopped when he saw a young man grabbing her arm. He felt an uncontrollable urge to throttle the man who dared lay a hand on her. He broke from the group abruptly, crossing the distance separating him from them, removing his jacket.

Both Brent and Rory swiftly followed.

"Uh . . . uh." Tiffany could not speak. She flushed feeling Alan's eyes fall to her breasts, which were partially revealed by the subtle opening of her shirt, but before she could respond to his questions, she felt a coat dragged over her shoulders. Turning in confusion, she found Clinton standing by her side, his arm possessively about her shoulders, pulling her against him.

Alan stared up at Clinton and released Tiffany's wrists, seeing the ominous glimmer in the gray eyes and the twitching muscle in the lean, hard jaw. Tiffany unconsciously rubbed her wrist. Clinton leveled his gaze to Alan. "Is there a problem, Tiffany?"

Tiffany stood speechless watching her dream vaporize into a living nightmare, then stammered, "I . . . ah, no."

Clinton drew her closer. Tiffany balked and stiffened at his high-handedness, wanting to explain, but unable to speak or move. "Why are you here? Who is this man? What is the quality of his life?" Alan demanded, stepping forward.

Clinton, filled with cold rage, answered in a voice that held a thread of challenge, "I am the man who brought her here. The quality of my life, sir, depends on the position she holds in it. I am her husband."

Realizing his folly, Alan lowered his eyes. He looked at Clinton and nodded his head, replying, "Excuse me, sir; if you require satisfaction for my error, I will choose my seconds."

Tiffany was slapped right out of shock and cried, "No!" Her eyes lifted to Clinton's, a plea of understanding in them. "He . . . he is Al . . . Marquess Thurston." She placed her hand on Clinton's chest, feeling the pounding of his heart. Clinton broke his stare from Alan and looked down at her, seeing her plea etched across her face.

He saw the lines of tension at her mouth and brow, the look of concern in her eyes, and he briefly wondered, Me or him? Clinton wanted nothing more than to ease her worry, erase her fear, reassure her. Lightly he fingered a loose tendril that fell on her cheek, then, cupping her chin tenderly in his warm hand, said "Do not fret, love, I concede!" Raising his eyes, holding Alan's, he added pointedly, "This time."

Brent and Rory slowly let out a collective sigh of relief.

Alan merely nodded in recognition.

Tiffany closed her eyes and sighed.

"Come, love, it is time we go. The carriage is waiting." Tiffany yielded.

"Good-bye," she whispered to Alan before turning, letting Clinton draw her away from her lost love.

Clinton placed a booted foot on the seat and the other on the carriage floor. Tiffany rested between his legs, glumly staring out the window. She felt the hard, unyielding muscle of his raised thigh as the carriage rocked over the terrain.

Rory and Brent sat across from her regarding her from lowered lashes as they carried on a quiet conversation with Clinton.

Brent produced a flask of brandy, pouring out three glasses, which he distributed to his brothers. Clinton leaned over, accepting the glass. Tiffany caught the clean, manly scent of him and shivered. His strong, warm hand touched her shoulder, and she turned to him. He offered her the brandy and she accepted, sipping the strong brew, seeking the soothing effect it offered. The fiery liquid rushed through her veins. She took another long sip, handing the glass back. He smiled at her as a rush of color stained her face. He lifted and drank from the same spot her lips had touched. Tiffany settled back between his legs and stared off. The rocking motion of the carriage was a balm to her, and the brandy soothed her. She worried at her slender finger, unmindful of those in the carriage. Her thoughts, far from the conversation in the carriage, dwelled elsewhere. She had always imagined their meeting, and in her wildest of dreams, she never thought it would be so disastrous.

She had wanted to see him again, to talk to him . . . Well, she hardly spoke at all, she never had a chance, everything had somehow gone awry. She felt Clinton press the glass against her lips; she allowed him to hold it as she drank deeply from it. She did not see Rory's cocked brow or Brent's incredulous look when Clinton silently requested a refill.

What did Alan mean by her being there and dressed like that? Of all the words she had dreamed he would say, those were definitely not ones she anticipated.

She snuggled closer to the warmth emanating from the body she rested against and continued her musings. Well, you ninny, what else would he say? she thought in his defense. He was as surprised to see her as she had been to see him. After all, he last saw her in England, and now to find her in France and married, of course he'd be shocked. She nodded. Yes! of course.

The brandy snifter appeared magically before her, and again she indulged herself, catching snatches of the soft conversation about her. "Great bloodlines, good form, excellent time and confirmation." She paid scant attention to it, for at the moment she felt so overwhelmed by the brandy, she could hardly think straight, let alone follow the conversation. Instead she allowed her thoughts to ramble.

I wonder why I thought he was taller? Now, Clinton . . . She smiled appreciatively, and sighed. Now, he is tall and so broad and so . . . Clinton! Why, he is the root of all my problems!

She frowned, marring her brow, and with a determined

set to her jaw, she stubbornly concluded that Clinton was the reason for Alan's response. She snorted aloud, a most unladylike sound, which caused Rory to draw his brows together and turn to her. Brent shook his head wondering at Clinton's wisdom of plying her with brandy.

Tiffany's thoughts continued. What the hell was all that nonsense about the quality of his life, and her position? He was an arrogant, domineering, high-handed man! Why, he had just about ruined her reputation today. Quality of life, my ass! She hiccuped, drawing another frown from Rory. She giggled, for some reason finding the whole situation at the moment funny.

The carriage's sudden lurch almost toppled her, save for the three pairs of hands reaching out to brace her. She gazed about at her brothers-in-law, seeing an assortment of looks etched on their handsome faces.

She recovered herself, feeling strong, warm arms encircled her, holding her securely. She awarded Rory and Brent with a lopsided smile, then shook her head in an effort to clear her blurry vision, and focused on Rory's face. She spurted out, "Rory, you look positively awful when you frown. Not fierce, like you think, just ghastly. Are you miffed that you lost two hundred pounds to me?" She hiccuped, laughing merrily.

"You know, Rory, Clinton said I could challenge you to a race." She turned her head quickly, bumping Clinton's chin. "Didn't you, Clinton?" she asked, her words slurring.

Clinton smiled down at her, "Yes I did, Princess."

Turning back to Rory, her movement caused yet another jar to Clinton's chin. "Sooo, what do ya say, Rorry?" She smiled smugly, snuggling against Clinton, hiccuping loudly. She giggled delightfully at Rory's frown. Brent drew his breath in sharply and rolled his eyes heavenward.

Rory seethed inside, his face devoid of the anger he felt. He leaned forward and lifted her chin with the tip of his finger. "I accept, any time; you name the date and place."

"I'll ride Duchess!" she squealed, suddenly turning to face Clinton, who dodged, avoiding the top of her head.

"And you—" she pointed a slender finger at Rory as she wavered back and forth, closing one eye, zeroing in on his blurry face "—can ride that redhead. I mean the roan you're so partial to."

Brent, Clinton, and Rory nearly spat out their brandy at her comment, knowing Rory did indeed have a preference for redheads in a more tender saddle than Tiffany referred to. All three laughed heartily. Tiffany looked befuddled.

The carriage came to a halt and the door was opened by a footman. Brent and Rory descended, followed by Clinton, who carried a giggling Tiffany through the foyer of Chablisienne. As he ascended the steps, still holding his wife, he turned to his brothers, asking, "Are you accompanying us to Richilieu's this evening? We are spending the weekend, and tonight is Tiffany's birthday dinner."

Hearing her name, Tiffany piped up. Holding her hand high and with a finger pointed to herself, a wide, lopsided grin on her face, she cried out delightedly, "I'm nineteen today, ya know?"

Clinton continued his ascent, with Tiffany leaning over his arm crying out to Brent and Rory, "Do you know what that means? I'll tell you. I am a woman."

Brent and Rory stood at the bottom of the broad, curving staircase. Brent regarded her, an eyebrow cocked, in humorous surprise, a smile tipping the corners of his mouth, when she exclaimed, "A woman of means, position . . ."

Shaking his head, Rory leaned against the baluster, hearing Tiffany's words, "A woman quite capable of controlling her own future, answering for her own actions . . ."

And as they disappeared out of sight, Rory, his mouth turned up in a slight smile, his left eyebrow raised a fraction, added, "And a woman quite drunk."

Chapter Twenty-Five

The well-sprung coach, bearing the Chablisienne coat of arms, traveled at a leisurely pace down the well-worn road. Tiffany sat quietly across from Rory and Brent, Clinton at her side, puffing slowly on a cigar.

Tiffany's headache, from which she had suffered all afternoon, finally ceased, but only after taking the snifter of brandy Clinton presented to her, remarking, "You always bite the dog that bit you." She had been unable to sort out the events of the afternoon, for there had been little time. Before she knew it, she was dressed and off to their host, who was renowned for the parties he gave.

She asked softly, "What type of parties does he host that are so legendary?" All eyes turned to her, for she had been, up to this point, silent.

Smilingly, Clinton regarded her, catching the glimmer of her diamond necklace, which he had presented to her this evening, the nineteenth stone added.

"He offers a variety of entertainment, an array of food, and a weekend filled with festivities. I believe, Princess, you will enjoy our stay."

The coach pulled up the long drive, the clattering of the horses' hooves echoing over the cobblestones. The coach drew to a halt and four livery-clad footmen appeared, opening the door and assisting the occupants in their descent.

While the butler procured her cloak, Tiffany took note of the opulence of the foyer. While she thought it beautiful, it in no way compared to Chablisienne or Wentworth. For some reason, she was pleased by this fact.

"Ah, Clinton, *mon ami.*"

Tiffany watched a tall, slender man with the lightest hair, almost white, approach them. His eyes were dark as currants, and his bronzed skin provided a striking contrast. Richilieu was taken in by the vision Tiffany presented. She was an alluring sight in white silk and satin. Her gown was trimmed with double ruffles at its base. Her shoulders and the graceful curve of her back were bare, and a white ruffle ran from off the shoulder across the plunging bodice, where the full, soft swell of her breast rose. The exquisite diamond necklace was the only jewelry to adorn her. Her raven tresses were dressed so they cascaded softly down her back; gardenias were arranged within the simple coiffure, with one pinned lovingly behind her small, shell-shaped ear.

Richilieu, a sophisticated man of reputation and experience, never lacking female attention and who, at the age of thirty-two, had managed to avoid the matrimonial state, was impressed with Tiffany.

In a low, smooth voice which sent shivers down her spine, he said, "Ah, so the rumors do not lie, you are indeed exquisite." He took her hand and bent over it, placing a kiss upon it. Clinton smiled at his friend's reaction, then introduced Tiffany.

"May I present our host, Tiffany, Robar Richilieu."

She smiled and curtsied prettily.

When the amenities were over, they strolled into the salon to await dinner. Rory and Brent went about their own devices.

Clinton handed Tiffany a glass of sparkling champagne. Tiffany, from lowered lashes, watched her husband, noting, as usual, his impeccable dress, which, as always, was simple yet elegant. This evening he dressed in black save for his white shirt and cravat. She noticed the heads of many women turn to regard Clinton; a twinge of jealousy touched her, as did a feeling of pride.

Chad Devonshire walked over to them, conversing about Kent and Alysse awaiting the birth of their first child, and then began to talk about business with Clinton.

Tiffany lost track of their conversation and sipped her champagne as she watched a group of newly arrived guests. Her eyes widened and she spilled her champagne. There, standing in the foyer, was Alan!

Clinton paused in his conversation when the glass fell to the carpet. He looked at Tiffany, seeing her stunned expression, and followed the direction of her gaze, coming to rest on Alan. The butler's timely announcement, ''Dinner is being served,'' and the pressure of Clinton's hand on her back brought Tiffany out of her state. Taking the arm he offered, she allowed Clinton to lead her from the salon to the dining room.

Clinton seated Tiffany across from him and took his seat.

Alan could not believe the transformation of Tiffany, and if he thought her lovely before, he now found her elegantly exquisite. He was unable to take his eyes off her and had to suppress an urge to reach out and touch her.

Discreetly, while arranging her napkin, from under lowered lashes she found Alan among the hundreds of guests.

Dinner was a never-ending affair, typical of French formal dinners. Tiffany found the meal tedious and wanted nothing more than to leave. *Le terrines d' alouetts truffes* was the appetizer, which she hardly touched, not favoring meat paste, instead consuming a glassful of the claret. She nibbled on the lobster. Taking a mouthful, she pushed it down with another gulp of wine. Her stomach knotted with fear, or was it the course of pheasant with fresh vegetables that turned it topsy-turvy? Her wineglass was again refilled by the waiting footman.

She toyed with the stem of the crystal goblet and casually stole a glance toward Alan. Alan happened to be looking her way, smiled, and then caught Clinton's gaze, which chilled him to the bone. There was no threat, no challenge, just a look that staked a claim and drew the line.

Glancing back at Tiffany, Alan saw a pleading look in her eyes.

Alan knew he had no rights to her. He had turned those rights over to this very man whose intentions he now questioned. Alan vowed he would not interfere, but he would, for old times' sake, offer Tiffany any refuge from any ill treatment the duke rendered to her. It was the least he could do.

Clinton regarded both Alan's behavior and Tiffany's. He missed not a detail nor stolen glance. For the first time in his life, he felt threatened. He had faced many over the barrel of a gun, and crossed many with a sword. But this was different, for the solution was not who possessed the strength or sharper wit or skill, but rather who possessed the heart. By the time the cheese and fruit trays were replaced with ice cream and kirsch, Clinton had his solution worked out.

On the other hand, Tiffany was more confused and frightened than ever. One part of her cried out to hold on while another cried out to let go. She knew not her heart nor its dictates anymore. She felt as if her foundation was like a sand castle, slowly crumbling with each wave.

As she walked with Clinton, his hand riding possessively on her back, she felt fear, not of him but of herself. As they entered the ballroom, Clinton put his hand under her chin, turning her toward him.

"Remember, Princess, your promise of long ago?" he asked softly as if aware of her quandary.

She looked quizzically at him, and he explained patiently, "The first and the last dance are mine."

As the music began, he extended his hand, and as soon as she touched the warmth of it, she felt safe.

* * *

Seated at the dressing table, combing her hair, lost in thought so deep, Tiffany neither heard nor saw Clinton enter and close the door.

He quietly leaned against the wall to gaze at Tiffany. He thought about the decision he had made at dinner this evening. After observing the stolen glances, obvious perusal, and reactions between Tiffany and the marquess, he knew what he intended to be the best course. He felt her battle her fear, and knew the time had come.

He watched her pull the brush through her locks, absorbed in her dreams, holding on to them; she was totally unaware of his presence. His eyes moved slowly over her form, resting on her dark mane which shone with rich luster, then moved over to her creamy shoulders exposed by the silk chemise she still wore. His eyes traveled to the pink-hued nipples which strained against the sheer cloth reflected in the mirror, down to her slim waist he could span with his hands. His eyes rested at her waist, thinking if he went through with his plan, her now slender waist in three months time would thicken, and her breasts, which were full, would grow heavier as her slender belly swelled with his child. There was no going back, he thought. It was a chance he must take, for he wouldn't allow her to rebuild any portion of the wall he had taken down. He would not allow her to hide from him and immerse herself in her dream.

He shook his head. No, he could see through her; just one look in her eyes told him the dream had become flesh and blood again. His threat now had a face he needed to erase from her heart. He smiled as he appreciated his uninterrupted view of her. It was time she realized that now was what mattered. She must forget the past. Ready or not, now was the time for her to give him her love. Tonight she would yield her heart. Tonight she would give him the chance to show her he could make all her love dreams come true if she'd let her true feelings come through. It was time for her to give him her love, open her heart and let him in, let him touch her inside.

Clinton startled Tiffany when he stood over to lean against the bedpost behind her. He caught her gaze in the mirror, holding it. Her cheeks pinkened and she felt as if he knew her thoughts and where they wandered to. Lowering her eyes, for she could not meet his knowing gaze, she whispered, "You startled me, my lord." When hearing no response, she raised her eyes to find him regarding her through the mirror.

Casually he withdrew a cigar, lighting it, continuing his perusal as a curl of smoke drifted upward.

Tiffany became nervous under his close scrutiny and worried at her lower lip. Seeking to break the unbearable silence, she chattered while her hands wreaked havoc with her hair. Finally, unable to bear it any longer, laying down her brush, she said, "I think I shall retire. I am tired."

In the span it took to say those words, she found Clinton smiling leisurely over her shoulder. He leaned over her, putting his cigar in the ashtray on the dressing table. Tiffany felt his warm breath, tinged with the smell of brandy and tobacco, caress her shoulder. She shivered, closing her eyes, trying to hide the effect he had on her. She opened them to find his gaze in the mirror. She watched him while he held her eyes, lowering his head and kissing her shoulder and nibbling at the slim column of her neck.

His breath was warm and moist against her skin, and she felt her skin tingle where his mouth touched. No matter how high-handed or ruthless he was, nor how angry and frustrated he made her, he only had to touch her and nothing mattered anymore. He so easily made her long for him and the unbearable pleasure he could give her. But not tonight, she vowed. She closed her eyes to deliberately shut out any awareness of him.

"No!" she whispered brokenly, causing him to stop, but remain poised watching her.

"No?" he whispered a breath away from her sensitive ear, causing Tiffany to lean her head against his mouth.

"Please, not tonight . . . Just leave me be, my lord, for tonight . . . please?"

He spoke softly to her reflection, "Princess, any night, save our first and this night, would I grant your request."

"Please, I am tired and wish to sleep," she implored, her eyes pleading with his.

"And perhaps dream, Princess? Dream of a love of yesterday, of days gone by?"

Clinton shook his dark head; his hand rested on her shoulders, his fingers played downward, just touching the swell of her breasts. "Nay, tonight above all nights, Princess, for tonight I leave my mark permanently."

Why wouldn't he let her be? Was she not a purchased wife? And a wife she had been; he had seen to that. All she had left was her dreams, and those he could not buy. She cried to him in the mirror, "What more do you want of me? Is what you have never enough? Will you not be satisfied until you have drained me and left me dry as dust to be blown in the wind? I have fulfilled your contract. You have the merchandise, my lord. What is it you want that I have left to give?"

Tears pricked her eyes, threatening to spill. She could no longer go on for fear of crying. She held his gaze, her bottom lip trembling in fear, fear she would be traitor to her dream.

"Something money can't buy, Princess." His hand slid down over her breasts, his fingers slowly circled her nipples. "I want you to love me."

She watched her nipples rise and strain against the sheer cloth, then raised her eyes, meeting his gaze. The sound of his voice, low and seductive, affected her deeply. "I want you, Princess, to take me deep inside you." His fingers moved, caressing her breasts, causing them to rise and fall rapidly. Her breathing became ragged.

Clinton continued, "Let me touch you deeper than

ever,'' as his hands played homage to her body. She closed her eyes against him, but his voice, lulling and filled with promise, continued, ''To leave my mark, Princess.''

Clinton created a quickening inside her. She could not speak, for her words would sound hollow. Instead she shook her head in refusal. She felt him move and come to kneel before her. He gently parted her thighs, lifting the edges of her chemise, and leaned forward. She felt his breath warm against the sensitive skin of her inner thigh before he lowered his mouth, covering her woman's flesh.

She bit her lip to suppress a groan and failed when she felt his fingers part her nether lips and his tongue stroke her most sensitive spot. Her belly quivered, its muscles leaping across the flat surface. Passion pounded the blood through her heart as she soared higher, reaching the peak of delight, forgetting all else. His stroking tongue sent pleasant jolts through her, and her hands, involuntarily, grasped his dark head, holding him, pressing him on. She opened her eyes, catching her reflection in the mirror. The woman in the mirror looked back through eyes dark with passion, lips parted, hair wildly streaming about her shoulders. She dropped her head back, moaning.

Clinton felt her tension, her fingers wrapped in his hair, the spasms of her muscles, and knew he would soon taste her release. He lifted his mouth and gazed up, hearing her cry of disappointment when he left her. He rose and stood above her, seeing her eyes glazed and dark with unfilled passion.

''Come, make love to me, Princess,'' he whispered hoarsely as he removed his cravat and began working at the buttons of his vest.

''Come, let me touch you,'' he taunted as he unfastened his shirt, ''deep inside you.'' He pulled his shirttail from his breeches and let his shirt fall open.

She was overwhelmingly aware of his hard, furred chest and stared at him with longing, aching for the fulfillment of his lovemaking. She felt the ache between her thighs, throbbing incessantly, and felt her blood race hot through her veins. She was taut as a bowstring; his words were promises she knew he would keep.

"Oh, please," she pleaded between breaths, begging him for release.

"Love me, Tiffany," he whispered, shrugging out of his shirt, dropping it to the floor.

She stared at the wide, firmly muscled chest. Her eyes followed the crisp black mat of hair that narrowed down over his taut belly, disappearing at the line of his breeches. She felt her own warm and thick moistness, aching to flow. Impulsively her hand moved, an instinctive gesture, to release herself.

"It will not be as good without me, you know." He rubbed his hand down the hair on his chest, watching her eyes follow its path down to the fastener at his waist.

Tiffany raised her eyes. He captured them with his. There was no denying the promise she read in those gray orbs. She didn't know if he spoke the truth, but trusted him. She wet her parted lips and again pleaded with him, her need reflected in her eyes. "Please," she whispered brokenly.

Clinton was not immune to her need nor her pleading and wanted nothing more than to sweep her up and make love to her, but he held fast. Their whole life depended on the few short steps she had to take. "I'll give you what you crave." He opened his arms to her. "Just love me, come love a man, not a dream."

She leaned her head against her shoulder, slowly rubbing it back and forth, and closed her eyes, imagining a hand moving over her, a tongue releasing her, yet still she felt no release, only raw hunger no dream could satisfy. Her hands moved slowly up and down her arms, teasing her raw nerve endings. She opened her eyes to find him bootless, his breeches undone and opened at his waist, revealing a wedge of black hair where she knew his manhood rested inches below. Love him? But how, she knew not.

"Come, Princess, love me, you know how." His voice was endearing, tempting. His words released her and she rose, holding his eyes with hers, and closed the distance between them. Her body ached with need and love she knew this man could give. She stopped a breath away from him and shrugged her shoulders, her chemise falling around her feet. Stepping over it, she came to him, reaching up with both hands, holding his face, which she drew down to hers, cupping his jaw with her fingers splayed over his cheek. Her thumb brushed his lips, which he parted, and moved seductively over them, occasionally touching the tip of his tongue. She moved closer, moaning when her sensitive breasts brushed against his hair-roughened chest. She pressed against him—flesh against flesh—man against woman. She stood on her toes and covered his mouth with hers, tasting herself on his tongue when she coaxed his to parry.

Clinton's groan gave her confidence and a certain power in her allure and she pressed herself against him, feeling his rising manhood against her belly. She ached. A burning fire spread between her thighs, urging her on. Clinton stood, arms at his sides, hands clenched. His body was like a bright flame which Tiffany stoked. He felt her trail kisses down his neck and twirl her tongue about his ear. He moaned and Tiffany became bolder with her newfound power, sliding her hands from his face, over his chest, feeling the heavy pounding of his heart. Her fingers lightly circled his nipples, which, to her surprise, rose proud, hard, like pebbles. Her tongue circled their hardened peaks and worked its own magic while her hands slid boldly down his taut belly, which quivered in spasms of anticipation. Lightly she teased the muscles, watching in fascination how they rippled. Her hand stopped at the waist of his open breeches. Clinton's sharp intake of breath caused a smile to cross her face. She slid her hands down the sides of his breeches, which fell. His manhood popped free, full and very potent. Clinton stepped back; Tiffany took in the virile form, missing no detail of his manly perfection. A sense of pride, of ownership, fleeted through her.

Weeks of abstinence, an evening of worry, a night of bewitching seduction, almost caused Clinton to lose control, but he waited.

Tiffany moved closer to him, rubbing her breasts against his hair-roughened chest, and then lower, until she felt his manhood slide between her breasts. He groaned. And when he felt her cup him and draw him into her mouth, he gasped. While she had not the expertise of a seasoned courtesan, her innocent ministration brought him to the point of where he threatened to spill himself.

He gasped out, "Don't, love . . . stop."

Tiffany wanted nothing more than to bring him the pleasure he so often brought her, and ignored his plea. She marveled at his size and the feel of him. When she felt him grasp her shoulders to still her, she fell back onto her knees and looked up at him wondering how she displeased him.

Seeking to reassure her, he drew her up against him, whispering, "No, love, you'd render me useless." His manhood throbbed painfully with his carefully leashed control, but he held her close, noting her breathing matched his own short, ragged gasps.

Tiffany wanted nothing more than to quench the burning between her legs and moved closer to him, rubbing against him.

Knowing her need, he lifted her easily up against him. She wrapped her arms about his neck, and her legs about his waist. He moved to carry them to the bed. Tiffany whimpered against his throat in frustration, feeling his hardness against her wet core. She arched against him, causing Clinton to lose his balance and fall backward onto the bed.

Beyond the limit of endurance, Tiffany straddled his lean sides and lowered her arching warmth on his engorged member.

Both drew in sharp breaths as one descended and the other rose to become one. Grasping her hips, Clinton rose, trying to give more of himself to her. Whimpering aloud and pounding on his chest, she cried, ''Please, you promised, please.''

With a growl, he tossed her on her back, thrusting deeply into her, feeling her widen and arch to meet his driving thrust, bringing him deeper into her welcoming flesh.

Clinton reared back, pulling her legs over his shoulders, and thrust deeply into her.

Tiffany felt his penetration, felt him touch her as never before, as no other ever would. And at that moment she loved this man. Their eyes locked and she whispered to him, ''You're so deep . . . you touch my womb.''

He looked down at her, into her eyes, and saw tears, her love, and groaned aloud, ''I shall fill it.''

And then she felt him bring her to the edge of climax and she cried out, ''I love you.'' His hand moved to hold her head as his body moved over her and she whispered, ''I love you.'' What she saw in the smoky gray depths of his eyes surprised her, the glistening of tears. And when the rippling convulsions of her climax brought him to spill his seed and fill her womb, tears slipped from the corners of his eyes as the woman he loved gave him her heart and he gave her life.

Chapter Twenty-Six

Morning came, and with it, bright sunlight, which streamed into the room, its fingers touching the faces in sleep. The chirping birds had long since risen, and the soft, insistent knocking disturbed the couple who lingered in that half-sleep state, comfortably and contently entwined about each other.

Clinton was the first to open his heavy-lidded eyes. He held his breath a moment to be sure the knocking was not his heart, but the door. He gazed down at Tiffany molded against his side, her leg straddling his thigh. His eyes roamed appreciatively over her naked buttocks and he would have continued, save for that incessant knocking. Clinton pulled the sheet up over them and called out, "Enter."

An impeccably dressed Mortimer rushed in, unusual for him since the valet was always quite stolid and pompous. Mortimer approached the bed a bit hesitantly, still not used to serving both master and mistress. He averted his gaze from Tiffany's form. His eyes betrayed his discomfort when Tiffany, in her sleep, moaned and sighed, snuggling closer to Clinton.

Clinton shot him a grin and asked, "Yes, Mortimer, what brings you here?" Clinton reached for a cheroot, which Mortimer quickly intercepted. While Mortimer never approved of the filthy habit, he was most grateful for the diversion from this most embarrassing situation. After lighting Clinton's cigar and procuring an ashtray, again Mortimer averted his eyes from Tiffany and stared at Clinton.

Clinton puffed leisurely on the cigar, noticed a flush creeping up his valet's face, and raised an eyebrow in question. "Er . . . Your Grace, Monsieur Richilieu sent me to see if you or Her Grace are ill." Mortimer wrung his hands nervously as Clinton regarded him with a puzzled look. "The hunt, Your Grace . . . 'Twas scheduled for early morn. They are awaiting you and Her Grace." Mortimer raised his eyes to include Tiffany, then quickly looked away when she kicked out a slender leg.

Seeing his valet's discomfort and always delighting in upsetting him, Clinton took longer than necessary to reply. "Tell Richilieu we will be down within an hour."

"Very good, sir."

Tiffany slowly drifted up from her sleep, hearing the closing of the door. Slowly she opened her eyes, still heavy with sleep, and saw Clinton lying beside her, smoking his cigar.

He smiled softly thinking how soft and beautiful she looked when she first awakened. She returned his smile, laying her head against his shoulder, snuggling against his body.

Clinton shifted his leg, which rode strategically between hers, brushing against her woman's flesh. Tiffany felt the thickness of his thigh against her and the beginnings of a sweet ache. Blinking away the remnants of sleep, she allowed her body to move against the pressure of his thigh.

Clinton smiled, moving his knee closer, applying delightful pressure, feeling her grow warm and moist against his leg. Reaching over, he pulled her beneath him. He was stopped by a knock on the door and called out angrily, "What!"

Mortimer's head peeked around the door; his eyes widened as his face turned crimson at the sight before him.

"What the hell is it *now!*" ground out Clinton.

"Ah, er . . . Monsieur Richilieu wishes to know which saddle to tack Her Grace's mount," stammered Mortimer.

"Hunter. Now, get the hell out of here!"

Realization slapped Tiffany awake. She sat up, the sheet falling to her waist, and covered her mouth. The hunt! She scrambled to get out of bed, but Clinton snaked an arm out, catching her about the waist and holding her to his supine form.

Looking down at him, love shining in her eyes, she said softly, "Clinton, the hunt. We're late. They are waiting."

With the cigar clenched between his teeth and a mischievous look in his eyes, he replied, "Let them wait, Princess, or let them hunt." Removing his cigar, but holding her, sure she would dash away as he reached over and put it out, a wicked grin lit his features as he said, "I've a need to improve my skills on a mount worthy to be ridden." Moving his hand down her belly, feeling the muscles jump under his fingers, he found her soft, moist essence.

"And you, my lady, need to improve your skills as a rider."

Tiffany smiled, then put her hands against his chest, pushing away, explaining, "Nay, Clinton. They will know. I will not be able to face them, nay." She shook her head.

"Princess, they already know. Why else would we be abed so late?" he reasoned.

Frowning at his words and shaking her head, she persisted, "Nay, they will only think we were tired and slept." She smiled brightly at her explanation.

"Like hell they will! I'll not let them believe I'm some tired old man in need of rest." He moved his fingers slowly over her moistness. "Nay, Princess, as you say, they will know, for there is nothing like the glow of a recently bedded woman, all rosy and radiant."

He lifted her, and just as the engorged tip of his member teased her opening, he said huskily, "Aye, Princess, they will see my mark on you this morn." Before she could utter a protest, he lowered her onto him, and a deep moan from her throat was her response.

Sure enough, as they descended the steps an hour later, Tiffany's cheeks bloomed like the petals of a red, red rose.

It was evident that everyone knew what had detained the duke and duchess this morn. The stares from the sea of faces awaiting them made Tiffany want to thrash Clinton. She colored fiercely, her cheeks becoming warmer when she caught Rory's smug smile, Chad's wide and knowing grin, Brent's infamous raised brow, and Richilieu's slow, secret smirk. And then there was Alan's look of disbelief.

The men, while awaiting the arrival of the women, stood outside drinking brandy served by numerous footmen. Clinton caught sight of the marquess who occasionally looked toward the front entrance. Clinton knew who the marquess was looking for. Brent watched Clinton watch Alan, and Rory watched Brent watch Clinton watch Alan. Exasperatedly, Rory threw down his cigar, shaking his head, thinking he didn't need any of this, and walked over to his mount.

Clinton knew the moment Tiffany exited by the look on Alan's face. Clinton moved toward her, coming to stand one step below, smiling softly, offering her a sip of his brandy. She took a sip as he held the glass to her lips.

Clinton reached up, brushing a lock of hair from her face, then lightly brushed her lips with his. Placing his arm across her shoulders, they descended the steps.

Most of the guests did witness the couple but thought nothing of their behavior other than it was apparent the duke and duchess had a *mariage de coeur,* definitely an unusual situation for the times. However, Alan felt their display was scandalous. What did he expect from the infamous duke of Chablisienne, whose reputation was notorious! Why, had he known the dukes of Wentworth and Chablisienne were one in the same man, he would never have given Tiffany over to him. Well, he thought, maybe not that, but I would have done something.

The call to mount brought all to their horses. The teams were chosen, and much to Clinton's dismay, Tiffany and he were separated. His displeasure stemmed from the knowledge of her fear of the kill and his need to protect her. To make matters worse, the guests had heavily wagered on the kill, so they would be riding for blood.

Clinton saw Rory was to ride with Tiffany. He nudged his mount forward, cutting Rory off.

"What goes, Clinton?"

Lighting a cheroot and offering one to Rory, he explained, "Keep an eye on Tiffany if we should get separated."

Rory puffed leisurely on his cigar, gazing over to his team, seeing the marquess. Turning to his brother, an eyebrow raised in disbelief, he cocked his head in the marquess's direction, "From that twit?"

Letting out an exasperated sigh, an expression of pained tolerance crossing his features, Clinton remarked, "Be serious."

"Then tell me the danger and I will keep her from it."

"The kill." At Rory's puzzled look, Clinton elaborated, "She cannot handle the kill."

It was hard to believe his volatile sister-in-law would be bothered by anything so trivial. He asked sarcastically, "What's she do? Go all aflutter and swoon?"

"Precisely." Clinton spurred his mount, leaving Rory muttering to himself as he made his way. "First we have an old flame, nearly a duel, and now the vapors—hell, I don't need this."

* * *

Tiffany was adjusting her stirrup when Rory pulled alongside of her. She decided she was in too good a mood to let him upset her this day and decided to ignore him.

The others shifted in their saddles, screaming out wagers to the bookmakers. Vanessa VanGard's throaty laughter broke through. "I heard the duchess is a fair rider. We should have no contest. I bet on my own team one hundred pounds."

"Precisely why I wagered against my own team," shouted Marcel.

Rory casually smoked, watching Tiffany stand in her stirrups, being sure they were even. He asked quietly, "What say you of this, Tiffany?"

After a moment in which she decided he was not mocking her, she answered, softly voicing her trepidation, "I find no sport in running down a fox. I can't stand man's inhumanity to animals and will not wager."

While it was common knowledge this was Tiffany's first hunt, why she had not hunted until now wasn't known. The fact that she was a superb rider was all her team cared about, that and winning.

The hound-master came over to Rory, asking him to join Clinton's team, for there was one too many on Tiffany's team. Rory had no recourse but to trot over to Clinton, shrugging his shoulders.

The horn was blown, the hounds released, and while the riders waited for the signal, Alan moved his mount alongside Tiffany. He smiled softly at her and her heart warmed, remembering the days of riding over their properties, leading him on a merry chase.

As if reading her thoughts, Alan said, "It will be like the old days."

"Yes, it will," Tiffany replied.

The report of the gun sounded and Tiffany dug her heels in. (She forgot the fate of the fox, feeling safe in the company of one who knew her so well, one whom she could trust.)

* * *

"Ah, Clinton, it would appear your wife's team will win, *mon ami.*" Clinton nodded. He was concerned, and both Brent and Rory could see it on his face.

Clinton's group had been misled on a false scent, and now they were farther away from the fox and Tiffany.

"Perhaps we should head yonder, where the baying is louder," suggested Chad.

Leslie Marshall called out as the riders began to move, "Gentlemen! Do you mind if I catch my breath? I daresay I am exhausted."

Rory rolled his eyes heavenward, thinking most of these people would starve if they had to hunt for their food. Knowing Clinton wanted to find Tiffany and realizing they were headed on another wild chase, he suggested, "If you chaps don't mind, I suggest we head east, for the hounds we hear now are just as lost as our own."

"I agree, let's be off," Clinton said.

"Just wait a minute, gentlemen. What's the fuss! We have no chance of winning." Leslie fixed her hair, adding, "And I daresay, the end is so bloody, I won't mind missing it."

Taking the proverbial bull by the horns, Clinton instructed, "Brent will remain with you, Countess, until you regain your strength. The rest of us will head off."

Tiffany saw the pack surround the petrified fox. She tried to turn her mount around to leave, but the throng of riders was rushing in, pressing her, their mounts crushing against her legs while she frantically sought to escape.

Her mount became skittish smelling Tiffany's fear and panic and began prancing in circles, slipping on the muddy bank.

The need to escape was overwhelming; a primitive terror born of fear overrode reason. She raised her terrified eyes in search of Clinton.

She found instead Alan and cried out his name. Alan

looked over at what he mistook as her cry of victory and shouted, "By Jove, you've done it, girl!" He called out to all in the confusion, "She's done it. We've won!"

The group moved in on her, shouting, "Bloody the duchess, bloody the duchess." Someone pulled her from her mount and drew her to the hounds. She heard the snapping, growling, vicious noise and watched in horror as the pack attacked and mangled the fox. Blood spurting from a severed artery splashed on her. She cried. The hounds tearing the body apart, fighting and nipping each other in the blood sport, caused the bile to rise in her throat.

She could not move and felt the throng of people push her closer to the hound-master, who turned, holding the bloody tail in an upraised hand.

"Tribute to the duchess," the crowd cried.

She closed her eyes and began to back away but was stopped by a wall of people pressing in.

"Come now, Tiffany, it's tradition, you know." Alan pulled on her hand. The hound-master reached up, smearing one cheek, then the other, with blood, still warm and fresh.

Instinctively she touched her cheek and looked at her bloody hand. She gazed down at her shirt, splattered with blood, then looked up at the crowd celebrating their blood sport. She backed away terrified, in shock, then turned, never seeing Clinton or Rory trying to push their way into the crowd, and screamed.

No one heard it, but Clinton saw her terrified face and silent scream.

She fell in her rush to be gone, slipping on the muddy bank. She scrambled up, bile rising, threatening to spill, and she ran.

Clinton followed and saw her stumble, nearly falling into a ditch. He pushed his mount to gain on her.

Tiffany ran, her hair streaming out, tears blurring her vision. She was very close to complete hysteria and unaware the ground sloped. Stumbling, she would have toppled down the steep hill had not an arm swooped down, lifting her up.

Clinton swung her across his saddle within the safe circle of his arms, bringing her close against his chest. Gently he moved his hand up and down her back until her sobs slowed, whispering, "Hush, hush." He kissed the top of her head and rocked her in his arms.

Her sobs slowed to gulps and hiccups. She turned her face in to his chest, feeling protected and safe.

"I . . . I . . . I'm going to be sick."

He swung down, and when her feet hit the ground, she ran, tripping over a tree root, sprawling to her knees. Nauseating bile rose as she heaved.

She felt fingers pulling back her hair as she emptied her stomach, leaving her weak. Clinton lifted her up, feeling her tremble.

Rory arrived and dismounted, taking Tiffany as Clinton remounted. Rory saw her bloodstained cheeks where her tears cut paths through the clotted blood. His eyes traveled over her bloody shirt. He handed her up to Clinton with a question in his eyes.

"Relay my excuses. I'm heading back."

Tiffany sat across his lap, locked in the shelter of his arms before a small fire which burned in the hearth. She rested her head against his shoulder, feeling him kiss the top of her brow, her eyelids, and the tip of her nose.

She was clean, warm, and safe. She drew up her knees, which poked out from under the lawn shirt she wore. Clinton casually caressed her bare legs. She sighed.

A soft knock on the door interrupted the silence, and Clinton called out, "Enter." Surprisingly, Mortimer and Germane entered, a look of concern etched across their faces. Mortimer placed a tray of brandy and glasses near the chair. Germane poured out two glasses while she stole looks at her mistress.

"Will there be anything else, sir?"

Clinton shook his head.

After the servants left, Clinton picked up the glass. "Here, Princess, take a sip." Dutifully Tiffany obeyed, and Clinton turned the glass to where her lips touched and drank as well.

Tiffany moved her hand soothingly over his chest. The feel of his hair-roughened chest gave her a sense of security and she felt safe. She accepted another sip of brandy, feeling its warmth spread into her limbs.

She leaned her head back against his arm, watching him finish the brandy. Feeling her eyes on him, he looked down and smiled softly, brushing a newly washed tress from her forehead. "Feeling better?"

She nodded her head and softly said, "It was horrible. All the blood. The poor thing was all mangled and . . ." She stopped, turning her head in to his chest, and began to cry softly.

"I know, Princess, it's all right now. Hush, love. You're safe now," he whispered soothingly.

She lifted her tearstained face to him and asked, "You don't think I am childish, do you? I just—"

"Hush, love. No, I don't think you childish, quite the contrary." He smiled and continued, "I knew about your aversion to the kill. I even know about your aversion to eating meat."

"How did you know?" she whispered.

"I love you. I made it my business to know all about the woman I love."

She snuggled against him, then remembered how every meal served always offered two entries, one meat, the other fish. She remembered all sorts of things—her breeches, the saddle, her bonbons, her violets. Things she took for granted, things no other, not even her father, had bothered about.

She moved his hand over her legs to caress her thigh, then travel over the triangle of curls, where it rested intimately. She lightly touched her tongue to his chest, circling his nipples.

Clinton's fingers moved till they found the source of her pleasure and began to caress her. When she lifted her head, he covered her mouth and stroked her till Tiffany was aware of only the pleasure she felt, and all images of the hunt disappeared.

Clinton rose, carrying his precious bundle to the bed, where he laid her down and joined her. Tiffany welcomed him with open arms and parted thighs and he reared over her, entering her slowly, finding her moist and ready for him.

He made sweet, gentle love to her, after which she fell asleep.

He lay back against the pillows on cradled arms, his mind and body weary. He closed his eyes, waiting for the much-needed sleep to claim him. His mind drifted over the recent events.

He felt Tiffany move close to him and snuggle against his side, then sigh. He smiled, for she had come to trust him, feel safe with him, and love him.

He cradled her against him, feeling her soft, silky skin. He felt her burrow closer to him for warmth. His thoughts drifted pleasantly as he prepared to sleep. She had given her love and heart to him. He'd known enough women to know, when a woman spoke, to listen to what she said with her eyes. He listened and saw moments of love and moments of lingering doubt. He was not discouraged, for he knew her love to be tenuous and fragile. Time and the child, and there was no doubt after this weekend there would be a child, would make it stronger and take deep root.

Before he drifted off to sleep, his last thoughts were that it would take a bit more time for her to lose any thread of doubt, any question of betrayal, and then all that remained was for Tiffany to admit she loved him above all else. This step was a step she must take alone.

Tiffany stood at the open window, clad in Clinton's shirt. Lifting her cup, she drank the sweet hot chocolate.

It was eleven in the morning and she had risen hours before and had drawn the curtains, shielding the bright sunlight from Clinton, who slept deeply.

As she placed her cup on its saucer, her eye caught a sheet of paper under the napkin. Her fingers lightly touched it. Then she picked it up, opening it. It read:

Tiffany

I missed you at dinner and hope all is well. I had hoped to speak with you more but I am departing this eve. Perhaps I will call on you in England. Until then, have care. I wish you the best.

Fondly,
Alan, Marquess Thurston

A tear slipped from the corner of her eye. She brushed it away with the back of her hand and lifted her eyes up as if to prevent the fall of more. Her dreams planned so long ago drowned with her unshed tears.

The note slipped from her trembling fingers, floated to the floor, as did her girlhood dreams of yesterday.

The world at this moment seemed unkind, unfair. A thousand "what ifs" crossed her mind. What if she had never left England, never met Clinton, never saw Alan again? What if time and circumstance had been different? Then, perhaps—but it didn't matter, for all the "what ifs" could never alter the present.

The fact of the matter was, destiny had taken control of her life, and few were masters of their own destiny. She was not one of the few, nor was Alan. The strong, ruthless ones turned the hands of fate to make their own destinies, and Clinton was one of those few.

And now it would seem her future lay with him. She had fought it, but could no longer deny she had come to love him. But was she more to him than a possession his ruthless nature desired, sought, and gained? Was she just another treasure bought and paid for to add to his worldly possessions? Nay, her mind screamed in self-loathing.

God, she had to believe him and believe he did not lie, nor betray her love.

The sound of stirrings brought her out from within herself and she turned to see Clinton move onto his back. A soft smile touched her mouth, she felt her spirits lift. As she moved toward him, she closed the door to a past that had remained open for so long.

Tiffany padded softly toward the foot of the bed, where she stood gazing down at Clinton. Her eyes traveled over his powerfully built chest, covered with a crisp black mat of hair, down to where it veed at his waist. Her eyes scanned the handsome, strong planes of his face and settled for a moment on his mouth, which she knew curled as if always on the edge of laughter.

She smiled her love at his sleeping form and thought how boyish he looked as a lock of hair fell onto his forehead; he was truly a magnificent man! Just looking at him, she felt stirring in her belly, a pleasant ache beginning in her center. She marveled over the effect he had on her even while he slept. She felt a need, as if nature called, to feel him inside of her.

Her fingers moved, working the buttons of her shirt, her eyes never leaving him. He stirred, causing the sheet to fall, exposing the lower half of his groin. His manhood rested in the nest of dark curls there; flaccid against his thigh. She marveled at its size and shivered in anticipation. A moistness began to flow within her and she lost herself in carnal images. She worked the third button with fingers that shook, and stopped, hearing voices in the drawing room.

Without a thought to her attire, she crossed the room in

purposeful strides, opening the door and entering the sitting room. Closing the door behind her, she turned to lean protectively against it and came face-to-face with Richilieu.

Germane and Mortimer gasped at seeing their mistress scantily attired in front of Richilieu.

Richilieu let his eyes appraise the delightful form. *Mon Dieu,* what a captivating picture she makes, he thought.

Remembering she was a duchess, and refusing to be daunted by his leisurely appraisal of her or knowing grin, Tiffany asked with as much dignity as she could muster, "Richilieu, is there something I can help you with?"

Smiling suggestively at her question, he remarked, "I came to inquire if you and Clinton would be attending lunch. You have missed breakfast and—"

Not allowing him to finish, she replied, "How kind of you, but we will be unable to attend. Perhaps your chef could make a tray?"

"But of course! Is there something special?"

"Yes, Clinton is fond of eggs and kidneys, oysters, and herring. Tea and perhaps a bottle of Bordeaux."

"And you, Duchess?"

"Some fruit, cheese, and a salad if your cook can manage it."

Bien, I shall have it sent up immediately." He turned, walking to the door, but was stopped by her words.

"No, monsieur, in about an hour or so."

He turned to see her close the door behind her.

He smiled, whistling as he left the room. He would probably not see his friend until dinner, if at all. Maybe this marriage thing was not so bad.

Clinton was dreaming he was sailing on the Aegean Sea when he first felt the stirring in his groin. He dreamed he shouted to Austin to let the mast out when he felt a growing ache in his groin. He groaned softly at the sensation. "Mmm."

Slowly his dream faded as his body responded and he drifted upward, as if coming from the bottom of a pool. He heard himself moan and felt his manhood grow hard and erect.

Slowly he opened his eyes, savoring the incredible sensations. His eyes focused on a dark head which moved slowly up and down between his thighs. "Ahhh," he moaned, reaching out to touch her shoulders. He whispered hoarsely, and somewhat stupidly, "What are you doing, love?"

Tiffany looked up, her hand continuing where her mouth had been, moving slowly upward and downward as she breathed, "Loving you, Clinton."

Her breathing sounded shallow, ragged, to him as his became rapid and harsh. His body was taut from the throbbing ache in his loins and the agony of the sensations she was creating within him. He managed to utter, "Don't, Princess," then moaned, "ahhhh."

"Let me love you, my lord." Her mouth closed over him, drawing him deep into the moist velvet sheath of her mouth.

He protested no more and yielded to her exquisite torture until he felt himself tighten and ache. "No, no more, love, no more." He grabbed her shoulders, stopping her, and pulled her on top of him. Their faces met. Tiffany saw the strain and concentration etched across his handsome features and felt the wild hammerings of his heart. She inadvertently moved, causing him to cry out, "Don't move, love, don't!"

Tiffany stilled. He opened his eyes and looked into hers, listening to what her eyes told him and her words confirmed. "Please, I need to feel you inside me, my lord." He closed his eyes, groaning at her words, trying to gain a measure of control over his desire, and would have succeeded had she not mistaken his pause and implored in a broken whisper, "Please."

Feeling her hard nipples brush against his chest, and his

manhood press against her belly, he whispered, "Do you wish to ride, love, or be ridden?"

His hand moved to her moistness, lightly stroking her source of desire, and not waiting for her reply, he grasped her hips, lifting her onto his erect shaft.

Tiffany moaned, gripping his sides tightly, setting the tempo to bring them to release. Clinton tried to still her movements, for he was close to his own release and wished to prolong their joining but was unable to stop the convulsive heave and spurted himself hotly into her welcoming warmth. He groaned deep in his throat, a measure of pleasure, a measure of disappointment in not bringing her with him.

Tiffany gazed at him with passion-dazed eyes. When he opened his, he looked up, seeing her unfulfillment and confusion; her lips still parted, her nipples erect, peaking from beneath the veil of her hair, her breathing still ragged.

He lifted her from him and brought her against him, and she rested her head against his throat. A moment of silence passed and he whispered against her hair, "Pleasant way to awaken, Princess."

Tiffany rested against him, feeling an ache, almost like a pain, throb between her thighs, but she managed to ask, "Are you hungry, my lord?"

"Mm-huh." He smiled, feeling himself begin to harden at her innocent, yet suggestive query.

Lifting her head, she said, "I informed Richilieu—" Before she could finish, he tossed her onto her back, raising her legs over his shoulders, and before his mouth closed over her, he said, "For you, not food."

He brought her to a much-needed release with his tongue, then plunged his eager member into her slick woman's flesh. And because he had already gained his pleasure, he was able to ride her into release after tumultuous release before he again took his own.

* * *

"I want to go home, Clinton," she whispered as she lay satiated in his arms.

"We shall leave for Chablisienne tomorrow, love. 'Tis too late today," he answered as his hand stroked her shoulder gently.

"Nay, I want to go home to Wentworth, Clinton."

Lifting her chin with the tip of his finger, gazing into her eyes, he said, "Then to Wentworth it is." He gently kissed her lips.

A gentle knocking at the door caused him to raise his head and call, "Enter."

Germane and Mortimer scurried in. Germane rushed to open the curtains, letting in the afternoon sun, while Mortimer directed a servant who rolled in a cart laden with an assortment of covered trays.

"Will you be bathing, my lord, my lady?" At their nod, Germane dashed off to the bathing chamber, ordering about the servants to make haste, lest the food got cold.

Mortimer opened the bottle of wine, allowing it to breathe.

The two servants were in harmony today and had put aside their differences. They were united in the cause to see to their lord and lady's comfort. Having done so, they withdrew.

On the way to their bath, Clinton stopped to view the array of food: oysters, shrimp, mussels, eggs, kidneys—an ambrosia of delights meant to appease the palate as well as augment one's sexual prowess.

With amusement he asked, "Who ordered this?"

Tiffany peeked over his shoulder, glancing at the array, and saw nothing amiss. "Richilieu, I believe."

Clinton threw back his head, and a throaty laugh escaped as he led Tiffany to their communal bath.

Chapter Twenty-Seven

"But why do you have to go? Can't Austin handle it?" Tiffany pleaded while helping Clinton on with his jacket. He turned to face her and she began to straighten out his cravat.

"Princess, Austin is tied up with the strikers, trying to negotiate a settlement." Lifting her face, gazing in her tear-filled eyes, he promised, "I'll return in three days, four tops."

Snapping her head away, not in the least bit appeased, she turned her back to him. She watched Mortimer direct the servants to carry out his baggage.

What's wrong with me? she wondered, her eyes filling with unexplained tears. God, I'm so weepy lately, she thought as she brushed a tear away. And so tired. Every afternoon I have to nap, and just this morning I nearly vomited when Germane brought me blueberries in cream. She shuddered in recollection and pushed the thought away, asking, "Why do you have to go?"

Clinton regarded her. His experienced eye traveled down her back, stopping at her slightly thickening waist. She had been excessively sensitive since they'd returned to England; her impulsive changes of mood—from exuberant to weepy—had not gone unnoticed by him. Her appetite was at times waning, then voracious. Even certain foods she normally turned her nose up at, she now could not have enough of. Then there was the greenish tinge that colored her face whenever he smoked a cigar. These were all clear, undeniable signs she carried his child.

Patiently he explained again. "Princess, Brent is in Genoa, Tristan at sea, and Rory is handling the spring foaling. That leaves no one but me. I must go."

"Then take me!" She spun around, no longer tiffed, but now imploring.

He saw the soft curve of her slightly rounded belly and the fullness of her breasts, noting the tiny blue veins more prominent against her creamy skin. Her nipples were darker and larger as they pressed against the sheer cloth of her shirt.

Running his hand through his hair, he patiently explained, "The roads are not safe, Tiffany. We have been plagued with a rash of robberies. I would not endanger you."

"I would not call two robberies in six weeks a rash!"

"No," he said in a voice she knew brooked no argument. Tears filling her eyes, Tiffany brushed past him, stomping out of the room, slamming the door behind her.

Clinton stood quietly going through his mental checklist: Clarissa had been summoned, Rory was about, and Keegan was instructed not to allow her to ride.

Shaking his dark head over the last item, he thought she certainly was not going to be happy over that restriction, especially since she was not yet aware she was with child. He considered telling her, for possibly she would then understand his concern, but he wanted her to realize her condition. Until she did, he would have to take measures to protect her and the child, for he knew not what he would do if he ever lost her. Confident in his decision, he left the room to search for her.

He found her where he expected, by the window in his study. He saw her shoulders trembling as she sobbed, and walked toward her.

Tiffany heard him approach and turned, wiping her tears

Tiffany heard him approach and turned, wiping her tears away with the back of her hand, trying to appear indifferent between her gulps and sniffles.

"I . . . would have thought, my lord, you left. It is past time."

He smiled at her pretense and extended his arm to her. "Will you not see me off, love? Why, in the days of old, the lady offered the stirrup cup to her departing lord with her blessing."

Pouting and sniffling, she replied, "In days of old, some lords gave scutage, my lord."

"Ah, my lady, I would never ask of anyone what I would not do."

Knowing his words to be true, she relented and walked to him. His arms encircled her waist, and together they went outside. As countless women before her, in days of old, she saw her man off and to battle without tears.

"What is the meaning of this! I want Xanadu immediately," she screamed at the young groom who stood with hat in hand, nervously twisting its brim.

"But m'lady, I have me orders."

Exasperated beyond belief, Tiffany waved an impatient hand at the groom, cutting off his words. "Yes, yes, I know. Well, we'll see about this."

Turning her head, her hair flying out nearly smacking the young groom in the face, she asked as she looked about, "Where is Keegan?"

"I 'eard 'e went to . . . Oh, there he be, m'lady." The groom pointed, relieved. Keegan appeared at the scene, for his lady, while normally a sweet thing, had turned into a regular termagant lately.

With purposeful strides, Tiffany moved toward Keegan. Just by the jaunty way she walked and the color on her cheeks, Keegan could see her temper rode high. He waited till she stopped before him.

"Keegan—" she pointed a finger at the retreating figure

of the groom "—that miscreant says you gave orders I'm not to ride."

Keegan saw the glimmer of challenge in her blue eyes but responded easily, " 'At's right, 'at's what I said."

"Why?" she asked disbelievingly.

" 'Cuz the guv'nor instructed it."

"He would do no such thing!" she screamed at him.

" 'Fraid so, m'lady," he answered, apologetically.

Pressing her lips together, she narrowed her eyes in anger. "Well, then, stand aside, Keegan. If you and that miscreant won't tack Xanadu, then I will!" She made to pass him, but he stepped in her way.

"Now, m'lady, I can't let ye do 'at."

"You would stop me?" she challenged.

He nodded his red head. "I'd do wonts necessary to carry out the guv'nor's orders."

She stood for a moment sizing up her opponent and then spun about, charging out of the stables.

"What the hell—" Rory ducked quickly, a priceless vase smashing inches from his head against the wall, as he entered the study "—is going on here?"

His eyes scanned the room quickly, taking in the books, the contents of Clinton's desktop strewn about the floor, coming to rest on Tiffany, ready to throw another missile.

Covering the distance that separated them in a few strides, he grabbed her poised hand holding the missile. "Here, here! Now, what the hell is the matter?"

Tiffany fell against him, breaking into heartrending sobs, her tears making wet spots on his shirt.

"I . . . I . . . just—" she gulped "—want to *riiidde!*" she cried.

Taking in the condition of the room as his hand moved comfortingly over her quaking shoulders, his eyes widened in disbelief at the havoc she wrought, and he asked incredulously, "You did all *this* because you wanted to ride?"

"Wouldn't," she sobbed.

"Wouldn't what?" he asked, confused.

"Let me ride," she cried, new tears falling freely on his already damp shirt.

"Who wouldn't let you ride?" he asked, becoming more confused by the moment.

Her head snapped up, hitting his squarely in the chin. Tiffany stepped out of the circle of his arms. She tossed her head and lifted her chin defiantly and spat, "Your *brother!*"

Confusion etched his face. "But he isn't here."

"I know that, you dolt!" she said just before she spun around, exiting the room, slamming the door behind her.

Shaking his head, Rory muttered, "I sure in hell don't need this."

The sun had risen above the horizon, sending tiny prisms of light through the study window. Clinton sat at his desk, going over the correspondence of the last few days.

He had arrived before dawn broke and had worked steadily since. He loosened his cravat and stretched back, leaning in his chair, his arms braced behind his neck, and closed his eyes. He had been apprised by both Keegan and a very confused Rory of Tiffany's recent tantrum, and he wondered how his volatile wife would greet him this morn. He did not have long to wait, for the slamming of the door caused him to sit up abruptly, his eyes flying open.

Tiffany strode into the room, her breech-clad hips swaying as she crossed the room, coming to stand before his desk, anger glinting in her eyes.

"You ordered I was not to ride?"

He withdrew a cheroot, lit it, and nodded affirmatively.

"Why?"

Sitting up, placing the cigar in an ashtray, he asked, "Some hot chocolate?" He poured out a cup, not waiting for her answer.

Tiffany saw the pot of hot cocoa, knowing he had anticipated her visit, and this knowledge somehow made her angrier.

The sweet aroma of the chocolate wafed up, teasing her nostrils, causing her stomach to churn in revulsion. She grimaced and shook her head but refused to be sidetracked. Again she asked, "Why?"

"Did you have breakfast already?" he asked, again ignoring her question, lifting a cup of strong tea to his lips.

The smoke from the cigar and the thought of breakfast made her mouth water in an awful way. She again shook her head, beginning to feel sick. Forcing her mind not to concentrate on her queasiness, she again persisted, "Why did you order I was not to ride?"

Clinton could see she was fast becoming ill and offered, "Take a seat, Princess."

"I do not want to take a seat, drink hot chocolate, or eat breakfast. I want to know why." Contrary to her words, she sat.

"When was your last monthly flow, Tiffany?" Clinton asked quietly, laying down his cup.

"What nonsense is this, Clinton? I never ride then. What has it to do with your orders?" she asked, bewildered by his question.

"Since when, love?" he repeated firmly, yet gently.

When it suddenly dawned on her, she paled. It had not come for six weeks, since before the weekend at Richilieu's. She sat numb before him, fighting her nausea and the truth. Standing on shaky legs, her knuckles white as she gripped the edge of the desk, she choked out, "Impossible."

The duke's eyes glistened with pleasure as he gently said, "Hardly, impossible, rather highly probably." And with unmistakable pride he added, "You carry our child."

"You planned this. You knew," she accused.

Grinning as only an expectant father does, he proudly stated, "I'd like to think of it as assisting nature in its cycle."

"Damn you! Think of it any way you want, I know better. Damn you and damn your child!" Her voice broke and she spun about, running from the room.

Running out of the house, she ran past Rory and Keegan.

At the edge of the headland, Tiffany stopped running. She wiped away the tears that were falling down her cheeks with the back of her hand and wrapped her arms protectively about her waist. Breathing deeply, she tried to calm herself.

Her mind screamed in anger at Clinton and herself. How could she have been so naive? Oh, how foolish I must appear to him. He had known what I had not! All the signs were there—morning sickness, frequent naps, cravings, erratic behavior. How could I have not known?

"Oooh," she cried, stamping her foot in anger as her tears fell softly. He had planned this, she just knew he had. He was high-handed enough and arrogant enough to believe he had the power over such things, and by God, if he just didn't! She should have known, for there had always been a prolonged absence from lovemaking after her flux, except . . .

"Oooh," she cried again, thinking he had already decided it was time for her to do her duty and present him with an heir! Another possession to add to his others.

She began to pace back and forth in agitation, remembering with startling clarity that weekend. While she seethed at his arrogance and high-handedness, telling herself he had seduced her, had she known the consequences, she would not . . .

She shook her head, and stopped her pacing. Nay, if the truth be known, she had been the seductress, not the seduced.

Her mind rebelled. *Consequences!* You ninny! You're having a baby, not a consequence. A soft smile lifted the corners of her mouth, and her hand moved to her belly. It was with wonderment she imagined a baby curled protectively within her, and amazement that she had been so unaware of it.

Her stomach rebelled as the queasiness came over her. Bile rose quickly and she covered her mouth and scrambled to a tree, dropping to her knees, becoming quite sick.

A strong, warm arm wrapped about her waist, bending her over as she heaved the contents of her belly.

"Easy, Princess, don't move. It will pass," he said gently, reassuringly. Tiffany complied with his request, grateful for his presence, and when her stomach stopped its fluttering and her head its spinning, she let him help her rise, and leaned against him with shaky legs.

"Take a sip and rinse out your mouth." Clinton tipped the bottle to her lips and she spat, a very unladylike gesture, but felt better for it.

"Feel better?" he asked, softly holding her steady. At her nod, he inquired, "Well enough to return?"

Again she nodded, then felt him lift her to his mount. He mounted behind her and nudged his horse forward.

Tiffany rested her head against his chest, quite weary. They rode slowly in companionable silence until she said softly, "I've behaved quite wretchedly this past week."

Clinton replied gently, "Expectant mothers are supposed to, Princess."

"You knew, didn't you?"

"Yes."

"Why didn't you tell me?"

"About 'my damn child'? Usually the radiant mother-to-be informs the father of his heir." He smiled down as she looked up to face him.

"The baby is not damned! You know well I didn't mean it. Don't you?"

"Yes, I know. How could I ever think the mother of my heir would think such?"

Tiffany stiffened hearing 'heir.' Seeking to understand herself and sort out her fears, she fell into thought.

Again she broke the silence and stated quite blandly, voicing her fears, ''You know, I will become quite fat and unattractive. No doubt you'll find me quite distasteful.''

He smiled down at her, imagining her belly swollen, and said, ''I expect you'll be quite rounded, but unattractive? Distasteful?'' He shook his head. ''Nay, I think not. I will no doubt still have my way with you—even if there is more of you,'' he added, grinning wickedly.

Seeing the unmistakable wide grin and glint of pride in his eyes, Tiffany took him to task, slapping playfully at him although she was quite pleased with his answer.

Smiling, she taunted, ''Yet you will have to abstain, my lord, sometime.''

Returning her smile, he countered, ''Aye, but I'll manage the drought.''

At her look of disbelief, he replied easily, ''I would ensure your safety as well as that of my heir.''

''I suppose your inflated male pride has not considered the possibility of a girl?''

A soft smile crossed his mouth, touching his eyes. ''A possibility, love, but highly improbable, for males run in the family. There has not been a girl for generations.''

Clinton gazed down, holding her eyes. ''But, love, if by some change of fate you present me with a girl, I promise you I will buy her a gilded coach with four dapple grays.''

She smiled up at him and said, ''Would you, really?''

''Have you a doubt, Princess?''

She shook her head. ''None, my lord.''

After a moment she laughed and Clinton asked, ''What's so amusing?''

''Poetic justice.''

At his puzzled expression, she explained, ''The Barencourtes defending a maiden's honor instead of taking it.''

Clinton threw his head back, letting out a peal of throaty laughter.

As they drew closer to the estate, Tiffany softly asked, ''Do you have no other children?''

''No, Princess, I have no bastard children I pay support for.''

Tiffany smiled, inordinately pleased by his answer, and snuggled against him, safe and much contented.

The entire household buzzed with celebration over the duke's announcement.

Mortimer waylaid Germane in the pantry and, in answer to her questioning look, produced a bottle of vintage champagne, which they shared. No one was able to locate the two that afternoon.

Clarissa had arrived to a much-delighted Tiffany, and tears of joy reflected in Clarissa's eyes as she regarded her charge, thinking her baby was soon to have one of her own.

Tiffany rested that afternoon while Clinton posted letters to all family members, announcing the news of their expected bundle of joy.

When he was done, he sat back and lit a cigar and sipped his brandy. He was much the picture of a proud expectant father, a grin splitting his handsome face. This is how Rory found him.

''Well, now, if you don't look like the proud father-to-be.'' Rory reached for a cigar and poured himself a brandy, seating himself in the soft leather chair and raising a booted foot to rest on top of the desk. ''Proud as the proverbial peacock, Clinton.''

''Your day will come, Rory. I only hope I'm there when it does.'' Clinton smiled as he leaned back in his chair.

Both men sat in companionable silence, celebrating as men for generations have done—smoking good cigars, drinking fine brandy, and getting quite drunk!

Clinton's mouth moved slowly down the column of her neck, placing small, shivery kisses with its descent. He lowered his mouth over a dark, taut nipple, sucking gently on it. Hearing her moan as he tugged upon it, he raised his mouth, whispering, "Does that hurt, Princess?"

Running her fingers through his hair she whispered, "Nay, not how you mean it."

He began again running his tongue over the nipple of first one breast, then the other. His hands cupped them, feeling their weight.

Tiffany moaned as she felt him slide his tongue down her belly and into her woman's flesh. She cried aloud as his tongue worked its magic and brought her to pleasure. And when he slowly, deliciously entered her, she cried out in a shattering release and shortly felt him spill his hot seed into her.

Clinton shifted his weight onto his elbows so she would not bear it and smiled down at her. "I love you, Tiffany." And while she did not return the endearment, he listened to what her eyes told him.

He slowly withdrew from her, savoring the sensation, and rolled off, bringing her to his side. He felt her fingers swirl within the hair of his chest. He was a much-contented man, and he need not count his blessings, for his greatest one lay safely against him. He would keep her always safe, for she was his life.

"Clinton," she said, softly, "I am frightened."

He knew she feared the coming birth, and drew her closer to him. "I will be there. Nothing, not death itself, will keep me from being there."

And, as always, she felt safe with him and was able to drift off to a peaceful sleep.

Winifred dabbed at her tears with her hankie. She reread Clinton's letter—Tiffany was to be a mother!

She decided she would leave France come late October and spend the holiday in England and remain until the baby's birth in January. She reconsidered, thinking perhaps she'd have her agent locate a small home there for her. After all, she'd want to visit her great-niece or nephew frequently!

"Jacques," she called while she made a mental list of things she must get in order.

"Pia, Pia donde esta?" called Evette. Tears of joy coursed down her cheeks as her hand held Clinton's letter. It was too good to be true—a brand-new Barencourte was expected come the first of the year!

There was so much to do: open up the dowager cottage she hadn't used in years, hire new servants, and locate Tristan. She had not felt so healthy and happy in years.

"Pia! Damn, where is that girl?"

Ali Khan nodded knowingly. "Ah, any day a man's seed finds fertile ground is a day of celebration. Thanks be to Allah. Perhaps that slave girl would assist you in your celebration. Who knows, maybe your seed will strike ground as fertile this night."

Tristan smiled, thinking not of what the girl offered, but rather proudly that the Barencourte numbers were increasing.

Brent, a disarming smile etched from ear to ear, sat at the club across from Percy.

"You've the smile of a cat that caught the proverbial canary. Give over, chap."

"Another Barencourte is expected at the turn of the year," he explained, his face beaming as if he had something to do with it.

"You don't say." Percy turned and called out, "Here, here, chaps, Clinton's expecting an heir come January. Pull out the wagering book and let's make our wagers, chaps!"

For once, Brent dismissed the odds and probabilities; instead he wagered purely on desire—fifty thousand pounds on a girl!

* * *

"Austin, my love, what a surprise. Do come in, darling."

"Put on your finery, Jezel." He picked her up, twirling her around and around. "Come now, Jezel, get dressed and hurry along." He patted her bottom as she rushed to do his bidding.

Austin threw himself into a nearby chair, a satisfied smirk etched on his face.

"Darling, what's this about?" Jezel called from her room.

"We are celebrating in style, love. The theater, dinner, drinking, and loving. Now, hurry along, Jezel."

"What are we celebrating?"

"Procreation," he shouted.

"What?" she asked as she appeared, a look of confusion crossing her delicate features.

"Another Barencourte's expected!"

"Bring out the oldest brandy, two bottles, man. Have one delivered to the duke of Wentworth and bring me the other."

William, as he waited for Godfrey's return, looked out over the property of his Cornwall estate, thinking he might return to Courtland Manor for the holidays.

Godfrey returned with the open bottle of brandy, pouring out a glass, handing it to his master.

"Have a drink with me, Godfrey."

Godfrey looked with startled eyes and poured a draft.

The earl raised his hand in toast.

"What is it we're drinking to, sir?"

Misty eyes regarded the servant. "To my daughter, you fool; she's going to have my grandchild."

Chapter Twenty-Eight

England, Summer 1819

The bursting blossoms of the wild roses of June in no way compared to Tiffany's radiant bloom: all blushing, pinks and reds.

Tiny fruits began to appear out of the blossoms, the bees were plump with nectar, and the birds brooded over their eggs while their mates brought them food. Tiffany, the fourth month of her pregnancy ending, shone with the sunny beginnings of life, growing in harmony with nature.

Sitting on the garden wall, she found that the sweet fragrances that hung heavy in the air threatened her queasy stomach.

God, she hated this accursed morning illness, she hated the lethargy, her moodiness. God, she hated it all!

A flock of birds flew overhead and she shaded her eyes and longingly watched them, envying their freedom.

She muttered to herself, "Can't go without an escort, must ride Sugar Plum, must use a sidesaddle—and on and on."

Everyone hovered over her, Clarissa, Germane, Mortimer. She couldn't move without someone asking where she was headed. She felt as if she were a child, not carrying one!

Even Clinton had turned into an overbearing monster,

placing more restrictions upon her freedom every day. Why, he even set Rory and Keegan as "guards" who no doubt reported her every action to him. Well, no more!

She heard the tread of footsteps and her lips tightened in rebellion, knowing for certain the "guards" had been set upon her. Lifting her skirts, she turned, fleeing from the garden, in pursuit of her freedom.

By noon the alarm was set off, for Tiffany was nowhere to be found. No one wished to be the bearer of bad news, especially since the duke had been extremely short-tempered today, demanding no interruption.

Standing outside the study door with fist poised to strike, Mortimer turned once again to Germane, who timidly nodded. He knocked.

"Enter," Clinton called out in annoyance. Looking up over the contract in hand, he glanced at Mortimer, asking more harshly than intended, "Well, what is it?"

"Her Grace is missing."

"Exactly what do you mean by 'missing'?"

"As in gone, without a trace, sir."

Standing abruptly, throwing down the contract, Clinton strode from the room.

Reaching the stables, his mood little improved, Clinton asked Rory, who just emerged from the stable, "Any mounts missing?"

A negative shake of his head was Rory's response, noticing the anger in his brother's face.

"Keegan, get my mount!" Clinton shouted.

"The chicken escape the coop again?" Rory asked lightly.

Impatiently slapping his gloves against his thigh, Clinton retorted, sharply, "It would appear so." Then he mounted and was off.

Rory and Keegan shook their heads, thankful they were not Tiffany.

* * *

"What a fine pair we make, Duchess; soon we'll be rounded and cumbersome." She patted the pregnant mare's head, which was lowered, munching the sweet green grass.

Walking barefoot through the meadow grass, holding the lead rope to Duchess's halter, Tiffany stooped to pick a flower, laying it in the basket hanging from her arm. She knew she had wandered outside her newly imposed boundaries, but didn't care. She was free again!

The pounding of hooves caused her to turn. Galloping up the crest on Mercury was Clinton, who reached her, pulling the stallion to a halt.

Duchess, scenting the stallion, began to prance and fuss. Tiffany tried to calm the mare. Duchess would have none of it, backing, thus pulling forcibly on the rope.

"Leave her. Let go of the rope," Clinton shouted at her, his voice edged in fear. Mercury began prancing, catching the mare's scent, and it took all of Clinton's control to hold him.

"I said let go of the rope, Tiffany."

Before she could, Duchess reared up, pulling the rope through Tiffany's hands, burning the soft skin. The mare's front hooves came down inches from Tiffany. Clinton reacted, moving Mercury forward, cutting the thrashing hooves from their target—Tiffany.

Tiffany cried out, "Clinton, she's running away, do something!"

When he didn't respond, she turned to find him glaring down at her. Leaning forward and in a stern voice with no vestige of sympathy in its hardness, he spoke, spacing the words evenly. "Madame, you have exceeded your bounds today. If you were not with child, I'd toss you over my knee and spank you as you deserve. You have been told, repeatedly, not to leave without an escort, not to go wandering about, to inform someone of your whereabouts. What you have done today is place yourself and my child in danger. You will not, I repeat, will not leave the confines of our home without *me!*''

''How dare you! I am not some errant child and will not allow you to treat me as such!'' she screamed back.

''Don't push me, madame. You behave as a child and should be treated as one. I will, if necessary, lock you in our room, thereby assuring myself of your safety and gaining some peace of mind, knowing that where I put you, I will find you.

Tiffany stood her ground when Clinton moved his mount forward, refusing to let him intimidate her. A not-so-nice smile crossed his face and he lifted her onto the saddle. He nudged his horse forward. Tiffany sat ramrod-straight to avoid touching him.

Tiffany's chair remained conspicuously empty at dinnertime. Clarissa had announced that Tiffany would not be down for dinner.

Rory finished his meal and, laying down his fork and knife, picked up his wine and regarded his brother.

''Well, brother,'' he began, breaking the silence, ''what are the new rules pertaining to Tiffany?'' Without allowing for comment, he continued, ''Are we to shackle her with ball and chain or perhaps just lock her in her room?'' Rory smiled at Clinton's narrowed eyes and proceeded. ''I'd suggest if you intend to lock her up, you consider barring the windows as well.'' Rory sipped his wine, gauging the effect of his words, and added, ''She is resourceful. Of course, I don't have to tell you that, do I?''

Refusing to be drawn, Clinton replied, ''She is not to leave the confines of the house without me.''

''Well, that certainly makes all our jobs easier since you're leaving tomorrow.''

''Don't cross me on this, Rory. I've listened to you plead her case all afternoon. Nothing has changed. You were not there when the mare nearly struck her down. As it is, her hands are badly burnt and cut.''

"I told you, Clinton, she's like a mare in season, skittish, restive, variable. Locking her in will not help."

"Believe me, Rory, I am aware of it. I am only pulling back on her bit; she'll have her head soon. A clearer one, I hope." He lifted his glass and finished the remnants of his wine.

"I hardly think she'll see it that way."

"No, I'm sure she considers me quite arbitrary."

"More likely tyrannical, I'd say."

"No doubt, brother, but my orders stand until I return."

As Clinton entered the sitting room, Clarissa walked out of the bedchamber carrying the dinner tray.

Eyeing the untouched plate, he questioned the wisdom of his actions. Clarissa put him at ease. "She'll not starve, Your Grace. What ye did was fer her own good. She's a bit headstrong, but she'll come around."

Clinton smiled down at the wrinkled face. "I suspect you're right, Clarissa."

He entered the bedchamber and stood at the foot of the bed, his fingers working the buttons of his shirt. He gazed down at Tiffany, who was sound asleep from the laudanum he had laced her wine with. His eyes were drawn to the white bandages on her hands. He was thankful that was her only injury.

He slipped into bed, pulling Tiffany into his arms. He smelled the fresh fragrance of violets, inhaling deeply, savoring the scent and feel of her in his arms.

He planned to be gone for a while and hadn't told her yet. He needed to clear up some business problems so he could be with her now as well as when the baby came.

Two weeks seemed an eternity without her, for he would miss her greatly. He wanted very much a memory to take with him to warm him through the long, lonely nights ahead. His manhood rose. His chest rumbled in silent laughter as he mused, If she thinks me high-handed, what would she think if I took her tonight, defensive and vulnerable as she is? He rationalized, If she protests, I will cease.

He lowered his mouth and captured soft lips in repose, which responded; gently moving the soft, pliant body, he slid into her. Tiffany moaned gently, wrapping her legs about him in a passion-induced dream. Her breathing grew ragged and soft mews escaped her throat. He brought them to a climax, flooding her with his seed. They lay entwined about each other.

"I've left your crackers and milk on the table, lamb," crooned Clarissa, who fluffed pillows about a drowsy Tiffany. "Now, don't forget to take them before ye rise. Won't be much longer, lamb, the sickness will be gone for good."

Tiffany had difficulty sitting up. She felt dazed. Everything was hazy. Giving up, she lay back against the pillows.

"What's the matter, lamb?"

"I'm so groggy. I can't seem to get my legs and arms to work together."

The concerned look vanished from the wrinkled face. "Oh, not to worry, lamb, 'tis only the laudanum."

"Laudanum? Whatever are you talking about?"

"His Grace put some in your wine."

"And you let him?" Tiffany asked, incredulously.

"Of course, lamb, 'twas for the pain in your hands."

Managing to sit up, Tiffany was instantly confronted with another realization—she was sticky! Her eyes widened. Why, that arrogant beast. Not only drugged her but taken her as well.

She tossed the covers off, stood on wobbly legs, and shrugged into her robe. Tiffany left the room with one purpose—to find Clinton and tell him exactly what she thought of him.

* * *

Upon learning Clinton was gone and noticing a servant posted at each door, Tiffany stormed up to her room. She remained closeted for four days, unaware Alan Thurston had come to call. As she refused to speak to anyone or open her door, Alan's message was never received. However, by the fifth day, feeling her solitude sharply, Tiffany emerged to wander silently through the manor. She moved listlessly from room to room, feeling the void of Clinton's presence. The anger she felt for Clinton turned toward herself when she admitted how very close she had come to injuring herself and the baby. The anger quickly turned to sadness, knowing they had parted with harshness between them. She yearned for the time to pass and waited anxiously for Clinton's return. In the meantime she sought the study, knowing she'd feel closer to him there.

Sitting behind his desk, her chin in hand, she smiled, content with the thought Clinton loved her and, more astonishingly, she loved him. A gleam lit her blue eyes; thinking of images of a quiet, moonlit supper and a night of passion quieted her mind, and for the first time in five days, tomorrow couldn't arrive too soon.

Deciding to play solitaire, Tiffany opened the desk drawer, looking for a deck of cards. Shuffling the papers within, she removed a stack of them.

"Ah, there you are." She snatched the cards, knocking the pile of papers to the floor, "Bloody great!"

Bending to retrieve the loose papers, she paused noticing a large folder marked "THURSTON PROPERTIES."

Curious, she opened the file and began to read.

"It can't be true." There in her trembling hand was a betrothal contract, dated April 10, 1818, signed by her father and Marquess Winston Thurston in proxy for Alan.

Sitting back, disbelief etching her face, the paper slipped from her fingers, floating unnoticed to the floor. She withdrew the other contract, dated the same day, but—she'd recognize that bold signature anywhere. Clinton!

She blinked, clearing the tears from her eyes, and saw

a draft for 150,000 pounds. She closed her eyes to block out the truth and opened them again to see the foreclosure notice on Thurston Manor held by the Barencourte Bank.

Tears slipped from the corners of her eyes, falling on her hand. Standing up, she turned to the window, dejectedly, resting her head against the pane. Thoughts ran helter-skelter while her hands fisted in anger and denial. Betrayal was a bitter pill to swallow. Deception even harder.

He had purchased her and used another's misfortune to ensure his end, making her trust and love him. She had given her heart to him; now she cried with self-loathing. When her tears were spent, she turned from the window, walked to the desk, shuffled the papers back into the folder, and replaced it in the drawer. She stood just as the pasty-faced Bartholomew announced the arrival of Marquess Thurston.

When he saw the pale, tear-streaked face and bandaged hands, Alan's smile faded. He waited until the stodgy butler left before walking hurriedly toward her, asking, "Tiffany, what's wrong? You look dreadful."

"Oh, Alan, thank goodness you are here. You must help me," she pleaded as tears fell unchecked.

"Of course I will. Tell me, what has happened?"

"I need to leave here before Clinton returns. I will go to Aunt Winnie. She will know what to do."

"Now, wait a minute, Tiffany. I cannot whisk you away from your husband. Why, that wouldn't be proper."

"Is it proper for a husband to lock his wife in, Alan? Is it proper for him to post guards at every door? If you'll not help me, I'll escape anyhow."

Alan saw her distress as well as her determination and knew her to be headstrong and foolish enough to leave on her own. Perhaps it was his sense of chivalry, or her desperate pleas, or his guilt that overrode reason—in any case, he consented.

* * *

Rory stopped at the drive, recognizing Thurston's carriage. "What the hell is that twit doing here?" he muttered, climbing the steps to the manor. At that moment a hurried Alan exited, stopping abruptly when coming face-to-face with Rory.

"Well, Thurston, what brings you to our neck of the woods?"

"I . . . I just returned from the Continent and thought I'd pay my respects." With that, he turned and tripped while descending the stairs.

Rory moved to Alan's side and called to one of the servants.

"Are you all right, Thurston?" Rory asked, thinking Thurston to be quite clumsy. "What the hell happened?"

"Must be my new boots. Slippery, you know? If you gentlemen would be so kind as to assist me to my coach."

Rory watched the carriage amble down the drive. Chuckling to himself, he thought Thurston ought to change his boot makers, as they hardly had a shine.

He turned to the butler. "Clinton's expected this evening. I've received word."

"Very good, sir, I'll inform the cook."

Handing his hat and coat to Bartholomew, Clinton headed to the staircase, taking the steps two at a time. Turning down the hall, he covered the distance to the bedroom in long strides.

Germane gasped in surprise when Clinton opened the door. She quickly curtsied. Clinton nodded, impatient to see Tiffany, and about to enter the room. He was stopped by Germane. "Her Grace is not here."

"Do you know where I might find her?"

"No, Your Grace, perhaps Clarissa knows."

As Clinton descended the stairs in search of Clarissa, he met Rory. "Ah, the prodigal son returneth. What did you do, work around the clock? I understood you'd be gone two weeks.''

''I managed to accomplish far more than I anticipated.''

Entering the study, with Rory in tow, Clinton scanned the room for Tiffany, adding, ''Brent and Austin are expected. I received word just this morning.'' He accepted the glass of brandy Rory handed him.

They drank in companionable silence until Clinton asked, ''Where is Tiffany?''

''About, I suspect.'' In answer to his brother's unasked question, Rory expounded, ''She's fine, a bit subdued. Stayed hidden but came out today.''

Clinton smiled. ''Nothing unusual happen?''

''She didn't escape, if that's what you mean. Threw no tantrums that I know about. About the only unusual occurrence to my way of thinking was a visit from the twit.'' Rory laughed, recalling the incident, adding, ''Actually, the twit's visit proved to break up an otherwise dull afternoon.'' Rory's chest rumbled with laughter as he filled Clinton in on the marquess's mishap.

Bartholomew entered, announcing dinner.

Upon entering the dining room, Clinton noted Tiffany's absence and demanded, ''Where's the duchess?''

The footmen, serving girls, and butlers looked at one another and then turned to Clinton.

Icy fear twisted his heart and knotted his stomach as he read the answer in their eyes. He abruptly left the room, summoning Bartholomew.

''Thank you, Clarissa, that will be all.''

''But . . . but where can my lamb be?'' Clarissa sniffled. ''She didn't take her shawl.'' She wept softly, leaving the study.

Clinton, running his fingers through his hair, leaned forward in his chair. In a controlled voice he stated, ''Send the stable hand in, Rory.''

Rory stood at the mantel listening to Clinton ask the

same questions over and over again. The stable boy was dismissed.

Suddenly the study door was thrown open by a swaggering Austin, followed by Brent. "Jesus, Clinton, terrific homecoming. We're greeted by weeping servants and hysterical maids. Where's the funeral?" Throwing himself down in a nearby chair, one leg dangling over its arm, he looked from Rory to Clinton.

Brent, realizing something was amiss, inquired, "Is it the baby?"

"No" was all Clinton said.

"Where is the radiant mother-to-be? We've brought some special tidbits to tease that finicky appetite of hers and those unusual cravings expectant mothers have."

From his station at the mantel, Rory dryly replied, "We seem to have temporarily misplaced her."

Brent furrowed his brow; Austin jumped to his feet and demanded, "How in the hell do you misplace a mother-to-be?"

Clinton filled Brent and Austin in, concluding, "One thing is for sure, she did not leave here alone. There is no mount missing, and since search parties have not found her, it's safe to assume she did not travel by foot."

"I'd say the marquess's visit has something to do with her disappearance," commented Brent.

"And his fall was a ruse to divert the servants," added Rory.

"I'd bet my life on it, especially in light of Rory's observation of the twit's boots. You really should have killed him at the race, Clint," Austin heatedly remarked.

A muscle twitched in Clinton's jaw, his voice cold and exact. "He has her."

"Well, man, let's not sit here! Let's take back what's ours and rid ourselves, permanently, of the twit," Austin declared, standing up, ready to do battle.

"Wait a minute, Aus." Grabbing his brother's arm,

Brent turned to Clinton. "Are you saying she was abducted or she went willingly?"

Shaking Brent's hand off, Austin shouted, "What the hell difference does that make? She's a Barencourte, carrying a Barencourte. She belongs right here!" Austin pointed his finger to emphasize exactly where "here" meant.

While his brothers argued heatedly, Clinton absently looked at the sheet of paper he picked up from the floor. He stated irrevocably, "Tiffany took advantage of the marquess's presence and sought his aid."

Rory looked puzzled, asking, "Why the hell would she leave? Certainly not because—"

An impatient, angry Austin interrupted, "It makes no difference, I tell you. The fact of the matter is, she's not where she belongs, whether she was taken or not! The marquess is as good as dead for interfering." He looked at Clinton and added, "Let me kill him for you, brother."

"Now, wait a minute, Austin." Grabbing his arm again, Brent stated, "If and when it comes to that, which I highly doubt, it would be Clinton's pleasure, not yours."

"Our honor, the Barencourte honor, deserves satisfaction, and I tell you I intend to . . ."

Clinton tuned his brothers out, keeping his own consel while Rory and Brent attempted to appease Austin. By the time Austin was appeased, Clinton had set the wheels in motion to locate and capture his quarry.

Clinton spun around, hearing Austin call him. He turned from the window where he had remained through the night, awaiting word.

"Captain Faulkner sends this message, Clinton: 'The duchess of Wentworth has booked passage to France."

"And the name of the ship she's on?"

Austin smiled broadly. "The *Tiphanie.*"

Clinton's face split into a grin, the first one in the last twelve hours.

"We ride to London, Austin. Tell Keegan to bring the carriage as well. I'll not have her ride astride, but in comfort."

Austin smiled, turned, and whistled as he left.

The sun broke the horizon as four horsemen galloped down the road. A black, well-sprung coach followed in their wake, its coat of arms: two lions rampant on a field of *noir,* the mark of cadency, the File, the sign of a first-born son, gleaming as the first ray of light appeared.

Chapter Twenty-Nine

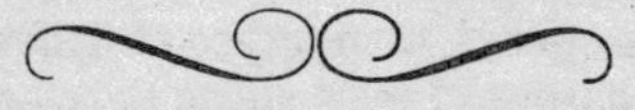

London, 1819

"Feeling better, Tiffany? I do hope you're not already seasick. We do have quite a journey ahead of us," remarked Alan, noting the greenish tinge to her face.

"The tea the captain sent is soothing my stomach," she replied softly. The smell of lemon oil and sandalwood pleasantly teased her nostrils. Lifting her eyes, she studied the cabin. The floor planking was dark mahogany, and the paneling the same rich wood. A wide window seat with plush cushions afforded a view of the murky water of the harbor. Oriental rugs graced the floor, adding warmth to the cabin. The bunk that nestled against the wall was covered with warm, plush blankets. It appeared the captain had given his lavish accommodations to her. She was about to comment when she heard a knock on her door. She called, "Enter."

Captain Faulkner entered; after nodding to Alan, he turned to Tiffany, inquiring, "Do the quarters meet with your approval, madam?"

Tiffany smiled. "Yes, Captain, they are lovely. It was kind of you to give me yours."

"Madam, these are not mine; they belong to the owner of the yacht. And you, Marquess. Are your quarters acceptable as well?"

"Certainly, Captain."

A moment passed. The captain looked upon his passengers and then he said, "I came by to inquire if you'd both care to join me for dinner."

Feeling the beginnings of hunger gnaw at her stomach, Tiffany readily agreed. "That is quite kind of you, Captain."

"I am afraid, Captain, that I will have to decline your most generous offer." Alan turned to Tiffany, explaining, "I have some business I must attend to before we set sail." Glancing back toward the captain, he added, "I trust Her Grace will be safe on board in your company."

"Most assuredly, Marquess."

"Well, then, if you both will excuse me, I shall be going now. I shall be back before morning." With that, he took his leave of them.

Austin and Brent watched the marquess leave the yacht. A devious smile lit Austin's face and he nodded to Rory, who shadowed the marquess.

Austin moved up the gangplank, meeting the captain. A short but successful conversation ensued. When Austin turned to leave, Brent could not miss the wicked grin or mischievous glint in his brother's eyes. Brent thought it was going to be a very long night.

As Tiffany emerged onto the deck, the waning afternoon sunlight momentarily blinded her. She paused and felt the captain stop behind her.

"I thought, my lady, that while you were taking a bit of fresh air, the cabin boy would ready your bathwater."

Tiffany smiled up at the tall, ruggedly handsome face of the captain, noting his long sideburns and trimmed, full beard. "That was so kind of you. I imagine you have many duties to perform without having to see to my comfort."

"On the contrary, madam. The owner has a well-manned crew, which runs this ship efficiently."

Tiffany gazed about, admiring the ship. "It would appear the owner takes pride and has spared no expense."

"Indeed not, madam. This ship is a gift to his wife."

An incredulous look crossed Tiffany's face. "You mean this yacht is purely a pleasure vessel purchased for his wife?"

The captain nodded.

A call from a mate forced the captain to take his leave. Tiffany wandered to the upper deck and looked down at the activity below. Idle sailors lingered against rows of riffraff. The dock was alive in a chaotic sort of way. Having her fill of the sights and sounds, she moved to stand at the prow.

Her hair blew back with the slight breeze. Turning her face to the sun, feeling its warm caress, she grabbed the rail to balance herself against the sudden gentle rolling of the anchored ship.

Lifting her head again into the breeze, she closed her eyes.

Feeling a sadness in her heart, Tiffany tightly shut her eyes, trying to prevent the tears from falling. Behind her lids, smoke gray eyes and a mouth whose corners tipped in smile appeared.

"Princess!"

Eyes flying open, she felt a momentary jolt of happiness, then turned, gazing down from her perch to the deck below. Smoky gray eyes and a mouth whose corners pulled up into a smile greeted her.

"Well, well, Thurston. Fancy meeting you." Rory moved uninvited to the table Alan occupied. Straddling a chair, he drawled, "Why, wasn't it just yesterday, or was it the day before, you were at Wentworth 'paying your respects'?" Rory paused, stopping a passing serving wench to retrieve his mug of ale. After drinking and slamming down the mug, which caused Alan to jump nearly out of his skin, Rory asked casually, "So what brings you to London?"

"Ah . . . I . . . er, that is to say, I have business to attend to."

"Really?"

Refusing to be intimidated, Alan gathered courage and asked pointedly, "What business brings you here?"

"Why, my brother's, of course."

Alan's head snapped from left to right when Austin and Brent suddenly appeared—drawing chairs, flanking him. Austin straddled his, crossing his arms across its back, leaning toward Alan, while Brent sat stretching his long legs before him. Both brothers turned, grinning at him.

Alan looked nervously from brother to brother as introductions were hastily made. He cared not much for the secretive smile and glint of danger in the probing eyes of Austin's, nor was he at ease with the almost too casual smile of Brent. Alan wished to be anywhere but here, but could find no plausible excuse to leave. Instead he asked, "What brings you chaps to London?"

Austin lit a cigar, blowing a curl of smoke at Alan; he replied in a silky voice, "A bit of Barencourte goods is missing."

"Surely you chaps have insurance to cover the loss?"

With cigar clenched firmly between even white teeth, Austin stated, "That's not the point. We Barencourtes are a possessive lot and like to keep what's ours."

Brent casually added, "Besides, the 'goods' are priceless. Worth far more than its weight in gold."

"Or someone's life, for that matter," added Austin, a grin of pleasure etching his face as he regarded Alan.

"We intend to recover it," Rory added, stopping a serving wench, ordering another round.

"No matter what the cost or at whose it is," Austin stated quietly.

Alan did not miss the ominous quality of his voice, and swallowed hard.

* * *

"Go away, Clinton." She watched him move up the gangplank.

"Not without you, Princess. You must know that by now."

"Oh, I know *everything,* you deceitful man."

"Yes, I know you found the papers, Princess. I know you read them." Clinton moved casually toward her. "Come down from there and we can discuss the matter."

"If you come a step closer, Clinton, I swear I'll jump." Turning, she looked down at the dirty waves lapping against the sides of the ship, and the bile rose in her throat.

Clinton did not miss the ashen hue of her face, and moved. He knew she would not jump, but he feared if a roll hit the ship suddenly, she'd be tossed over. "Come down off there and we shall discuss this intelligently."

Tiffany stubbornly refused, tossing her head.

"Madam, if you do not come down off of there, I shall advance, and when I reach you and after I bring you to safety, I will thrash you for putting yourself and the baby in danger."

Tiffany believed him. To salvage her pride, she negotiated, "I shall come down only if you step back and promise not to whisk me away."

Clinton smiled at her words. "You have my word as a gentleman, Princess. I shall step back." He did so. "And I will not whisk you away unless you want me to."

Moving down the steps toward him, she exclaimed, "Want you to! Are you mad? I ran away from you."

"Aye, that you did. Are you well? You look tired." The purple circles under her eyes and her pale skin prompted him to ask.

His voice was like a soothing balm to her low spirits. She nearly drowned in the smoky depth of the eyes that held her. She wanted nothing more than to lean against him, knowing his broad shoulders would never tire with any burden. She wanted it all to be as it was before. But the wound, though small, was still tender, and her anger still new. Stepping back, she replied sharply, "I am not fine. You have seen to that! You lied to me, deceived me, and betrayed my love. Damn you, Clinton, I don't want to love you anymore! I can't even believe I could love such a deceitful, ruthless man as you."

Tears of anger welled quickly; she brushed them away and turned to hide their flow, lest he see.

"Is it so bad loving me, Princess?" he asked gently, his voice like a sweet caress. "What difference do the papers make? Of what consequence are they?"

"I believed," she stammered, "believed I was more to you than another conquest, another infernal contract." She rallied. "You lied to me, betrayed me; I am nothing more than another possession you wanted and ruthlessly obtained."

Leaning gracefully against the rail, arms crossed negligently across his chest, Clinton replied, "I never lied to you, Tiffany. I may have deceived you by not telling the all of it, but lie, nay, I did not." He shrugged. "As to being another possession, make no mistake, Princess, you are mine as much as I am yours." Pausing to brush an errant curl from her face, he continued, "I don't regret the measure I took to have you."

Tiffany gasped at his casual and self-righteous attitude over what he had done, and slapped his hand away. "You conceited man. You are despicable. You pulled on the strings as if we were only puppets, never giving the freedom of choice."

Clinton turned her to face him. "Make no mistakes, Tiffany, the marquess had a choice in the matter."

Breaking from him, she cried, "Choice. You made sure no one had a choice—not Alan, not his father." Shaking her head, tears spilling, she added, "Or me."

"Perhaps you should speak with the marquess about his choice in the matter."

"He is a victim, just as I. How can you so easily dismiss your own ruthlessness?"

A smile etched his face; easily he replied, "I had no other choice. I wanted you, above all else." He lifted her tear-streaked face. "And I love you above all else. If you were one bit honest with yourself and gave up this childish charade, you'd admit that whatever it is I've done matters not, for you love me as well."

She angrily spun away from him, heading toward her cabin, but was stopped by his words and did not mistake the promise etched in them.

"Tiffany. I give you tonight to make your choice. Tomorrow I'll make it for both of us." He pushed off the railing and departed.

She stared after his retreating figure till he disappeared in the crowd.

Pushing the empty plate away, Tiffany, full and contented, sat back.

"Oh, Captain Faulkner, your chef outdid himself." She smiled, thinking the salmon tender, the shrimp delicious, and wine delicate. "I could not eat another bite."

The captain motioned for the first mate to clear the plates. "Do you mind if I enjoy a cigar with my port, my lady?"

"If you open the window a crack, I'd not mind." The mate complied and the captain lit his cheroot, the aroma wafting in the air, reminding her of Clinton's rich cigars.

The mate placed a plate of bonbons and chocolate mousse before her. Tiffany smiled at the captain and commented delightedly, "This is my favorite dessert. Perhaps I can eat a little more."

The mousse was sinfully delicious and the bonbons heavenly, and belying her words, she not only ate her mousse but the captain's as well.

The captain escorted a very full and drowsy Tiffany to her cabin. He made sure she was settled in before he left for the deck.

In the shadows he saw the tall, dark-clad figure of a powerfully built man move with easy grace up the gang-plank to the deck.

"She's asleep and settled for the night," the captain said as he pulled out a cigar, offering one to Clinton.

"Did she eat well?"

The captain smiled, wondering what the hell was going on, but being a seafaring man, did not ask. Instead he replied easily, "Everything, including my dessert."

The flash of white even teeth was seen in the night. "Good!" was Clinton's reply. He turned and disappeared into the night.

Fondling the ample bosom of the bar maid perched on his lap, Alan turned, blurry eyes focusing on Austin, who was between the ripe bosom of a serving wench, lapping up ale he purposefully ladled on her. He thought, The Barencourte brothers are an awesome lot. Pretty decent chaps.

"Ah, guv'nor, 'eres a room at top we can go fer 'is," she squealed, trying to get off Austin's lap.

"Aye, love, 'tis early yet. Perhaps later, you and your friend Sally—" he nodded to the wench with Alan, "—can entertain us gentlemen properly. What you say, Thurston?"

Alan blinked, clearing his vision. "Why . . . I thinks that's a rich idea, Aus."

"Guv'nor! Ye be expectin' Sally and me to take ye all on?" she howled, winking slyly to Brent.

"A ménage à trois, love. You ladies are skilled, are you not?"

"You be daft, guv'nor, 'eres six of us total."

"Ah, yes, love. Perhaps two ménage à trois!"

A shrill laugh escaped the heavily painted mouth, causing the hair on Brent's neck to stand at attention. He sat back, smoking his cigar, drinking his brandy, watching his brothers get Thurston roaring drunk. He idly wondered how Clinton made out and wishfully hoped Tiffany was in the

Barencourte coach heading back to Wentworth, though odds were against it. So Brent resigned himself to a long night.

Another shrill laugh reached his ears. He thought distastefully of the evening ahead. He would pull rank on Rory and go with Thurston, and leave Austin and Rory with the hyena.

Much later, Clinton entered the smoky, noisy inn and was directed to the private room in the back. Entering the room, he saw that seated at the table were his brothers. A very drunk and very disheveled Alan sat between Austin and Rory. Alan smiled crookedly at Clinton before his head fell upon Austin's shoulder. Austin shoved it off and it promptly fell against Rory's shoulder.

The two whores had finished buttoning up their dresses, catching the bag of coins Brent threw at them. As they left, Sally winked at Clinton and raised a brow. Clinton ignored her, instead reached over and poured himself a brandy.

''Well, brother, what we have here is a very drunk marquess,'' Rory remarked, pushing Alan's head back onto Austin's shoulder.

''Yes, Clint,'' chimed Austin, who pushed Alan again, but this time Alan held his head up for a moment and began to sing a bawdy ditty. Austin shoved Alan's face down on the table, silencing him.

''He has eaten, drunk, and been bedded properly. Although it would have been cheaper if we just killed him, to my way of thinking,'' Austin said as he reached to pour himself a drink.

Clinton smiled and shook his head. ''We promised you satisfaction, Austin. You assured me there would be no blood.''

''You would doubt my word? I'm merely saying it would have been cheaper to kill him, that's all.''

A loud bang on the rear door interrupted them. The door banged open, and in swaggered Tristan with two burly seamen.

"Ah, Trist, you got my message," Austin called.

A smile etched from ear to ear, Tristan walked over to the table, pouring a measure of brandy, and after sipping it, said, "I want you to know, Austin, your request pulled me from the thighs of a lovely wench." He took another sip and proceeded, "If it weren't for my sister-in-law, I'd have ignored it."

Tristan looked down at Alan, then up at his brothers, asking, "Who the hell is this?"

"This is your cargo, brother." Austin smiled at Tristan, who pulled Alan's head up, and Alan, with a lopsided grin, called out "Hallo" to Tristan.

Tristan released his hold, and Alan fell forward onto the table. Tristan motioned to the two seamen, who hoisted Alan up between them as if he weighed no more than an ounce, and walked out the door.

"What will you have me do with him?" Tristan asked.

Austin smiled. "Use your imagination."

Tristan winked at him, knowingly.

Tiffany sat up. Her hand moved to rest against the soft swell of her belly. She held her breath; a moment passed and a smile lifted the corners of her mouth.

Beneath her palm she felt the first stirrings; like the flutter of a butterfly's wings.

Lying back against the pillows, she felt the flutter again, and smiled. Their baby, her's and Clinton's. And as if in agreement, she felt the flutter against her womb once again.

She hoped for a girl. Clinton would be so good with a girl. And it would serve him and all the Barencourte men right, having to defend a maiden from the likes of their own kind.

She laughed, picturing Clinton, enraged over some ardent suitor, and Austin offering to dispatch him!

Yes, a daughter! Oh, with midnight tresses, smoky gray

eyes. She would have the deepest dimples and the Barencourte smile.

She worried at her lip realizing how empty her happiness seemed without Clinton.

Getting out of bed and walking over to the table, she poured a small glass of wine, hoping it would help her sleep. She turned, nearly stumbling on a packet of letters on the floor. She picked them up. Her eye caught the seal on a letter. The seal of the Barencourte Bank.

Again curiosity won over, and removing the documents, she sat at the table and read them.

Clinton walked to the study window, looking out over the cobbled stone street, now quiet save for the occasional sound of a carriage.

He, unlike his brother, was unable to sleep and would not seek his cold bed until he had Tiffany to warm it.

He smiled knowing tomorrow would soon be here, and with it, Tiffany.

He could have made tomorrow today, but he had seen how pale and weary she was. She needed tonight to rest, and time to sort things out. Tomorrow he would board his ship and take her home. He smiled, confidently.

Tiffany rushed out from the companionway and onto the deck with the realization that Alan never could love her as Clinton did, and more important, she never loved Alan and she loves Clinton. With those thoughts, she made her way down the gangplank and was startled to find Keegan appear before her, and briefly wondered where he came from.

"How . . . how . . . what are you doing here?" she stammered.

"The guv'nor had me wait here in case anything happened or if ye needed anything." He nodded toward the shadows, where she saw, under the streetlamp, the gleaming carriage bearing the Wentworth seal.

Turning to Keegan, she smiled. "Take me to him."

A broad smile broke his face as he agreed, "Right away."

He nudged the sleeping footman awake, who jumped down, opening the carriage door to assist Tiffany.

"Keegan," she called, "how long have you been here?"

"Ever since ye been on the guv'nor's yacht, lady."

"His yacht?"

"Well, 'tis yours really." At her incredulous look, he explained, "It's named for ye. Latin or French, not sure which, but it's yer name."

She gazed back at the yacht before ascending into the carriage, her eyes misting with tears.

Clinton leaned back in his chair. His steepled fingers brushed back and forth against his chin. A soft smile lifted the corners of his mouth. Closing his eyes, the image of a raven-tressed, gray eyed daughter appeared. A spitfire to be sure! Impetuously reckless, stubborn, and just slightly spoiled.

She'd have the finest coach—gilded, of course—with the mark of the File, and the softest of silks and velvets and the rarest of gems to adorn her. She would have four uncles and a father who'd gladly boot any overzealous suitor down the stone steps of Wentworth.

He leaned back in his chair, crossing his arms behind his head, a broad smile on his lips, thinking of the excellent child he and Tiffany would make.

The sound of a carriage stopping interrupted Clinton's thoughts. Rising, he walked to the window; pulling back the curtain, he smiled, watching Tiffany pick up her skirts and run up the stone steps.

The study door burst open wide, and there, at its threshold, stood Tiffany. Breathless, she paused, then walked grandly toward Clinton, who sat at the desk, his legs stretched casually atop it, crossed at the ankles, a cigar clamped between even white teeth, grinning back at her.

She stopped before him and quite openly studied him, raking him from head to toe and back. His grin broadened over her obvious appraisal of him.

"How dare you grin at me, Clinton! I should by all rights sail away on *my yacht* and be done with you, once and for all." Placing balled hands on her hips, she hurried on, "But you and those brothers of yours would only come after me—and while I might be damned for it, I'd be glad you did."

At her admission, his grin overtook his features. Her stormy blue eyes narrowed at him.

"But that does not change the fact that you are cursed with an inordinate amount of male conceit."

Clinton quirked a brow in mock disbelief, blowing out a curl of smoke, smiling.

"Along with innumerable other flaws; you're high-handed, manipulative, and terribly arrogant." She began to pace back and forth in front of him. "Oh, and let's not forget how terribly ruthless you can be. Or how tenacious! Why, you are an impossible man!"

She stopped. Turning to him, she paused, meeting his eyes. "But in spite of it all, I do love you. Above all else."

He grinned broadly, grinding out his cigar; rising and coming around the desk, he scooped her up and headed toward the door.

"Well, aren't you going to say something?"

"What's there to say, Princess?" He grinned. "It worked out exactly the way I planned."

Epilogue

Wentworth Estate, England
January 6, 1820

The sun's rays gleamed and sparkled off the icicles hanging from the cornices and gables, reflecting the colors of a prism.

On the ice-glazed drive stood a gilded coach with four dapple grays. The sun glinted against the gold-trimmed crest of two lions rampart on a field of *noir*—the mark of cadency—the File—the sign of the firstborn gleamed in the sun.

The gilded coach belonged to the newly arrived duchess:

BRITTANY ELIZABETH BARENCOURTE

The Barencourte men finally had a maiden to defend.